THEY WERE FLYING IN
ZERO VISIBILITY

Bracken said, "Try sticking your nose out again. I think that ship you saw was the *Ultima Thule.*"

"Sure." Casey broke into the clear at three thousand feet and there was the ship, just where Bracken said it would be.

"Approach with the sun behind you," recommended Bracken.

It was the order to strike, yet the words were casually spoken. Casey eased his thumb over the torpedo control button.

A sudden red glow burst from the bow of the ship. The flame rose to meet them and Casey considered it. A long yellow tail. An adaptation of a ship-to-ship missile.

"Tallyho!" Casey yelled for Bracken's benefit. He pointed the nose at the sea, thrust open the throttle, and with the wind tearing at his goggles, dived to meet the missile rising toward them.

WILLIAM STEVENSON

BOOBY TRAP

ZEBRA BOOKS
KENSINGTON PUBLISHING CORP.

ZEBRA BOOKS

are published by

Kensington Publishing Corp.
475 Park Avenue South
New York, NY 10016

First Zebra Books printing: February, 1989

Printed in the United States of America

CHAPTER 1

Professor Rutgers leaned over the cruise ship's rail to watch the parade trickle down the road to the dusty waterfront.

"A toy colony," said his companion, a narrow-chested young Frenchman. "A toy governor. And toy soldiers." The professor's fellow Americans applauded the bandsmen. "Poor guys," said a lady from Brooklyn as the pipers swung past. "They must be melting in those bearskins."

The only man who gave no sign of melting sat in the back of an open landau. Under the blazing sun, under an enormous plumed hat, he remained straight and thin as an icicle.

Black faces glistened under white helmets as the band wheeled around the flagpole near the ship's berth. The big drum struck a new beat, and the first note muffled the report of a gun. The icy little governor of the British Windfall Islands rose with a tiny jerk and toppled over.

"He's fainted!" said a short, stout girl from Maine.

"No," murmured the Frenchman, his mouth at Rutgers' ear. "He's been shot."

Any words between the two men were lost in shouts

5

from the other cruise-ship passengers, hardworking Americans who had saved all year for this short escape from drab routine. Professor Rutgers wished the assassination had been the work of a passenger hoping to add still more excitement. He feared not. He suspected the gunman had been carefully planted among the crew. It included lascars, those nomadic seamen who leave very thin paper trails for policemen to follow. It was not a suspicion he felt like voicing to the Frenchman.

He ran a practiced eye over the growing chaos. Guardsmen wrestled with panicking horses. Carriages piled up between the parliament buildings at the top of the hill and the quay. Dignitaries doffed their hats and dived for cover. The police were few and looked odd in their dark London bobbies' uniforms. A blimplike figure, scarlet of face, jogged up the incline, waving a baton. The band struck up a rousing march.

The professor checked the colonnaded buildings opposite. Could the shot have come from there? Someone among the gawking tourists would have unwittingly photographed the assassin. The professor knew exactly how to conduct the search. Unfortunately, this was Britain's turf, although lately it had fallen into limbo, living off America while psychologically dependent on Big Momma, a phrase Windfallers used to describe their Queen, in England. It was, thought the professor, ideally situated for a certain form of terrorism.

Professor Rutgers heard the Frenchman begin to utter another indiscretion. "If you please," muttered Rutgers, "I honestly prefer not to know."

* * *

At the other end of Great Sound, through which ocean vessels make passage into Nelson's Harbour, a girl scrambled over a clifftop and called to two men, "Did you see that?"

"Looks like *Britannia*," said Lord Bracken. He was on one end of a child's seesaw. He jumped off so abruptly that the large black man at the other end fell to earth with a bump.

"Hey!" protested Detective-Sergeant Churchill S. Winston.

"Sorry!" said Bracken. "Give me the glasses—quick!"

"It's not the royal yacht." The girl stood in her wet bikini, smiling, *"Britannia's* in the Bahamas all this month."

Her father kept the glasses on the elegant yacht until it vanished behind Drake Island. "She's flying the standard of the Republic of Sahara, with enough pennants for an emperor."

"Zia Gabbiya." Alison Bracken crossed the clifftop garden.

"The King of Terror," said the sergeant. "Devil's Godfather."

"Bloody silly names invented by journalists," growled Bracken. "They make him sound like Attila the Hun, and play into his hands."

"King Zia," said Alison. "Fits a tight headline, anyway."

Bracken tugged his beard. He was clad in shorts and nothing else. His body was tanned leather, and lean. His hair was a silver-black mane. He turned to the sergeant. "Do *you* think he's on board that floating brothel?"

Winston shook his head. The sergeant was formal in

the heavy, dark uniform kept for ceremonial occasions. What he shared with Lord Bracken was a piratical air. Both men had startlingly light blue eyes. In Winston, the effect of those pale eyes against ebony skin was to remind others of the intermingling of race and clan in islands with a long and often bloody history. "Zia wouldn't risk it!" said the sergeant.

"I think he would," said Alison. "We don't take his threats seriously enough to suit his ego. So he comes to us."

"We're too close to U.S. territorial waters," said Winston. "You're a good lawyer, Alison, but you don't know men like Gabbiya. He got permission for a goodwill visit *for the yacht,* not himself. He won't be lured off his own turf."

"And you're a good policeman but you don't know the world of commerce." Alison drew a towel over her shoulders and gave the sergeant a thoughtful stare. She was a pretty girl, but as careless about appearances as her father, particularly here, Pretty Penny, their home. It was a three-hundred-year-old Windfall-style cottage. That kind of antiquity provides a greater sense of security than wardrobes full of expensive clothes. She said, "Half the fiction library consists of American offshore companies in which Gabbiya has hidden interests."

They all knew the fiction library. In the law firm founded by Lord John Bracken, fiction was the whispered name for records of companies registered in the Windfalls to reduce or avoid taxes elsewhere. Bracken had withdrawn from the firm's daily affairs, claiming he wanted to retire, but privately he worried about offshore companies whose motives might be sinister. Alison, new to law, felt at least one member of the

8

family should remain among the firm's dozen ambitious young lawyers.

Her father said, "Gabbiya might stub his toes if he thinks his money buys *anything* here."

Then the phone on the veranda rang.

"Headquarters, I bet," said Sergeant Winston. "Wanting me to turn more somersaults for the tourists. This morning I escorted the town crier. Tonight, it'll be beating-the-retreat."

"Say you're busy detecting," recommended Lord Bracken.

"They'd never believe me." The sergeant reached over the rail for the phone. "The last bit of detective work I did was five months ago. Oyez Lem broke into the dinghy-club bar. He does it every year on his birthday." His voice trailed away.

The others did not hear the words that followed. Suddenly the phone was slammed down and Winston headed at a run for the tiny blue-and-white Panda police car parked behind the stone buttery. "The governor's been killed!" He flung the words back at them.

"So it's starting," murmured Alison

There was no mention of assassination in the local broadcasts that evening. Instead, there was an announcement from the Prime Minister, a black taxi driver who also held the tourism portfolio. The governor had died unexpectedly after opening the new session of Parliament. In the Windfalls, there was no minister for defense, on the theory that the best defense was to maintain overseas confidence and keep the tourist dollars flowing. Big foreign corporations were now an even larger source of revenue, but the pleasantly quaint tradition continued of regarding the Minister of Tourism as the chief bulwark against misfortune. Islanders, hearing the Premier's version of events, understood that he spoke as commander in chief for tourism, and dismissed the rumors of a gunshot. The poor old guv had been felled by a stroke, they agreed. Thus was born a new reality, unlikely to spread panic abroad.

Professor Rutgers heard this version at dinner on board ship. He took a turn on deck. The Frenchman was nowhere to be seen, which was what Rutgers expected. He spent a long time staring at the large steam yacht which had appeared unheralded in mid-harbor and now lay at anchor, festooned in lights. He knew it belonged to Colonel Zia Gabbiya, dictator, terrorist, ideologue. But he was sure Gabbiya was not on the yacht. Not yet.

A month later, Lord Bracken finally got back to his pals in Washington. They were Smithsonian experts in the restoration of old airplanes, and Bracken dropped by for some further advice.

By then, the murder of the Windfalls governor was forgotten. It had not been possible, of course, to hush it up completely. Americans lumped the Windfalls in with other troublesome spots, all former British possessions dangling down the eastern seaboard: places like Turks and Caicos, whose Chief Minister had been arrested in Florida for smuggling drugs, and Grenada, where U.S. forces had kicked out the Cubans. If Americans thought about the Windfalls at all, they thought of them as stuck in another century, and harmless. In this, they could not have been more wrong.

A flying dinosaur was flapping above the Washington Mall as Bracken left the air-and-space-museum. He stopped to watch. It was a test flight of the Smithsonian's model of the biggest reptile ever to terrorize the skies. The reconstructed pterosaur turned above the White House and headed back over the crowd of spectators. It looked like a hang-glide crocodile.

"Reminds me of my old Stringbag," said a short, stout man who had appeared at Bracken's side, and who wore a rather dashing eyepatch.

"How very odd," replied Bracken, keeping his eyes on the monster above. "It reminds me of mine."

The two men, one tall and bearded, the other stubby and bald, squinted against the fall sunshine and followed the model's progress. It would flap and glide, flap and glide.

"Those Smithsonian fellows didn't do a bad job," said the stubby man. "One of paleontology's great mysteries is how that thing ever got airborne."

"I felt the same way about my Stringbag," grunted Bracken. "The chaps who built that model are helping me rebuild mine."

"Your Stringbag?"

"Yes. I crashed her in the sea during the war, and fished her up later."

"Fished her up, eh?" The stubby man stuck one hand inside his blue serge jacket and gave a short whistle. Bracken smiled to himself. Probably there were no two other men on this entire continent who had ever piloted aircraft that so resembled, in size and oddity, the flying dinosaur. The Stringbags struck from secret places against Nazis and Japs. The flying dinosaur dominated the skies until 60 million years ago, when something better had come along.

"Does me good to see these old girls fly again," said the stubby man. "Makes me feel less of an old fogey. Not so much of a useless tit."

"Our biggest mistake is throwing away the old weapons," murmured Bracken.

The other man gave him a keen stare. "Look here, old man . . . Got time for a drink?"

"Don't mind if I do," said Bracken.

They knocked back more than one drink. Bracken had to race to the Capital Hilton, at Sixteenth and K, to catch the Washington Flyer bus service to BWI Airport. He could not afford the outrageous taxi fare; nor could he afford to stay overnight. His trip was made practicable by a British Airways unadvertised and, as it happened, soon-to-be-suspended service. It offered a one-way fare of ninety-nine dollars, a giveaway ticket compared with its U.S. rivals, but a means of filling seats for the short Windfalls hop before the long haul to London. He barely made the flight.

"Welcome home, Lord John," said the black immigration officer on his arrival, showing that special warmth reserved for locals. Few knew him by his title outside the islands. Nobody would have used the endearing term Lord John except an islander.

He pulled his old moped out from the cargo shed, chewing an unlit cigar with the ferocity of a man warned to stop smoking. He had started smoking a pipe when he was eighteen, to give warmth in the open cockpit of a Stringbag. Complaints that he was a fire hazard had not stopped him. Now, finally, his doctor had.

He puttered through Nelson's Harbour, his mind still burning with what the man with the eyepatch had told him. It was near midnight when he reached Pretty Penny. He found a note from Alison in the kitchen. "I'm sailing the Dragon over to Wreck Cay to stitch that tear in the rudder and fix a strut. If it's not too late, could you pick me up?"

Bracken grinned. It could never be too late.

He took the runabout and putt-putted with easy confidence down the chain of islets. Alison was a good sailor, but she disliked maneuvering the old and leaky Dragon home through hidden shoals in pitch darkness. She would have set off while it was still light, which meant she must have made more progress with the final repairs on the Stringbag. The warplane stood now on top of abandoned Wreck Cay. This is near the tip of the Windfalls' southern tail, where it vanishes into the sudden abyss of deep ocean. Ever since events led Bracken to resign from his law firm, he had spent his time, and the small income he drew from the company, restoring the Stringbag, hopping over to the Smithsonian for advice on adhesives and engine parts, on fabric or wood replacement, on a thousand small matters that would have astonished the airplane's deck handlers of more than forty years ago. They could not have foreseen a day when the Stringbag as a class would be dead as the Dodo, the pieces scattered to the four winds.

The Stringbag on Wreck Cay kept Bracken sane. Or so he thought, pulling himself hand over hand up the cliff face by way of iron spikes. He couldn't remember when he'd last heard the old lady called by her correct name of Fairey Swordfish. The first aircrews swore she was held together by string. Hence Stringbag. Even before she flew the first time, in 1935, her class was obsolete. Yet she had survived as the indestructible workhorse of the British Navy through all the years of war at sea. Bundled up in Stringbags had been a lethal mixture of torpedoes, rockets, bombs, antishipping flares and World War I machine guns, with assorted odd bods crammed into vast and windy cockpits, their young faces sticking out in the wind.

She was, reflected Bracken, a pirate's delight. Crewmen long dead would have been mystified by the lengths he'd been forced to go to restore his own machine. Stringbags belonged to a piratical era of self-sufficiency. Their methods of attack were unorthodox and depended upon surprise. They had been flown from carriers to otherwise inaccessible airstrips in remote lands. They had attacked German battle cruisers in the English Channel, every Stringbag lost but the enemy shaken. Stringbags had inadvertently shown the Japanese how to attack Pearl Harbor, in the way they knocked out the Italian fleet one year earlier. They were terrifyingly slow. That, however, had been turned to advantage.

Bracken was an acting-temporary-unpaid midshipman pilot when he first scaled the flanks of a Stringbag to the open front cockpit. He'd never really thought of himself as more than a midshipman, even after he took command of a squadron at the age of twenty-three. He'd always shown an animosity to titles. The islanders called him Lord John out of affection for his forebears, who had earned King's honors. They had been licensed with letters of marque. They were pirates.

Most of his Stringbag mates had been killed long ago. He had given this little thought until his chat with the man in the Washington Mall.

He found Alison at the top of Wreck Cay, stitching canvas in the light of hurricane lamps. "You're carrying devotion beyond the call of duty."

"I'm doing this to save your life," she said, looking up. The long climb had not left him as frighteningly breathless as in the past. She had pleaded with his doctor: "Frighten Daddy into being sensible!" The doctor soon discovered problems likely to shorten Bracken's life, not only because of recent drinking bouts. The doctor had encouraged Bracken to take up a full-time hobby. The hobby became an obsession to restore to fame the big old biplane that by the end of the war had been upstaged by all those sexier jobs: Messerschmidt jets, Sea Vampires, Hellcats and Corsairs, Sea Furies and Barracudas, whose very names mocked the poor old Stringbag.

Alison went along with this exhausting hobby because it was "putting lead back into the old man's pencil." She drew the line at letting him fly the machine again, though. Now she sniffed the air.

"My God," she said. "You smell like the inside of a brewery."

"Ah, yes, well—" Bracken looked around. An absurd impulse. The nearest other human being had to be on Grand Windfall, across the sound. The restored Stringbag was concealed in a wooden hollow at the end of an ancient ropewalk. Nobody had reason to be lurking here. Nevertheless, his voice dropped. "This is absolutely confidential, right?"

"Right," said Alison. "Provided it's not a top-secret excuse for you getting sozzled."

"I met this chap. We did knock back a few," admitted

15

her father. "But all in a good cause."

"Cause?" Alison froze. "There's only one cause I care about. That's to keep you alive."

"This should do it," lied Bracken. "It's simply a matter of keeping an eye on Zia Gabbiya."

Alison sat back on the bamboo mat. "Gabbiya's not here."

"But his killers are."

Alison took her time digesting this ambiguous statement. "A man in Washington," she said slowly, "asks you to keep an eye on the Devil's Godfather? That means the CIA."

"Wrong. Downwind Dalrymple."

"Who?"

"Vice-Admiral Dalrymple. He's attached to some British mission there. I knew him as a snotty called Downwind."

"What," asked Alison, "is a snotty?"

"They called us that, as midshipmen. We wore little brass bells around our sleeves so they couldn't be used to wipe the snot from our noses. Dalrymple was called Downwind because he did the impossible in an emergency and landed downwind in a Stringbag, in half a gale."

"Now this ex-snotty wants you to get rid of Gabbiya!"

"I never said that!" protested her father. "He just wonders if Gabbiya had any links with the governor's murder."

"So you're a free-lance spy for an idiot called Downwind?"

"That's no way to speak of your old dad's old comrade. If London doesn't care what happens here, you can't blame us for filling the vacuum."

16

"Suppose others have the same idea?"

"No covert operation would be sanctioned by an American Government on British territory."

"Ho, ho, ho!"

"CIA's forbidden by executive order from carrying out executions."

"Funny you should talk about *execution,*" said Alison.

Her father knew her technique for worming things out of him. Sometimes, he thought, there were things out of which he wished to be wormed. "If that's a proper sentence." Unconsciously, he spoke aloud.

"What?"

"Just mumbling."

He and Alison were very close. She jumped up, and he knew she'd read his mind again, "So, the bastard *is* coming!" She faced him, hands on hips. "You'll be in some unholy mess if you get involved. Gabbiya would love every government with a grudge to send in their liquidation teams, each unknown to the other, and make royal asses of themselves in front of the whole world."

"That's just what old Downwind wants us to prevent," murmured Alison's old dad.

CHAPTER 2

Professor Rutgers was back in his secret Washington cubbyhole.

"I don't know what we're looking for," said a visitor. "I do know what we don't want." He nodded at his controller of Personnel Discovery (PDC-1), who handed the profile to the professor.

"The man mustn't be a fanatic," said the chief. "No grinding cigarettes against the forehead to prove willpower, eh?"

"Try for a woman, then," suggested Rutgers.

"We have a policy against women killers," said the first of the two visitors. He had been sent by the director of central intelligence to this scruffy walkup over a Chinese restaurant near Wisconsin and M, in Georgetown. That fashionable quarter was known as Jaw-Jaw Town for leaking government secrets. This became an asset. Nobody took the gossip too seriously and little men in nondescript offices were too commonplace to be worth noting.

Rutgers stared at the file. "I've always thought the female of the species more deadly than the male. But don't quote me. I don't want to be tossed back into academia for offending Those Who Must Be Obeyed."

The first visitor grinned. He had started out as a lawyer. He recognized the reference to London's Old Bailey. He said a few words of reassurance, for he knew how Rutgers swung between dislike of bureaucrats and distaste for scholarly retreats. Then he left with his companion. Rutgers listened to the footsteps echoing down the darkened stairway. He sighed and spread out the candidate profile under his desk lamp. It was always the same. The profile was the barest outline of the department's needs. The candidate must not stand out in a crowd, must dislike bureaucratic procedures, must have absolutely no political or media contacts . . . Full of contradictions, it gave little indication of the task contemplated, although the first thing PDC-1 had said was "I thought you'd have more of a suntan." *Someone* knew the Windfalls to be the scene of operations. That was the trouble with deep-deep-cover assignments, the so-called Double-D-C's. To save the CIA's *official* officials from having to tell embarrassing lies to the White House, to the Senate Intelligence Committee, to the layers of subcommittees within the Task Force on Combating Terrorism, it was necessary to play silly games.

Rutgers chewed the end of a pencil. Here the candidate profile asked for a man of mature judgment, no vices, no grudges, and *no* family. It was almost a contradiction in terms. Where did you find a man old enough to shoulder responsibility and show both aggressiveness and control, but without a family?

Even the Info-Access Ultra-A System, which in effect thumbs through files like an old-fashioned archivist, is foiled by this sort of request. I can do better, thought Rutgers, on an underwater archaeological dig. If I have any claim to intellectual brilliance, it's in the business of re-creating history from the few surviving clues. If I dived on a two-thousand-year-old wreck with this much information, I'd fish up something more substantial than what lies in prospect now.

The phone disturbed him. A man's voice said, "The great man wants you. Yes, I'm aware of your high-priority whatsit. That's why he wants you. Pronto!"

The wheels were finally turning.

The great man was mercifully brief.

"This conversation," he said, "never took place. Right?"

"Right," said Rutgers, doing his best to look like a man who would never even dream of writing his memoirs.

"I liked your assessment on why they hushed up the murder of the governor. But it was an outside job. You're sure of that?"

"Going by guesswork."

"As a scholar, you made your name with guesswork." The great man's smile flashed on and off. "JSOC would like to hog this one," he added abruptly.

Rutgers looked neutral, but his heart rejoiced. Joint Special Operations Command, at Fort Bragg, in North Carolina, had nurtured a Delta Force, confined to hostage rescue in cooperating host countries. The great man's few words meant JSOC saw a situation developing in the Windfalls that might expand the Delta Force role. When rivalries pitted Pentagon against CIA and set special strike forces against turf-conscious defense chiefs, the Double-D-C's could maneuver between. When politicians grew restive about insufficient consultation on White House wishes regarding secret activities, then the high-profile departments were frozen. Which, again, left more room— His meditations were interrupted by the great man.

"Colonel Gabbiya." Said with half a smile. "If we don't get him, JSOC might turn this into another Grenada. And we might as well fold our tents . . ."

Rutgers listened with half an ear as Gabbiya's name flung open the archives of his mind.

". . . If anything overt ends in shambles, State will say they told us so. We'll be back to the Munich theory of quiet diplomacy and Hitler's a decent chap if you handle him right. . ."

Rutgers let the fathead keep on talking. He'd already gotten the message.

Get Gabbiya.

Get him with as little fuss as possible, without tossing the hardware around sea and sky. Get him without fighting the bureaucracies' lawyers, or the nervous Nellies surrounding the antiterrorist task force. Get him without stumbling through the thickets of secretaries of State, Treasury, Defense and Transportation, the directors of the FBI, Office of Management and Budget, and National Security Council, the Attorney General, chairman of the Joint Chiefs, and the President's chief of staff, all of whom are required to pass judgment on intelligence missions. Get the bastard the way Rutgers had dreamed of getting him for his own deeply personal reasons, without wasting energy and time on those dozen leaky committees that oversee the directorate of overt/covert operations.

Just . . . get Gabbiya. Get him without the preliminary whys and wherefores and whereases and whereins of politicians fearful of laws written in happier times when none foresaw the cowardly warfare of those who would advance over the bodies of women and children, who regarded prisoners as negotiable items . . .

It made Rutgers' task of finding a candidate for the profile a whole lot easier. Usually he made a point of not knowing the mission for which the candidate might be required. This time it was plain as the purple-veined nose on his face.

They were asking for a vacuum man. Someone who was not a criminal, yet someone who had lost the best years of his life. That was the only kind of man who acquired no responsibilities, yet balanced between skilled aggressiveness and a mature coolness.

The profile would be filled. Though not the way the great man intended. I'm looking, thought Rutgers, for an old-fashioned American hero, the kind that's no longer in style here in trendy Jaw-Jaw Town.

CHAPTER 3

"I am not," declared Colonel Zia Bel-el-bey Gabbiya, "the Devil's Godfather."

"No," said the girl. "Of course you're not."

He sat in a gold chair dead center of the blue marble floor. White columns separated him from the desert and the starry night. The palace pavilions were like Bedouin tents of stone.

He wore his ivory uniform, the one you see in the newspaper pictures, with heavy gold epaulets and the breast plated with medals. A military cap perched on the famous mop of curly hair made him Golliwog Gabbiya. He had coined his own nickname. He could afford it. His skin was no more than dark tan. When black African leaders addressed him as Golliwog, they did so with roars of sycophantic laughter, because they all took his money, which is better than taking offense.

He was looking through the latest batch of videotapes from Washington. They were network news shows. He doubled up with mirth until he came to the U.S. President's advisor calling him "Godfather of the Devil." This was followed by an ABC "Nightline" debate among ex-premiers, terrorist experts and assorted politicians from the West. The topic, as it so often was now, concerned how best to dispose of Gabbiya, King of Terror. They wrung their hands, but made clear their fear of direct action.

Then he heard Mrs. Thatcher say that the Fascist Left "works with terrorist states like this monster Gabbiya."

"She's not only wrong," complained Gabbiya, "she's ungrammatical."

The girl hushed him.

"But does the hag mean *I'm* the monster, or the state?"

"You, obviously."

"Who does she think *she* is?" demanded Gabbiya.

Mrs. Thatcher, on the tape, was laying into him. "Gabbiya finances terrorist gangs within our own borders," she declared. "He works with crime families. He subverts our unions."

"And I could buy your Bank of England tomorrow if I felt like it," interjected Gabbiya.

The girl's lip curled while the TV panelists tiptoed around disposing of such a monster. The Americans quoted the presidential order forbidding assassination. The French wondered how civilized nations could commit uncivilized acts, even against a barbarian. The Brits hedged.

"I don't see why you give a damn what the Brits *call* you," said the girl. "They're terrified of *acting*. Sahara's too big in their economy. Oh, they *talk!* But they don't say anything about the killing of their Windfalls man, do they? They can't afford to connect you with *that* assassination! They'll never touch you."

"I had to put it to the test."

"How many test runs do you need?"

Gabbiya laughed. "You're a clever girl, Lani. *You* work out the answer." He had a darkly humorous face shaped like a rectangle, with vertical lines bracketing sensuous lips. The lines curved when he was amused. As a matter of fact, he was amused most of the time. Unlike most men of seemingly limitless wealth, he never ran out of amusing things to do, and what amused him was the conduct of each battle in his war of revenge. He shouted at the face filling the TV screen, "Great American Satan! You're frightened fartless. You won't have the guts to go after me either." He made a lewd gesture. "I've got the lot of you by the balls."

He knew all their tricks. They had bombed his head-quarters on the pretext of punishing terrorists; and when world opinion turned against such naked use of power, they tried other methods that drew criticism from Americans at home. Now they would try to get around their own legislation by luring him into a third country, where a well-paid third party could knock him off. He had read in a Washington *Post* exposé the pro-posal put forward by the director of central intelligence to the White House, and it had given Gabbiya the idea. He would move into a third country, then secretly con-trol it himself, and knock *them* off. Humiliate the great American Satan once and for all.

He was not a monster. The monsters were the white imperialists who kept his land in poverty. Once, he had been forced to survive by doing stupid monkey tricks. He had lived as a boy magician in a mud hut with three camels, a horse, five goats and some geese. He was one of a family of seven, for whom a feast was stir-fried camel's liver and sweet tea. His theater was an alley between lofty white-walled houses of coral rag tied with

27

square beams and decorated by wooden lattices and carved doors of two-leaved teak with fine brass hinges and ring-knockers of hammered iron. The streets were floored with damp sand solidified by time, silent as the tread of carpets. The people who came to see Zia the boy magician had scarred and hairless faces. They dressed in red cotton shoulder shawls and little round skullcaps. They were hypnotized by his magic, enchanted by his words. They so loved his deceptions, they could not help loving the deceiver.

The girl he called Lani knelt when Gabbiya rose. "Did you work out the answer?" he asked. She regarded him from under lowered eyelids. "Yes," she said. "You need me to make a final test run before you move into the Windfalls yourself."

"Uncanny!" He stared, and then threw back his head and let out another roar of laughter. "With our magic, we could have conquered the world, you and I! We could have produced the greatest mind-reading act in history."

"We *can* conquer the world," Lani whispered.

She waited until he had swept out of the inner palace, and then she returned to the technical journals and catalogs scattered across the great bed. She leafed through pages of Zia's particular brand of pornography: illustrations of new weapons of war. She pretended to read the snake-oil pitch for Exocet, Gabriel, Harpoon, Otomat, Shield. They might have been the brand names for rubber goods, for erotica. They were, in fact, missiles and decoys for sale to any billionaire with cash to put on the barrel. When she was sure Gabbiya was back at his magic, she slipped from its place between the pages of a Swedish arms magazine

28

the letter she wanted to read again. It was from Gabbiya's oil-and-gas corporation in Ho Chi Minh City — Saigon.

"I am the soldier of Almighty God!" Zia Gabbiya intoned. "I will destroy all who do not shout Allahu-Akbar."

"God is great!" responded the men at prayer in the Bir-el-Abed mosque.

"Death to America!" called Gabbiya.

"Long life to the Great Protector of the Faith!" they roared back.

A few minutes later, Lani appeared, suitably shrouded. She stood at a careful distance between the uprights of a black doorway. What she saw now was the man who could have brought the Arab revolt to full glory while tribes still swept on camelback across seas of sand. He looked so tall, like a slender pillar in his white silk robes and his brown headcloth bound with the gold and scarlet cord. His hands rested on a silver-hilted dagger. His eyes were hooded, his face colorless as a death mask. His body had now become strange to her, and tense. The figures in the prayer room looked up at him in silence with steadfast gaze.

He is not a monster, she thought. He's a quick-change artist. He directs the mass attention one way while he performs sleight of hand. He does it all for the faithful, from North Africa through Persia to the Indonesian Archipelago and Australia's doorstep. He conjures out of thin air those vast images that place his name on the tongue of the muezzin, and guarantee headlines in every newspaper. He does not wish to rule by force the vast Islamic crescent, though he's strong enough to swing that mighty Moslem sword across half the world. He's too wise, too magical. He knows empires are unwieldy things. Empires decay. They crush their rulers. What Gabbiya does here, in Sahara, commands another kind of obedience. Nobody goes in physical need, and he nourishes their spiritual bodies with grandiose dreams. All problems he can solve with the brains he buys.

She had seen former chiefs of intelligence come to bow and scrape in his presence, to collect his gold. Their state secrets cost him less to buy than one percent of a day's interest on his more conservative holdings; and their treacheries incurred no punishment at home, for they bartered away everything in the guise of consultation."

Once, he was limited by the oil market. It no longer mattered. He had purchased the services of the world's best financial brains, and they had shown him the best trick of all: how to make money spawn money. His affairs of state were conducted through banks. Sahara's embassies did little more than act as storefronts, with flunkies serving Gabbiya's whims and his overwhelming need to know what the rest of the world said about him.

No, he wasn't monster. Lani prepared to leave. She had lived so long in the mental and physical costume of the Arab that sometimes she wondered if she had lost contact with her own culture. Yet she knew she could not altogether vanish into an Arab skin. She had been given a duty to perform. But she had been out of touch too long with those who instructed her. They held her life to be too valuable to put it at risk. They needed her intact, for some as yet unforseen task. She was alone between two worlds, and her body went through one set of motions while her mind frequently observed the performance with contempt. She saw everything through opposing windows, her eyes and his. She saw that the monsters were those who had corrupted his people, interrupting the centuries of lean living. The monsters were those who sold him ultramodern hospitals equipped with medical mercenaries whose methods of birth control included tearing the heads from newborn infants. She had seen this for herself. She had met the nuclear physicists who, because the money was right, told him how and where to buy the ingredients for bombs. She had watched recruits from secret armies abroad, teaching his young terrorists new forms of mutilation. They were the monsters. They told him he could buy their icebergs in Greenland and tow them into his North African harbors, to become a source of fresh water. He was a magician, and the trouble with magicians is that they are the most easily conned by the conjurors.

"But I work for those monsters, those conjurors," Lani reminded herself, as she was obliged to do almost every night now. She had heard the warning shuffle and stir of feet in the prayer room, and she silently withdrew.

He was still young-looking.

He strode from the mosque and called, "Bring me the horse, Szeik!"

His favorite Republic of Sahara documentary film showed him astride the Polish stallion Pterskov out of three-times U.S. National Top Ten mare Pritski. He had his own program to restore the bloodlines of the Arabian horse world, corrupted by America. America corrupted everything, everywhere. On Pterskov he had shaken off the humiliation of the mud hut and the camel dung to proclaim the sacred rage of Islam. On Pterskov he paraded before his troops while they swore fidelity to the Great Islamic Crusade against satanic influences, and the holy war against America. He had paraded the horse because he wished to remind them that the toys of modern warfare must never blind them to their own true past. Each man must every morning ride the wind.

It was almost morning now and the wind was rising out of the gap between desert and fading stars. The horse stood in the dark moon gate. "The Lord has chosen you," whispered Gabbiya while the horse bent this leg and then another, arching its white swan's neck. "Fly without wings," said the Great Protector of Islam as he sprang into the saddle. "Be victorious without the sword."

Upon the wind he rode, solitary in the desert, and listened to the voices of his ancestors.

He returned refreshed, certain that the final act must begin. The girl waited.

She thought: He's made up his mind, then.

She could read his mind like an open book. She hoped she was not as vulnerable. That joke about adding mind reading to his bag of magic had cut too close for comfort.

She knew what he liked best after these wild desert rides, and she had prepared herself accordingly. There would be the terrible struggle of body and willpower, the slow surrender. She had discovered Gabbiya's vast repertoire of magic. She could still surprise him by pulling a new trick of her own. She was going to need all her ingenuity today. She felt his eyes exploring her.

"You must leave for the islands the moment your papers are in order," he said, and wondered if he should tell her it might be months before he followed. He fell back onto the bed. One of the new eunuchs, castrated after his return from two years of private school in England, began removing Gabbiya's boots. The lad's eardrums had been punctured at the time his testicles were cut off. He would never dare try to lip-read the words of the Protector. Still, Gabbiya's thoughts were best kept to himself for now.

He rolled onto one elbow and studied Lani, a feast spread for his delectation. Should he later confide the great secret? It would inspire her to new heights of sexual invention. She knew already that he could do what he wanted with the Windfalls. He could start a panic. Incipient destructive instability. That's how it was described to him by the best of the world's financial whiz kids that money could buy. "Think of the world economy as an airplane," this commercial wizard had told him. "It keeps flying on wings balanced upon national debts and deficits. It will stall and crash if the airflow breaks away at any point along the wings, because the balance is already too delicate for safety. The Windfalls could be such a point of stall, of incipient destructive instability." Even on the largest map, the islands were an insignificant dot. Brigandage and the courage of explorers had made them a major crossroads of ancient commerce. Today, what had been the haven for ships laden with gold was now the haven for large corporations escaping taxes. Panic here would spread like a fever. Gabbiya knew how to start it. This much he had allowed Lani to learn.

But there was now a greater secret. Should he tell her? A sweet dilemma. His mouth watered.

And if she was a spy?

Why, then, so much would be added to the exquisite humor of things. If the United States really had the best intelligence system in history, it must know Gabbiya held the Windfalls hostage already, through his bankers and offshore companies, reinsurance and shipping agencies, trusts and brokers. If the American Government learned of a greater danger, it could never act decisively, with media and legislators clinging to its coattails, against Zia Gabbiya, descendant of those who commanded ships of the desert and of the sea. No wailing mothers, no timid politicians, hampered him. He had the power, at will, to revive a war in the seas around the Windfalls that Americans thought was long ended. He had taken a British sea cadetship, had served a year in warships of the Royal Navy in that fantastic time when London thought it controlled Sahara. *He* knew that the true value of the Windfalls lay in the seas around.

As a cadet in Britain, he had also mastered some jolly funny naval expressions. If the girl was a spy, she could only assist the Imperial U.S. Presidency in falling flat on its fat face. "We were twenty days at sea / When the captain turned to buggery," he sang to himself. He gave the eunuch a genial kick of dismissal. The lad groveled, backside waving deliciously.

"Stop," Gabbiya signaled. The boy paused. Several notions ran through Gabbiya's head at the same moment. He turned to Lani. "We'll make him watch."

"So he can give a full account to the servants' quarters?"

"He won't be able, not when I'm finished." Gabbiya caught a glint of emotion. Fear? Compassion? "He's already lost his balls and eardrums." Gabbiya raised an open palm. "What is it Shakespeare says about the last stages of man? Without hair, without teeth, *sans* everything?"

Poor little eunuch, thought Lani, and she faked an ecstatic wriggle of her hips. Poor boy! And poor me! Another of my communication lines down.

She dared not plead for the lad. Perhaps she could make Gabbiya stop at merely cutting out his tongue.

CHAPTER 4

The search for the vacuum man drove Professor Rutgers into what must have appeared, to Those Who Must Be Obeyed, as a frenzy of action. She nipped in and out of the run-down Georgetown office with an irregularity he knew would infuriate any TWMBO tails. *If* he was being tailed. He had to face the risk that others had gotten wind of a Double-D-C operation. The joke was that the bold *Get Gabbiya* order was almost certainly being watered down. Rutgers sensed it. He sensed a swing back in favor of the regularized irregular services. Overt/covert operations had upset Capitol Hill again. Instead, there was a Special Forces buildup underway. A team of SEALS, Sea, Air and Land Soldiers, had embarked on a submarine equipped to release and recover them underwater. Task 160, the Army's not-very-secret helicopter unit, was being redeployed. Combat Talon helicopters were moving out of Fort Worth for unknown destinations. Rutgers had friends everywhere. He knew the signs.

He hoped, but he was not very confident, that this was not going to blow up into a full-scale combined-ops project of the sort ending in charges that the War Powers Act had been violated again. The consequences would be worse this time, if Gabbiya was the target. Sahara's President was not entirely the posturing fool the Pentagon took him to be. Gabbiya would certainly have arranged for any new U.S. strike force to collide violently with U.S. allies. But warnings to this effect from outside the services would be interpreted as civilians timidity. Anyway, Rutgers' job wasn't to resolve rivalries. The more overt secrecy the better! The more informers the better. One went with the other. The greater a nonsecret secret, the more that politicians and journalists felt compelled to shout it to the world. The results made it easier for those who really did have something to hide. The clients of informers had lost the knack of searching below the surface. They were spoiled by having officially unacknowledged secrets handed them on a platter by nonexistent sources who would deny everything if hauled before congressional investigators.

"You can accomplish anything, provided you don't care who gets credit or blame," he consoled himself. The advice came from a superior officer of long ago — a modest intelligence analyst in the field. He had cracked codes said by Washington to be impregnable. Intelligence officials had robbed the combat agent of all credit for a major victory. He'd been speared like a frog and hung out to dry by jealous deskbound rivals. He had kept his self-respect, though. In the end they could not keep him from contributing to his country's preeminence in the field.

The vacuum man would need some of this same stubborn integrity. He must be safe from surveillance. Rutgers winced when he thought of those ambitious men who would see the chance for promotion in a large-scale, overt intervention. *They* would be the likeliest to have Rutgers tailed.

He saw no sign of tails. He was indulging in fantasies, which was part of his Double-D-C job. He was supposed to imagine an enemy's many possible actions, and it was natural to let his imagination roam over what his own side might also do. He really didn't believe we'd be so mad as to *invade* the Windfalls.

All the same, he approached the vacuum man with stealth. He laid false trails among the friends he kept in Washington's many nooks and crannies. He already knew where to put his hand on an old-fashioned American hero.

Pete "Cat's Eyes" Casey flipped through the order books. Demand was again exceeding the supply of Spad beer. Not bad for a small newcomer in a land of giant breweries. He had started the venture with Bingo Harriman after their release from Hanoi's Zoo. They had borrowed the brand name from the A-1 Skyraiders known to their fellow naval pilots as Spads. The two men drew just enough from the business to cover living costs. Otherwise, profits were plowed back into the brewery, in trust for the buddies they knew were still alive and held against their will in Vietnam, Laos and Cambodia.

The two men were liked around town for their reserve. Folks in Raleigh, Virginia, were glad of the boost Spad Beer gave to local employment. Few in town knew about the secret Forget-Me-Not Fund through which other veterans helped finance the brewery; and those few saw no cause to talk about it to outsiders. Officially,

Casey chose the place for the fresh and sparkling Appalachian waters, and Bingo for the cheap land whose slopes were suited to a certain amount of terracing and rice farming. How Casey and Bingo came by their expertise in these matters may have been the subject of local gossip. Not a whisper escaped into the wide world outside the community. It was a two-hour drive from Washington, but light-years away in philosophy. This was the true and compelling reason Casey and Bingo picked on Raleigh, Virginia.

Casey was a long-legged man with an awkward stride caused by the brutal treatment he received after parachuting from his jet over North Vietnam. He was still thin as a bean pole. Other prisoners had ballooned after they got out. Casey stuck to the monkish discipline forced upon him by ten years in the cages. His dark hair had first turned gray. Then it reverted to the dirty blond of early childhood, for no medical reason that he could discover.

He was in his bare office when the intercom buzzed.

"Mr. Casey?"

"Yes, Carol."

"There's a man here to see you. A professor . . . Rutgers?"

Casey hesitated. Professor? His guard came up. "Tell him I'm busy." He swiveled away from his desk to stare out at the mist-laden hills. There was a slight drizzle. Sometimes he yearned for the sun. Sometimes the damp gloom reminded him too much of the deep jungle. Still, it was this year-round rain that gave Spad its much publicized spring waters.

Professor? Professors who arrived without warning, in his experience, wanted similar things. They had started prodding his psyche when he came home from the Zoo. He lumped them in with the eggheads in Washington who had run the war into defeat. They talked a good game. When it came time for decisive action, though, they found a dozen reasons to do nothing, rather than take responsibility for innovation. Lessons learned by the men in the field were wasted.

The door to his office opened. He turned, eyes cold.

"Sorry," said Carol. "Either I got here first, or he would." She kept her voice down. "He's quite harmless and I'll stay."

Despite himself, Casey smiled. Carol could terminate any conversation by the strategic employment of her notebook. He stood up, unprepared for the untidy figure who bustled in. Rutgers wore a tweed jacket over what looked like faded pinstripe pants, a stringy red tie with a red-striped shirt and a *detachable* white collar already flying free from its stud at the back. He had graying locks and the creased, pugnacious features of a navy warrant officer. Nothing about him seemed to Casey to add up. He was either muscular, or plump. He was either sartorially inventive, or didn't give a damn about clothes.

"What are you a professor of?" Casey demanded belligerently.

"Oceanography. *And* history."

Casey sat and tried to get the split image into focus. "They go together, of course." But he knew the sarcasm would run off this man like water from a duck's back.

Rutgers took a chair. "That's right," he said.

"You don't look like a man who'd spend a lot of time underwater," said Casey, still probing for a way to knock the man off his perch.

"But I do. There's a whole new world of history beneath the sea. I reconstruct an era from the shards left in ancient wrecks. Prosopography, it's called."

"Proso — ?"

"Just a fancy word, stolen from wartime intelligence, which stole it from old history profs like me." Rutgers leaned forward, playing the eccentric scholar. "You take some monster from history, see? You build up a profile of him from surrounding bits of information. Slowly you get a picture of his habits, temperament, the way he treated his lackeys. It's an art. Apply it to tyrants today, and you can predict how they'll act, how they'll respond and what you can do to make them stick their necks out."

This professor had said enough. Casey glanced at Carol, sitting in a far corner, taking notes, and gave her a nod of dismissal.

"Thanks," said Rutgers, relaxing.

"How much do you know?" asked Casey.

"About the Forget-Me-Nots, we've heard about a couple of tyrants in Hanoi who continue to give you the runaround. I think I know why."

Casey noted the switch from "we" to "I." He waited.

"About oceanography. I know your partner and yourself went through the Navy's program at the Scripps Institution, in California, just before you were assigned to the Gulf of Tonkin. You both fantasized in the Zoo, to survive solitary. What you fantasized came out of that brief period of underwater research."

Still Casey waited.

"You also kept your sanity by performing mental arithmetic. When your partner joined you in the cages, you were calculating natural logarithms to two decimal places in four or five iterations with a stick in the dust. Mr. Harriman's nickname of Bingo, incidentally, comes from his habit of stretching fuel past BINGO, which is the point of return to the aircraft carrier. Bingo flew at speeds and ranges outside his aircraft's envelope of performance. He did it once too often and that's how he came to join you in the Zoo."

Rutgers' voice was a low, pedantic singsong. Casey had to lean forward to hear, as if he were attending lectures again. The man seemed to have it all wrapped up, even to the way Bingo and Casey tried to make good use of their limited opportunities when the Communists thought they were losing the war and it might be prudent to improve prison conditions. The two pilots had learned about rice farming, and Casey already knew something about how Japanese beer got its distinctly crisp flavor from rice. Like many long-time navy pilots, the two had acquired degrees in engineering and applied physics and were astronaut material. But when they were finally released, they concluded outer space was for younger fliers. They'd explore the neglected world of inner space. For reasons connected with their decade in prison, their interest ran to underwater communications. They were back in America, working on a fresh approach to sonar and the use of sound waves, when the first hard news emerged from Indochina that American prisoners still survived.

At this point Casey interrupted. "You've demonstrated enough. Now let me tell you what *I* learn from all this bafflegab. You're part of that goddam establishment that washed its hands of the missing-in-actions."

"Men thought to be MIAs may be live prisoners," Rutgers cut in. "I'm not among those who tried to suppress the truth. My career doesn't depend on lies issued as official fact years ago. I have seen satellite scans of the territory where our men are still held. I have seen field reports. *And I need your help.*"

Casey's laugh was hollow. "That's a joke! Our veterans have pleaded with presidents, with national security advisers, with DIA and CIA and maybe even JC Himself. Now, just like that, out of the blue, you want us to help you, after you rejected us time and time again."

"Not me."

"C'mon!" growled Casey. "You're all hand in glove."

Rutgers stared down at his grease-stained tie. "Three months ago," he said softly, "you paid a visit to the Windfall Islands."

Casey froze.

"What you did there wasn't illegal," continued Rutgers. "But it wasn't exactly legal, either, was it?"

"I looked into the formation of an offshore company. Nothing wrong with that. Some of the largest corporations in the world keep their head offices there."

"But they don't have secret funds," said Rutgers. "Dollars waiting to be moved to Asia if ever Hanoi decides to do business."

"I can't imagine a prisoner wanting us to sell American honor to get him back," protested Casey. "Any money we might spend would go to finance escape and rescue."

The two men locked eyes. Rutgers studied the lean, firm jaw, the sharp blue eyes and their surrounding whites innocent of any sign of illness. Yes, thought Rutgers, this is my man.

The professor emerged from the brewer's office an

hour later. He had broken rules, played a hunch, done it personally and without authority. He was climbing back into his black sedan when someone he took to be Bingo Harriman went hurtling into the building.

"What was that unfrocked priest doing here?" Bingo asked Casey.

"More like an unmade bed, I thought," said Casey, considering. "There is something of the confessional about him, now you mention it. I wish to hell we'd never met!"

"I knew it!" Bingo raised his hands to fend off the bad news. In the days when they had flown out of naval air stations, it had always been the chaplain in his black sedan who brought news of a fatal crash. "Tell me the worst," said Bingo.

But Casey felt unable to tell him all of it. Not yet.

The professor knew there were those who called him Rotgut. In their company, and because he had so little regard for them, he cultivated this resemblance to a partly inflated hot-air balloon. He was not a windbag, however. He never appeared on Capitol Hill, and only occasionally at the secret convocations across the river. Whenever he could, he escaped back to the oceanographic institute in California where he got on with his research in peace.

His independence salvaged him from the Wrath of God, which was what they called any sign of displeasure from Charles de Wrathe, the Double-D-C's coordinator.

"It's not your job to charge around the countryside inventing stories," rumbled De Wrathe.

"The invention was necessary," replied Rutgers. "You guys hand me a profile to fill. I root around and find an exact fit. After all, I *am* your expert at getting inside the heads of the inaccessible."

"You psyched out Augustus and how he maneuvered around Julius Caesar. But nobody's alive to contradict you," said De Wrathe. "Anyway, you got two summers free diving in the Med out of it. I'm still not sure those wrecks added to *our* store of knowledge."

A pained expression settled on Rutgers' face. "Everything counts. Every tiny bit of broken pottery tells a story." The trick in handling the great man was to blind him with science. "With Pete Casey, one accidental bit of information was the clue. Whoever fit that profile still had to be so highly motivated, nothing would hold him back. Once I had the clue, I invented — no, dammit, I merely *embroidered* a little on what we know already. Whatever Zia Gabbiya's planning in the Windfalls, it's in collaboration with Hanoi."

"That doesn't give you the right to say MIAs are involved."

"But they are," said Rutgers, "I can't prove it, but they are!"

De Wrathe was on delicate territory and he looked away. "Worst of all," he rapped out, turning back to Rutgers, "you should *never* have seen them in person."

"I saw only Casey," Rutgers said calmly. "And that was absolutely necessary. It was the only way I could have gotten that tiny, accidental bit of extra information."

"The clue. So? What *was* the clue?"

"You know better than to ask," Rutgers said sententiously.

De Wrathe reined in his temper. There was nothing else he could do for the moment. If Rotgut were a full-time employee of the agency, if he lived for nothing else, if he could be kept under control by threats about the size of his pension, then it would be worth arguing. But Rotgut was a contract man, and in this affair for personal reasons. He was most dangerous of agents from the viewpoint of his own masters. He had alternatives. De Wrathe had only one way open: use Rotgut and then get rid of him.

"Perhaps you will let me ask you this, then," said De Wrathe. "What's going to motivate Casey?"

"He's sick of seeing this country being kicked around," said Rutgers. "He figures the rot set in when we abandoned our prisoners. It becomes a corruption of all our American values when we watch our own nationals terrorized abroad, our embassies bombed with impunity, our interests damaged because no politician has the common integrity to take the heat if the blow is struck and then goes wild."

"He told you that?"

"I know my man. He didn't need to tell me."

"Permit me, then, to ask you this, too," said De Wrathe in his silkiest tones. "Casey has a partner. How can you be sure he won't confide to this partner? After all, the cover story will be that Casey's returning to the Windfalls on company business."

"Casey will find something to tell Bingo Harriman."

De Wrathe sighed. "No wonder vets make lousy businessmen."

"They make reliable buddies," retorted Rutgers, wondering what a life long bureaucrat like De Wrathe really knew about running any business unsupported

47

by faked expense accounts and siphoned government money. "If I'd let you send some fat-assed whiz kid," he added, growing suddenly heated, "can you imagine Casey listening? He commanded pilots who were launched by catapult to their deaths. They were killed attacking targets designated by those same whiz kids, thousands of miles away, with no knowledge of the terrain and no experience of flying except the launching of paper clips with government-issue elastic bands. Casey listened to me because it takes one to know one." He sat back, folded his hands across his stomach, and defied the Wrath of God.

De Wrathe concentrated on opening the middle drawer of his desk. "I take it neither is married?"

"They *were* married." Rutgers looked at the ceiling. "Casey's plane was seen exploding after a raid on Nam Dinh. There was some argument about reporting him missing or killed in action. Squadron commanders avoid stating a pilot is killed in action for several reasons—"

"I thought Casey was a squadron commander."

"He was. He'd discussed with other pilots the dilemma. If a man's reported killed, the enemy can do what it likes with the poor devil. But also, if he's reported killed, his wife's automatically a widow. She can collect benefits, remarry, get on with her life. Casey and Bingo made it understood, if they ever went down, they were dead."

"A coldhearted decision."

"I would have called it heroic." Rutgers swallowed his anger. "Being killed in action relieves the government of any obligation to get you back." He looked at the great man's uncomprehending face. "Casey takes a keen in-

48

terest in MIAs. Not unnaturally. He won't tell Bingo anything that might jeopardize the safety of the living dead."

De Wrathe took out a folder. He watched the professor watching the ceiling. "Not a word spoken here gets out," said De Wrathe. "I've as big a stake in total sanitation as you." Their eyes met. "Now hear this and hear it good. If Casey goes, he goes on his own hook. Nobody will know anything about him if he's caught. If his name comes up, we'll disown him. And he's got no authorization from us for using deadly weapons. Nobody gets killed in action on this one."

"Meaning we can't kill them but they can kill us!" retorted Rutgers, confident there would be no hidden microphones in this office, which was unknown to even the most covert of the overt side of the agency. "Well, Casey's no innocent. He knew we only need to find out how many Gabbiya means to kill of ours, so we have the right number of coffins ready." And with that final piece of sarcasm, Rutgers took his leave, thinking he'd really extracted more from the situation than he had any right to expect. The main thing was to get Casey rolling with a fair bit of backup. Casey would make his own decision about who might get killed in action, regardless of directives.

The thought occurred to Rutgers when he got inside that De Wrathe was making a similar calculation. It relieved the department of all responsibility.

"Rotgut probably figures I'll tell you the truth anyway," Casey told Bingo some days later.

"Rotgut?"

"I checked a few things out," said Casey. "This Professor Rutgers is a bit of a joke at the oceanographic center, where he's called Rotgut. My own feeling is, he plays the fool to the hilt. He's okay. He seems to understand about the Group."

The Group was how some pilots thought of themselves. They took their cue from the aviator-author Antoine de Saint-Exupéry, who wrote about flying before jets were born, and yet seems to have said everything. "My love of the Group," he wrote, "is my substance. I am of the Group and the Group is of me."

"Of course the professor understands," said Bingo. "His own son was one of us. Trigger Tony."

"Tony Rutgers?" Casey was appalled. Trigger Tony Rutgers had been directed from Washington to fly a mission way outside the envelope. "How the hell did I miss that?"

"The only reason I caught it was, I just got a report leaked by the DIA." The Defense Intelligence Agency had its own sources of live-prisoner sightings from Vietnam. A sympathetic DIA colonel had slipped Bingo the new list. "They put a question mark against Tony's name in the old column of KIAs, and penciled it among the MIAs, pending verification."

The colonel had taken a risk. If word got out that Tony Rutgers might be alive, the reaction among veterans' groups could be politically bad. The list had been passed to Bingo because the colonel trusted the Forget-Me-Nots' discretion. Casey was glad he had briefed his partner fully. He had waited to get Bingo where they could talk freely, without making too big a thing of it. They were driving from the plant to Raleigh when he seized his opportunity. "So how'd you feel about me spending more time on the islands?" he prodded Bingo.

"It makes sense from a business point of view. But why'd Rotgut come to you? It seems too neat."

"You know those guys."

"No, I don't," said Bingo. He was feisty wee man from a Scottish mining town in Pennsylvania. "All I had to do with the breed was with our own Navy Intelligence, and they were fully operational, not flying desks back home. The only thing excuses Rotgut is, he had a son who was one of us."

"Maybe that put him on track. Maybe he worked backward, from seeing the threat in the Windfalls. His pals in some other agency, FBI or Internal Revenue perhaps, would run through names of Americans looking to do business out of the islands."

They drove on in silence until finally Casey said, "He seemed to know I got information out of the Zoo."

Bingo frowned. Getting information out of the Zoo had been the single most dangerous task a prisoner could undertake. The Navy had improvised a method by which Casey could report back to Washington the identities of prisoners. Once a man was known to be alive, representations could be made to the International Red Cross asking that he be treated in accordance with international law. Vietnam's Communists did not acknowledge that law, but world opinion became a consideration in how Hanoi then treated a prisoner whose existence was now publicized.

It had been a coup, to get Zoo information out. It was accomplished with the help of relatives in the United States; by a painfully slow method of doctoring what little prisoners' mail got through, sometimes with the help of Westerners who visited wartime Hanoi with dreams of moderating its policies. For prisoners who collected data, discovery meant death. Casey had performed this seemingly impossible task for nearly four years, assembling facts on new prisoners through an ingenious system known among navy pilots as the Smitty Harris Tap Code.

Bingo looked vastly unhappy. "If Rotgut knows you did that, he thinks you're crazy enough to do anything."

"Now you sound like the trick cyclists," said Casey. After the Zoo, he had faced psychiatrists Stateside who had refused to believe anyone could behave as Casey had and keep his sanity.

"It's obvious this is why Rotgut came to you," muttered Bingo.

"He thinks I'll snoop around the islands and see what happens if Gabbiya shows up. That's all."

"Until you're asked to pull the trigger."

"No chance."

"So you don't think Gabbiya should be destroyed?"

"If an elephant runs amok and keeps killing, someone has to shoot him." The savagery in Casey's voice was directed at the impossibility of answering Bingo's artful question. "What makes us different from Gabbiya is that we don't use his methods. I'm not another Jackal," he added, naming the legendary arch-assassin of modern terrorism.

"Yet Gabbiya's using our old buddies as pawns?"

"So Rotgut says."

"If that's true, do you really think Rotgut's government bosses would have the guts to do anything about it?"

"No." Casey's grip tightened on the wheel. "They've

done nothing about the guys we left in Vietnam—" He let the indictment hang between them.

"So nothing's going to happen in the Windfalls," Bingo said. He cheered up. "A fox like Gabbiya won't chance being caught in an open field. So what are we talking about? An expenses-paid vacation for one."

"It could run into months."

"Heck," said Bingo. "We needed to get off our butts with this offshore company anyway. What about building a brewery out there? They don't brew beer in the Windfalls. But if they're like the rest of the Caribbean, I bet they guzzle it by the barrel."

CHAPTER 5

Lord John Bracken hoisted another tankard of beer while he waited for his daughter at the Royal Windfalls Yacht Club. Lush green lawns ran down to the crowded docks. The harbor spread out before him, small islands in the distance. There were no commercial buildings to be seen; no vulgar hoardings; nothing to offend the eye except Colonel Zia Gabbiya's yacht. It was back.

"Bloody disgraceful." Bracken wiped the beer from his beard and motioned for Alison to join him.

She had already seen his scarlet face and guessed its cause. "You're going to bust a blood vessel." She glanced out to sea. "It's only a yacht, not a battleship."

"I hear she's got a moon pool midships for divers."

"Bar gossip?"

"Yes," he admitted. "But bar gossip among sailormen, lassie!" The bar was a sore point. It was strictly Men Only. The place for women was clearly labeled Ladies Annex. After Alison's first attempt to break the centuries-old taboo, she had complained, "You treat women as if we belong in a zoo." Bracken had stuck to his view that men had the right to a refuge from wives. The club had finally yielded the lawn as a common

55

meeting ground.

He signaled a waiter to bring Alison her usual pre-lunch gin and tonic. "Some members have taken a closer look. That ship seems as old as *Britannia*, but they say she's crammed with every mod con."

"Sort of a Q-ship?"

Bracken pondered this. Q-ships were the armed merchantmen whose disguise caught German U-boats napping in two world wars. "It's a fair analogy," he admitted.

"She's obviously got range. She also comes and goes as she pleases. Doesn't anyone clear her?"

"The owner has HM Customs in his pocket."

"Oh?" Alison's instincts as a lawyer were aroused. "Have you spoken to anyone?" *Anyone* was shorthand for Government House.

"Waste of breath. Anyway, I leave that sort of thing to you nowadays." Bracken swiped up another tankard, blew off the froth, and took a deep swallow.

"There's one bit of unfinished business you can't palm off on me," said Alison. "That American who makes beer in Virginia. Peter Casey? He not only wants to incorporate. He's applying to start a brewery here."

"Smashing idea!" Bracken's face brightened.

"I'm glad you like it, because he wants to see you."

"Not me, dear. He's doing business with John Bracken Partners. And John Bracken being retired, you're the next in line."

"You started the paperwork." Alison made no attempt to hide her dismay. "I was planning tomorrow to make myself scarce."

"He's coming here tomorrow? Great heavens! It's

56

months since he first talked to me. I've heard practically nothing since."

"That's another reason you'd better see him. There's something not quite right."

Bracken sighed and looked into his daughter's cornflower-blue eyes. Sometimes she was too like her dear mother for comfort, in looks and in perceptions. "There's nothing strange about Casey's revival of interest. You know the government's setting a quota on new offshore companies—"

"No! That's economic suicide."

"Not for the companies already registered. Their value multiplies accordingly. Gabbiya owns a lot of them, so he's that much richer."

"Gosh!" Alison put a hand to her face. *"That* explains the new directorships! Gabbiya's been putting government ministers on the boards of his cutout companies. He'll buy control of the legislature that way. No wonder this American is rushing here. He must be another of Gabbiya's cover men."

"Hold on!" protested Bracken, who seemed to remember that he'd taken rather a liking to the American.

Alison refused to stop speculating. "He telexed something about setting up a research project, too. It all smells fishy."

"With your keen sense of smell, you'd better deal with him."

Alison set down her drink. "Very well, I will! I'll settle that young man's hash."

Bracken shuddered. When his wife, God rest her, assumed such a stance, he had always dived for the Men Only bar. "I reckon I'll just have a quick one for the road." He got up.

"I thought you were standing me lunch?"

Bracken retreated a prudent step. "I see the latest addition to our legal brains trust heading your way. I fancy he'd like to ingratiate himself with a junior partner. *He'll* buy you lunch." He gave a cheery wave to the spectacled youth picking his way across the lawn. "Morning to you, Forsyth-Smith! Sorry can't linger!" He turned his back and grinned fiendishly at Alison, who pulled a face. "All yours, daughter dear . . . Oh! By the way." Bracken pirouetted around again. "Casey's not a *young* man. He's about the age you like 'em."

Bracken kept out of everyone's way during the following days. He had fish of his own to fry. He called Downwind Dalrymple a couple of times, and then was favored with a visit from a Queen's Messenger of the British embassy in Washington. "You blokes have it soft," said the courier. "It's cold enough on the Potomac to freeze the balls of a brass monkey."

"Cut the cackle and gargle," ordered Bracken.

The courier was his own vintage and offered gossip in payment for the whisky consumed. "They've gone nuts in Washington over bloody titles. Dukes, princes, knights . . . The Concorde ships 'em in at the expense of the American taxpayers. Costs them six million bucks to get a dozen duchesses together with some exhibition of noble ruins."

Bracken let him ramble on while he scanned Dalrymple's handwritten warning. ". . . almost certain Gabbiya's men tapping overseas calls . . . We'll have to fight the bastard on his own level, not with high tech but booby traps." Vice-Admiral Dalrymple had commanded forces during the third jungle war in Malaysia, the final war that Britain won largely by telling nobody about it while the war in Vietnam was being lost on worldwide television. That, anyway, was how Dalrymple saw it. He was not popular for this: London had become caught up in the fad for fighting wars by publicity. Whatever Dalrymple did now to help Bracken was strictly unofficial. Even the Queen's Messenger had simply stopped off during a routine run with sensitive dispatches for London. "Ironic," Dalrymple's note ended. "With all our technological advances, we're back to cleft-stick messengers."

From time to time, Alison appeared at breakfast before Bracken's daily sail to Wreck Cay. She seemed preoccupied. Bracken smiled to himself. He knew Alison.

Two Sundays after he got Dalrymple's message, she joined him in church. Bracken enjoyed the tranquillity of the old Scottish kirk, the reassurance of gleaming white gravestones bearing the names of close-knit families like his own. He loved to bellow the old hymns. He even enjoyed the parson's sermons, delivered in a soft Scots burr. He cherished the sense of continuity, the disconnection from a modern world gone mad in the aftermath of lost values. He was, as Alison had anticipated, bubbling with good spirits when they stepped out into the hot glare of noon.

"I was wondering about Casey," she said. "You don't mind me bringing him over to Wreck Cay?"

Her father stopped dead on the gravel path, causing momentary confusion among other worshipers. "I thought you planned to settle his hash by now."

"Okay." Bracken admitted defeat. "He *does* turn out to be the age I like 'em." She tugged him forward. "Satisfied?"

Bracken savored his brief triumph. "But . . . Wreck Cay?"

"I'd like him to know you better."

"Ah."

"And you're a bit of an ogre anywhere else."

"Oh?"

They retrieved their mopeds from behind the hedgerow. "He's rather in awe of you," said Alison. "He's only seen you behind a desk. And anyone who flew old war relics must strike him as . . . well . . ."

"A relic?" Bracken grinned. "I take it you no longer suspect he works for—" He jabbed a thumb earthward.

Alison looked up into the heavens. "My only fear is, he might be too much of an angel."

Bracken pulled his crash helmet down over his head, then paused. "You coming home?"

"I kind of said I'd take Casey to the nautical museum."

He finished strapping the helmet. "You don't dislike him, then?"

"He's a smasher."

"Then, by all means bring him over to Wreck Cay," said Bracken, kick-starting the moped. From the way he gave his daughter a wave and roared off, she knew he was unusually cockahoop about something.

Casey felt like a truant. It was now midwinter in Virginia. His heart bled for Bingo, for it was also midmorning in the middle of another workweek. Casey

60

had to remind himself that he was working, really, even while he sat on the yacht club lawn to keep yet another date with Alison. The legal proceedings to incorporate a Windfalls branch of Spad Beer had been started through Alison's father months earlier. Casey had been taken aback when he learned his company's business was being passed over to the girl. She seemed too young, too darn pretty, to be a lawyer. At their first meeting, though, she had been helpful with the brewery proposal. She had also asked shrewd questions about the ocean research project, provisionally titled INSPAD for Inner Space Development and inspired by Professor Rutgers.

When Casey had described how INSPAD began as a dream shared in prison with his partner, Alison said, "I thought Hanoi's prisoners couldn't talk with each other."

"We found ways. Sort of a Morse code." Casey's reply had been guarded. He wasn't exactly tailored for the role of an undercover man.

Alison had her father's sharp ear for dissemblers. She continued to cautiously explore his mind. If Casey justified their frequent lunches and dinners as business, it became for him very pleasant business indeed; and Alison had a guilty sense of enjoying their times together far beyond the call of duty.

So it came about, two days after talking with her father at church, Alison turned up on the club lawn wearing an old shirt over weathered jeans.

"Sailing's the order of the day," she said defensively, catching an odd expression in Casey's eyes. "So I threw on my old togs."

"Shouldn't you be in court later?" Casey was trying to

catch his breath. Old togs on Alison did more for her than furs and diamonds on a New York model. "Don't you have torts to untort? No malfeasances or *in flagrantes?*"

She grinned. "No. No wig and gown. No commissioning of oaths. Just a day with ole Cat's Eyes." She saw him start. "Father found out your navy nickname. That's why I want this talk to be on the water. You can't keep anything secret for long around here, not on dry land, anyway."

Casey sighed. "My partner said this would happen."

"What?"

"Swanning on the high seas. Lotus-eating. Lizard-lounging." He followed her down to the boats bobbing in the basin. The islanders were dedicated water babies. The docks were loaded with spars, upturned dinghies and canvas under repair. At every mooring danced sailboats and runabouts. Casey thought it wasn't a bad way to rot, intoxicated by the sun, pickled in beer, in the company of a beautiful blonde. Bingo would never believe this scene was work—the girl in worn jeans cut above the knees to reveal golden legs, breasts untethered and bursting to get out of what must be her father's shirt. Alison in full legal fig was a severe figure. Now she was—well, a *figure.*

He recognized in Alison a skilled sailor. She handled the Dragon effortlessly. The design was obsolete, the wooden hull patched over many times. Sail and rigging would win no prizes at a fashionable regatta, but she was beautiful in a classic sense, and practical. That seemed to Casey a satisfactory way of also describing the girl. She had stowed a luncheon basket forward of the cockpit. Strapped on top was a folded copy of the

New York *Times*. He suddenly realized he hadn't seen an American newspaper in some time.

She caught him appraising the boat and said, "The Dragon was bequeathed to Daddy by a client who couldn't pay his legal bills. The boat was a mess, but it was all he owned when he died."

"A painstaking job to fix up?"

"Painstaking is the operative word. My father was no great handyman before he gave up the law."

"And why did he?"

"That's important to you, isn't it?"

"If Spad Beer has a future here, I really should know." He had avoided the issue until now. But if Alison had staged this outing in order to talk frankly, he might as well speak first. "Did your father's retirement have anything to do with political changes here?"

They had sailed into the lee of Gabbiya's yacht. The wind vanished. The sails flapped. A tiny frown creased Alison's brow and she made a show of nursing the Dragon through the patch of still water. A mild current was carrying them back into the harbor breeze. For a moment, the sailboat floated small and helpless under the black hull with an inscription painted on the stern: *Qurqũr*." The vessel's name was repeated in dancing golden Arab script. The only sign of life was the brief flash of binoculars above.

Casey knew the girl was using the distraction to avoid answering his question. It could wait. He was too interested in this yacht. Close up, she seemed the size of a Yankee clipper. There were several levels of deck. Rotgut had said *Qurqũr* was Arabic for some ancient form of sea vessel, reflecting Zia Gabbiya's efforts to identify himself with the great Islamic empires of another age. The huge ship hung over Casey, and he had the uneasy sense of unseen eyes watching him from the brooding silence.

Then the wind freshened, the mainsail filled, Alison hauled in the sheets and cried *"Lee-oh!"* making Casey duck as the boom swung over. He found himself too busy for further talk until they were out of the harbor and running before the wind along a chain of tiny, bare islands.

"I'm taking you to Wreck Cay," Alison said when he joined her at the tiller. "That's where my father now does his 'painstaking work.' It's the best way I can answer your question."

He knew he would get no more from her. "How long has Gabbiya's vessel been in port?" he asked instead.

She regarded him with amusement. "How do you know it belongs to him?"

"Everyone talks about it," he said quickly.

"They do? My impression is, almost everyone avoids the subject." She stretched. "These islands were very free and easy in the old days."

"They still seem that way to me."

"Yes, but you're an expat."

"You mean, a stranger?"

"Expatriate. From outside. Horrid word at the best of times, but here it implies much more. We're tight-knit and clannish. We curl up when danger threatens."

"And it threatens now?"

"The danger's growing daily." She pointed a toe at the New York *Times*. "Friends bring me that newspaper. I can't buy it here any more."

"Why not? Censorship?"

"In a way. The two distributors canceled several foreign publications a week ago, saying there wasn't enough demand. Both distributors were purchased a month ago by another Windfalls stationery firm which recently acquired two new directors. They can outvote the rest of the board. The two new directors are respectable Windfallers who'd fallen on hard times. I was surprised they could find the money to become majority shareholders. What they'd done was sell themselves to an expat."

"An expatriate named Gabbiya?'

"Gabbiya wouldn't be directly linked. He uses stooges. That yacht symbolizes the way he works. It appears. It disappears."

"And when will *he* appear?"

"I suppose that's what you're here to find out."

The challenge was unmistakable. Casey stared at her, and remembered Rotgut's advice: "Stick close to the truth in your story. When you're sure you've found a potential ally, trust your judgment." Casey felt he understood Alison as well as he had ever understood any woman. He was too old for infatuations. He had an automatic resistance to pretty faces. Still, if he should need a buddy to fly cover, he'd pick her. He had always recognized a good wingman when he spied one. No higher praise would have occurred to him than that.

He leaned back. Alison was taking a sudden interest in coming about and was busy with sheets and sails.

He was learning quickly about these islanders, thanks to her. Visitors, unable to see beneath the surface, assumed Windfallers had only an eye for money. The instinct was said to go back to when a drunken English captain became separated from a supply fleet with provisions for the settlement of Virginia and wrecked his vessel here. The survivors lured later ships onto the same reefs, plundered the wreckage, and laid the foundations of an economy. During the American War of Independence, islanders sold British gunpowder to the Americans and made the British Navy pay to victual British warships sailing against those same Americans. They nursed the healthiest skepticism of London, Washington, and all bureaucrats. This they inherited from forebears who had once ranged up and down the New World coastline as agents of the City of London's Company of Adventurers and Planters. They were adventurers in the freest sense, at one time governed by the Virginia Council, though an English king kept rights of veto. Their spirit infused an old document preserved in their centuries-old parliament: a report from the crews shipwrecked on the Windfalls in 1609: "This being still the Atlantic, the balmy climes are like more unto the bordering Carib. Though there be no fresh water, rain may be catched from the skyes. The islands are free from any creeping beast or hurtful venoms. There is much fragrant cedar and yellow woods for shipbuilding if enough of us may live. Food is abundant, such as turtles with sweet oil and wild hogs grown fat on berries, seabird eggs aplenty and a palmetto with head big as any cabbage. If there be any impediment to bright hopes for the future, it is that we do seem far from any succour and all of us are laid lowe with ailments and woundes . . ."

Alison, whose ancestors might well have waved lanterns to draw cargo-laden vessels onto the hidden reefs, had quietly indoctrinated her client in her people's secret ways. When Casey, with infinite delicacy, brought up the mystery of the murdered governor, her reply was brisk: "Our peculiar ties with England required us to invite Scotland Yard to help investigations. The Home Office in London then sent us a bill for the first month. We refused to pay and Scotland Yard withdrew its heavies. We said fair enough, *you* appointed the late governor, he's yours. If you don't care who killed him, neither do we."

"But you continued your own inquiries?" Casey had asked.

"Of course, although our police are hardly geared for terrorism."

"Terrorism?"

Alison had nodded. "It was an outside job, calculated to send us a message, that the Windfalls are on their own in a crisis."

Casey saw that British possessions in this region were adrift. American security impelled Washington to assume defense responsibilities. The action in Grenada, however, had a shocking aftermath, for the British viewed it as a direct challenge to their sovereignty. So the Windfalls remained in this dangerous, unacknowledged limbo. "There's a precedent," Alison had told him. "A few years ago, another British governor, in Bermuda, was shot dead with his military aide. The killers were caught and hanged. Everyone got back to making an honest dollar. London submitted the customary Scotland Yard bill, but I don't believe it was paid. Bermudians must have figured their own investigation yielded entirely satisfactory results. No foreign terrorists. No panic. No loss of tourism."

It occurred to Casey that while she was educating him, Alison had been also gathering up new information on Gabbiya. Once again, Casey's eyes fell upon the rolled-up copy of the New York *Times* strapped to the picnic basket. Very odd. Telephones tapped. Foreign papers unavailable. "What about TV and radio?" he asked out loud.

Alison, her arm draped over the tiller, smiled as if she knew where his thoughts had been. "The local radio's run by a broadcasting commission, and it's easy to censor news. A TV satellite dish supplies the community by cable, and the input also comes under the two-man commission's scrutiny. The commissioners are handsomely compensated for doing nothing as directors on several of Gabbiya's front companies. And individual ownership of satellite dishes is banned—on environmental grounds . . ."

She broke off. "Wreck Cay dead ahead."

Casey found himself squinting at an island with plumed trees crowning black lava cliffs.

"We'll have to sail 'round," said Alison, and Casey resumed his role of deckhand. Wreck Cay was protected by an outer ring of reefs. On the other side of its lozenge shape were mangroves marking swamps from which escaped an evil odor. "During the Boer War," Alison called out, "the British put child prisoners from South Africa here. Impossible for them to escape."

The mangrove trees grew several feet high, their fleshy leaves shining a sinister green. The smell borne on the breeze came from the oozing black soil. Casey was not sorry when bright, sandy beaches appeared.

Alison came up to a mooring. He helped her furl the sails. "I'm for a swim," she said and thereupon confirmed his first suspicion, that she wore nothing under her sailing clothes. "We skinny dip here all the time," she said, and dived over the side.

He was self-possessed enough to note that her extraordinary figure was tanned deep bronze from top to toe. "When in Rome do as the Romans," he told himself, and followed her.

Nothing seemed more natural. Swimming naked beside her through the warm waters of a small bay was paradise after the stinking mangroves. She led him to shallow water, heated by the sun all the way down to the beds of sea grass. She stretched full length, the water barely covering her. Casey floated alongside. He felt as if he wallowed in hot springs on a bed of velvet.

"You asked me why my father retired suddenly." Alison rolled onto her back, raising herself on her elbows. She seemed unconscious of the water lapping around her breasts. Casey had come to rest a judicious distance away, the sun's reflected glare half blinding him. The girl's voice continued softly. "He was the first to see the possibilities for the islands in offshore-company trading. That was years ago, when he wanted to free young English entrepreneurs from the punitive taxation of London's socialist governments. He got laws passed that opened up a business alternative to our dangerous dependence on tourism."

A school of tiny fish invaded their small world, skipping in silver clouds and producing expanding ripples of water that felt to Casey like gentle fingers stroking his body.

"He didn't mean this to become a tax haven for cheats and crooks," continued Alison. "You've got to understand this about my father: he's straight as a die. He saw the Windfalls serving a purpose like that of— say, Hong Kong, a crossroads of free commerce, though for us it could never be more than modest. He was wrong. Places like Hong Kong became politically insecure. Big international corporations shifted their head offices here. Modern electronics made it all suddenly feasible. Tons of business can be conducted instantaneously through one girl secretary working a telex machine, provided there's a sign outside the door insisting this is headquarters of Worldwide Waffle Traders Inc., or whatever. You see the possibilities?"

Casey, squinting in Alison's direction, answered yes, and tried not to sound ambiguous.

"We still monitored the foreign companies pretty closely." Alison shifted position. "Then too much money poured in too quickly, and we're not big enough to handle sharks. Dirty dollars came in for laundering. The temptation's been too great for some islanders. Daddy felt the offshore company records contained fiction that was turning into docudrama."

"Wouldn't he be better off doing something about it?"

She shrugged, and her breasts shimmered golden in the clear water. "The noose is drawn too tightly. Even I didn't realize till now. It's too late." She touched his arm with the tip of one finger. The contact was like an electric shock. "To do anything legal," she added.

"And illegal?"

"Ah." She stared at him, her pointed eyes now changing color from the green of the sea to the cornflower blue of the sky. "As a lawyer, I shouldn't voice an opinion. But the history of these islands —"

"Is piracy, plunder, and homemade rules," said Casey. "You've instructed me well." He was also recalling Rotgut's words: "Forty Thieves, that's what the top island families are called. The Forty Thieves take a percentage from any business registered in the Windfalls.

70

The Forty Thieves make the rules, and any time some smart Yankee lawyer finds a loophole, they change those rules. You can't score a goal, because they keep moving the goalposts." Casey smiled up at the girl. "If your father's afraid Gabbiya will ultimately control things through these companies, why doesn't he get the Forty Thieves to make some new rules?"

"Because Gabbiya's compromised so many of them." The answer was jerked out. Alison ran her finger along his arm and over one shoulder, tracing a jagged scar. It was the largest of burn scars he'd suffered after ejecting over Vietnam. His captors had eventually covered the burns in mud, leaving it here until maggots multiplied beneath, eating out the rotten flesh. A French-speaking Vietnamese doctor had claimed it was from his old colonial masters in Paris that he had learned about this nauseous remedy, used among peasants.

"Let's drop Gabbiya," said Alison. "I want you to enjoy the day. When you first arrived, you were like those Americans who can't seem to stop running. I found myself wishing I could shoot you down . . . Oops! Sorry! *Shoot down* isn't very diplomatic."

He had never told her exactly how he had been taken prisoner. Yet obviously she knew. He said hastily, "Your father. Let's get back to him."

She withdrew her hand. "He's up there. We'll find him soon enough. First, some lunch." She scrambled to her feet and ran for deeper water. When Casey reached her, she shouted, "Race you!" and made for the boat in a fast crawl.

He tied with her at the mooring. She clung to the buoy. "Casey?"

He was hanging to the bow of the boat, and turned

his head.

"Casey. I like the sound of that better than Cat's Eyes. Casey, I'm not a cock teaser. Swimming back just then, I suddenly thought you might get that impression. I feel very natural with you. All my gang and my family have swum here nude, ever since we were kids. But I don't want you to think—"

He reached out and pulled her toward him. "Let's not complicate things," he said, and kissed her.

On board the boat, she put out hefty sandwiches and beer. It was clear she had grown up among men.

"What about your father?" asked Casey.

"He cooks his bangers and mash up there on a stove. He'll let us know when he's ready to see us. He's turned terribly hermity."

They wrapped themselves in towels, gorged, and became drowsy in the heat.

"Another reason it's taking so long to finalize your incorporation," murmured Alison very much later, "is, they're trying to figure how patient you'll be."

He opened one eye. "I rented Backgammon from that South African on a six-month lease. That's a measure of my patience."

"Mmm. You don't mind more business talk?"

"That's what we came here for. Originally."

"I don't yet see what good this INSPAD project does. Won't you have your hands full with building the brewery, if you ever get permission?"

Casey stiffened. "I've explained our interest."

"Frankly, I think it serves another purpose."

Casey said nothing.

"My father also thinks you might be here for other reasons. He's a bit bonkers these days. He's into synchronicity. Know it?"

"Similar events that don't seem linked by cause and effect."

"Goodness!" said Alison.

"Like E.T." Casey elaborated. "Remember the little extraterrestrial who was befriended by a small boy named Elliott? When E.T. saw a girl kiss a boy on TV in Elliott's house, away at school Elliott stopped scuffling with a girl and kissed her."

"Gosh!" said Alison.

"Of course it could be telepathy."

"Daddy has other ideas."

"So have I." Casey laughed at the way Alison's eyes flew open in astonishment. "There's a lot of solid scientific work on the subject. Wolfgang Pauli, for instance. He discovered the quantum mechanics exclusion principle. He's done a monograph on synchronicity."

"You sound exactly like my father. What on earth got *you* interested?"

"When I was in the Navy, we talked a lot about mind-controlled cockpits. Pure fantasy. But later, in prison camp, I'd think about it. There wasn't much to oil dried-up minds. One day I got the most precious gift, an equation tapped out in prisoners' code . . ." He stopped. "I'll explain sometime. Meanwhile there's a tall, bearded skeleton up there on top of the cliff, showing its teeth."

Alison did not even bother to turn. "That's him," she said. "Father."

The man on the cliff whistled.

"We'll have to swim," said Alison. She rummaged

inside a bag. "Trunks for you. Bikini for me."

Casey found it instructive that she hadn't mentioned them earlier.

The more she listened to the two men, the more uncanny seemed the resemblance. Alison's father was much older, of course, sitting on the clifftop like some old salt, an unlit cigar sticking out of the foliage of his beard, a knitted sailor's hat on his gray head. Casey seemed like a kid beside him. What intrigued Alison was the way their minds worked in parallel.

Casey was enjoying this first encounter since he had approached John Bracken about Spad Beer's offshore plans. Then Lord Bracken had made at least some concession to appearances, wearing an unpressed suit, crumpled yacht club tie, and shoes without socks. Now, clad only in faded khaki shorts, he seemed all bones and beard. Despite his retirement, he still seemed willing to discuss Spad Beer; and sprinkled his advice with asides about the danger that the Windfalls would get the reputation of other tax havens already infected by the dirty dollars of organized crime. "Then," said Bracken, "there will be an international crackdown. We'll have lost our money-making capacity *and* our self-respect."

"Is that what Zia Gabbiya wants?"

Bracken turned on Casey a pair of very pale blue eyes filled with curiosity. "Is that what you've learned?" he shot back.

"I know practically nothing."

Bracken nodded. The two men were at an impasse.

Alison said, "I don't think you two trust each other enough yet." She got an angry glance from her father.

74

Ignoring it, she jumped up. "I want you to see what my father's escaping into, Casey."

"Escaping?" echoed Bracken, rising.

"Yes. Running away, into second childhood."

"You said it was saving my life!" objected Bracken.

"It's also removing you from the political battle," retorted Alison, moving away.

Casey listened to their bickering as he followed them into the interior. They seemed to argue for his benefit. As if, in this way, they could coach him. Perhaps this whole day had been carefully planned. Perhaps Alison's little lessons in Windfall ways had been leading up to this. Suppose Bracken was himself selling out to Gabbiya, and hoped to bring Casey over?

It was difficult to imagine. Bracken had become a skinny hermit, scrambling over crags and bashing a path through thornbushes with his stick. He was nimble as a goat. He moved with the energy of someone meeting trouble head on, and not at all like a man of devious ways.

CHAPTER 6

"My very own dinosaur!" Bracken said proudly.

Casey gaped. It stood in a shallow valley at the top of the island. Its four olive drab wings were concealed under the carmine flowers and polished broad leaves of royal poinciana trees. It looked at first like an armor-plated dragonfly of absurd dimensions. The nose pointed along a well-trodden path. The three-bladed propeller was too high to swing by hand from the ground.

"What, besides a dinosaur, is it?" Casey asked.

"It was designed as a torpedo-spotter-reconnaissance plane, a T.S.R. We called it the Stringbag."

"How the devil did you get it here?"

"Fished bits of it up from the sea, where I crashed it long ago. That's a ropewalk." Bracken indicated the shadowed path. "Back in windjammer days, islanders made rope by *walking* the fibers backwards, twisting them under tension, a mile down to the slipway. I reversed the process and walked my bits and pieces up from the sea."

"You didn't put them together here, though?"

"In a shed, hidden in undergrowth." Bracken waved toward some rotting vegetation. "I rolled the old girl out just now for a breather."

"So she can be seen from overhead?" Alison asked.

Casey caught a flash of something between father and daughter, and Bracken said, "Nobody'll pry round here."

Alison said, "The ropewalk's long enough for an airstrip. The shed used to be a *cordelier*, for twisting the rope strands mechanically instead of walking the rope. But the demand for rope ended with the days of sail. An attempt was made to start a floatplane service in the islands. The planes were kept in the sheltered bay, with the *cordelier* as a hangar approached by a sea ramp. The Second World War stopped all of that. They say Wreck Cay wrecked men's hopes because —"

"Because of its name," Bracken interrupted quickly.

Again Casey sensed tension.

"You're the first outsider to see her." Bracken moved around the big biplane, kicking the outsize undercarriage wheels, testing guy lines, checking flagged rods that held the moving surfaces rigid against high winds. "I get a bit of help from our dockyard, and from your Smithsonian chaps. None have seen her though." He stopped and fixed Casey with eyes of hooded intensity. "You do know about the Stringbag?"

"Not really."

"No, of course not. Your navy was fully stretched in those days too. More's the pity. If your chaps *had* been paying attention, there'd have been no Pearl Harbor."

"How's that?" Casey asked politely.

Bracken described the Stringbag attack on the Italian fleet a year before Pearl. "The Japs in their Berlin embassy went down to see the damage and figure how we did it. German intelligence even sent questionnaires to their agents in America, based on what the Stringbags did and how such an attack could be sprung

78

on Hawaii."

He was not boasting. Casey understood completely the pride prompting Bracken, the wistful need to restore the honor of this wood, canvas and baling-wire warplane.

"Is she flyable?"

"Pretty much," said Bracken. "That's why I staked her out. She needs to get some air in her nostrils first."

"What if a gale springs up?"

"Stringbags weather any storm. This one's lashed down because she'd kite in a blow. Landing her on deck, I sometimes needed men on each wingtip to hold her down." Bracken shook a strut, demonstrating its strength. "She's shipshape and Bristol fashion . . . and ready."

Ready for what? Casey wanted to ask but thought better of it.

They left John Bracken fiddling with the huge, eight-cylinder Bristol Pegasus engine. It was like a steam engine compared with the sleek turbines of Casey's era. Bracken had to climb a ladder to get there.

"Don't you go thinking he's an old fogy," warned Alison when they were back on the Dragon and underway.

"I'm one myself."

"Don't dismiss the Stringbag as a blunderbuss, either." She brought the Dragon up into the wind for the long tack through the reefs. She seemed oddly defensive.

"Talking of a blunderbuss," said Casey, to lighten the mood, "did I really see a crossbow leaning against the—what is it?—*trestle footing?*"

Alison laughed. "You soon picked up the lingo."

"Your dad did a pretty good job of showing me how she flies. He named every visible part."

There was a tiny dimple of triumph in each corner of Alison's mouth. Casey had absorbed those strange names! He *must* be hooked. She said, "He'll show you how to fly her yourself. When she's ready."

Ready? Again Casey bit back the obvious question. Instead he asked, "And the crossbow?"

"Oh, that's my department. We don't permit firearms in the islands. A crossbow doesn't rate as a firearm. I keep it for protection."

"Against what? People don't even lock their doors around here."

"But small islands like Wreck Cay are tailor-made for terrorist landings. And HMG won't take the danger seriously."

"HMG?"

"Her Majesty's Government. All they're good for nowadays is an occasional royal visit. One governor they sent us was then canned for fiddling his entertainment allowance. The only people who really understand us in the United Kingdom are the Navy, and they've been pulled out of here. The Navy *made* policy here! Daddy's a throwback. His ancestors had roving commissions as privateers, and the family's first knighthood was one of those that James Stuart used to hand out like lollipops when he was king in the 1600s. Simple prizes for making use of simple weapons. It's in our blood. Americans wouldn't understand."

"Some do," murmured Casey. "Those of us who saw a bicycle economy absorb the blows of bombers. The bicycles cost the Communist Vietminh very little. God knows what the bombing cost us. But I question if your dad's Stringbag qualifies as a simple weapon. To me, it looks more like a complicated, heavy-duty truck. If any tiny part falls off, the whole thing goes down."

"You're wrong. Complicated, no. Handcrafted, yes. She's like a Rolls-Royce, the coachwork and all lovingly put together."

He was disturbed to see tears in her eyes. A brisk wind had come up and she pretended to shield her eyes against the flying spray.

"Sorry if I get overdramatic about that Stringbag," she said after a while. "It's my father's lifesaver. He's been very sick. Then he got depressed over what's happening here, and it nearly destroyed his will to live. He's a fighter, but he couldn't see how he could fight Gabbiya's wealth and cunning."

"Gabbiya doesn't seem to have broken any laws."

"Not until he's ready to act."

"*What* action?"

"Impossible to guess."

"He doesn't *own* the Windfalls. If he tried to operate as King of Terror, he'd get his comeuppance." Casey made it sound flippant. "He'd come up against the Queen of England."

"No, he wouldn't," said Alison. "The history of the Windfalls is one of piracy. 'What we have, we hold.' That's also the motto of the British Navy. Well, the Navy's been kicked out from here, so *they* don't hold it. London listens to our parliament, but stays uninvolved. Parliament only talks money. And money talks. When Gabbiya's ready, he'll make clear his financial stake in the Windfalls, and how easily he can start an economic crisis that will spread worldwide."

"Synchronicity," said Casey.

"You've come to the same conclusion?" Alison glanced automatically into the cockpit, where her New York newspaper had been wedged under the transom. She said impatiently, "Come on, Casey! You knew exactly what I meant when I was the first to speak of synchronicity . . . Similar events and similar thoughts that don't seem linked by cause and effect."

Casey found himself staring at the newspaper Alison now withdrew. She had folded it to a column reprinted from *Harper's* and written by that magazine's editor, Lewis Lapham. The CIA, he suggested, tongue-in-cheek, had made such a persuasive mess of things lately that the time had come to transfer the business to the private sector. If America owed its greatness to its entrepreneurial genius, why allow its safety to remain in the hands of muddled bureaucrats?

Casey, slowly raising his eyes, wondered what he should acknowledge.

"You're an angry man under that calm veneer," said Alison. "You're like my father."

"Your father, you said, couldn't see how to fight a terrorist like Gabbiya."

"Not until now," Alison amended. "When he salvaged the Stringbag, he was just messing about like a kid with a boat. Now he thinks he's found the one weapon Gabbiya can't control."

"Good God!" Casey stared at her.

Alison gave him a bleak smile. "I've no intention of letting him use it. I'm too grateful just to see him come alive again." She shivered. "It's late. I'm supposed to be at a bar association dinner tonight."

The wind had shifted with the onset of evening and

now blew into Nelson's Harbour off the open sea. The final run to the club was a broad reach. With the wind full astern, there was little sense of speed. It was Casey's mind that was racing. Why had she shown him the Lapham column? Did she thing something crazy had happened? That the CIA had been *deregulated* and Spad was part of a "black" operation run by free enterprisers?

Did she know more than Casey?

He was hauled next day before a government committee to determine if Spad's plans to build a brewery might cast a small shadow on the Windfalls' independence. That struck him as an odd preoccupation, if the islands were being bought out from under their feet by Gabbiya. A three-man board questioned him in the vast auditorium of the town hall. Nobody else was there except Alison.

"We wonder," said the beefy-faced chairman, "why brewers would dabble in something esoteric like oceanography."

Casey was taken aback. Why were they zeroing in upon INSPAD research proposals, slated for a later hearing? He glanced at Alison, who was scribbling on her legal pad.

"Why pick on these islands for your research?" asked another committee member.

"The Great Meteor Seamount, south of the Azores, is linked to certain phenomena in this region," Casey said. "There are lava eruptions along the mid-ocean ridges that throw up magnetic minerals. My partner believes there may be an abundance of mineral concentrates on the seabed here. I confess this seems to have little connection with the brewery business—" He paused, hoping for at least a friendly chuckle or two, but none came. "It's really a kind of hobby with us for the moment," he finished lamely, catching sight of Alison's note, which said, *You don't have to answer.*

The chairman's red face vanished behind a large handkerchief with a loud *"Harrrumphhh!"*

"Can we turn to my client's more immediate concerns?" Alison inquired sweetly. She was looking particularly perky. Any committee not actually dead on its feet couldn't help but be charmed, thought Casey.

"*Our* most immediate concern is water," said another member. "Every drop has to be collected from the sky."

"I fully understand, sir," said Casey. "Rainwater's ideal for Spad Beer."

"Our taxpayers would resent your use of it in periods of drought."

Casey almost asked *which* taxpayers in a land where there was no income tax. He almost said it was the foreigners like himself who kept the islands afloat. Instead, he observed mildly, "We proposed a water catchment, as in Schedule D."

"Our people won't consult your Schedule D," objected the chairman. "They will simply see you've got water. And they don't."

"We deliberately provided for emergency supplies to the public," Casey replied patiently. "We aim, sir, to be known as a public-spirited organization, and genuinely so."

They stared at him in silence. Finally the chairman consulted a file and muttered, "Bottling. Your use of crushable bottles is condemned by the environmentalists . . ."

By lunchtime, Casey knew he was in trouble. The only thing saving him was Alison: not because of her charm, but because of the committee's respect for the Bracken quickness of wit. They were leaning over backward to be courteous about a conclusion already arrived at: dismissal of the petition to build a brewery.

Alison wanted to use the break to clear up some office routine. Casey took the opportunity to call Bingo in Virginia. The connection seemed unusually bad. Casey huddled inside an unventilated booth in a corner of the town hall's vestibule, and found himself staring up the wide staircase where portraits of past mayors marched up the white walls. The mayors all seemed to regard him with the same stern eyes, which said, *Don't try to put one over on us.* The first mayor, who was the nearest, had Bracken in his name and looked like Alison's father. He must have been three hundred years dead, but there was a lively gleam in his eye. Casey couldn't read the nameplates under the other portraits, but several had that piratical Bracken look.

"Bingo?" Sweat ran down Casey's face. The air conditioners in the building seemed to have broken down. "You've got to consult the professor for me." He had to wrap it in the language of a prisoner of war. "It's urgent. If we want the go-ahead for Spad, we might need to drop the research project."

The partners were old hands at conveying much in little. Bingo read him loud and clear. "Just one thing," warned Bingo.

Casey listened and was shocked. It took a moment to disentangle what Bingo was trying to say. Their technical adviser had left Washington a week ago to see Casey.

There was only one technical adviser: Professor Rutgers. *And he'd been here a week?*

The connection began breaking up. Casey pushed out of the phone booth, gasping for air. He was soaking in perspiration. Something known as "Windfall dust" must have been accumulating in that booth. It gave Windfallers asthma, though they'd never admit it for fear of denting the tourist trade. But it wasn't the dust now. It was the feeling the booth had given him of being back in the isolation pit, just his head sticking out of the ground and the Tonkin Delta for company, steamy and desolate. He had to get his breath. He leaned back against a pillar under the mocking stare of generations of mayors.

The walls closed in, and the mayoral portraits turned into thin faces under pudgy blue caps. Big Vien shrieked something in Vietnamese. Big Vien! Who debated French philosophy one moment and turned into a frenzied Marxist the next. Casey smelled the Zoo's peculiar odors, the human sweat, the red Tonkin mud, the incense sticks persistent even in Ho's paradise. *Claustrophobia,* they had warned him on the flight home: That will be one of the long-term consequences. Claustrophobia. When it hits, resign yourself. Tell yourself it's like catching a cold. It will go away.

He sank onto the bottom step of the immense staircase and lowered his head. The burn scars were hurting again, but the images had gone. He was in the town hall at Nelson's Harbour, not in solitary, not under torture. The telephone in the booth was ringing. He forced himself upright, ordered himself to pick up the instrument. There was nobody in sight, it was lunchtime, the huge teakwood doors were tight shut and the whole place was stifling hot.

"Yes?"

"Are you okay?"

It was Bingo. The old bastard. Always there when you needed him. "Sure I'm okay."

"My phone went dead, so I raised holy shit with the operators."

"We'd said all we had to say."

There was silence from Bingo's end. Only Bingo Harriman could make a silence speak volumes.

"Okay," Casey said finally. "Spit it out."

"The Duck," said Bingo.

"Got you." Casey felt his whole body turn suddenly cold. An invisible hand lightly touched the back of his neck. The Duck had been a private way of referring to their chief tormentor in the Zoo: Big Vien.

"Don't drop the INSPAD project," said Bingo. "It'll make great duck soup."

"Right."

"Just in case you miss the prof."

"Right."

"Right." Bingo cut the connection.

Casey stepped out of the booth, breathing heavily. Pure coincidence? Synchronicity? No need to weave fantasies. Their minds had been running in parallel, that was all, and the logical figure waiting for them both at the end of the run was Big Vien: Nguyen Khac Vien, whose commonly used middle name and whose voice in French or Vietnamese sounded like the quack of a duck.

He stood for a while staring blankly at a poster. "Windfalls Annual Arts Festival," it read. "Under the Patronage of the Acting Governor . . ." Pasted across it

in a diagonal slash was the one word: CANCELLED.
Too bad.

Big Vien in cahoots with Zia Gabbiya? That must be
what the professor had told Bingo. It must be what the
professor wanted to discuss with Casey. But there
would be more to it than that. Professor Rutgers had
always emphasized the vital requirement to avoid direct
communication, let alone face-to-face meetings, except
in real emergencies.

Bingo, after today's first phone conversation, realized he possessed information that Casey hadn't received *because he hadn't seen Rutgers here.* Once Bingo had
woken up to the implications, he quickly restored the
overseas connection. He, because of Rutgers, did not
want Casey to let the committee kill the INSPAD project!

The big doors rattled and creaked open. Alison
walked into the vestibule behind a man carrying a ring
of big keys. She spotted Casey and hurried over. "They
locked you in! I'm so sorry."

"Why should you be sorry?" He was still stunned by
where logic was taking him.

"It's early closing today—Thursday. I should have
reminded you. Shops and government offices pack up.
That's why the committee's in such a hurry. The members resent being made to work—" She broke off. "My
dear, you're *soaked!* Are you all right?"

He saw now that someone, excessively zealous, had
turned off the central air conditioning. In a way it was a
relief. At least he knew he hadn't relapsed into that
humiliating postprison period of panics and nightmares.

"You could have died in here," said Alison, only half

joking. The sun pouring through the high greenhouse roof of the closed vestibule had sent the temperature soaring. "Let me—"

He interrupted her. "Can we get an adjournment?"

"Probably." She looked at him in surprise. "I thought you were in a hurry to have Spad Beers approved."

"Not without INSPAD," he said grimly. "The committee took the initiative in mixing the two. Let's hold them to that."

Her gaze strayed to the open door of the phone booth. "I see." She moved away, and he heard her speak to the man with the keys. Then the gentle hum of the air conditioning started up again.

He still felt weak. Perhaps the fear of a *return* of fear had caused his knees to buckle. Big Vien! He'd waited a long time to come back at Casey. All these years. Years of continuing imprisonment for men Casey and Bingo had left behind.

What *was* Rotgut up to?

Casey returned to the hearing in a mood he recognized could be self-defeating. Alison had said he was a deeply angry man under the veneer. She hadn't seen anything yet. Most of all, now, he was angry with himself for having relaxed too well, for having joined the lotus-eaters.

Alison was right about the committee's resentment. The members turned up looking flushed from a liquid lunch. Their first questions were abrupt. Casey was even more abrupt in his replies. This seemed to fluster them. Perhaps they had expected him to crawl. He grew more taut. The chairman pointed out that, originally, Spad merely sought incorporation. Now it wanted to brew beer "on the premises." What else did the company have up its sleeve?

"INSPAD," Casey declared.

"We disposed of that this morning," grumbled the chairman.

"Oh no, sir. You raised it this morning."

"It is, however, a separate issue."

"It was, Mr. Chairman, until you brought it into this discussion."

"Mr. Casey, this is not exactly a discussion. My colleagues and myself have a very important decision to make."

"Then I humbly suggest—" Casey was stopped by Alison's hand on his arm. He turned to shake it off. Before he could resume, she cut in.

"A week's adjournment," she called out hastily. "I think that would meet your general convenience, Mr. Chairman. The committee has nothing on the agenda for that day—"

"We expected to dispose of the matter today, Miss Bracken."

"My client, with respect, wishes to consider certain adjustments," Alison snapped back.

They growled and mumbled among themselves, but they could not with dignity deny an application for adjournment from someone of Alison Bracken's impeccable island background.

"What adjustments?" asked Casey when they were outside again.

"I don't know." Alison steered him toward the waterfront. "You nearly blew it in there! What the hell's got into you? And don't sulk! Those bastards were ready to close you out. They're afraid to make it obvious. This is, if you'll pardon the expression, a parliamentary democracy. They don't want awkward questions raised in public." She was in a raging temper. It matched Casey's own. He was suddenly sick of this toy-town version of Royal England, its phony Olde Englishe pubs with names like Ye Olde Ram's Bottom, and committee members who dressed in shorts, knee-high socks and buckled shoes and wore a false air of genteel poverty. He'd lost patience with the lotus-eaters who could brush a murdered governor under the carpet and paste CANCELLED over his successor's public appearances. He stopped.

"What's cancelled the acting governor?" he asked.

Alison, whose own angry thoughts had been moving in another direction entirely, swung to face him. They were standing where the traffic policeman in his pointed London bobby's helmet was perched on a podium in what was known as the birdcage, at the confluence of Palace Rise and Harbor Road. He had no traffic to direct, but there he was, white gloves and all; and at that moment he seemed to Casey to sum up all his own frustrations.

"I'll tell you what's cancelled the acting governor," said Alison. "Bloody Gabbiya! He's arrived."

Casey's heart jumped.

"You mean here, in the islands?"

"My father just told me," said Alison. "He was all steamed up. One of his pals in Immigration tipped him off. He didn't have details." She broke off. "I don't think we should stand here talking." She made him cross to the big stone quays. "You mustn't go off the deep end." She looked up at him anxiously.

The absurdity of the phrase made him laugh. "That's the deep end." He caught her by the shoulder and nodded at the flat patch of sea caught between the empty dockside and a breakwater pointing like a finger into the harbor. "Do I look as if I'm going to jump?"

She laughed with him. "You had me worried. When I got back after the lunch break, you seemed . . . shaken. You let your anger show for the first time. It frightened me."

He tightened his hold on her and they moved toward the breakwater. It was one arm of a storm shelter for small boats. The afternoon was late; there was a heavy stillness in the air. Storm clouds gathered beyond the harbor mouth, shielding the sun. A strong smell of spices drifted on the first breeze. For a moment Casey could imagine himself back in the North Vietnamese port of Haiphong, after his first interrogation. The moment passed.

"I guess I owe you an explanation," he said.

"Only when you feel ready."

"Let's walk."

They moved out onto the breakwater. Was he ready? What, really, could he tell her? She'd already as good as accused him of being secretly more interested in Gabbiya than in Spad's future here . . . He thought: I don't really know much. I don't know why Rutgers invented INSPAD. Alison could be better informed than I am. That second possibility had occurred to him before. Perhaps she was willing to trade? Any temptation to open negotiations was pushed into the back of his mind by the sudden appearance of a woman.

"The Irish Girl!" exclaimed Alison. She kept her voice low, although the woman walking toward them was still a distance away.

Casey supposed she had come upon them so suddenly because of the strange light flooding the sky. The Irish Girl moved in her own cloud of diaphanous veils. Behind her, the huge thunderclouds were swiftly expanding, their anvil heads flushed pink. She wore a white dress of finespun muslin. Her slim body, backlit, was clearly naked. Casey thought of the desert nomad in an engraving from Sir Richard Burton's *The Kasidah of Haji Abdu el-Yezdi*. Erotic poetry from an Arabist might seem an odd association, but it sprang to mind as readily as the name of Zia Gabbiya. The woman seemed both brazen and chaste. Her long black hair swung and flew behind her. There was wildness in her, and yet something tentative. If the breakwater had been wider, if she could have passed them without acknowledgment, Casey felt, she would have gladly done so. He was surprised to hear Alison say, "Miss Blake?"

The woman stopped. A smile transformed her bronzed features.

"I'm with John Bracken Partners," said Alison without giving her own name. "I recognized you from the immigration pictures."

The woman seemed on tiptoe, ready to fly.

Alison turned to Casey. "This is Mellanie Blake, from Killarney."

"A long way back it was." The woman looked up at Casey with an intent expression. "People call me Lani."

Casey took her hand. "I'm Pete Casey. This is Alison Bracken."

"Yes." There was an absence of curiosity in her soft voice. She looked away to where small puffs of orange cloud were reflected in the calm waters. A few windsurfers struggled to catch the dying currents of air in mid-harbor, their sails painting rainbow colors against the gathering darkness of the cays. Where the thunder-clouds grew up from the horizon, long streaks of lightning waved silent fingers.

"Well," said the Irish Girl. "I'll be running along, then." She seemed to float away.

"Why did you call her the Irish Girl?" asked Casey moments later.

"She had trouble with immigration." Alison spoke quickly in a tone of disapproval. "She was on an Eire passport when she arrived here weeks ago. Forsyth-Smith, one of our younger lawyers, was called in. He spent quite a long time on the case. He also turned all pale and moony. He said her boss overseas called her the Irish Girl. He keeps singing 'When Irish Eyes Are Smilin'.' He's become a regular pain in the neck."

"Who hired the lawyer?"

"Someone in Beirut. But I shouldn't be telling you all this. It's a matter of confidentiality."

"Then, don't tell me."

They were near the end of the breakwater. After a silence, Alison said meekly, "It's important to you, isn't it?"

"I should think it's important to you." Casey turned. The Irish Girl was watching from the steps to the quays.

"Okay," said Alison as if her mind had been made up suddenly. "Forsyth-Smith is known as Mr. Four Five Six around our office. They say he looks after that number of Mideast companies in the fiction library. The Irish Girl flew in here for one of those companies jointly controlled, hands-off, by Zia Gabbiya and Edgar Geld."

"E. P. Geld, our American tycoon?"

"There's nobody else by that name."

"So why the holdup?"

"Not everyone here," said Alison cautiously, "is corruptible. Ordinary folk are aware of a possible sellout. Our low-level customs and immigration people are strictly honest. They're not sure if that can be said for the new Minister for Immigration. They detained the Irish Girl so they could make 'further inquiries.' She was on Interpol's watch list. They started to check with Paris. Then the minister intervened."

"Forsyth-Smith spoke to her boss in Beirut?"

"Several times. The man insisted all the necessary papers had been filed a long time ago. We have several ways of controlling outsiders here, as you've discovered."

"You mean, the rich are one category, skilled workers another, Portuguese laborers a third?"

"More or less. If you can afford the murderous price of a residence 'available to expatriates,' you're wealthy enough to be tolerated. If you can prove nobody among the islanders can do your work, you fall into the second category. If you're a dumb beast of burden from the Azores, and no threat to anyone, you're in the third category, here under contract. The Irish Girl is in the second category as—" Alison hesitated, then laughed. "Well, get this! She's here as a deep-sea industrial diver."

"Isn't it possible she is?"

"Didn't you see her face, her body? She's deeply tanned, all over. Professional divers hardly get the sun on their faces. No," Alison said firmly. "They picked a trade for her least likely to be competition for the locals. They followed the form. Advertised the job in the local rag for the prescribed three issues, and demonstrated to

95

immigration that nobody here could do that particular task."

"Did you see the advertisement?"

"No. Immigration took the minister's word for it."

"Did you find out why she was on the Interpol list?"

"Yes," said Alison. "But this conversation is an unfair trade. It's one-sided."

She walked the few remaining steps to the end of the breakwater and stared down at a powerboat bobbing on the end of a line.

"What can I offer you in return?" asked Casey. He saw dive tanks in the after well of the boat. The tanks were dull black and rolled gently with the motion of the boat. Lodged between two of the tanks was a larger object.

"Just level with me," said Alison. "Whose side are you on?"

"Yours."

"Something drives you. It has nothing to do with me."

"You're wrong. It has to do with you *and* me. All our values."

"That doesn't tell me much!" Alison broke off and stared into the boat again. "Isn't that — isn't there a man there?"

Casey braced himself on a bollard and tried to make out the shape between air tanks. The sky had darkened. Thunder growled in the distance. He ran down stone steps to the boat's bow line, fastened to an iron ring. The stern was secured to a white buoy. He pulled on the bow line and the buoy ducked under the surface as the boat rode forward. Alison took a grip on the line while he prepared to jump. She was standing one step beneath him, and water washed over her shoes. The steps were all slippery with sea moss. The stone wall of the breakwater was covered in tiny shells like thorns, and crabs scuttled over them, making little clicking sounds.

"Let's leave!" Alison cried out suddenly.

But Casey had already jumped. He worked his way to the after well. "You're right, it's a man," he called back. "But he's dead! The head's bashed in."

"Then, leave him!" Alison looked around the storm shelter. There was nobody to be seen. "You can't do anything. Let's go. Please!"

This was utterly unlike Alison. Casey could not move. "We can't just . . . run away," he said quietly.

"No. No, of course not." Alison clung to the line as if she needed the connection with Casey. "But be quick. Then let me deal with it my way."

The last words were for the moment lost on Casey. The man was face down. He was dressed in a black neoprene diving suit, feet still encased in diver's bootees. The balaclava hood, though, had been wrenched back from the head. The hair was matted with blood and seawater, and Casey thought he saw white bone shine through. He turned the body over. Even in that eerie light between dusk and dark, he recognized Professor Rutgers, old Rotgut, the man who had started this whole affair.

CHAPTER 7

"Slipped, banged his head on the valve of the air tank," said the black police sergeant without even blinking.

Casey stared in disbelief. "If you believe that, you believe in the tooth fairy."

Alison touched his arm. "Sergeant Winston knows his stuff."

"You go on home, sir," said Winston. "We'll take care of this."

The rain had started. Between the police boat and the stone steps, men in gum boots moved in weighty silence. Casey allowed Alison to drag him away. "The victim isn't from here," she said. "Much better to call it an accident."

"Is that what we know as British justice?"

"What's the alternative? Let all this go up in flames?" Alison gestured at the white tower of the old town hall as they climbed past the deserted fish market. Floodlights caught a riot of color in the botanical gardens, where a plaque recorded their founding by Sir John Bracken MacAlison-of-that-Ilk in 1757. Casey felt surrounded by ancestor worship.

"The sergeant," Alison was saying, "just came back

from an antiterrorist course. He doesn't want to see here what's happening in Grenada, or in Central America, or in former British possessions in the region."

"Then, why doesn't he pick up the Irish Girl?"

"That might be what Gabbiya wants us to do."

Casey's head spun. He had not recovered from the spectacle of Rotgut under the police lights, his pink body plumped up like stuffed turkey and spread on the slit-open dive suit as if it still preserved him in the pink of life. There had been a lot of quiet talk between Alison and the sergeant while Casey had time to wonder what had happened to the prof's pinstriped pants. What right did he have to turn up in this other, bizarre disguise? "Recognize him, do you, sir?" the sergeant had shrewdly inquired, and Casey had quickly answered, "Never saw the fellow in my life."

Alison took him to the parking lot. She was driving the office car this day. "Come on home," she said. "You need a drink." When they were clear of Nelson's Harbour, she added, "You did recognize him, didn't you?"

He knew it was just a lawyer's probe, but now he was certain he needed more information from her than anything he could offer in return. "Yes," he sighed. "I knew him."

Alison compressed her lips. She was going to have to winkle this out bit by bit. "Did he have anything to do with your special fund?" she asked crisply.

He sat up. "Fund?"

"The Forget-Me-Not Fund. Only, it goes under another name in the bank here. Very fat it is, for such an ordinary private account with such an ordinary name:

100

James Jonathan J. Smith."

"He wasn't an ordinary guy," Casey said wearily.

"Killed in Vietnam?"

"Caught, escaped, tortured and escaped again. Last sighted two years *after* the war ended. It's really a trust fund . . . How did you know?"

"I told you, Winston's a *very* good detective."

"So what's he going to do about . . . about this latest killing?"

"We'll go about it our own way."

He noted the "we" and said, "Same way you did the governor's murder?"

Alison eased the car around a horse and cart blocking half the narrowing lane. "Perhaps."

"Perhaps?" Casey groaned. "Perhaps you're too worried about the tourist trade to do anything."

"We think about it, yes," retorted Alison. "Like the other countries round here, we used to look to Mother Britain for security. You may laugh at the old colonial ties, but Big Momma *did* recognize her obligations. Now our only security lies in overseas confidence. Other islands lost that, and went bankrupt. Look at them now — *scorched!*"

Casey was jerked upright by the venom behind the last word. It described what Ho's successors had accomplished after the Americans left Saigon. Ho's men had certainly scorched Vietnam.

Alison gave him a quick glance. "Your dead friend was a Dr. Earle Rutgers," she said softly.

Casey studiously watched the way she negotiated a bend. The car bucked under arched trees. The rain was coming down in buckets and the headlamps danced between hedgerows sewn with honeysuckle and olean-der.

"This Dr. Rutgers was into undersea research," Alison went on, her tone neutral. "He came to it through his work as a historian. He was very useful to the CIA. He could look at a tyrant from a distance in time or geography and, by a kind of remote sensing, make astonishingly accurate projections."

"Oh." Casey's manner was neutral.

"Yes." Alison wound down her window. The tropical rain had brought a sudden rise in temperature, and it was hot inside the car. "I'm quoting from a confidential report, courtesy of Detective-Sergeant Winston."

"You just learned all this?"

"No. I've known about Dr. Rutgers' presence for several days."

Casey swore under his breath. "You should have told me!"

"I didn't know you knew him."

The questions hung between them. Casey lowered his window. With the slanting rain came an intoxicating perfume and the peep of tree frogs.

"The sergeant," said Alison, "made the connection because he's learned Dr. Rutgers put a substantial deposit into the account of your Mr. Smith. The sergeant already knew you'd got withdrawal rights."

"So much for banking confidentiality." Casey huddled deeper into his seat. "Hell, I didn't know Rotgut was stuffing that account."

"I'm glad you confirm it! I thought for a while you might be working for Gabbiya. Then I was afraid you were some kind of mercenary. You called him . . .

102

Rotgut?"

"It doesn't seem very funny now," Casey said miserably. "How was he depositing the money?"

"In hundred-dollar bills. What's the fund for?"

Casey thought about Rotgut's son, Trigger Tony Rutgers, maybe dead, maybe rotting still in a Vietnam cage. "You've heard about funds for the preservation of wildlife? Well, this one's for the preservation of *our* lives. Our way of life. Our friends who thought they were preserving our way . . . Guess it sounds all Yankee-doodle-dandy to you, but some of us still believe in that kind of thing."

His face was wet. He stared out into the rain. Tall pampas grass nodded behind red-headed poinsettia in the light from a cottage. In Washington, something called the Polar Express had paralyzed the capital with snow and ice. He wondered who was there to mourn old Rotgut.

Lord John Bracken let his daughter set forth the facts. He had opened a rare bottle of purser's rum. "As Provided Her Majesty's Navy," it said on the bottle.

The rum took the curse from the chill in Casey's stomach. It had to be a very fine old rum. He didn't think the British dished out rum at sea any more. One more capitulation to American sea power. How the old sea dogs like Bracken must hate it. Behind his head was an oil painting of a Royal Navy privateer escorting a captured American vessel into the Windfalls during the War of 1812.

Casey had not seen the cottage before. Its name,

Pretty Penny, struck him as affectedly Victorian, on a par with the islands' masquerade as a little bit of jolly old England. He entered the cottage by the traditional "welcome-arms" stairway to an open veranda. The rooftop was in the Windfalls' icing-on-the-cake style, lime-washed to purify rainwater collected along narrow "steps" leading to gutters and pipes down to a water tank.

Inside, Pretty Penny justified its name. A warm smell of cedarwood infused the book-lined living room built around the universal fireplace, where logs blazed. A tray ceiling trapped the day's heat; the night often turned chill. With the passing of the storm Casey had already noticed a drop in temperature.

The firelight bounced off polished brass and gleamed along waxed panels of oak. Bracken occupied a large easy chair with shining leather arms and bow legs. Alison crouched by the fire.

Casey's thoughts had been flapping around like a barnyard hen dodging the ax. Now they came to rest, joining him in a comfortable old cottage chair covered in brightly flowered chintz. A brass-ringed ship's chronometer ticked, giving a sense of unhurried contemplation.

But Rotgut had been murdered! The barnyard hen gave another flap. Casey felt another flush of guilt.

"Nothing like a spot of rum to chase away the whim-whams," Bracken said, watching Casey through the foliage of full beard, side-whiskers and uncombed hair. "When Their Lordships of Admiralty did away with the rum ration, they banished sunshine."

Casey wasn't listening. Who were Rotgut's bosses?

There must be someone in Washington who knew how Rotgut intended to use INSPAD. Had Rotgut been working on his own, or with some free-lance bunch? *Was* free enterprise running a denationalized CIA?

Alison finished telling the story. Lord Bracken asked, "Where did this Irish Girl come from?"

"The dive boat," said Casey, alert again.

"She could have been just walking along the break-water," protested Alison. "Like we were."

"She's a diver," said Casey.

"Not the kind to drive a sledgehammer through a man's bean," said Lord Bracken.

The hen had started flapping around inside Casey's head again. He held out his glass for more of the black rum, and took a long swig. He blamed himself for letting the easy lifestyle of the islands seduce him away from his job. His job hadn't been Spad Beers — he'd put in plenty of time on Spad's innocent business matters — it had been to help Rotgut. He'd failed Rotgut. He felt like a wingman who dozes in that fraction of a second when his fellow flier is vulnerable and takes a hit.

"Mellanie Blake," said Bracken, "was diving off Wreck Cay yesterday." He relished their surprise. "I ticked her off for diving without a partner."

"Those reefs are dangerous," said Alison. "Why would she dive there alone?"

"Trying new gear. She said."

"What kind of boat?" asked Casey.

Bracken described it.

"Sounds like the one with the body." In his mind's eye, Casey saw the hen flapping again. With the next words, he brought down the ax and severed its head.

"Confirm that and you'll have the Irish Girl."

"And maybe do exactly what Gabbiya wants," said Bracken.

The headless hen still jerked. Casey looked from father to daughter. "Alison said that earlier. Why?"

Bracken uttered a deep sigh. He stood. His hair was such a haystack, he seemed to reach to the cedar beams. He wore old khaki pants tucked into muddy Wellington boots, and a loose safari shirt. "Alison agrees with me, nothing should be done in haste." He swiped up the rum bottle and swung in onto Casey's side table. Casey appreciated for the first time the man's workmanlike, powerful hands. "I've an errand to run," said Bracken. "Make yourself at home."

It should have been an invitation easy to accept. The room was snug. The fire had chased some of the cold fear out of Casey's bones. A question of simple terror would have been less damaging to his self-respect. Things were more complicated than that. He felt he'd wasted valuable time while others — Rotgut, the men in Vietnam — depended on him. He'd allowed himself to get too deep into the local politics of his company affairs. On the other hand, he reminded himself, improving Spad's prospects here was what old Rotgut had wanted . . . *Suppose our own people killed him?* The sudden, intrusive thought made him jump up to hide his turmoil. Outside the cottage, the putt-putt-putt of Bracken's moped receded.

Alison misread Casey's alarm. "He'll be back. There are others in this."

He let the words sink in. Of course! There must be others, besides these two, conspiring to foil Gabbiya.

How else would the police sergeant already know so much about Professor Rutgers? He heard Alison offer to show him around the cottage, as if she suddenly remembered her duties as a hostess. Something in her voice, though, made him stifle his impatience. He needed friends. Rotgut's death meant he was cut off from outside help. The only motive he could imagine for killing Rotgut would also provide a motive for killing himself, Casey. He wasn't afraid of death, but he was afraid of giving Big Vien a final victory. And Big Vien was in this, somewhere, *INSPAD will make great duck soup.* Those were Bingo's last words. Make duck soup of the Duck, of Big Vien.

He heard Alison politely repeat her invitation to tour the premises. "I'd like that," he said, suddenly waking up to her need to tell him something more. "There's obviously more to this cottage than meets the eye."

She took him through the rambling rooms. He had to duck his head under the cedar lintels over the doorways, although inside each room a tray ceiling soared into shadows. Lanterns in wall brackets guided them. Alison said, "There's a power cut. Daddy wouldn't install a generator. He secretly prefers oil lamps." And indeed the flickering illumination only reinforced a cozy sense of contact with a secure and unalterable past. It explained, Casey supposed, the self-assurance of father and daughter in the face of a major crisis. In their own odd, understated fashion, they were fighting for their lives. He saw that now.

Not that they couldn't save their lives by just getting out. They could. In terms of material wealth, they had little bag or baggage to take with them. The way they lived was not ostentatious. Most Americans would find it boring, perhaps. No television. No kitchen aids of more recent vintage than a manual coffee grinder that looked a hundred years old. The floors were wide cedar planks. There were a few fine old carpets. He guessed some of the furniture would qualify as antique, although much of it was awkward and seemed to belong elsewhere. The Brackens spent most of their time outdoors or messing around in boats.

Alison led him back to the central fireplace and drew his attention to the painting of the privateer escorting an American warship. "That's Dockyard," said Alison, pointing to the shore base in the picture. "Nearly sixteen thousand American fighting ships were captured as prizes in the West Indies and the Great Lakes when your country and mine were enemies. Now we're allies, at least in theory, Dockyard's closed." She turned away. "You Americans forced the shutdown on us. You'll discover someday what a mistake that was."

"You love this place, don't you?"

"It doesn't look much, but it represents everything. Pretty Penny was built by an Elizabethan captain of privateers. In another age, he'd have been called a pirate." Alison took her father's chair, and it was Casey's turn to sit on the stool by the fire. "He made these walls from coral rag and limestone, all quarried by hand. The quarry became the water tank we use to this day. He shaped the ceilings like upside-down trays. They fit into the steep-pitched roof, built to collect all the rainwater we need. He built for the way we live now."

"What was this privateer's name?"

"Sir John Bracken."

"I should have guessed," said Casey.

"Not really. Another of the privateers, a son I think, bought his way into the House of Lords or whatever they had in those days. Daddy's nobility doesn't come from honest adventuring, so he ignores it. He'd rather be a privateer. That gives him a special dispensation, if not by law, at least by tradition. He feels at one with Hawkins and Drake, Walter Raleigh, Frobisher and Grenville. Theirs was the genesis of Anglo-Saxon law in America, though they broke laws to establish it. They set the precedents. They justify any action my father takes now to protect what they handed down to us."

What we have we hold. Casey remembered the proud boast. "You're all in this?" he asked. "All the islanders?"

"Not all." A cautious note crept into her voice. "Obviously some at the top have been quietly selling out. And I'm doing my damnedest to make Daddy stay on the sidelines."

That was a surprise! Casey withdrew his hands from where he had been rubbing them together in front of the fire.

"I don't want him at the pointed end if it comes to a battle royal," said Alison.

"You think it will?"

She shrugged. "Your President launched one military operation against Zia Gabbiya. It doesn't seem to have worked. I think Gabbiya's chosen to meet the next challenge his own way."

"And us?"

"I told you earlier, I was afraid you were either with Gabbiya or a mercenary. I did some digging into the background of your company, the Virginia company. Know what I found?"

Casey waited.

"Of course you know. The directors and shareholders are all former navy fliers who served in Vietnam, except for a few women. And the women are widows or wives of the killed or missing."

"That's no crime."

"Gabbiya would think it is. What I can find out, his agents can find out. They must think you're a commercial cover for a new kind of CIA based on the old World War Two pattern of OSS and the British SOE."

"SOE?"

"Special Operations Executive." Alison ran one finger along a bookshelf. "Their agents were amateurs in sabotage and subversion, but they were professionals in private life—*not* bureaucrats too worried about pensions and promotions." She withdrew a plain book between brown covers. "Here's a privately circulated memo on SOE's wartime ops. I can't imagine how this much got into type. Islanders are secretive by nature— in the Windfalls and in the British Isles." She thrust the book at him. "Here, bedtime reading."

He took this as a sign he should leave. She detained him. "You're alone in that big house?"

"Backgammon? Yes. There's just a daytime staff."

"Be careful." She raised her eyes. "Gabbiya's never been directly involved here till now."

Casey's head jerked back. So much else had happened, he had almost forgotten. "You're sure he's here?"

"That's what my father's gone to confirm. He doesn't

trust the telephone. He's beginning not to trust anyone outside a very small circle."

"I hope I'm one of the trusted?"

Alison did not answer. She said instead, "He doesn't know I told you about Gabbiya being here, and I'm not sure he'd want you to know. Well, not through me, anyway."

"Zia Gabbiya's not someone you can hide, exactly."

"Zia the magician, I've heard him called. He can make himself invisible. He's got two ships to help: the yacht, and a research vessel, the *Ultima Thule*."

"I don't care how magical his invisibility," said Casey, "he's looking for trouble."

"Right! Deliberately looking. To draw out his enemies."

"That can't be the explanation."

"He drew Rutgers back here!"

"Back?" Casey set his empty glass down. "Look, I'd better go." He was afraid now of revealing too much of what he knew—and did not know.

"Rutgers was here before, according to immigration. I'm surprised you don't want to know more about him. Where he stayed. And when he came."

Casey waved aside the provocation, thinking he would get the answers somehow from Bingo. He said again, "I must go."

"I'll drive you. I want to see Winston. Maybe *he* knows Rutgers' movements."

He was glad of the ride. The rain had started again and the house he had leased was on the north shore, two miles away. In the car he said, "Gabbiya's a fool to expose himself to his enemies in neutral territory."

"A third country. That's the expression. There's said to be a *covert* American plot to tempt Gabbiya into a third country. Instead, he chooses the third country to tempt *your* agents into the open. Like Rotgut."

"Rotgut wasn't my agent."

"You all say that, don't you? Standard operating procedure. *Disown if caught.*" Alison drew up outside Backgammon and put a hand on his arm. "I'm all for secrecy. We're fighting this war together. But our most powerful ally — your government — can't undertake a covert operation without broadcasting it to the world before it happens. The source of the leak and the newspapers that publish it don't care about the damage. Now they've given Gabbiya his best chance yet to make America look helpless in the face of terrorism."

The wipes squelched back and forth across the window. The rain drummed on the car's roof. A dog barked. Casey hunched his shoulders, feeling hopelessly at sea. How to explain that he really knew very little, that he'd come here because Rotgut wanted him merely to look around in the course of business? He prepared to run for shelter.

"Casey?"

He turned.

"You're a good man," said Alison, reaching out to kiss him. "Don't take chances —"

The house was in darkness. Like many costlier homes in the islands, this one was built to take advantage of the sea and presented to the landward side a solid white wall interrupted by porthole windows and a door surprisingly small for what the rental agency had called "a superior luxury accommodation." Most days, Casey walked around to the spectacular "back," where lawns and a large swimming pool overlooked a sheer drop to a small private beach. Tonight, for some reason, he preferred to go in by the front door. This mild eccentricity may have saved his life.

He was feeling distinctly queasy. He was not sure if his judgment of Alison was colored by his growing affection for her. There were moments, like just now, when she seemed to be trying to provoke him into indiscreet responses. If she suspected he was with a free-lance version of the CIA, all her talk about Washington's worrying inability to keep secrets had a purpose.

The dog's barks began to get on his nerves. He realized with a start that the animal was a responsibility that went with the house. She was a large white Alsatian, and she had been locked up inside. The moment he opened the door, the bitch rushed out into the darkness. He saw her white shadow vanish around a corner of the house, shrugged, and stepped inside. "Josh? Mary?" He did not expect an answer. The elderly couple also came with the lease. In the work-rich islands, they regarded their housekeeping job as a kind of inheritance to supplement much-better-paid work at the nearby golf club.

Casey headed for the library. It had been designed as the centerpiece of the house by the owner, a South African who had made millions from diamonds and who had a natural instinct for that secrecy whose absence in Washington Alison mourned. The library had been made into a kind of giant safe. To reach it, Casey had to pass through a system of wood-paneled steel doors. Inside, there were real and false bookshelves. The walls were steel behind walnut paneling. There were no windows. Light switches gleamed eerily. Casey ran his hand over one and the room was flooded by indirect lighting. The library was the perfect retreat. He did not think of it as an armor-plated sanctuary, but as a place to sit and think without distraction. Tonight, however, he had an odd sensation of being watched, of some unseen presence.

What if Alison was right?

What if Zia Gabbiya felt he must humiliate America on a big scale? Official Washington denied the President's reported authorization of black operations against Gabbiya through a third country. Alison had imagined Gabbiya saying, "I don't believe the denials. I'll provide the third country, and provoke Washington into some half-assed 'secret' operation. There'll be such a domestic crisis, the leaders will be forced to intervene militarily on a big scale. *Then* I pull out the rug from under the economy and America will be blamed for the global consequences."

But how did Big Vien and Hanoi come into it?

Casey moved restlessly around the room. He was still holding the cardboard-bound book Alison had given him. The bulk was a British Government memorandum: "Special Operations Directive for 1943." Later pages seemed to consist of postwar comments by the SOE chief, General Sir Colin Gubbins. Casey's eye was caught by a passage: "I came to secret operations as a professional soldier, out of the company of men who

114

trusted one another. I learned the best agents were amateurs who had survived the jungle of civilian life by *not* trusting one another." A little farther on, Casey read, "The best saboteurs come from civilian life. An insurance adjuster, for example, knows what to look for when he investigates a fire claim, and so discovers how best to start a fire without being caught. A first-class subversive is likely to be a political journalist in peacetime who knows the weak links in a nation's political chain of armor." The last sentence had been underscored.

Casey's curiosity was piqued. He decided to go to the kitchen and make himself a sandwich. The moment he passed out of the library's cocoon, he heard the piercing cries.

The cries came from the garden facing the sea. They sounded like a child in agony. Casey skidded through the front living room. The big glass sliding doors were still wide open. He shot across the patio. There the sound was almost unbearable. The pool lights had been left on, throwing up a green illumination that in the circumstances was more ghastly than decorative, for there was no other light to moderate the pool's sickly hue. Near the gnarled old Indian laurel tree beside the stone wall along the clifftop, something writhed.

Casey retreated as jaws cracked shut and teeth ripped his sleeve. The dog, in pain, was ready to tear at anything in reach. The white furry coat twisted and jerked, but remained transfixed to that part of the garden where the stone path from the front driveway ended in a wooden footbridge. Anyone entering the house this way had to cross the little bridge to reach the flagstoned patio.

There were flashlights in the garage. Casey got one and shone it on the dog. The white coat was flecked with blood. The beautiful head angled back, exposing a throat stuck full of what appeared to be porcupine quills. A stake had split the chest, driving up between the forelegs. It was impossible to approach the animal from any direction without encountering the desperately twisting head and snapping jaws. The howls were heart-rending.

So far as Casey knew, there were no guns in the house. He certainly had no weapon in his own possession. Yet the dog had to be put out of her agony. There was only one place to call: Pretty Penny. The voice that answered was John Bracken's. Casey hurriedly explained the need for a shotgun. "I'll be right over," said Bracken. He could hear the dog's cries.

He showed up moments later on his moped, carrying a crossbow. It took a moment to fire the dart into the animal's hindquarters. Seconds later, she collapsed. Bracken walked up to her and gingerly touched her foam-flecked muzzle with the crossbow's stock. The dog whimpered, and bubbles broke around her nostrils.

"Poor bitch!" said Bracken. "Can anything be done?"

"I doubt it." Casey was kneeling beside the tranquilized animal. His voice was strained. "This looks like a *panji* spike."

Bracken tried to roll the dog over.

"I wouldn't touch it," warned Casey. "Those are bamboo spikes. They're almost certainly infected. The dog's done for, anyway."

116

"I'll take your word." Bracken reloaded the crossbow and fired a bolt between the dog's eyes. He knelt by the dog, then turned away and asked gruffly, "What's a *panji* spike? Sounds Indian."

"It was, originally. From the Punjab. The bamboo's tempered over fire, hard as steel, then smeared in excrement. The snares came in various shapes and sizes. In tin cans. In foot traps, with altering jaws so you hurt yourself more pulling yourself out than getting in. If a man had stepped into this, the central spike would have come straight up between the legs, into the crotch."

"And where did you come across them?" asked Bracken.

"In Vietnam," said Casey.

Bracken stayed only to make sure the house was secure, and to have a short conversation with Sergeant Winston on the kitchen phone. "She's with you? Good. And remember, deal with this discreetly."

He hung up and turned to Casey. "Alison went over to the local police station. She was drinking cocoa with Winston. I didn't think there was any point alarming her."

Casey was relieved the girl was safe, but his voice was sarcastic. "Another case to be brushed under the carpet?"

Bracken avoided his eyes. "For the moment, yes."

"Meanwhile I have to explain to the owner how his guard dog died. Unless, of course, by the time the owner returns here, I find he's also sold out to Zia Gabbiya."

117

"What's that supposed to mean!" The tall Englishman whipped round.

"I don't know." Casey dropped his hands helplessly to his side. "Whenever bad things happen around here, everyone's outraged but nobody actually wants to *do* something about it."

"Maybe you and I should have a private talk," said Bracken. "Just the two of us. Over on Wreck Cay. I'll come round for you bright and early. Tomorrow. Down on your beach."

Casey stood looking down at the beach long after Bracken had left. Even on a dark night, you couldn't really miss that beach, coming in by boat. Bracken seemed to know it well. Well enough that he hadn't even bothered to say he was coming in by boat.

Whoever had set the *panji*-spike trap, the hallmark of irregular warfare in Vietnam, had come in by sea. And they were not after the guard dog. They were after Casey. Otherwise, why had the dog been locked inside one part of the house while the quarters fronting the pool and the sea were left wide open?

CHAPTER 8

The high-pitched hum of an outboard running at full revs jerked Casey out of a deep sleep. It had been almost dawn when, restless and frustrated, he threw himself into a patio sofa. Staying inside the house had brought on the old feelings of claustrophobia. His attempts to call Bingo Harriman were met with the same response: "We are experiencing difficulties with overseas circuits . . ." In the end, the operators had not even answered.

The tousled head of John Bracken appeared over the garden parapet. "Beautiful morning, Casey!" A long leg was hoisted over the wall, followed by the other. "Great Scott! You slept out here all night?" Bracken followed the other man through the kitchen to the staff washroom, where Casey stuck his head under a cold-water tap. "Dammit, I should have made you come home with me!"

"That's okay." Casey toweled himself dry. "I needed time alone."

"But suppose they'd come back — ?" Bracken waved in the direction of the dead dog.

"I was hoping they might," Casey said grimly. "Coffee?"

"I've food and drink in the boat." Bracken moved toward the pool. "Strictly speaking, we should bury that poor beast first."

"I thought of it. I thought," Casey added curtly, "of a lot of things."

Bracken turned. He was wearing shorts, sandals, and an old beach shirt, but with the early sun behind him, his beard and hair flying, he looked slightly ominous.

"And one thing I thought about," continued Casey, "was keeping myself square with the law hereabouts." He pointed to the dog. "That needs to be reported to the police."

"Already taken care of," Bracken said cheerfully. "Now come on, old lad." He was halfway over the wall again.

"A moment ago, you were talking about burying the dog. What's the hurry?" Casey moved to the sea wall and gazed down with some envy at an old Zodiac drawn up on the sand.

"I like a bit of sea room when things get hairy." Bracken hesitated. "Look, I shouldn't rush you. Alison's dealing with the cops, and then she has to put in her day at the courts. I thought it was a good opportunity for us to talk."

There was a note of appeal in Bracken's voice.

"Okay," said Casey.

They were like a pair of schoolboys playing hookey, it seemed to Casey. He felt grubby in the same clothes he had been wearing the previous day, but it was the grubbiness of rebellion. He threw his shoes and socks into

120

the rubber boat and helped Bracken manhandle it into the water. By the time they cleared the headland, they were perched together sipping hot coffee from a thermos, the wind and sea in their faces, Bracken's huge corn-beef sandwiches on the wooden thwart between them. Casey felt he could breathe again. Neither man spoke much until they tied the Zodiac to the stone wharf at Wreck Cay.

"I didn't want to alarm Alison, but the Irish Girl's appearance here was never a coincidence," said Bracken as they slowly climbed the ropewalk. "She came to spy out the land."

"Why pick on you?" Casey had to raise his voice to be heard above the squabbling kiskadees, whose black and brilliant-yellow wings flashed through the trees.

"The way I see it —" Bracken was breathing heavily and had to rest on a tree stump. "Well, some weeks ago, there was this helicopter buzzing around. You know flying's forbidden over the islands? Commercial airliners have to approach and take off over the sea. So the public asked questions when this chopper comes over for an entire day. Government said they'd hired a New York publicity agency to take the Windfalls' picture for overseas advertising. That was a lie. It was a security measure, prior to Gabbiya's arrival."

Bracken took out a cigar case and offered it to Casey, who was leaning against an outcrop of lava rock. Casey shook his head. "Wise man," Bracken said mechanically, and stared at the cigars before putting them back. "I have to tell you, for a time I thought you might have been the pilot. This was before Alison changed my mind about you. The helicopter was doing the survey for Gabbiya's Ministry of Enlightenment, which is double-talk for Sahara's security and intelligence. Alison doesn't know that."

Casey wondered how a father and daughter who were so close also managed to keep so many small secrets from each other.

"I reckon my Stringbag showed up on the aerials," said Bracken. "Gabbiya's Ministry of Enlightenment probably didn't have experts working on the aerial photographs for a while; and even then, they wouldn't have spotted the old girl at first. She was not very visible, the day of the helicopter." He got up and resumed the gradual climb.

"You blame Gabbiya for everything?" Casey had been wrestling all night with evidence that some rather unpleasant Vietnamese know-how had been employed to kill the dog.

"Zia Gabbiya ought to be shot." Bracken spat out the words. "Same way we should've shot Hitler before there was no way to stop him. Sorry, Casey. Not done, is it, to voice such things these days? Not in America. Not in Britain, either."

Casey mumbled some suitable response. He was trying to remember how much he already knew from Alison, and how much she had asked him not to let Bracken know he knew. It was very perplexing.

Bracken took the noncommittal response to mean skepticism. He said, "You Americans are the chief victims," in a scolding tone. "The cases become worse each year. Hundreds killed in suicide and truck bombings.

We've had our share, too. We had a gunman in the Saharan embassy in London killing our police officers, our people kidnapped in Beirut, Brits held hostage in Sahara until Gabbiya's crooked diplomats were let free in London. After a time the memory gets fuzzy. Shipjackings. Bombings against U.S. installations all over the world. Gunfights between airline hijackers and antiterrorist forces. And always the same fanatics proclaiming their faith according to Gabbiya."

They had come to the end of the ropewalk. Casey said quietly, "There's really no need to instruct me. We had the same problem during the war in Vietnam. The bureaucrats would never face the facts. Today you still can't get agreement to state the facts."

"Which are?"

"That Gabbiya for years paid to have people trained in Vietnam." Even as he spoke, Casey saw what had been staring him in the face all along. Vietnam had developed to the highest degree the art of terror as a psychological weapon. He'd seen it himself. There was always a practical purpose to the methodical beatings of Americans, the torture, the seemingly aimless delight in prolonging agony in some and visiting sudden and violent death upon others. The aim was to gain control over the minds of the survivors. Somehow, the Hanoi regime was bringing its psychological warfare closer to American shores, via Gabbiya.

He became aware of Bracken's intent stare. He was still not ready to volunteer more than he had to. He said, "If you think Gabbiya knows about your Stringbag, shouldn't you do something to protect it?"

Bracken threw back his head and roared with laughter. "Already have, dear boy. Look!"

Casey looked. The shallow valley faced them. Where the Stringbag had been there was now nothing but a canopy of vegetation alive with the tumbling kiskadees, the winged clowns of the Windfalls, crying, "Ha-ha! You-missed-me!"

"You put her back in the hangar?"

"No," said Bracken, vastly pleased with himself. "She's right there in front of you."

They descended into the bowl and Casey saw how it was done. What appeared to be thickly leaved vines were horizontal and formed precise squares. "Camouflage netting. Where . . . ?"

"From Dockyard. From stuff cached there after the Falklands. Our navy lads weren't too thrilled about the base being officially closed. So after that little war, they decided they didn't want to get caught so far from home again without reserves. There's a petty-officer storekeeper still guarding surplus from World War Two, and they just added to his little treasures without burdening the paper-pushers in London with the uncomfortable details."

The explanation seemed uncharacteristically long. Casey wondered what Bracken was trying to say. "Couldn't you have wheeled her back into the hangar?" he asked. "That's camouflage enough."

"No. The old girl's fully operational. And inside the hangar, there's the risk of fire." Bracken was watching him closely now. "All we need is a torpedo and rockets." He sat on an upturned bucket half buried in grass, took

124

out his cigar case again, and this time stuck a cigar between his teeth. But his eyes never left Casey's face.

"A project like this contains its own logic," he said. "Those camouflage nets are an example of the sovereign power of causality."

Casey stared back.

"We think things happen by coincidence, but often events are on parallel tracks. The Harrier jump-jet pilots from the Falklands who tipped me off about the camouflage were following a logical sequence in their own minds." Bracken's voice sharpened. "They had to deal with stupidity at home, cunning enemies in the air, and they were looking out for themselves." Bracken bit the end off his cigar, and added abruptly, "Alison tells me you're a student of synchronicity too?"

Casey, wary, answered a simple "Yes."

"Remember your Schopenhauer? He was wrong, but *everyone* remembers him. He said, 'Coincidence is the simultaneous occurrence of casually unconnected events.' "

Casey had an impulse to add the response he had once given Big Vien to just such a remark. Then, to his utter astonishment, Bracken repeated it. "A German philosopher has no place in today's technology." The words were an eerie echo from days spent in the jungle with Big Vien, who had interspersed brutality with this kind of strange talk. In the end, it hadn't seemed strange talk at all to Casey. He had seen its purpose. He had also glimpsed Big Vien's one great weakness: intellectual vanity.

But Lord John Bracken had no problems with his

identity; he had no need to prove himself superior to a captured enemy. He had restored an old warplane with enormous ingenuity and hard work. Now he was saying there was some natural law which brought him to his purpose. He spoke of the paradox of certain extrasensory perception tests — the "E P R paradox." A famous 1982 experiment in Paris established that once two particles had been near each other, they would continue to affect each other simultaneously, no matter how widely separated they later became. Big Vien's philosophical discussions had predated that experiment, but now Casey had the odd sensation that he and Big Vien were two such particles.

And Bracken was saying his old Stringbag and himself were also two such particles. They had fought together in war. For forty years the Stringbag lay under the sea . . . Suddenly it was clear what Bracken thought the old warplane was destined to do.

"You know Gabbiya's here?" Bracken's sudden question dragged Casey back from his disturbing speculations. He thought quickly and decided he'd better tell the truth.

"Yes, Alison told me."

"But she didn't want me to know she told you, right?" Bracken searched the other's face. "She's terrified I'm going to try something—"

Casey wanted to avoid Bracken's confidences. He turned and declared he could see the warplane now, under its new camouflage.

"Never thought *why* I should rebuild her at the time," mused Bracken. "But she'll fly again soon. Just one

126

more torpedo drop."

Casey blocked out Bracken's last sentence and moved away. The Stringbag's olive drab fabric was overlaid with wartime khaki and jungle greens. She seemed to strain at the leash against the lashing cords. "We kill murderers," he heard Bracken saying behind him. "Why don't we execute men like Hitler, *before* the slaughter begins? Men like Gabbiya. We pussyfoot around, we invent weasel words like 'low-intensity conflict' when we're really talking about a dictator and his reign of terror. King Zia!"

"I'd better be getting back," said Casey. "I have to call my partner."

Bracken gave him a sly look and stood up. "You won't get much help from that quarter," he said. "Your President announced today the dismantling of a deep-deep-cover department, following newspaper disclosures. And anyway, all overseas circuits are going to be out of action from now on."

The enormity hit Casey when he was on his own again, back inside Backgammon.

The noble lord had flipped his lid. If Lord John Bracken flew that antique against Zia Gabbiya, it would end in fiasco. Alison was right about one thing: King Zia's reign of terror would be helped immeasurably by the failure of an attempt on his life. But it wasn't the Americans that would invite the humiliation. It was her own father.

Zia Gabbiya was making himself a target. He must

have made certain, then, that he would escape. There would be public outrage, and of course U.S. intelligence agencies would be blamed. Politicians would take fright amid sensational "revelations" about unauthorized black operations. Antiterrorist task forces would come under attack, obliged to disclose every detail of their work. There would be another brutal, hasty, *suicidal* dismissal of the true professionals, with even more devastating effect than the purging of the CIA during an earlier wave of hysteria in the 1970s. The tragedy of these upheavals was that the really good and dedicated became frustrated by those ill-conceived restraints put on them by a fearful bureaucracy.

It would be a considerable victory for Gabbiya.

But Gabbiya had something more in mind. His allies were in Vietnam. Big Vien. The Duck.

In Backgammon's library, Casey tried again to put in a call to Raleigh, Virginia. This time, when he did get the Windfalls operator, she was even more peremptory than before. No circuits were open, "owing to technical difficulties." Bracken was right.

Casey threw himself into his landlord's black leather recliner and impatiently pushed buttons on his landlord's custom-made "entertainment center." Bracken's daughter had said all news coming into the islands was unobtrusively controlled. Bracken had said the U.S. President was making news today in a manner that ought to please Gabbiya. So let's see, thought Casey. Let's see if something to Gabbiya's taste wins the local censor's approval. He hopped from tapes to radio to cable-vision. A large TV set rose from its recess in front of him.

He had to sit through commercials and part of a syndicated soap that left his mind free.

The notion of the Stringbag bucking the wind at a stately eighty miles an hour to slide a rusty torpedo into Gabbiya's floating hotel . . . For crying out loud! The odds were all against Bracken, even if he found a torpedo. Probably even the torpedo wouldn't work. And if it was serviceable, Gabbiya must surely have a ton of miniaturized gadgetry on board the *Qurqūr* designed to foil attack.

"I've played executioner before," Bracken had said, looking wild-eyed in the half-light on Wreck Cay. Now his words sounded perfectly sane, divorced from the hairy eccentric who spoke them. "I gunned down a Nazi bigwig in a transport plane between Hamburg and Oslo. I'd been given exact details of his route. Your chaps did such jobs too. Remember Tom Lanphier and the American fighter pilots — *your* navy, Casey — shooting down the Jap admiral, Yamamoto? Cold, premeditated murder? Or a blow that saved God knows how many young American lives? Yamamoto was in supreme command of the combined Pacific fleet, and his death was devoutly to be wished. The intelligence operations were brilliant, the long-range air attack precisely delivered, and Yamamoto never knew what hit him. And wasn't he, back then, the embodiment of evil, same as Gabbiya? Try telling that to nail-nibbling desk jockeys today! They call in their astrologers, their naysayers, their seers and students of chicken entrails. By the time they finish cogitating, the moment's gone and the story's leaked . . ."

The word *leaked* was echoed from the television set. Someone—Dan Rather? Peter Jennings? Casey was so much caught up in his thoughts that he didn't know—someone had said something about a leaked press report. Then the screen turned to black before a local commercial appeared. He waited. The tail end of another news item, then a reporter speaking from the White House: ". . . Hardest hit was a department most Americans have never heard of, known as the Double-D-C, for deep deep cover. Evidently under past public pressure, a department in one of our intelligence agencies burrowed out of sight. Into deep deep cover. Agency heads are quoted today as saying they knew nothing about the Double-D-C's black operations, such as one code-named Seaspray. It was the leaking of Seaspray to the media earlier this week that prompted the President's action. The chairman of the Senate Intelligence Committee is demanding an immediate public inquiry." The Senator appeared on screen: "We cannot accept the White House denials . . . Ignorance is no defense . . ."

The news item that followed was a follow-up to the redefection of a top-level Soviet diplomat whose spying activities in the United States had produced some meaty confessions. Now he had gone back to Moscow in a blaze of publicity, casting doubt on his revelations and the competence of the CIA. Another humiliation for America. The item was telecast in full, but the unseen censor cut swiftly to another local commercial before the news anchor could finish the sentence: "Another skyjacking victim was buried today at Arlington—"

Casey heaved himself out of the chair. The censorship was crude. Yet the censor must have considerable power. Why wasn't there any public protest? Alison had said Windfallers were accustomed to amateurish broadcasts, and perhaps most of them put it down to poorly trained technicians. The wealthier expatriates presumably still got their news by other means, and didn't care about mismanaged local collaboration.

Casey walked to the living area facing the sea and checked the bolts on the sliding windows. It was long after sundown. He turned on the outside security lights. He made another tour of the house to make sure doors and windows were shut and locked. It had been drummed into him that Windfallers never needed to lock up their homes. A note in the kitchen, however, now warned: "Please take every precaution. A police patrol will check outside periodically through the night." It was signed by the black sergeant, Winston. He wrote in a surprisingly fine hand. He signed himself Churchill S. Winston. Casey had already been told that the sergeant's mother had given him that impressive name to make up for the absence of a father. He smiled at the recollection: some islanders might be secretly supporting Gabbiya, but it was a sure guess that Detective-Sergeant Churchill Spencer Winston would be on the side of the angels with his own supporters.

Police patrols . . . They would create a problem. Casey had been toying with a plan that was so unthinkable, he suspected he would be glad of any excuse not to

131

put it into operation. There was a Boston whaler in a boathouse on the beach. In it, Casey could speed under cover of the night to Wreck Cay, and there—

The idea was revolting.

There he could set fire to the Stringbag.

It would be easy enough. Bracken had shown him around the old warplane. Alison had shown him the several approaches to Wreck Cay.

It would be like stabbing them in the back, after they had entrusted him with information known to nobody else.

Yet—the newscast, everything he'd learned from it and recent local events, told him loud and clear that Gabbiya had set a trap. The Stringbag would spring it.

Casey walked back into the library and began pacing the huge Persian carpet, his mind working while his eyes took in the delicate patterns worked so cunningly through the thick pile. He remembered Alison's ambivalence, her fears for her father, and it began to seem to him that she might *welcome* the intervention! But—set fire to something her father had so lovingly restored over such a long time? At once his feelings swung the other way. Lord Bracken had flown that aircraft in combat. He'd described how youngsters, still in their teens, died in it when he crashed. The Stringbag was a pilot's airplane. It had become an essential part of Bracken himself. They even looked alike!

Casey paused. He was letting his imagination run away. There was a clear and visible danger to American interests and Lord John Bracken posed it.

No, no, he thought. I'm getting things upside down.

Gabbiya's the danger.

How he wished he could talk to someone. That had been, after all, the purpose of his coming here. To learn all he could, and report back to—? To who? Rotgut? But Rotgut was dead. Almost certainly, his associates were scattered to the wind by the new White House directive. This Department Double-D-C must have been the group running Rotgut. *There was nobody to talk to!* Except Bracken.

He started pacing back and forth again, his arguments swinging to and fro in rhythm. Bracken had to be neutralized. Yet it was ironic; for he and Bracken were, in Bracken's odd phrase, synchronized. They had both lived on the leading edge. The leading edge was the first section of an aircraft's airfoil to confront the opposition of the elements. The leading edge of Americans at war was the navy task force, and the leading edge of this task force was the fighter pilot.

And we're on the leading edge, here and now, in a war against terror, thought Casey. There aren't enough men like Bracken, willing to fight. I can't just strike him out.

The carpet was enormous, and the patterns reversed themselves. The hanging gardens of Babylon were discovered to be hanging the other way when you changed direction. Trees and flowers grew along gentle blue streams which flowed any way you wanted, so that the scenery reflected itself, and the trees and flowers were suddenly growing upside down. His footsteps traced the classic forms until they came to a stop at the liquor cabinet. This time, instead of turning, he opened the cabinet and poured himself a very large bourbon. It must have been this kind of mental turmoil drove Bracken to drink not wisely but well.

There was no denying it; he'd needed that drink. He was finding it difficult to sustain the arguments against burning the Stringbag. Already part of his mind was working out how it could be done. There was a streak of obstinacy in Casey. He knew this about himself, that this stubbornness often proved a weakness. When his mind became set on something, he had trouble letting go.

He poured himself another drink and recrossed the carpet. Something in the rich pile glittered briefly. He knelt. Whatever it was had fallen between a camel's bell and the *Haram,* the Mohammedan holy of holies. He felt a sharp nick and found a tiny piece of fine silver wire sticking to the tip of a finger. *"The tinkling of a camel's bell."* The line flashed through his mind. Arab studies had been optional during his service in the Mediterranean. He had taken Arab poetry and history to chase away boredom, and discovered an interest. He saw that the weave and woof of the carpet came together in one glorious classic poem like an illustrated medieval tapestry. There were a lot of Persian carpets around, inferior, imitative, hastily produced like a magician's sleight of hand to catch the boom market of the recent past. This one was genuine, rare, the kind of thing to be found only in a sultan's quarters. What was it doing here, this pure piece of Islam?

He took a thin paper ticket from his pocket and wrapped the sliver of silver wire in it. There was no particular reason for doing this. The ticket came from his last ferry ride across the harbor. It was quicker, sometimes, to ride the old ferryboats than drive all the way around. Then he thought: I'd better check ferry times. If I cross tonight in the whaler, I can't risk being seen by gossiping ferrymen.

He realized a decision had been made. Well, at least the decision to go to Wreck Cay. He could still back away from the unthinkable when he got there.

He'd better have some sort of excuse, just in case. Night fishing? Islanders said the big fish swam into the main channels on such starry and moonlit nights as they'd been having lately. There was a deep storage cupboard near the anonymous landlord's collection of old books on Africa, containing fishing tackle and other sports gear. Casey helped himself. Then, feeling hangdog about it, he moved to the kitchen for matches. He took three big boxes of those large kitchen matches you still find in hardware stores. All he needed, for what he had in mind, was a cheap lighter or a folder. Taking all those extra matches was overkill. Overkill was the curse of the pilot who wasn't sure of what he was doing, thought Casey, but he took them all the same.

After you have done a certain amount of sport diving, the ancient and honorable art of angling with rod and reel somehow loses its appeal. You know what the fish are doing down there. You grow to like them.

Casey also knew a mysterious force came into play. Telepathy, if you will. Once the determination to catch a fish has gone, the fish refuse to bite. Maybe they figure the game's not worth the candle if the angler's heart really isn't in it.

He puttered along some reefs, the 35-horsepower outboard burbling at his back, and pretended to troll. Yet he couldn't kid himself. The only thing that mattered was getting to Wreck Cay.

He was distracted by another piece of the puzzle to add to all the other bits. His landlord. He'd never seen him. This South African diamond millionaire might not even exist. He'd only accepted the word of a local realtor. The lease had been handled by a local lawyer. He tried to remember who'd recommended the place. Was there something questionable in the arrangement, explaining why Rotgut had never attempted to reach him? Could he be sure Rotgut hadn't tried, anyway? And what the hell was Rotgut doing with the Forget-Me-Not Fund? "Shouldn't I be finding answers to these questions instead of toying with arson and a half-assed fishing expedition?" He had no chance to examine that final query. A strong wind blowing down Great Sound had started to pile up water along the reef. He nosed out into the channel, where it was rougher but free of hidden rocks. He saw, by the flashing light of Needham's Point, that he was heading straight across the sound to Wreck Cay. Just by chance. Of course.

He hadn't been out alone on the open sea since—well, the Gulf of Tonkin. He laughed to himself, crouching in the stern of the Boston whaler. The waves were marching down the sound, and the blunt-nosed boat hit them head on, the bow lifting at each crest.

The wind curved up each wave's back and caught the boat under the bow. Each time, he felt the stern dig in. Once, the boat seemed to be dancing its tail on ice. His heart in his throat, he reduced the power and wrenched the engine's steering post back and forth to avoid dropping sideways into a trough. It was a lot easier to play the swashbuckler in his old Black Knight squadron, catapulted from a carrier into the stormy Tonkin night, than chug through these rough waters with only a tired outboard between yourself and the wet.

The whaler got out of hand and slewed broadside to a giant wave. There was more physical labor required to shove this chunk of fiberglass through the ocean than "doing a bolter" under full power after missing the carrier's deck arrester gear. Pilots wired to measure fear by the wingless wonders of psychiatry had made the needles jump, not dodging missiles or dogfighting, but in carrier night landings. Casey wondered how far he would make the needles jump now.

Courage came more easily when you were wired up, playing to an audience, or observed by fellow pilots. He missed the Group. He missed the terror and the ecstasy of the catapult, the harsh acceleration, the wind knocked out of you, your vision shrinking close to blackout, and then the slow reawakening in a soft-breathing womb with umbilical cords of oxygen and reassuring voices from fighter control. You were scared, but your finger was on the trigger. You balanced between care and belligerence. You were the ultimate paradox: the knight in armor who moved cautiously, the predator in a romantic search for a damsel in distress. Now no womb, no voices; just yourself and the wind and the rain. "To give and receive. To be more than yourself. To be part of the Group." Casey looked up at stars beginning to show through scudding cloud, and suffered a brief stab of nostalgia. He missed the cat shots. He missed the Group.

The outboard's stick jerked violently as if to say, "Pay heed!" The motor raced as the prop hung in the air, then gave an almighty cough so that Casey was certain his heart had stopped beating. Cold water sloshed around his rump. The whole weight of the boat surged aft and she sucked herself out of another wave and smacked down into a valley of slack water. He thumped the top of the outboard, felt the prop bite, heard the most inefficient engine known to Christendom resume its soft grumble. He told himself this design of boat was unsinkable, but he didn't believe it.

The lee of Wreck Cay was calm. The tide was high, allowing him to drive straight through the gap in the reef Alison had shown him. There was a moon of sorts. Its silvery path led him up onto the beach. He tipped the motor, jumped out, dragged the light whaler farther across the sand. He took a line from the bow and secured it to a palm-tree stump. He knew the way up the cliff face where Bracken had driven in black iron spikes. He grasped the first, then dropped back. Matches! He returned to the boat and groped in the locker for the big boxes. When he took hold of the spike again, he thought, but for that brief interval, he could have continued to kid himself: Winds, tide, a fishing trip, gone awry, had brought him by accident to this place. He almost, at this point, threw the matches away.

He had to feel his way up, spike by spike. The lava rock had sharp, sometimes razorlike edges. Thorn and spiky cactus tore at him. Near the top, he extended his hand above his head in another search for another spike.

Another hand enclosed his own like a steel trap.

The unknown hand was joined by another, just above Casey's wrist. His arm was being pulled from its socket. He raised a leg, found a rocky purchase, and pressed down hard. He came over the top so fast that one of the grasping hands let go to grapple with him. Casey's head was lowered as he shot forward, and his skull sank into flesh. The assailant grunted. Casey jabbed his fist at a point below the stomach and heard the grunt become a scream. He was on afterburn, and took aim at the white blob of a face. Something cracked. The man toppled. For an awful moment, Casey thought he had knocked him clean over the cliff. He found him, instead, flat on his back in a bed of bracken, out cold. In the dark there was little to see except the crumpled form. Then the Come-By-Chance lighthouse sent its beam sweeping across the sound in slow rotation. Reflected back from dispersing overcast was an illumination sufficient to tell Casey the man who had attacked him had the features, the short black hair, the flat, splayed feet, and the black cotton jacket and trousers of what could only be a Vietnamese.

Casey ran inland, freed from any doubts. If Big Vien himself had appeared before him, he could not have been more certain that Hanoi was in this up to its ears. If the Duck had men here, the Duck *must* know about the Stringbag. There was a Vietnamese saying, "Make the enemy use his strength against himself." It was a Communist adaptation of the traditional art of self-defense. Here it could mean, "Make our enemy's friend use his Stringbag to humiliate our enemy."

He crashed through the lush vegetation, skidded and tripped, and cursed himself for not having memorized better this approach from the beach side. He plunged into the bowl where the Stringbag had been lashed down, found her where she had been left that afternoon, and hurled himself onto a lower wing. He grasped a strut here, found a foothold there, felt bracing wires cut into his hands as he slipped on the damp wing surfaces, and slowly hoisted himself up by the intercockpit fairing to where he could claw at the handhold behind the upper-wing center section. If he remembered Bracken's description correctly, there should be a twelve-gallon gravity fuel tank incorporated in the center section of the top mainplane. He did a split, positioning one foot on either side of the gaping front cockpit, and found the fuel cap. A shaft of moonlight broke through the clouds and pierced the overhead camouflage netting. He glanced down. If he started the fire in the gravity tank, he would have a long way to go before he could run clear: down past the coffinlike cockpits, through the massive girders angling out from the fuselage, through the rigger's nightmare of wires. He would by lucky not to hang himself, or dangle like a side of beef over his own barbecue.

140

His hand slid over the wet skin. He tore a fingernail against the jagged edge of the fuel cap. He twisted off the cap, still awkwardly balanced, and laid out the matches. He wobbled uncertainly while he dragged out a handkerchief, soaked it in gasoline, and twisted it into a fuse to be strung out over the wing. It just might give him time to get back to earth before the poor old girl went sky-high. He felt like a Visigoth about to destroy a work of art.

The first match flared. The forest held its breath, and he had no need to cup the flame. Even the gentle soughing of the wind in the tall casuarina trees disturbed no air here. The smell of the warplane was overwhelming: that special combination of oil and metal.

I can't do it! The flame died.

A navy plane is like a woman you will always love. She has a special aroma, a particular magic. The older she is, the stronger the passion. She has an identity, a history of devotion. She will have been part of other men, but these are men you trust with your own life. You are grateful to her for looking after them, for bearing them up into spheres beyond mortal reach. Destroying a navy plane is worse than scuttling a battleship. Other kinds of aircraft may evoke strong emotions among other kinds of pilot. All Casey knew was that, as a navy man, he was paralyzed by sentiments he would never outgrow, aroused by a machine he had never flown although it sprang from a tradition with the power still to stir his blood.

He leaned forward, his face against the wet fabric of

141

a wing. He heard a faint whistle as if something had flown past his ear. He heard a soft *plop!*

"Don't move!"

Alison! Her clipped voice was clear and unmistakable. Light splashed along the underside of the upper wings, wavered, then rested on his precariously balanced figure. He squinted into the glare.

"Don't touch anything!"

He withdrew his hand from the gravity tank. He had never felt so ridiculous in his entire life. He wanted to say something light, but no words came.

Another voice. "Come down the starboard side. *S-l-o-w-l-y.*" It was Lord John Bracken. Casey had never known the human voice could convey such fury without being raised much above a whisper.

Carefully he bent his legs. He had no burning desire to hear again that sinister whistle of a missile shaving his earlobe. He remembered how Bracken's crossbow split the dog's skull. He transferred his weight gingerly and exaggerated every movement so that his intentions could not be mistaken. He could not imagine how he had made the ascent so swiftly in the dark. Returning back down was, even without the hazard of two enraged armed watchers, by-guess-and-by-God. He felt like a tired chimpanzee.

"You bloody bastard!"

Casey rocked queasily on terra firma and faced the wrath to come. He said, conscious of how foolish the trite phrase must sound, "I can explain."

Bracken let fly a string of oaths.

Desperation drove Casey. He shouted, "I nearly

killed a man to get here."

"A man? What man? *Kill* a man? You heard that, Alison?"

"I did."

"You and me!" Bracken spluttered. "We're the only men on this blasted island—"

"Hush, father!" hissed Alison.

Branches snapped. Casey pressed back against the bottom foothold jutting out below the fuselage. Alison's flashlight pinned him like a moth to a board.

The light went out. Someone was crashing through the undergrowth as if drunk. Casey could see Bracken in the gloom, but Alison had gone. Seconds ticked by. The noises continued. Casey thought he heard the hiss of a drawstring, and winced. He heard, without doubt, a grunt. It seemed familiar. It had to be the Vietnamese. Poor bastard! It must be getting monotonous.

"Got him." Alison's matter-of-fact voice came out of the shadows.

Casey started forward.

"No you don't!" Bracken's arm suddenly barred the way. It was surprisingly strong.

There was another pause while Alison could be heard crashing around. The flashlight came on. She said, "Winged him, but he's out."

That was when Bracken allowed Casey to move forward. Some of the rage had ebbed. Casey had been vindicated.

They stood looking at the man held in the circle of light from Alison's torch. "I near killed him when he tackled me," said Casey. "What hit him this time?"

143

"A very small dose." Alison raised the crossbow and Casey saw why her aim was so accurate. The flashlight was attached to it like a gunsight.

"And that's what you fired at me?"

"A *very* light tranquilizer," said Alison. "You'd have come round in no time."

"After dropping a mile?" Casey waved at the Stringbag's topside.

"Nobody makes a free fall from up there," Bracken assured him. "Had a fitter tumbled once, got caught in the crosswires. He was so tied up in 'em, and I was in such a hurry, I took off with him still rigged to the yardarm."

It amazed Casey that the fiery lord with the nimble tongue could now coo gentle as any dove. "Astonishing," he said, "what a visitor from Hanoi can bring in the way of enlightenment."

"Is *that* what he is!" Bracken looked more closely. "Kind of a Buddha lighting our way?"

There was something of the Buddha about the man in repose. He had the broad, flat features of an Annamite, the full belly of an oriental power broker. Casey had felt the physical strength in the man's grip and he guessed there was that other kind of strength, mystical or political, denoted by the timeless symbolism of the fat Buddha. Casey had seen the Buddhist tolerance of pain reversed, and he had been the recipient of the pain dished out. He was not deceived by this Buddha's disarming obesity. "Tie him up!" he warned.

"There's rope over there," said Bracken. "In the bottom panel of the fuselage, astern of the cockpits, starboard side."

Casey stumbled back to the plane. "It's where the ballast weights are kept!" called Alison.

Ballast? All these nautical terms . . . you'd think it was a boat! Casey found the rope and got back to find the other two straddling the man. The crossbow light shone directly at his chest. The man half rose and then slowly rolled over like a baby trying to crawl. Bracken dropped onto him, hands and shoulders, knees on rump, and took the rope. He began trussing the man with swift competence, reeving the manila hemp about the upper arms, around the neck, down to the ankles, clinching shoulders and arms tighter until the prisoner came to full consciousness with a grunt of pain.

"Easy!" protested Casey. Men like Buddha had done the same to him in Hanoi's Zoo. The memory could only arouse compassion.

Bracken stood, remembering Casey's experience and recognizing the fellow feeling. "Right," he said. He was breathing much too heavily. He took one end of the rope and tied it to a tree. "Let's get out of earshot."

"He probably doesn't speak English," said Casey, for it had been his observation that Hanoi's men spoke French but hardly ever any English, and then only with great difficulty. But something in the way he said this rekindled Bracken's former anger.

"I don't want to take the chance," said Bracken. "You speak it. It's from you I want to hear."

CHAPTER 9

Casey meant to tell the truth. He wasn't bound by any official secrets act. He hadn't engaged in secret activities. "But it's obvious now," he said "when Rotgut came to see me the first time, he was with a secret department. Now it appears to be disbanded, so even if I wanted to go that extra mile, I've nothing to back me."

"Go what extra mile?" Bracken asked suspiciously.

"I thought I spoke plainly enough," answered Casey. "Rotgut cast around for the right man to find out Gabbiya's latest plans. Rotgut picked a candidate he figured would go further—" He broke off. "Oh, come on! Rotgut and his bosses expected me to react the way you've reacted. You're fighting the same battle . . ." And then Casey put his foot in it. ". . . however clumsily."

"Clumsily!" exploded Bracken. "You nearly buggered up the only weapon we've got!"

That was when Casey deviated a little from his honest intent. "After I knocked out Lord Buddha back there, I figured I'd better check the Stringbag," he lied.

"Lighting matches?" Bracken was working up another rage. Alison intervened. "Casey, why *did* you come here?"

"I saw a newscast. It said this covert outfit—

147

Rutgers', I guess—was finished, *kaput!* I had a hunch. I tried phoning the cottage. You weren't there." It seemed a fair enough assumption, another sensible lie. Manifestly, they'd been away on Wreck Cay. "I felt uneasy." That was true. "I thought I'd find you here."

"You've got a nerve!" said Bracken. "Sergeant Winston's at the cottage! If you'd called, he'd have told you *we* were at the yacht club!"

"That's odd." Casey could only brazen things out. "There was no answer . . . Your number *is* 44050?"

"You're one digit out," said Alison. She turned on her father. "And you're becoming paranoid—"

"I never expected to catch a *navy pilot* sneaking around, *spying.*"

"You're no slouch in the Gestapo game!" Casey rejoined. "Friends in Immigration, pals in the police, bankers who report on confidential funds."

"Your damned Forget-Me-Not Fund cried out for investigating!" bellowed Bracken.

"I explained it to Alison."

"I don't believe the explanation," said Bracken. "Why would Rotgut put in twenty thousand dollars? It's hardly chickenfeed."

Casey was struck by a new possibility. "Chickenfeed? That's what one intelligence agency feeds enemy agents to mislead them. Rotgut never contacted me. Why? Because he found I was under surveillance by the Gabbiya crowd! Maybe he carried that money for some other purpose. He stuck it in the fund after he discovered Gabbiya's men watching the fund too. Chickenfeed would put them off the track. They'd think the fund was to finance some CIA operation."

"Isn't it?" asked Bracken.

"Of course it's not!" cut in Alison. She was playing light over the distant prisoner, but her attention came back to them with a jerk. "For a time I did wonder if the fund and Spad were all a cover. But that's nonsense. Still, Casey's only guessing—"

"I'm guessing, with few facts to go on," admitted Casey. "The truth is, I'm on my own. I can't even reach my partner. And I seem to face an old enemy. Forget Gabbiya—next to Hanoi's Zoo, he's a dove of peace."

"Dammit, laddie," said Bracken. "You're not on your own."

Tempers were cooling again. Alison, welcoming a diversion, whispered, "Looks like Buddha has something to say."

The prisoner had rolled to the extremity of the rope and was jerking at it so violently, the tree to which he was tied had started to shiver. Alison walked over, and the others joined her. "He's trying to kill himself," she said in awe.

Casey knelt. The man had contrived to get the rope wound around his throat. Casey loosened it. He began to say something in Vietnamese, the phrases returning automatically. He stopped. Better the man should remain unaware of who Casey was. He switched to French.

Buddha could not see his face. He listened, and answered in the kind of French common among students who had gone to Vietnamese Catholic schools, rather than to Paris. The two men talked quietly while

149

Bracken fidgeted. Finally, Casey rose. "That dart terrified him," he told Alison. "He thinks he was stung by a snake."

"The drug wears off quickly. He shouldn't feel anything."

"He thinks he does. These people are tough in their own jungle. This isn't his jungle, and he's badly frightened. He says he had a terrible vision, a monster—" Casey's eyes strayed over to where the Stringbag's huge shadow crouched in a deeper darkness. "I told him we'll give him a medicine to cure him."

"I don't have an antidote—" Alison began and then turned, exasperated with her own stupidity. "Yes, of course." She ran back to the Stringbag and rummaged through a parachute bag lying under the tail. She came back with a syringe from the first-aid kit. Before the prisoner could resist, she stuck the needle into his arm. "Tell him that will fix things."

Casey watched the man's face slowly relax, the gray pallor of fear recede from under the yellowish skin.

"If you've got more questions, ask them fast," said Alison softly.

Casey took her advice. He knew how ancient superstition still moved close to the surface of Marxist doctrine. Had the man faced a brutal interrogation, his devotion to the new religion would have given him the fortitude to remain silent. The belief that he had been struck by some unknown serpent in a strange land, however, summoned up atavistic fears of black magic. Casey spoke quietly with him, and after a while he left Buddha and joined the other two. "What did you give

150

him?" he asked Alison.

"A single shot of morphine. Enough to make him whoozy, nothing more."

Casey nodded. "Turn him loose. Then set fire to the Stringbag."

"*What?*" Bracken turned apoplectic.

"Or let him think that what you first expected is really happening."

"You're mad."

"No. Come over here." Casey led them back to the black cavern of trees sheltering the warplane. He had secured the prisoner so that he could not hurt himself. "Buddha's from the research ship *Ultima Thule*. I think he's truthful about Zia Gabbiya. He's never heard of him. The ship's carrying a Vietnamese crew, but the deck officers and skipper are white. He says they're Russian, but I'm not sure of him in this respect. He was sent to find out more about the aircraft. He rowed to the next island and swam the rest."

"What's this got to do with . . . with . . ." Bracken failed to get the words out. He gestured helplessly above him. He was leaning against the tail plane. He could have been, with his wild hair and beard, a ship's mop hung out as a signal to other captains to drop by for a wee dram o' scotch, thought Casey. He was like part of his aircraft; or a squeegee, sayk, stuck on the stern to swab down the afterdecks, for the fuselage at this point had the slab-sided look of a medieval hull.

"I'm not saying we *have* to burn it," Casey repeated.

"You're damned right you're not! I'm going bounty hunting in this thing." Bracken smacked the flat of his

151

hand against the tail plane.

"You're not," said Alison.

Until that moment, Casey had been grateful for her presence. She moderated her father's irascibility. But the last words inflamed Bracken again. "I'll fly her, blast it, if it kills me!"

"It will," Alison assured him. She turned to Casey. "My father came here tonight to start fueling up. I came — I'm sorry, Daddy, but you must understand how serious I am — I came to plead with him. He absolutely must not fly the Stringbag. He's not a well man. Suppose he became sick in the middle of the mission—"

"What mission?" Casey felt he was losing his wits.

"Against Zia Gabbiya," Alison whispered. "Father doesn't know when, nor how, but he thinks he has the firepower. He just needs to get the weapons over here."

"I don't know what Gabbiya could do to you," said Casey, "but I know what your own laws—"

"Ha!" barked Bracken. "I'll be within the law. Bounty hunting."

"*Bounty?*" Casey clutched his head.

"It's *your* tradition. Bounty hunters are 'licensed to kill predators.' It's the killing of predators I'll be doing, Casey. Using a letter of marque. It authorizes a vessel in the service of Her Majesty to attack enemy ships. This—" Bracken thumped the taut fabric. "—is a vessel of the Royal Navy." And indeed, where his hand fell, Casey read in the lantern's glow the aircraft serial number and the words ROYAL NAVY.

Alison said, "He's right, unfortunately. The Crown can issue a letter of marque making any ship a privateer, a legalized man-of-war. Lord knows when it was last done." Her tone altered. "Casey — ?"

"I cannot and will not fly this thing," Casey burst out, anticipating her.

"So you really want to make a bonfire out of my father's work?"

"No!" Casey looked up in despair at the forest of spars and rigging. "Let the prisoner think I did what I set out to do. He saw me sneak ashore. Fake a struggle between us. Then let him escape. He'll report the Stringbag's destroyed." Casey paused, listening to renewed cries from Buddha. "Do it now! Before he scares himself to death." He knew the only way was to stampede Bracken and the girl into doing what was needed.

He returned to Backgammon with the dawn, the fire imprinted on his mind. Alison and her father had dragged the prisoner farther off so that a firebreak could be cut with tools from the hangar. Casey had been shaken by the collection of equipment there. It suggested Bracken had logistical support from somewhere.

They had staged the fight, Lord Bracken playing his role as an outraged aviator roaring at the villain Casey, who "escaped" and quite by accident stumbled across the prisoner as the first flames showed through the brush. Buddha was still shivering with fright. Casey pretended sympathy and freed him. The man had to swim a narrow strait to the next cay, where he had left a small rowboat. By the time he reached the boat, the blaze lit up the sky. It worked like a charm. The fire must have looked like a major disaster for the Stringbag, but it was restricted to a small area, feeding itself on aviation juice from drums that Bracken had ferried over to begin fueling the plane.

The way Alison and her father whooped and hollered—Casey grinned at the recollection—must have convinced the escaping prisoner that their panic was genuine. In fact, they had moved with awesome efficiency. It was hard to reconcile this cool competence with their piratical notions. *Letters of marque?* They were up against a master terrorist, and perhaps against Vietnam, the Marxist power that once withstood American military bludgeons. Against all Gabbiya's technology and Vietnam's fanatical manpower, Bracken proposed to invoke letters of marque? Casey walked straight through the house to the library and searched the shelves. Here it was, in Bartlett's dictionary of phrase and fable: *marque*—a medieval word going back to Old French and Early Germanic, and once meaning reprisal, or to seize as a pledge. Only hopeless romantics would think they could sail—no, *fly!*—the Stringbag into action on such dubious authority. And who would pilot it? Not Bracken, with his bad heart. And not, thought Casey, *me*.

He wished now he had accepted Alison's invitation to breakfast at Pretty Penny. Her father hadn't pressed. When Alison suggested Casey move into their cottage for safety's sake, Casey had dismissed the dangers. Bracken, still on edge, snapped, "Okay, go be a bloody hero!"

154

Casey wandered back through the kitchen onto the patio, and called for Josh and Mary. Neither had been visible since the business with the dog. His nerves began to crawl again.

"Commander Casey?"

He jumped.

"Forgive the intrusion." The man who stepped delicately past the flowering rhododendrons was tall and wore his clothes with the casual elegance of the very rich. Worn sailing togs. Scuffed white kidskin shoes. Creamy-white ducks. "I tried your front door. But you know front doors around here. Nobody uses them."

"Did you," asked Casey, "consider the bell? At the end of the drive. Quite difficult to miss, actually."

The man stared at him as if this method of address was itself a violation of etiquette. "I'm Fetherstone," he said after a decided pause.

"Really? And what do you want?"

Fetherstone's brow wrinkled at the crudity of the approach. "I bring an invitation," he said in a drawl between a Boston and an Oxford accent. "From Edgar P. Geld."

Casey looked around him. "Is something missing? A fanfare of trumpets, perhaps? Who the hell is Geld?"

Shock was the only word for Fetherstone's reaction. Shock, and then disbelief. "You tease, of course, Commander." He laughed. "Mr. Geld is willing to see you *now*."

"But I'm not."

"Not ready?" Fetherstone cast a disapproving eye over Casey's muddied clothes. "In the circumstances,

Mr. Geld won't mind."

"You misunderstand me. I am not willing to see Mr. Geld." Casey knew very well who Edgar P. Geld was. He had no compelling urge to meet outside the gossip columns a man for whom he had a burning contempt. Fetherstone bobbed for his Adam's apple, and swallowed. "Mr. Geld is only here for the day. He has no time to waste."

Casey smiled. "Then, for goodness' sake, don't you waste it for him."

There was no doubt Fetherstone or some other flunky would be back. From the side of the garden, Casey watched the man depart in a white BMW with tinted glass. That meant Geld's establishment enjoyed exemption from the local restrictions on cars, which had to fall within narrow limits of size and origin. Presumably, if the rumors were true, Geld's privilege derived from Gabbiya's hidden power. It seemed an unlikely alliance.

Alison had spoken of an intermingling of business interests. Casey returned to the house, intending to phone her, and then changed his mind. He might as well try Bingo Harriman again. The operator who responded was almost insolent this time, and dropped into the local patois: "No, sah! Dere be no telephone circuit to d' United States. Nor London, nor Europe neither . . ."

The recital increased his sense of isolation. He walked away from the phone in disgust. It seemed an instrument of betrayal. He went to the garage, where a battered old Aston Martin went with the lease of the house. He felt distrustful of it and wheeled out his own rented moped. He putt-putted across the island and killed the flywheel motor before leaving the bike at the end of the lane to Pretty Penny. It had occurred to him that Alison might be catching up on sleep.

She wasn't. "Gosh, you startled me!" She seemed uncharacteristically flustered. She had been sitting at a small table on the open veranda, and scooped up some papers as she climbed the steps.

"I just had a bigger surprise," said Casey. "Fellow called Fetherstone came calling." He described what had happened.

"Jeff Fetherstone! That's quite an honor! Neither Master Geld nor his minions are known to see the light of day before noon."

"Why *Master* Geld?"

"He's never really grown up, has he?"

"I don't know. You tell me."

"He's a prize prick!" said Alison, abandoning all maidenly pretense. "That's priceless, to send a suck like Fetherstone to your place at crack o' dawn. Must be urgent. Look, sit down, I'll make some tea. Then I'll tell you—" She swung back. "Tea, or something stronger?"

"Tea. The sun's hardly up. By the time it's below the yardarm, I'll be in my bunk." Casey caught a glint in the girl's eye that baffled him. He wasn't familiar these days with the female mind, or he might have wondered if Alison had her own notions about what use can be made of bunks before sundown.

"I bet you haven't had breakfast yet—"

"No, please, don't think of it, even." He silenced her concern. "I think better on an empty stomach."

He sank back in the big, old-fashioned garden chair and lifted his feet onto the veranda rail. From there, he could look through the arching oleanders toward the sea. Why couldn't we all live in unassuming cottages where a man could put up his feet and listen to the nightingales instead of police sirens? Here the grass was hummocky, the garden a wilderness of wildflowers and vegetables, and there was no danger of landscape gardeners disturbing the peace to blitz the lawns into conformity with neighbors. He glanced sideways at the small table and wondered idly what it was Alison hadn't wanted him to see.

She came back with a tea tray that also held a plate of fruit. "Daddy turned in, or he'd join us. He says an apple a day keeps the doctor away. Wish it were true."

"You're very worried about him, aren't you?"

"Terribly." Her eyes clouded over, and then she sat down and said briskly, "Milk and sugar? Right. Now, about the frightful Master Geld."

"No, let's get back to your father for a moment," Casey insisted. "Why did you let him go so far with this airplane restoration?"

"I told you, it began innocently enough. He had a compulsion to do it, and I thought it would be good therapy."

"You're sure he had no sense then of Gabbiya's intentions?"

158

"Gabbiya wasn't known to be—" Alison broke off, closing one eye while she considered her next words. Casey knew the unconscious mannerism by now. It signaled Alison entering a mood of legal caution. "Well, Gabbiya was certainly low-profile. In retrospect, knowing now some of his front companies, he must have been burrowing away a long time." Both eyes flew open. "Maybe my father guessed something odd was happening. Never underestimate your old man, Casey."

"I never did," said Casey, remembering a father who had also played the cards close to his chest.

"In these past few years," Alison continued thoughtfully, "Gabbiya's been winding an awful lot of reputable American corporations into his own operations. I can track it, you see, through our fiction library. That's why I know Edgar Geld. I had the misfortune to handle his companies' legal affairs in these islands. The Parasite Islands, he calls us. Not Paradise, but Parasite. Parasites being the tax dodgers, and islanders like me. He couldn't bring in his own lawyers, because *we* keep tight control under our own laws. In the States, those lawyers of his surround him, cut him off from normal human contacts, convince him there's a world of human animals out there all waiting to grab his money. It's a laugh, really, Geld calling *us* parasites! His wealth derives from ancestors who invested shrewdly in land and railroads at the dawn of American industry. With that kind of money multiplying away, the man buys all the experts he needs."

Casey thought of how Gabbiya was said to boast of buying the world's best brains too. Perhaps there was really no big gap between them, after all. He said, "Zia Gabbiya worries me, but Geld scares me."

Alison showed open astonishment. "Geld's too big a coward to hurt anyone directly. He's too frightened of losing property in some act of revenge. He's boarded up against human contacts, except for the sycophants around him. He comes to the Windfalls once a year, *for one day only.* For that, he keeps Rose Hall Great House. It's a marvelous old plantation and cost him a bomb. He needs a residence here, you see, to meet tax requirements and pipe a lot of his international profits through the offshore companies. He flies here to arrive at daybreak, sleeps the day, leaves at night in his own jet."

"Why would Gabbiya need him?"

"To disguise the multitude of companies owned here, for a start. Their joint ventures go under the various corporate names associated with Edgar P. Geld. I suppose Gabbiya wants the islands to seem normal. Geld's reputation helps fill the glossy magazines with high-society crap about the rich and famous coming here year after year. That draws all those middle-class American families attracted by the Old World charm, tennis and snobbery. He needs *Town & Country* to go on featuring those posh weddings complete with coach-and-four and quaint churches. Gabbiya needs us to continue looking high-class respectable—" Alison stopped as if she was afraid of saying too much.

"But if he now owns the place?" prompted Casey.

"He *owns* it, if you weigh his money against that of all others. His money buys influence, bends rules, but the government here still has sweeping powers. It's a colonial government, but you Americans don't always understand that an old colony like this has great independence. If the Windfalls had wanted to put Edgar Geld off his land, it would have deported him. There'd be no appeal—in the old days. Now, in partnership with Gabbiya's billions, that begins to look less likely. A sufficient number of corrupted politicians and officials could sweeten the lives of Gabbiya and Geld."

"You mean, Zia Gabbiya himself taking over would have been too big a challenge—?"

"For London, yes. For the United States, too. Look how you intervened in Grenada. There was a British colony, but your forces moved in without clearing it with London. Grenada had shown its hand too soon—or rather, the Communist-supported government there wasn't smart enough to conceal Cuban help."

"Gabbiya's not a Communist."

"He doesn't need to be." Alison stood up. She seemed to have arrived at a decision. She said, "Let me get you some more tea."

Casey sat back. The scissor-grinding buzz of cicadas in the nearby cedar forest started up as the sun burned the mist off the water. He fought against a sense of well-being. Life had taught him this was when trouble struck. And yet, Alison was finally telling him more than she ever had before.

She returned, carrying the papers he had seen her remove so swiftly on his arrival. She laid them out on the table. "Sergeant Winston left this report for me. There's no point concealing things like this from you."

161

She shuffled out a strip of 35-mm negative film and some color prints. "The man who shot the governor," she said, "posed as a seaman on a cruise ship. I'll explain later about Winston. For now, just accept that he's got good connections abroad. After the assassination, he had his men check among tourists for anyone who might have snapped the gunman." Her fingernail tapped a blurred closeup of an Oriental raising a pistol. "That's the assassin."

The photograph might have seemed fuzzy to most, but Casey had no need to look more closely. "Has the sergeant shown this to anyone else?" Casey asked.

"No," Alison said calmly. "Winston trusts nobody in authority. Only three of us know—and now you."

The light had gone out of the day for Casey. He sifted through the rest of the tourist's photographs. The man in the uniform of a cruise ship's lower-deck crew, a man who could be mistaken at a distance for a lascar, was the Vietnamese they had called Buddha.

"He tried to get you with that *panji* booby trap," said Alison. "Why? What have you got that Hanoi doesn't?"

My honor, thought Casey. It would have sounded melodramatic to voice this to Alison. But he knew Big Vien, who had failed to break Casey in prison, and later showed a deadly compulsion to prove his superiority even from a distance. Big Vien saw Casey as a symbol of American willpower; if he could humble Casey, he would humble America. It seemed much too vainglorious an idea to confide to Alison. It required too much explanation, otherwise Alison must think he had a colossal ego. The fact was that it had been Casey's

162

absence of ego, a self-effacement said to be an exclusive Communist quality, that humbled Big Vien in the Zoo. And the Vietnamese wanted revenge, not only against Casey but against the American people he symbolized.

That was how it appeared to Casey at this particular moment. So, to answer her question, he simply shook his head in wonder. And all he said was "Let's find out what dragged a great American tycoon into such company."

CHAPTER 10

"Well, there it is, E.P.," said the Irish Girl. "The Great Protector of Islam wants to see you. Now."

Edgar P. Geld regarded Mellanie Blake with an expression of total shock. He had just received Casey's rude rejection of his own summons, couched in similar terms. Geld was not accustomed to being rejected. He was not accustomed to being summoned by others. He was not accustomed to Lani in this role. The last time he had seen her, she had been a convenient piece of tail in Manhattan. Now she had turned into a dragon.

A dragon, moreover, with real fire in her belly.

"Gabbiya," she had told him, "expects you to deliver Casey to him, *discreetly*." And when Geld said that was impossible, she had answered by placing before him a loose-leaf file whose contents he was forced out of horrified curiosity to look at again.

If Geld had been in a more reflective frame of mind, he might have noted a certain irony in receiving, here within the cavernous central hall of the Great House of Rose Hall, a messenger from the Great Protector of Islam, for the house was once in the gift of the Lord Protector and dictator of England, Oliver Cromwell. Rose Hall dated back to the time of the English regicides, the king killers who delivered Charles I to the axman in 1649. It was one of many estates scattered throughout the islands off the American eastern seaboard awarded the regicides for their dark deed. Such estates had the additional virtue of keeping the regicides at a distance from England and vengeance.

Geld sat in a Spanish leather chair, at the opposite end of the main hall to the gigantic fireplace. The hall, indeed the house, had been built around the kitchen, which occupied pride of place, with butcher-block tables gleaming pots and pans hung on thick stone walls concealing an adjoining staircase for kitchen staff.

Lani sat in the same kind of self-important chair, showing a curious contempt for the manorial splendor in which Geld felt obliged to live for one day a year. He was hunched over the file she had given him while she studied the central hall, rising three stories, one end absorbing the flow of the kitchen into reception and dining areas. Once, there would have been straw strewn over the flagstoned floor and hounds to snarl over discarded meat bones. A minstrels' gallery ran all the way around at mid-level. The whole place was maintained by a near-invisible staff so that the owner could satisfy those general tax requirements that applied to all the presidents of Windfall-registered companies.

If she had not disliked Geld so heartily, she might have found his present discomfiture amusing. He was discovering data in the file that told him things about his commercial empire that even he did not know, and his codfish eyes bulged. He wore a clipped black mustache, so sprightly it seemed almost possible he changed it once a day. He dyed his hair black. He could pass for forty; naked, he looked closer to sixty. His tastes were an odd mixture of vulgarity and discrimination, in women as much as in furnishings or clothes. He was like an ancient emperor who relied on others to guide him. Unable to kill off the slaves who created this environment, however, he fired them instead. He had homes on a grand scale in a dozen countries. The interior designers he hired were dismissed on completion of a project. There were always others eager to serve the great Geld. His face was like a sixteenth-century Italian portrait of a merchant who lacked a unifying taste: half was brutish and cunning, the other half sensitive and almost refined. His hair was parted down the middle as if to make a judicious separation between the two halves, and this gave him the comic air of a seedy *boulevardier* from another age.

He looked up, finally. "Lani, trust me. I'll find a way to get Casey to you before nightfall."

"Colonel Gabbiya," she said, becoming formal, "is past the trusting stage. He wants you to deliver Casey in person."

Geld leaned forward with that unconscious movement of the short-sighted. He was in fact wearing new contact lenses of an unnaturally vivid blue. They were giving him trouble. He intended to change both them and his optician when he got back to New York, but not the color. The color, like the mustache, the designer clothes and the nurtured tan, were symptoms of unease about what people really thought about him. Few knew that he cared. Lani had made the discovery, but still she could reflect that nothing would ever shake Geld out of his arrogance of wealth. It was his indiscriminate use of wealth in meeting his whims that helped cut him off from normal human contacts; that and the lawyers thickly clustered about him to keep away the gold diggers. Lani had been the exception to the rule adopted after his fourth divorce: one woman, one night, and no repeats.

"These documents mean nothing," he said with a show of bravado.

"Try telling that to your Justice Department."

"I'm not responsible for what a small subsidiary's been up to—"

"Peregrine Holdings (Windfalls) Limited will come under investigation tomorrow as a laundromat for the cocaine trade." The words tripped easily off Lani's tongue. "You can argue it's minuscule in your scheme of things. You can plead ignorance. You can shelter for a while behind a dozen cutouts. But once the Justice Department plods forward, it works slow but it sifts small. There will be questions about other companies, and more questions about the concealment of trading with a government America still doesn't recognize— Vietnam—not to mention the provision of arms through third parties."

Geld glanced quickly to left and right. He had given orders to leave them alone. Lani luxuriated in the idea of Geld spending the rest of his life looking furtive.

"Lani," he said, "you don't understand financial matters. If Gabbiya does this to me, he'll suffer tenfold."

"Yes," said Lani. "But he's not an American, subject to American law."

Geld's face glistened. "Peregrine enjoys the protection of British law."

The girl laughed. "Who gets protection here will soon be a decision for the Protector. The British will

168

rubber-stamp what he says, because it will be said through parliament here."

A silence fell between them. In the grounds outside, Geld's men kept watch, and wondered.

It had never before happened that Edgar P. Geld paid court to any man. Nor had he taken another's transportation, not taken any step to gratify another's wishes. He had taken other men's women, however; any subsequent uproar could be muted by money. Now he'd clearly taken one girl too many.

The only consolation, he thought, climbing stiffly into Zia Gabbiya's helicopter, was that when he had taken Mellanie Blake those many times in Manhattan, he had penetrated the Great Protector's domain in an unexpected way. He had done business before with Gabbiya, on advice and at a safe distance. Now it seemed the Geld empire was more intricately involved than E.P. himself had previously understood. But nobody could take away from E.P. the fact that Gabbiya's girl had responded sexually in ways flattering to E.P.'s male ego. Never had he risen to such heights of performance, which was why he had broken his own rule about one woman, one night, and no repeats. It was, in its way, a triumph for someone whose accomplishments were otherwise attributable to the family name.

The girl crowding in beside him brought the heat to his cheeks again. She rested her hips against his scrunched-up legs. He was too vain, too filled with self-satisfied memories of his conquest, to come to grips yet with the obvious: that Lani had been bait.

Lani, familiar with the small conceits of men, waited

for the generators to come on and circulate cool air within the bubble. The sun was reducing E.P. to the mewling schoolboy of the bedroom. Even if refrigeration finally chilled some sense into his addled mind, she doubted if he would be sufficiently disillusioned to face the truth and become enraged. He seemed more likely to present Gabbiya with the interesting challenge of trying to nail Jell-O to the wall.

She watched the Great House of Rose Hall fall away, and glimpsed the white faces of his personal guard. They were E.P.'s nursemaids, stunned to see baby lifted from the cradle by strangers. "Get on with your usual routine," E.P. had instructed an astonished major-domo. The orders mostly concerned a tiny island which at low tide was linked by a spit of sand to the Rose Hall estate.

The pilot, for his own inscrutable reasons, circled the island. E.P., knowing little about aeronautical imperatives, wondered if it was by design. He peered down at the cable car linking the grounds with what had become his Achilles' heel. He wished he knew how Gabbiya had discovered it. The facts were explored in one of the documents Lani had brought with her this morning — rather more extensively explored than in any previous communications from the Protector.

Colonel Zia Gabbiya, Great Protector of Islam, self-proclaimed Great Guardian of the Republic of Sahara, "one man and one nation indivisible," watched the Bell Jet Ranger helicopter flutter across the harbor named after Britain's greatest admiral, Lord Nelson. It pleased him to see his pilot flout local flying restrictions. The time approached when Nelson's heirs must learn to live by Gabbiya's own golden rule: the man with the gold rules.

"Most thoughtful of you to come," said Gabbiya, although Edgar P. Geld had been virtually marched into the *Qurqūr*'s chief stateroom. Its latticed windows leaned out, flush with the stern, so that sunlight bouncing up from the sea came dancing across the gold-leafed ceiling.

Geld suavely matched the Protector's manner. "It's the least I can do. Welcome to my neck of the woods, Colonel."

Lani, coiled on tasseled cushions, studied with cautious amusement this first direct confrontation between two latter-day monarchs. The Protector wore his Sunday uniform, a white tunic with embroidered and exaggerated shoulders under a white cloak thrown back to reveal red shoulder boards set vertically with the gold insignia of the Supreme Commander of Sahara Combined Armed Forces, and a cascade of self-awarded medals for bravery and disregard for personal safety in the pursuit of duty, including an unearned British Victoria Cross and an equally undeserved U.S. Distinguished Service Medal with assorted Bronze Stars. The effect was somewhat spoiled by white balloon pants and bare feet. Gabbiya squatted on an immense gold cushion. His visitor, more modestly accoutred, stooped to listen from the height of a chair modeled upon the King George I Shepherd's Crook, popular enough in the 1700s without its present incongruous leopardskin cover. The coral-stone deck resembled desert sands.

"*Your* neck of the woods?" Gabbiya showed even rows of dazzling white teeth.

"I virtually own the place," said Geld. "If I pulled my money and companies out, the Windfalls would fall apart. And the government here knows it—"

"And within a few hours, will also know that *I* own *you*."

"Your kind of rough stuff might work a good distance from America, but not here, an hour's flight from Washington." Geld was recovering his poise. "You trying anything here, you'll get hammered."

"A threat? Or an invitation?"

Geld ignored the smile. "Zia, King of Terror!" He held out his hands as if reading a newspaper. "Our smart-ass editors long ago figured how to compress you into a front-page flare. ZIA DEFIES UNCLE SAM. They'll inflame the public, force the politicians to act."

The Protector threw his head back in a paroxysm of laughter. "They have nothing—*nothing* to hammer me with. The armed forces cannot move without giving offense to London. Washington can't risk offending her best ally by staging another Grenada-style invasion."

"That was clumsy," conceded Geld. "Nobody in Washington took seriously the British monarch's position there."

"She's also Queen of the Windfalls. And my palace informants tell me she's made very clear that *any* U.S. military intervention here would be regarded as an act of war, whereas my presence is financially to the Crown's advantage."

Geld stiffened, and Lani disguised her surprise by examining the gold threads in the tasseled cushion.

"Money," said Gabbiya, "buys anything. But you have to be ruthless, Mr. Geld. Ruthless in getting the help of those who can be subtle in the way they run your errands." Then he mentioned the name of an old man, a man whose fortunes had been founded by a father who supplied Russia with badly needed technology in the early days of revolution, and sold on Russia's behalf the high-value, small-bulk goods during the West's economic embargo that fetched huge prices and valuable hard currency for a Soviet Union otherwise near bankruptcy. Furs, jewels and art treasures had bailed out the Kremlin and established a commercial empire this old man now commanded with as much authority in the Soviet bloc as in America. An old man with delusions of statesmanlike grandeur who knew that to win the respect of royalty he had only to shovel a few million of dollars into a prince's pet charity . . . "We have yet to find a brain that cannot be bought," said Gabbiya, as if he and the old man were together in the business of exploiting greed. "Royal brains are best for manipulating the elitists, for few question their authority. A handful of silver purchases my royal authority, though it be denied Americans."

Edgar Geld shifted restlessly in his King George chair. A lecture on the power of wealth was not what he needed. He said in an effort at self-assertion, "The people, nonetheless, identify you with every crazy terrorist act. You start boasting this way around here, you'll find we Americans have a new line in antiterrorist forces."

"I would be delighted to meet them. Those who've survived your presidential purge."

This time Lani made no pretense of disinterest. Zia Gabbiya had turned to watch a large parrot working its way down a rope by the windows. She glanced quickly at Geld. Had he paid attention, he would have seen

173

something like a mute appeal in her eyes. Instead, Geld asked, "What purge?" and the girl relaxed as if this were the question she had secretly wished on him.

Gabbiya held out an arm. The parrot half jumped and half flew to perch there in a flurry of gaudy feathers. "Your country has no forces suited to fight my kind of wars," he said contemptuously. "Your covert, your black, your special strike forces have lost their claws. They were torn out in a typical excess of American *'democracy'.*"

Lani quickly rose and coaxed the parrot away from Gabbiya. He smiled at her. "You're lucky you're not an American secret agent," he said softly. "You'd have no one to report to." She smiled back, her black eyes impenetrable, and moved swiftly to her former position, one that made her part confidante and part courtesan. This time the brief gestures were not lost on Geld. "I, too," said the American, "can and do buy bodies." He stared angrily at Lani.

"But you cannot win their devotion to an ideal," said Gabbiya. "Your President Johnson expressed the crudity of Western technique. 'When you've got their balls,' I believe is the way he put it, 'you've got their hearts and minds.' " Gabbiya made a plucking motion. "That may work for some, but I know great scientists who would place themselves at my disposal for a touch of idealism, a little luxury and a great deal of flattery . . . Or the price may be provision of some as yet secret medical technology. Say, for the desperate father of a demented child."

The last words brought an ugly flush to Geld's face. "Someday," he said in a strained voice, "my men will find your weakness."

"Meanwhile, I know yours. I want Casey."

Lani watched the sudden transformation in Zia Gabbiya, the color draining from her face. The dictator was no longer playing games.

"I can't just"—Geld gestured helplessly—"just *pick him up*. Why don't you get him with some of those magical powers you boast about?" Any defiance left in him seemed to die.

"Your good name is required for this," said Gabbiya.

"Haven't you traded enough on my good name?" asked Geld, thinking of business partnerships consummated between branches of his corporate empire and that of Zia Gabbiya. What Lani had brought him this morning was a record of collaboration between other subsidiaries of which Geld had never heard. If the papers were to be believed, Zia Gabbiya's high-priced financial whiz kids had infiltrated the Geld corporate structure and engineered deals that threatened what had always seemed an impregnable fortress on the American commercial landscape. Americans do not like the unauthorized sale of equipment to Communist countries. They do not like the transfer of classified weapons to Communist countries. They do not like investment analysts who suddenly turn into defense analysts writing reports for Communist countries. And they do not like big corporations providing cover for dealers in new hard drugs like "crack" who move the stuff through offshore islands by way of offshore companies. All these offenses could be charged against Geld's empire, thanks to Zia Gabbiya's agents.

Geld did not yet know the extent of the damage. He had to assume the dictator was not bluffing. What he did know was that enough of his corporate activities intertwined with those of companies controlled at a distance by Gabbiya to make it entirely feasible that the corrosion had spread throughout his interests like one of those diseases that began in North Africa — bilharzia, wasn't it? — and moved slowly but inexorably by way of rivers, tributaries and streams until it poisoned the entire continent.

The worst poison of all had been indicated by Gabbiya's reference to a demented child. *There* was the foulest infection! Edgar Geld looked up. "You want me to bring you Casey so that you're not directly involved? But I plan to leave here tonight."

"You'll need more time than that just to get confirmation that my hired hands have outwitted yours," said Gabbiya. "You'll find communications out of the islands are — ah, interrupted. However, for your phones and telexes out of Rose Hall, there will be special dispensation."

"You're mad! You can't *isolate* the Windfalls!"

"I don't intend to try. Just exercise a certain discrimination about what comes in and goes out," said Gabbiya.

Lani, sensing some dying spark of resistance in Geld, said, "The Great Protector is in no hurry."

Unctuous bitch! thought Geld, shifting his gaze in her direction. She knows, in one matter, it is myself who is in a hurry.

"I am not, as she says, in a great hurry," Gabbiya confirmed. "However, one of those extremely expensive brains of mine does advise that I'm on a twenty-four-hour countdown. So, though I'm not in a hurry, I apparently need Casey delivered tonight. And only through you."

"But—"

"*I'll* provide that offer he can't refuse," said the Great Protector.

Noon was Zia Gabbiya's favorite time for fun, followed by sleep. He lived by the sun. It struck down into the swimming pool amidships. He liked the ripple effect on the marble mosaic on the floor of the pool. It was copied from the Toreador Fresco from Knossos. In every line of the bull, and in the muscular figure tossed over the bull's back, there was the same projection of barely controlled power.

Gabbiya at noon enjoyed going naked. He could stand for minutes at a time admiring his own strong body. It offered reassurance. Whether he clothed it in Bedouin rags or in operatic uniforms, it remained unchanged. As a poor magician, he had enchanted the people by his trickery so that they could not help but love the trickster. Whatever flamboyance he conjured up to disguise the raw savagery of his body, he was so enchanted by his own illusions that he could not help but love himself.

Lani knew his habits. She stood naked on the other side of the pool. Naked, she could be mistaken for a Bedouin youth. Until she had arrived in North Africa, Zia had renewed his youth in that of boys and young men of a certain immaturity. He loved the cleanness of limb, the suppleness, the sense of rediscovering himself. The spoken legends of his own people acknowledged a special bond between the great warriors and the boys who refreshed them. In women, Gabbiya had taken only a certain animal pleasure until Lani came.

Women had seemed a species apart, until Lani came.

She plunged into the pool and rose out of the azure water as if emerging from the bull's massive phallus. There! That was the sort of thing she did! You were never quite sure if she had planned it that way. She was beguiling, she was boyish, she was clever, she was a witch.

She crouched with her damp face against his thighs. She was like one of the golden black-maned lions in the mountains of his own country. She was neither boy nor woman. Sometimes, lying with her, he felt he had invented her.

A musical chime filtered through the privacy wall. A voice chanted honorifics and a message in Arabic. "No," he said, addressing the polished teak. "The deputy governor, I do not wish to speak with. I know he leaves for London tonight. No more calls until I have eaten." He turned off the intercom and said to Lani, "He goes to London. He's been told what to do. He will retire a rich man. Why does the fool risk exposure by calling now?"

"Because he's nervous," said Lani.

The pool area was beyond prying eyes. The sky was empty, for only his own aircraft could intrude.

"So?" Gabbiya stretched full length on a wide banquette behind the fountains. Lani curled up against him like a cat.

"E.P. will do what you want," she said. "He's never been exposed to direct sunlight. He's the most underexposed man in captivity."

"And now he sees the light?"

"He's blinded by it. He cannot see a way to stop you ruining him. In matters of accountancy, nobody comprehends arithmetic better. About human beings he knows nothing. About profit and loss, he knows almost everything *except* the human factor. He thought he could build safe, obscure partnerships with you, never expecting where they might lead." Lani stirred her tight buttocks against him. "You blinded him where it counts, though he still has enough vision to see riches. I bet by the time he left here, he could give a fair assessment of the market value of everything in the stateroom."

Zia dribbled his fingers along her thighs. He had the lightest touch of any man. "If he is a cash register, why does he waste emotion on an idiot child? My people suffer from no such weakness. They put their weaklings out to die." He sensed her sudden tension, and her effort to conceal it."

"Is there hope? For the child?"

"If the silly little man does what I ask."

"You're still the magician," said Lani. "In such things, too often, you deal in illusions."

Gabbiya laughed easily and dipped his free hand into a marble bowl of warm oil. "No, this is not nonsense. I can provide a Russian who has worked miracles in mind control. This type of idiot child—"

"Idiot savant!"

"Well, *savant*. It's possible to bring about a semblance of normality. Or to drive them to the extremes of despair." He felt her muscles harden at these words, and he began to spread the oil like a nurse with a child. The oil was scented with a perfume of his own Paris expert's creation. One of his hands burrowed like a furry animal between her slippery thighs.

Lani shifted attention. From long practice, she could detach mind from body. She ran through the conversation between the two potentates. She had been shocked by Gabbiya's disclosure that American covert operations had been suspended. She knew how well the Protector could perform sleight of hand, but in this she was sure he spoke the truth as he knew it. And Gabbiya's sources were, well, as he said, the best money could buy. The news left her in a state of mind she knew to be dangerous.

Yet she could do nothing. Zia long ago had told her to practice her skills on Edgar P. Geld. It had not been difficult. E.P. was known within an exclusive Manhattan circle to be an admirer of women. He liked to keep up his public reputation for dating stunning girls. He had what the high-society madam of that exclusive Manhattan club called the repetitive "Wham-bam! Morning, ma'am!" simplicity of a rabbit. When Lani was left out in the city gardens to play, however, she had turned E.P. into the busy little bunny in the story who, rushing from female to female, hits a stone ornamental cottontail, who brings him up short with "Wham-bam! . . . Aargh, goddammmmm!" Lani wasn't made of stone, but she knew how to make careless ramming painful, in an addictive sort of way.

The last thing Lani needed now was to have Zia divine how successful she had been with E.P. It was one thing to go out on a job for Zia, and quite another to have the victim still leching after you. Zia thought his precious documents had gained her the private audience with E.P. this morning. Maybe. She knew E.P. well enough to guess his initial reaction had been one of secret rage and resistance. Her appearance had knocked him off balance; and, in an unexpected way, had given Zia's veiled threats a fresh authenticity.

She felt her legs uncoil. They had a will of their own now. Her nipples seemed ready to explode. One of the Great Protector's less odious oddities was his pleasure in giving pleasure, provided there was a challenge. The seduction of other women had always been a disappointment for him, Lani guessed, because they were too eager to capitulate. She herself fought against every kind of response to titillation, measuring out each small surrender to maintain the illusion of strength yielding to strength. She wanted Zia never to forget she was his match physically and intellectually. Each encounter was a contest ending in renewed proof of Zia's superior skill. Each time must be for him like breaking a wild horse again. Once broken, she would sink into the cries which for him were the most powerful aphrodisiac. For him, the challenge was never to be reduced to the whimpering submissiveness that made other men so controllable, such weaklings, in their relations with women.

"What's your real reason for wanting Casey?" she asked.

She had deliberately chosen the moment when he must know she was at the brink of the first clitoric orgasm. It was her demonstration of will. He stopped the motion of his hand. "I want to test Washington's resolve," he said, and laughed inside himself. Delightful! If the gods chose a companion for King Tantalus it must be this creature whose fruit receded when you reached for it and advanced when you withdrew. He drew back a fraction and felt her slight adjustment. "And then," he added, "there is the lesser matter of discovering Mr. Edgar Geld's limits. What do your informants say about the child?"

This time she could deal with it and betray nothing. "She plays exquisitely, as always, both piano and harp. And, in between, is lost in her own, unhappy world, the most solitary of living things." Lani twisted her head. "Can your tame Russian do more than merely bring her mind under control?"

Gently he massaged her back, working his way back to where he had detected already the first tiny squirts betraying her body's dissolving resolve. More exciting than the trite emissions of a boy were these vaginal explosions. He had never believed it was possible in a woman. He said, "My Russian perfected his art on American prisoners in Vietnam." Then, with practiced deliberation, he removed what Lani sometimes called his emotional armor, and mounted her.

Lani had disciplined herself to keep at the core of her being, during such moments, the knowledge of her true role. She was able to conceal her reaction to her lover's last words in the vigor of her physical response, beguiling him into the quite reasonable conviction that he was still in command and that it was she, mere woman, who had lost control. He bore her up on a rising tide of lust and she suffered the first concussion of delight.

The real Lani floated away like an astral body separating from earthly flesh. *He wants Casey for the Vietnamese*, she thought. Casey meant nothing to her. It was just a name to which she had briefly put a face. The implications were enormous, though. She had believed Gabbiya's objectives were precisely as defined by his money experts: to bring about a Western financial disaster. The experts had argued that the world economy was profoundly distorted by debt and showed serious symptoms of overspeculation in foreign exchange and the turnover of bank deposits in New York, far out of line with the true levels of economic activity. Anything could start the crash. That *anything* could be the deliberate crippling of financial institutions doing global business through the Windfalls. She remembered how one of the money men had employed aeronautical terms to describe it: "The West can be likened to an airliner at the point of stall, near *incipient destructive instability.* It doesn't matter where the airflow breaks away. Once it does, the whole thing crashes. Offshore capital that flows through these islands can be compared to part of the airflow, and if it breaks away in the Windfalls it begins to peel away everywhere, *irreversibly!*"

From this, Lani had deduced that there were certain aims Gabbiya shared with Vietnamese military leaders still thirsting for revenge. Now she wasn't sure.

Zia rolled away from her. Quickly she detained him. She knew what she was about to do was dangerous. She had no choice. She let her hand slide from his arm to his back, and down to his tailbone. She massaged the coccyx with the palm of her hand, her fingers gently enclosing his damp testicles. She made her actions appear to grow out of an inexpressible gratitude; the danger would come if he got the impression she had not been satisfied. Slowly she coaxed him back. She was testing her willpower against his. She felt him falling in with the game, and the danger receding. His pride now rode upon her ability to bring him to new heights of savage vigor, and upon his ability to remain on the crest of sensation and reverse the tables. Soon the first stage was accomplished and she felt the renewed explosions inside her own body. She must resist, only to collapse before he did into total submission. He was laughing, relishing the game, filling her with quick bursts of violent energy, falling just short of physically hurting her. Now to tackle the second danger. She had always avoided prompting him into indiscretions, especially in bed. She must do it this time, and risk the fate she had seen his inquisitive boys suffer because they were foolish and asked a question too many at a time too delicate. In Sahara, they were put into iron cages and left slowly to die in the desert air, their rotting bodies carrying the message: "Death to spies." Lani had little doubt Gabbiya could mete out the same punishment here. There was no security in her being filed away somewhere as a visitor to the Windfalls, though her subsequent departure would normally have to be registered with Immigration, or her disappearance explained. Immigration, at the top level, was already indebted to the Great Protector in ways that would prove embarrassing if they were ever made public.

She fought him while through her mind floated the image of a skeleton in an iron cage suspended from a gibbet. They fought until she felt he was no longer able to hold off a climax, and then she collapsed amid cries of ecstasy. He crouched over her, flaunting the ponderous machinery of sex. His face glowed with pride. He was caught. They renewed the game. She had seldom leapt from one orgasm to another in such number that she felt faint. She floated above the lesser ecstasies until she judged the moment right for another vast surrender. It was as if she had individual control over a series of smaller muscles and could, upon command, bring them together in one giant convulsion. Oh, her body loved it, no doubt of that! This was what made her brilliant in her chosen profession. She would have enjoyed such a struggle with that Russian they talked about, the one who had sharpened his mind-control skills in Vietnam. When it came to mind control, she could teach him a few things!

And now the iron cage hung directly over her, blotting out the sun. She felt Gabbiya exhausted by her side. Any moment he would climb, shouting and laughing, to the platform above the pool. His dive would signal the crew that it was safe to resume their duties on the main deck. Privacy time would be over. She whispered into his ear those things she had never voiced before, knowing how quick he was to suspect motives. She would take the chance. He was smiling at her flattery, and pretending not to luxuriate at her cunning touch while already his treacherous body quivered again. His eyes were closed tight against the sky's glare and so she could not read their expression when at last she asked him, leading up to the question by way of idle comment about E. P. Geld: "The American they say was killed accidentally— Did he have any connection with Geld?"

Only the slight flutter of eyelids informed her that she was right: that the question was very dangerous. Then a tiny dimple formed in each corner of Gabbiya's mouth. "What you really want to know," he said, "is this. The man's name was Earle Rutgers. There was no connection with Geld. If Rutgers' bosses knew half the truth about Geld, they would put him in front of a firing squad. But Rutgers' bosses might just as well be as dead as Rutgers. They formed a CIA section operating beyond all oversight committees and any form of public scrutiny."

Lani lay very still. Zia sat up abruptly and stared into her eyes. "I made sure the story of that CIA section leaked to the press. The section's job was to study and then get rid of me. Instead, I got rid of them. They don't exist." He began to laugh. "If you were an American spy, you would have been working for them too. If you were an American spy, you would be without help of any sort now. Not even Casey could help you."

"You're a wonderful man," said Lani, her blood running cold at the extra risk she was now running, "but you do boast. How could even you, with all your hidden power, 'get rid of' a section of the CIA?" She waited, almost afraid to breathe.

But the Protector appeared to take the question as coming from a naive admirer. "Americans get into covert warfare with both hands tied behind their backs. Their hands are tied because anything covert is at once splashed across their newspapers. Once Rutgers' department became a subject of public debate, it was finished."

Lani shivered. "Be careful," she pleaded. "Perhaps there are other departments."

Zia ran the tips of his fingers along an imaginary line from the glistening bushy triangle, across the miracle of her taut golden belly and up into the valley between her breasts. His fingers lingered and then proceeded down again. Lani closed her eyes, knowing the pendulum of his hand reflected the pendulum of his mind. He did not like women, because they clutched. She had taken care never to clutch until now. She had to show concern for his safety or he would start to consider the other and

186

obvious explanation for her curiosity; yet, showing that concern, she might antagonize him with the threat of possession. His fingers continued, the caresses built up. She opened herself to the bolts of lightning about to strike again. She sighed. A little poetry was in order. "I am your creature," she said, outraged by the extravagance of her own language. "If anything happened to you, my body would die of thirst. There is no man, no god, who could move me as you move me. I am proud when you lead your secret armies into war. All I ask is that you never underestimate your enemies."

"It is good advice," said Zia after a moment. He never could resist poetry. Unlike personal sentimentality, it made no real demands. "But don't worry. I know my enemies better than they know me."

He rose. She regarded him with lazy eyes, still as a lioness, letting him understand her independence. She caught a flicker of indecision in his face; something she had never seen there before. It frightened her. "Get dressed," he said, and he began putting on his bathrobe.

CHAPTER 11

Casey was grappling with the mystery of E. P. Geld when he arrived back to discover the white BMW had also returned to Backgammon. The car sat in the shade of the poinciana tree whose scarlet flowers and bright green, feathery leaves drooped over the intruder like an enormous beach umbrella. The royal poinciana was called in these parts the *flamboyant*. Flamboyant might describe Zia Gabbiya, but the BMW was a courier from E. P. Geld, whose style was not. For the second time that morning, Casey was aware of a terrible, unreasoning apprehension. As he had told Alison, "Gabbiya worries me, but Geld scares me."

He walked around the house to the patio and was pulled up short by the spectacle of two men leaning against the cliff wall. Then he saw two more beside the trellis. The four men wore identical coffee-colored seersuckers. Each kept one hand in a bulging pocket. A fifth sat in the glider beside the wooden gazebo from where a soulful visitor could contemplate the infinity of sea. None of the uninvited visitors contemplated anything at this moment except Casey.

The man in the glider was very fat. When he heard Casey's exclamation of anger, the fat man said, "Take it easy, man." His gaze slid over Casey's shoulder.

Casey swung around. Fetherstone stood on the pathway, smiling. "An invitation you can't refuse," he said. He lifted a briefcase and shook it as if there were a gift inside and he were Santa Claus.

Casey looked him up and down. He wore the same seersucker uniform as the others, including red and black striped tie. "You all go to the same English prep school?" he asked.

The man in the glider chuckled. "Yeah, man. What's it the Limeys call it? Eton? Yeah! That's it, Eton."

"You must be head prefect?" suggested Casey. "Are these your fags?"

The fat man spat. "Hey, now — !"

"Can it, Herman!" said Fetherstone. "In England, they call the little guys who run errands 'fags.' " He turned back to Casey. "None of us runs errands for anyone."

"Except for Master Geld," said Casey.

"Sit down, Casey," said Fetherstone.

Casey remained standing.

The fat man in the glider rose. The suspension chains rattled and the wooden couch groaned in relief. "I'm E.P.'s security chief," said the fat man. "When he says sit, you sit."

Casey took a stiff-backed wrought-iron chair. It felt good to have the metal against his spine.

Fetherstone put the briefcase on the round, glass-topped table. "Look inside," he said. "A present from Uncle Ho."

"Ho's dead!" Seized by a sudden dread, Casey reached out.

"The guys in there are not." Fetherstone's words were scarcely more than a whisper and vanished on the wind before they could reach the ears of the others, who were craning forward, fascinated by the way Casey moved convulsively to open the briefcase. He pulled out the neatly bound papers. He glanced rapidly down the first page, turned to the next, flicked it over, and went to the one after that. The sun burned the back of his neck. It shone so fiercely, he had to shade his eyes against the glare bouncing back from the white paper. He turned page after page. The names were all there. So long thought dead, these were the names of pilots now said to be alive, if you could believe Big Vien.

There was the name, at the end of each sheet: Pham Quac Vien. Big Vien!

The E P R paradox. Once two particles have been near each other, they continue to affect each other simultaneously, no matter how widely separated they become.

Big Vien, the distant particle.

Casey got a grip on himself, as he had when he faced Big Vien in the Zoo, outside Hanoi. He had beaten him then in the battle of wills, as he would beat him now.

But the other names! They brought tears to his eyes. Trigger Tony Rutgers! "Claws" Cameron, Gurowsky of the Black Knights, Leslie "Baa-Baa" Lambe, Tex Grainger . . . Until this moment, rumors of sightings and gossip about what the Pentagon knew but wouldn't tell kept these men alive only in the minds of the For-get-Me-Nots.

There was no way Casey could jeopardize these men, he suddenly realized.

And that was what Big Vien was counting on!

Casey waited a long time before he put the papers back in the briefcase. Then he said, his voice neutral, "How do I know this is for real?" He ignored the fat man and addressed Fetherstone.

"E.P. will vouch for it."

"I don't give a f—" Casey stopped himself. Anything he said or did from now on could break the slender thread that just possibly kept the men alive. "—a fig for any source other than the Communist government of Vietnam."

"That's what E.P. will give you," said Fetherstone with an expression that said he knew Casey had been about to commit *lèse majesté* against his master.

Two blue-and-white-striped police cars were parked front and back of the BMW when Casey and his escort rounded the house.

"Anything wrong, Mr. Casey, sir?"

Casey met the piratical blue eyes of Detective-Sergeant Winston.

"Thank you, no," said Casey. "Should there be?"

"Saw the Land-Rover in the lane, sir," said Winston. But what his eyes said was, Don't be a fool. This may be your last chance.

"The Land-Rover's ours," said the fat man.

"And who might you be . . . sir?"

"Rose Hall estate."

"That, I used my powers of detection to solve," Winston smiled politely. "Dat be what it say on de panels." He slipped into the local patois. Casey recognized the tactic. Windfallers were skilled at using it to shut out unwanted company. "*Now* da question I be axing is, who might *you* be?"

"I don't have to answer that," said the fat man, and tried to step around Winston, whose arm shot out, quick as a viper, stopping the fat man dead in his tracks. The fat man shook himself free.

Winston licked the end of a pencil and resumed writing laboriously in a notebook. "Motor-vehicle un-ah-licenced for da travel on da public 'ighway," he said slowly. "Ah-blocking da lane with said vehicle. Said vehicle carry no license plates. Is said vehicle yours . . . sir?"

The other men clustered around the fat one. All looked indignant and hot. Behind the steering wheel of each police car sat a constable, black woolly head lying back, mouth open, an arm hanging out the open window.

"I do not possess a car," the fat man said after a moment of what might have been silent prayer. "However, the BMW could be registered in my name, perhaps."

"And dat name is . . . ?"

The fat man glanced around. The only cops he had

193

ever been able to tolerate at close range were dead or bribed.

Fetherstone came to his help. "My name's Geoffrey Fetherstone, officer. I am well known in the islands. I am vice-president of several companies registered here. You will find my name on the leading charities including your own police widows' and orphans' fund. The Land-Rover belongs to Rose Hall estate and the BMW is one of several cars used by the secretaries." He inserted himself between the fat man and the sergeant. "The chief justice will vouch for our bona fides. I shall speak highly of your devotion to duty, Officer, when I see the chief justice at the club tonight. We shall be playing snooker, I believe, with your police commissioner. I'm sure he will be glad to hear my recommendation that you receive a commendation. I believe that would mean a bonus—"

Winston paused from taking another lick at his pencil. "Spell dat out, please."

But Fetherstone caught a warning note in the request. The police sergeant was not one of the corruptible. The sergeant was one of the stupid bastards who would charge him with attempting to bribe—"Yes, Officer," he said smoothly. "I spell my name F-E-T-H-E-R . . ." He faltered when he saw the sergeant was writing nothing down.

Winston addressed the fat man. "Where de driving license?"

The fat man was very red now from the heat. Sweat ran down his face. "I don't have it with me."

Winston pressed down with his pencil into the open notebook. "Driving . . . without . . . da . . . license." He looked up, his tongue still sticking out of the corner of his mouth. "You got ennything at all shows you got enny call come to dese islands and jest go 'roun' breakin' our laws?"

The fat man had been prodded beyond endurance. He lifted a thick, hairy wrist bracketed in gold and consulted a minicomputer display. "We're late," he said to Fetherstone. He faced the sergeant. "My name, you will find with immigration under special residential permits: Herman Schroeder."

The name made Casey look more closely at the fat man. Thin reddish hair, dark jowls, small brown rat's eyes in deep folds of flesh. Smart work, Sergeant Winston! You got it out of him, and I am properly warned!

Winston saw the flash of recognition in Casey's face. He had only wanted Casey to know the company he was keeping. "Dat be all, den," he said. "Until you be 'earin' from us, dat is." He stood aside while a flustered Fetherstone ushered Casey into the BMW.

The first police car rolled forward at some unseen signal from Winston. The second police car reversed a few feet. It was quickly, efficiently done. The BMW could swing out now. Casey was surprised at how swiftly the seemingly sleepy constables had moved. Now they resumed their indolent air.

Sergeant Winston leaned an elbow on the roof of the second police car. It was a small English Mini-Motor, but you still had to be pretty big to lean on it that way.

195

He watched the Land-Rover lurch off in the wake of the BMW and he said to nobody in particular: "Us jungle bunnies ain't showed you nuffin' yet, Shitface Schroeder, however much you grease the bosses' palms." He had spent four years with the London Metropolitan Police. He had taken the special course the U.S. Navy provided for friendly foreign police forces cooperating in antismuggling operations: it included the world's toughest scuba diving. He was waiting to take up a scholarship for the study of law. You had a wide choice of foreign education if you were a Windfaller. You could learn just about anything about everything concerning the world outside the islands; but you made it difficult for the rest of the world to come here and learn anything about you. All you had to do was talk funny to the foreigners.

Herman Schroeder! That went some way to explain a few things, thought Casey as the BMW delivered him to Rose Hall. The name and face were too well known. There could be no mistake. Schroeder had entered the American language as synonymous with a certain kind of union corruption. Workers who had been *schroedered* were those whose trade union was sold as a franchise to anyone with enough money and with the urge to make handsome new profits. Then Schroeder had gone too far, the law had caught up, and he had gone to jail, but not for long. Casey had never known how, but Schroeder had suddenly emerged from one of those fancy prisons for the well-heeled criminal and promptly vanished from public view.

The Great House of Rose Hall stood in a sharp-edged world of jungle greens. It looked a cross between Elizabethan manorial and California Spanish. The main entrance had huge mahogany doors hanging on big brass hinges. The stone walls were so thick, the temperature seemed to drop twenty degrees the moment you stepped inside. The floors were polished mahogany. Doberman pinschers loped through the central hall, where blood-red double-flowering bouganvillea drooped from huge Chinese pots along the minstrel gallery.

Casey was taken into a solid stone chamber which had been designed two centuries earlier to project into the path of seasonal storms like a cutwater, sloping knifelike to meet the oncoming gales. In this snuggery, previous occupants would huddle when warned of approaching tropical storms. Here, louvered windows could be barricaded instantly. The walls were loopholed with vertical slits. The place seemed ready to withstand a siege.

In this fortlike atmosphere, Casey was left at an oak table to leaf through original cables exchanged between Hanoi and a colorful variety of business organizations. He had the eerie sense of watching while Big Vien laid out his cards. The game was to guess what other cards Big Vien was holding from sight.

The whole thing was another of Big Vien's tricks. His agents in America would have little difficulty in obtaining the names of the missing from Forget-Me-Not circulars used to lobby Congress. Here were precise names, of men whose memories were kept alive because groups of veterans thought their government had failed—for whatever reason—to prove the men were dead. It was a Vietnamese trick, a clever one, well up to the standard of psychological gamesmanship set up by Big Vien in the Zoo's heyday. Big Vien had always included a tantalizing clue to something outside the immediate area of discussion to hook his quarry. The hook now was Gabbiya. For the life of him, Casey still could not see what interests Big Vien and Gabbiya shared to such an extent that American prisoners would be used by them. *To hold America hostage!* The words flashed through Casey's mind at the moment a figure stepped out of a recess in the wall and said, "Satisfied?"

Without lifting his eyes from the cables, Casey said, "I'd have to deal directly with this man who signs himself—ah, Pham . . . Vien, is it?"

"He has a title."

"So I see."

"Well?"

"Well, what?" asked Casey.

"Don't you want to go to the cablehead?"

Casey stretched. His eyes met those of the other man. There was no need for introductions. Edgar P. Geld was a society magazine's candid camera shot come to life, a Trotskyite stereotype of a Wall Street bloodsucker. You could not help recognize E.P., though he never gave interviews and took no part in public affairs. What he did provide was fodder for gossip columns, a feast for pavement photographers. "E.P. never repeats himself," a sob sister had noted. "You don't have to look for him in the scandal sheets under the hair dryers with the blue-rinse brigade. When a gorgeous girl goes by, E.P. won't be far behind. But not with the same girl twice."

If Geld saw in Casey's expression some hint of contempt, he had been too long surrounded by sycophants to recognize it. To the contemptible, contempt is the invisible ingredient in the air they breathe and goes undetected, ununderstood. As Big Vien used to say to his prisoners in their stinking cells, "If you live in a fish market, you don't smell the fish." It had been meant as a consolation.

"What's at the cablehead?" Casey finally asked, resenting the fact that E.P. had forced the question out of him.

"Zia Gabbiya, this end. Vietnam at the other."

"I'd better speak to my partner," said Casey, hoping E.P. had been exempted from the communications blackout, like Gabbiya.

Geld must have anticipated the request. He walked over to a boxlike structure. "There's a private line in there."

The telephone cabinet was a padded version of a Regency-style sedan chair Casey had once seen serving as a phone booth in a London pub near Shepherd Market, where whores congregated. Probably E.P. had purchased that very same booth, maybe with some high-class harlot inside to match his tastes. He had to be used to buying whatever he wanted. It made E.P.'s apparent kowtowing to Gabbiya so much more odd.

He got through to the Spad Beer plant in Virginia through an unseen operator with no trace of a Windfalls accent. He asked his secretary, Carol, for Bingo Harriman. She said, "Oh, Mr. Casey, he's been so worried about you. He's been trying and trying to put through calls. He's sent telexes to the company office in Windfalls—"

Casey cut her short. "Where is he, Carol?" He was terrified that Bingo might have found some way of entering the islands, and of entering a trap. His voice carried a note that Carol recognized. She became businesslike. "Mr. Harriman went to see the company lawyers in Jaw-Jaw Town." She had even fallen into the discreet evasions adopted after that first visit from Rotgut. The company lawyers in Jaw-Jaw Town could only be some of Bingo's contacts in Georgetown: senior bureaucrats sympathetic to the cause of the Forget-Me-Nots.

Carol answered the next question before he could ask it. "He didn't leave a number where I could call him."

That was a clear warning that whoever Bingo was with, he shouldn't be telephoned. Perhaps—Casey cheered up at the possibility—he was with Rotgut's departmental colleagues. Perhaps the President's decree had been cosmetic, to pacify a public incensed by the leaked report of a covert operation in another part

200

of the hemisphere.

"When he calls in," said Casey, freshly inspired, "just tell him I'm very excited about the new brand name Tony suggested: Donald Duck Drinks."

It hardly mattered if the line was tapped, thought Casey after he had left the booth. If they sensed he'd passed a message, there was nothing they could do. Carol had taken it all quite calmly, although she must have wondered about this new soft-drink line called Donald Duck. She was one of the few secretaries these days with shorthand. He hoped she'd transcribe "Tony" accurately. Bingo would certainly pick up that reference to Rotgut's son. Bingo would draw the right conclusions. He knew the ropes. He would again harass all concerned with Vietnam, ignoring fancy titles, dodging the guards around the mighty. He would beard the secretary for international affairs in the White House. He'd tackle the principal adviser to the President on prisoners of war. He'd tax the POW/MIA Affairs Office, in Defense. He knew how to weave through the crossfire of agencies scared of scandal, afraid to admit any suggestion of cover-up. Bingo had seen how such issues were trivialized in Washington, where all that seemed to matter was who won, who lost, in the daily skirmishes of parochial warfare. He cursed the way reputations could be still made or broken by Vietnam. Careers were built on the supposition that no live Americans remained in Vietnam. Proof to the contrary threatened promotions and healthy pensions. No administration wished to be seen as powerless to reclaim

Americans, from Teheran or from Hanoi. Better for everyone, said Washington cynics, to bury the proof with the men.

Well, thought Casey, I'll find out about *proof*. Bingo will regain his reputation as a crazy who keeps shouting about Americans rotting in jungle jails. Heads of departments will vanish from their desks again, held up at meetings or out of town. Eventually, though, they'll reappear. And Bingo will be there, patient, polite, inexorable.

Because Bingo knows *the Duck is drinking*, once the easiest warning to pass around the Zoo. It had meant Big Vien was switching from hard to soft tactics. Deals would be offered with a smile and a cigaret, as if past horrors never happened. Now, to Bingo, it would mean the Duck had made himself known directly to Casey. And the Duck wears a smile!

I'll know, thought Casey, I'll know when I meet Zia Gabbiya, if a deal is being offered. Zia has secured his place in history along the same trail of blood and hate. If Zia receives me with a smile and a cigaret, it will be Big Vien with another face. And when the Duck is drinking, every man sups with a long spoon.

Lord John Bracken sat on the child's seesaw in Pretty Penny's garden, with Sergeant Winston at the other end to counterbalance him. Bracken wore his favorite old sailing shirt over ragged shorts. Winston had removed his formal cap and tunic but retained white

202

shirt, black tie and dark blue trousers. Neither man wore shoes. Alison, mixing drinks and watching from the kitchen, thought Churchill Spencer Winston the more lordly: a case of names shaping character.

Bracken said, "Casey said nothing more?"

"Nothing."

"He seemed scared?"

"He's not that kind of man."

"No, I suppose he's not," murmured Bracken, fingering his beard. "But Alison told you he came here and he said he was scared. Takes courage to admit that. Guess you're right. He's not scared."

"Shaken, more likely," said Winston judiciously.

"He recognized the name of Schroeder."

"I saw it in his eyes. He knew."

"Knew what?" asked Alison, wheeling the drinks trolly across the hummocky grass.

"Herman Schroeder did time in America for union racketeering," said her father.

Alison sat on the nearby stump of rock polished by generations of wriggling children and brooding parents. "What rackets?"

"Embezzlement of union pension funds." Winston grinned at her. It was funny how Americans carried their interpretation of freedom to such lengths. "You can buy unions, like you'd buy a franchise for Kentucky Fried Chicken. Schroeder was a union expert who bought unions for the mob, then maximized the profits so they could be sold for ten, twenty times the price. Unless the profits were such that the mob benefited in other ways." Winston reached over and helped himself to rum punch and a meat patty.

"It's hard to believe," said Alison.

"It's well documented." Winston flexed his legs, and at the other end of the teeter board, Bracken gentle rose and fell. "Five leading mob families have controlled certain unions since the 1960s. They'd buy a franchise through someone like Schroeder. I know a bit about it," he added modestly, "because we did an investigation when the union organizers first moved into the Windfalls, trying to herd the local guilds into some amalgamation with a funny smell to it."

"I don't question your sources," said Alison. "I just can't believe even a Schroeder can get away with it."

"Money has a habit of defeating justice," pointed out Bracken.

"You put the finger on it." Winston munched his patty and gazed reflectively at Bracken.

"Do you suppose," asked Alison, "that Casey's scared of what a Schroeder-controlled union could do to Spad's business?"

"It's possible Schroeder still has power in the States," said Winston. "But no, I don't think that's why Mr. Casey went along with those Rose Hall thugs."

"How do Schroeder, corrupt union power, Zia Gabbiya, E.P. and the Vietnamese fit together?" Alison stared at each man in turn. "Let's try some deduction. Schroeder was jailed?" she asked Winston.

"For embezzling a $75 million fund relating to strike insurance and pensions for one union local in New

York State. He had total discretion on whatever part of the fund he invested, and took a commission. He wouldn't have been caught if an informer hadn't grassed to the police. See, the corruption crosses state boundaries and cuts across so many police jurisdictions that someone as powerful as the governor of the State of New York seemed unable to stop Schroeder. Every investigation got snarled up in conflicting jurisdictions."

"I thought they had a strike force over there for that sort of problem," said Alison.

"A strike force is created for specific problems by the Department of Justice in Washington." Winston stared down at his bare feet couched in grass. "They gather intelligence, but most of the time they don't have the powers necessary to act. 'It's like dealing with a passel of foreign countries, each jealous of its sovereignty.' " Winston looked up. "That's what was said to me by the FBI. A deputy director was explaining that the federal government is just as tied because of state's rights as it's tied when trying to work with us here. I still have old friends over in Washington from the days when we could cooperate . . ." The sergeant's face shone with amusement. "It's nifty to have a *black* old-school-tie network, eh?"

Alison brushed aside the sarcasm. *"When you could cooperate?"* she echoed. "What does that mean?"

"All the old informal arrangements, between here and Washington, set up when London ran things here on a tighter rein."

"Broken?"

"Bit by bit, very quietly."

"Nothing said?"

"Not yet."

"Why?"

"Hey!" protested Bracken. "You're not in the courtroom, Alison."

"That's okay," said Winston. "I don't mind. I've only just started to see what was happening . . . Schroeder was bought out of jail by someone in E. P. Geld's employ. Release was conditional on Schroeder getting out of the States, which was fine by those concerned. They wanted him here, fixing the unions, so E.P.'s hotel interests would be safe from any threat of strike. That's what E.P. thought, when he got to hear of it. By now, he'll have discovered Schroeder's release was arranged by one of Zia Gabbiya's men, working inside the Geld organization. The FBI believe Gabbiya's front companies have been buying up certain unions already in America."

"You mean key unions could be sold to a terrorist?" Alison's eyes popped.

"Schroeder was in jail, otherwise *he* would. You have to understand. These are *businessmen*. They get into union operations, and when the investment's maximized to the fullest, and someone comes along with a fantastic bid, they sell. Even to the King of Terror." Winston paused and cocked his head. " 'Course, you're not supposed to know 'bout none of this, missie," he teased.

"What a way to control a country," mused Alison.

"It's been tried before," interjected Bracken. "But for purely political reasons . . . I thought something was odd when there were all those meetings about forming a general workers' union in the Windfalls."

"If you quote me," said Winston, "I'd have to deny it. But Schroeder's men worked hard on the local guilds, and now the guild members have united and elected a president. The next thing, we'll have an island-wide general strike. Whenever Zia Gabbiya decides—"

"Electing a trade-union leader isn't exactly some harmless little matter not worth reporting," said Alison. "I don't understand how it's been ignored. It's not like electing a president of the yacht club, is it?"

"Commodore!" exclaimed Bracken, catching Winston's eye. "Commodore, not president." As if by common consent, each man cautiously rose. Bracken swung a leg over the seesaw and said, "The yacht club, eh?"

"The yacht club, Lord John." Winston became very formal.

"You're not dragging in the commodore?" Alison looked shocked.

"The commodore is vital," Bracken said soberly.

"But he's *eighty-five!*"

"I'm not asking him to fly the bloody Stringbag," said Bracken. "He just has to sign the aircraft's letter of marque."

CHAPTER 12

Casey clenched his fists behind his back and reminded himself that although Zia Gabbiya was a snake, a mass murderer, a dictator with boundless ambitions who would stop at nothing to humiliate his chosen enemy, America, he also held a key that might unlock certain prison doors. So take it easy, Casey told himself, matching smiles with the Great Protector, who had received him on board the *Qurqūr* in a teak-paneled private cabin. Gabbiya's opening words were flowery and intended to be flattering. Casey found them condescending but forced himself to grunt reasonably civil responses.

His senses were abnormally alert. Since his first look at the *Qurqūr*, he had reasoned out her history and potential, drawing also on the local public library's surprisingly good research section. He could pinpoint the Quebec shipyard where the vessel first took shape as a Canadian wartime navy frigate, before her conversion to a luxury schooner. When the ship's helicopter brought him aboard, he had noted features that were not to be found in any shipping registry. Inside the cabin, he felt engulfed in a rich man's taste fashioned by some expensive interior decorator, except for the crossed Syrian swords and a pair of fine Damascus pistols hanging on either side of a Queen Anne walnut kneehole desk. Directly above the desk was an El Greco which Casey seemed to recognize as the *Madonna Supported by an Angel*. But he could have been wrong.

"And of course I know the circumstances in which you earned the Congressional Medal of Honor," Gabbiya was saying. "It grieves me to put a man of such courage in the position of begging from former enemies."

"I'm not begging!" snapped Casey. He moderated his tone. His own feelings were of secondary importance. If he indulged in stupid displays of temper, others would suffer. "It's a question of obtaining information. If those men are alive, I want to know what has to be done to get them out."

"I'm sure there's a basis for negotiation," said Gabbiya, looking pleased. He reclined, in what seemed to Casey to be a striped nightshirt, on a sofa under the study's single porthole. Once, this must have been the captain's cabin, when the ship was a fighting frigate: a cabin occupied in a time of common integrity by a man of honor: a man serving the cause of duty and freedom and human decencies. He fought to contain his anger, and leaned back in the chair Gabbiya had offered him.

"So when do I start negotiating?" asked Casey.

Gabbiya looked over his head at a brassbound ship's chronometer. "They'll be in the middle of tomorrow's working day in Saigon."

Casey noted that the Great Protector scorned the

name: Ho Chi Minh City. "You're in contact?"

"I have offices in the old American embassy. It was taken over by the State Petroleum Agency. I occupy a modest corner . . . Paracels Petroleum." He watched Casey expectantly.

"Paracels?" Casey saw no point in dissembling. "I thought the islands were in dispute between Vietnam and China."

"Because of big oil reserves under the sea." Gabbiya spoke the words like a schoolteacher approving a boy's precocity. "It is one of my special interests, resources under the sea."

A warning light flickered in Casey's head.

"My communications are at your disposal," said Gabbiya. "As they are also available to the government of Vietnam." He pressed a button, reaching back to do this, long fingers groping along the edge of the desk. "You have heard of Armand Hammer?"

"Hammer?" Casey's face remained expressionless while his mind flipped through the new possibilities. Hammer's Occidental Petroleum had offices in Moscow and Peking. Hammer was one of the world's richest men after doing business with the Communist world since before Stalin. He was the Soviet's showroom capitalist, whose immense wealth might lure other capitalists to look for equally big profits. He was living proof, as the Soviets loudly proclaimed, that the West needn't take Soviet propaganda too seriously: businessmen could safely trade. Only under their collective breath did the Soviets repeat that capitalism would sell them the rope with which to hang capitalists. Finally Casey said, "Who hasn't heard of Hammer?"

211

Gabbiya nodded. "He's small potatoes, compared with me. Vietnam needs my technology, my experts, to develop the Paracels. We'll supply the whole Third World."

"Hammer's more than oil."

"And so am I. The Soviet bloc, the Eastern Reds, they all need big infusions of hard currency. I supply it. Petrodollars are out, Commander Casey, but my dollars multiply without oil."

"What are you paid in?" asked Casey, not really expecting a reply.

"Booby traps," said Gabbiya and smiled at a youth in sailor's uniform who had come at the Protector's summons. Gabbiya spoke in Arabic to the boy, turned back to Casey and said, "Draft your message."

The boy stood simpering. Casey took up the pad at his side while Gabbiya ran an appreciative eye over the tight bellbottoms and buttonless jerkin.

Casey thought: *booby traps?* Gabbiya hates America enough to fall for Hanoi's boast that guerrilla warfare and terrorism—booby traps—can bring down American technology. But Gabbiya's no simpleton. Rotgut's analysis showed a far more complex man than the world sees under simplistic headlines. Gabbiya wants to go down in history as the prophet who brought Islam to full flower. Like all the great dictators, he's also a magician. He performs on the world stage the way Harry Blackstone did in small American theaters: through diversion. He cooks up a deceptive crisis over here while preparing the big bang over there.

Casey waved his pencil like a man in the throes of mental composition, making a preliminary jab at the notebook, crossing out, filling in, while his thoughts raced. Behind him the clock softly ticked. He jotted down a tentative phrase, then a terse request for confirmation that the names he had seen were indeed those of Americans still in Vietnam. He addressed his message to the chief of Communist agitprop in the Hanoi of the 1960s, Pham Quac Vien, whose name reappeared on the telexes from Ho Chi Minh City. He signed the message with his full name, knowing Big Vien would expect it.

Big Vien the Thimble Man was said to be closer to Ho than even Premier Pham Van Dong at the time Casey locked horns with him. Casey had been caught organizing three escape attempts, and keeping up morale among fellow inmates at the Zoo who were undergoing torture. He was brought out of solitary after what seemed months, blinking because he was unused to the light, dizzy because his limbs had been confined. He had peered at Big Vien, ears sharpened by solitude. He heard for the first time, in the clack of Vietnamese, the man's full name. It was then he realized he'd been in the hands of that Paris-educated intellectual who was the subject of so many navy briefings before Casey's capture.

Vien wanted to talk, in the way that Zia Gabbiya later talked: courteously, as if there had been no past horror. Vien had talked all night. Casey had made Vien show off his intellectual prowess, his familiarity with Schopenhauer, his friendship with Albert Camus, his quarrel with Plato's definition of justice. The beauty of it was, Vien had been obviously convinced that *he* was making progress in breaking Casey.

It was no skin off Casey's nose. Anything was better than going back down the hole. They had traded quotations and revived some great debate in Piraeus among Greek philosophers twenty-four hundred years earlier. It was all college-level Western philosophy for Casey. For Vien, it was a chance to lay the groundwork for psychological games to come. He had to prove that Vietnam's Communists had pondered the West's philosophical arguments, and found them wanting in the light of Ho and Marx, Lenin and Engels. Casey had not been cooperative. He had previously refused to broadcast recantations; refused even to broadcast to fellow prisoners, knowing the seemingly harmless circulation of "news" was the start of a slippery slope to collaboration. Casey had resisted the temptation to appear before the Americans who came to hold hands with the enemy in Hanoi, though it would have offered a chance to convey reassurances that he was alive. Casey won both Big Vien's respect and his hatred. The philosophical discussions were the preliminary to Vien's renewed onslaught against Casey's resolve. Casey had become the ultimate challenge to Vien's belief in the whole totalitarian technique of brainwashing. "A man must wash his brains as often as he washes his face," he had advised Casey. "It is our philosophy, and puts the West's traditional thinkers to shame."

And so, composing his telex for Gabbiya's men to transmit, Casey added the phrase which, if answered, might confirm it was really Big Vien at the other end. *What a coincidence,* he wrote.

Zia Gabbiya did not ask what the inserted words might mean. That in itself struck Casey as significant. Zia merely scanned the message and turned it over to the waiting sailor. Then he invited Casey to stay for dinner.

Again, Casey felt he was back in Big Vien's company. The offer of a cigaret and rice wine after all the cruelties; a display of *bonhomie* before the return to cold brutality. This time, though, Casey had to accept the pretense of hospitality. He had to have Vien's reply.

The situation was eased by Mellanie Blake's unexpected presence at a meal laid out in the stateroom at the ship's stern. It wasn't what Casey regarded as a lavish Arab repast. The dishes were small and not memorable. He supposed Gabbiya had some purpose in that, too.

Lani offered a diversion. The moment the word flashed through Casey's mind, though, he remembered Rotgut's analysis of Zia Gabbiya's experience as a boy magician. If Lani was there to divert, Casey knew how to handle it. He watched her with unconcealed curiosity. Did she know they had discovered Rotgut's body soon after passing her on the breakwater? Perhaps she, and Gabbiya, wanted to find that out. For the first time, Casey saw that Alison and the black sergeant might have been smart to hush up Rotgut's death. It kept the enemy guessing.

Gabbiya suddenly turned off the talk about his Vietnam interests. He said, "I gather Miss Blake is known here as the Irish Girl. You will have heard that, Commander Casey, just as you will have heard of the problems she had getting into the islands."

That was Lani's cue. Without waiting for any response from Casey, she said, "The International Criminal Police Organization has me on a wanted list."

"But why?" Casey had never heard the answer from Alison.

"I've been with the Protector a long time. Agencies"—Lani lingered over the word—"agencies like INTERPOL are afraid to touch Colonel Gabbiya, although they spread it around that he's responsible for most of the terrorism in the world."

"Which is drivel," said Gabbiya. "They have no proof, nothing to connect me with a single act of terror."

"They're afraid to touch him," Lani resumed, "but they harass employees like myself. I have never been in trouble with the law."

Casey thought: It really is like the Zoo, where they could make you believe black was white. Truth, Big Vien had said, is whatever serves the revolution.

He smiled. They were all sitting on cushions and helping themselves from small plates of food arranged around what looked like a samovar. Lani was wearing a filmy ankle-length dress similar to the one he had seen her in before. It still, as before, revealed more than it concealed.

"I hear you may be having trouble with the law," murmured Gabbiya, scooping up a handful of spiced grains of rice.

"INSPAD," volunteered Lani. "You've had trouble getting it registered. The matter can be resolved, as it was in my case."

"A little money in the right quarter," appended Gabbiya.

"Why should you help me?" Casey watched the Protector dip slender fingers into a bowl of water where small pink flowers floated.

"Then we can go into partnership."

"With INSPAD? It's not for sale."

"Everything has a price with you Americans."

"Your friends in Vietnam may have told you so," Casey retorted. "It's not true."

"Even when I pay in human lives?"

Casey froze.

"Lives like Tony Rutgers?" prodded Gabbiya. "Or 'Claws' Cameron? Or Lieutenant Gurowsky of the Black Knights?"

Out of the corner of one eye, Casey caught a glance from the girl. Warning? Concern? He kept his face rigid. He fought to hide the emotions aroused by the names. "What's so interesting," he managed to ask, "about INSPAD?"

"The research your people have done."

My people? Casey concealed his puzzlement. "My people are me and Bingo."

"It's the deep-tow equipment," said Gabbiya. "The dolphin sonar. We particularly like the advances made in towing unmanned submersibles. Manned vehicles can't be utilized as economically. There's always this absurd preoccupation with human lives. The operators refuse to launch if conditions seem the slightest bit dangerous." He seemed unable to stop, or hide his enthusiasm. "Your detection gear is superior to anything else on the market. Nobody else has the capacity to search so deep and so far—"

Casey listened in amazement. These were INSPAD ideas, draft proposals, odds and ends on the drawing

217

board. Their fulfillment required scientists of a very high caliber. The difficulties were enormous. Between the concepts and their realization stretched endless hurdles. Yet Gabbiya seemed to think INSPAD was fully operational. It was absurd.

"You're exaggerating INSPAD's capacity," he said cautiously.

"No!" Lani interrupted firmly. Her dark eyes fixed Casey with an intent stare. "We have records of secret CIA funding for your project."

Casey suppressed an exclamation of disbelief. Lani had spoken the words with such deliberation, they seemed to carry some hidden message. He said slowly, "You can't expect me to comment on that."

"Of course not," said Gabbiya with manifest approval. He clapped his hands. "You play backgammon, of course, Commander Casey?"

Casey nodded, and wondered if this was another hint of hidden knowledge. But Gabbiya had signaled for a short-legged games table to be moved over: a beautiful piece of marbled craftsmanship. "A couple of games," he said, "and by then we should have confirmation Vietnam has received our cable. While we play, you consider my offer."

Casey glanced at Lani, but her face was enigmatic. He remembered Bingo saying INSPAD would make great duck soup. Had someone deliberately fed the Soviets or their Vietnam client some cock-and-bull about INSPAD being a CIA cover? If that was the case, why *not* barter it for American lives? INSPAD was worth nothing, held no secrets, but it might waste an awful lot of Big Vien's time. The ideas rattled in rhythm with the shaking of the dice.

* * *

"Bloody impertinence!" growled the commodore of the yacht club. His name was Sir Everard "Chilly" Chillingham. In his mid-eighties, he still roared to work on an overpowered moped, a crash helmet his only concession to prudence. He was also known as the Ancient Mariner in acknowledgment of his days as a boy seaman at the Battle of Jutland, some seventy years ago. He was virtually the islands' treasurer, as chairman of the Windfalls National Bank, founded by his great-great-grandfather. Thus he was also called Moneybags. "Bloody cheek!" he added for greater emphasis.

"What is?" Bracken peered along the club bar at the old man.

"This so-called lightning strike! The telecommunications section of this new general workers' union has closed down. But, *as a concession to the national economic welfare,* they're graciously pleased to let the bank continue transactions! Piffle! I'd use couriers. I've done it before. Now the blasted transport workers have practically closed down the airport! Prime Minister won't interfere. Doesn't dare. His brother's the new union's new bloody president. Baaahh!" A shower of froth flew from the top of his beer tankard. "Cheers!"

"Cheers!" said Bracken, thinking Winston had been right in his facts but a trifle behind the action.

Chilly's scarlet face finally rose like the sun over the rim of the tankard. The Adam's apple in his scrawny neck went up and down. "Tonsils. Needed wetting. Thirsty work, counting other people's money." The thought of what the union was doing to that money—

which, to Chilly's mind, was workers' money—started him off again. "The silly buggers have said certain offshore companies can go on running their communication lines, but not all! You can guess who the favored ones are?"

"Covers for Zia Gabbiya?" hazarded Bracken.

Chilly nodded. "We're running out of time," he said mysteriously and rubbed the side of his nose. It matched his red complexion and continued the theme of ruptured blood vessels that covered his pouched face like a fine net. He was an erect old man with a fine head of silver hair and faded blue eyes. He loved the Windfalls; loved their history, their people, their quaint traditions which were not quaint at all to him, who understood their origins. He was like an old salt who nurses the wind in his sails, who coaxes his vessel through tricky currents and treacherous winds because he knows heroics won't keep the boat afloat, but who will also gamble all knowledge and instinct to take the one chance of making it through a gap in the reef. That was why Bracken had herded him into the bar, away from the horrors of Gourmet Night in the Ladies' Annex.

"Must sound funny to you," said Chilly, "wishing the money didn't keep rolling in."

"Dirty money?"

" 'Fraid so. We set up barriers against money-laundering operations. Now our own enforcers seem to be taking bribes." He peered across the open-sided bar at the arc lights sputtering into life above the floating docks. "Shouldn't tell you this, old boy. No one else I dare trust. Had a visit from the American tax men. Nice fellows. Told them we survive on confidentiality.

220

They understood. Said they'd been tipped off to some shenanigans. Said it was just a friendly call to remind me what happened to offshore companies in Turks and Caicos, and to those banks in the Caymans, when they woke up one morning to find they'd been turned into laundromats." Chilly raised his tankard and his voice together. "Well, cheers again, old boy." The barman drew abreast. "Time for another?"

"Why not?" said Bracken.

The barman knew the drill. He poured a measure of gin for Bracken and one of scotch for Chilly. He put ice in Bracken's drink, mixed with tonic. His hand hovered a split second over Chilly's scotch. The old man jumped. "Steady, Simon! No ice, eh? Haven't sold out to the Yanks yet."

"You haven't knowingly sold out, you mean," said Bracken when the barman had vanished again.

"That's what bothers me," Chilly conceded. "Look at this!" He flourished a copy of the Washington *Post*. "One of those Yankee tax men gave me this. He said, 'You're safer under the big umbrella.' Now, what do you suppose he meant by that?"

Bracken stared at the front-page headlines: TAX HAVENS GO THROUGH WRINGER—THE OFFSHORE LAUNDRY RACKET. "Billions of dollars are lost to Internal Revenue each year and more billions of crooked dollars join them in Grand Cayman, this British colony, 460 miles south of Miami, which lives off tax avoidance. There are more than 18,000 foreign corporations registered here, more than one for each resident. There are more banks per capita than anywhere else in the world."

Bracken looked up. "You're our *only* resident bank,

221

Chilly. So what's this to do with us?"

"What that Yankee tax man was telling me — warning me — was this: Go with Gabbiya, the big umbrella man, before we squeeze the Windfalls next."

"That's funny advice, considering the source," murmured Bracken, and read on: "Federal investigators believe the crackdown on illegal schemes by which Americans avoid taxes will have major repercussions. Cayman islanders say a crackdown would destroy their livelihoods . . ." He put the newspaper aside and contemplated a ring of water on the polished teakwood bar. He had come here to force Chilly to finally grapple with the unthinkable. Now, it seemed, someone else had already started the process. Bracken wondered how to come directly to the point without repelling Chilly, who had an old-fashioned sense of banking ethics: for there was no question Bracken couldn't act until he had the old man's cooperation.

Soon Chilly said, "Often wish meself in your shoes, John. Look at you, never obliged to buy a suit from one decade to the next, never forced to keep up appearances. Where else in the world can a chap please himself how he lives? We'd all be poorer if chaps like you get pushed out of here." The old man moved toward the patio. "Let's sit outside a spell, eh?"

The noise from Gourmet Night was growing louder. From the kitchens came a rising clatter of dishes. Chilly's retirement to the darkness above the docks would seem an act of self-preservation to most onlookers. To Bracken, it signaled the banker's anticipation of his own need for greater privacy.

"Bankers," said Chilly, "ain't supposed to have blood in their veins. Money's money. It knows no moral scruples, so they say. But my roots are here, John, just like yours. Even if banking was all I'd known, I'd still want to keep the soil of these islands clean and sweet. You helped us do a fine job, setting up a system where money could generate energy, the way it's suppose to do." He tapped the *Post* angrily. "I don't want us to have the sleazy reputation of other islands, where drugs, mobsters, gun-runners, *crooks* wash their dirty cash . . . I want our people to prosper, but not at any cost."

"You know you're in good company?" Bracken asked cautiously.

His companion turned sharply, the silver hair catching a thin beam of light from the bar. "I've heard whispers, John."

They sat for a while, listening to the soft lap of water and the singing of the wind in the rigging of boats below.

"I went into parliament for the rough-and-tumble," said Chilly. "I enjoyed being Speaker of the House. We had some jolly good free-for-alls. We were fighting over how best to preserve the best of the past. But parliament doesn't count now, does it?"

"So a growing number of *ordinary* folk are saying," murmured Bracken, still taking his time.

"It's not only parliament," continued the commodore. "This new police commissioner has some odd ideas about how to apply the law. Customs and Excise works to new rules that bother the old-timers. I know them, you see, the little chaps, the mailmen, the constables, the low-grade customs officers. They see me about small loans. They don't mind my questions, because a banker's supposed to ask questions before he commits to a mortgage, ain't that so?"

"It is, Chilly, it is," breathed Bracken.

"Shouldn't be talking this way to anyone," said Chilly, "but you're different, John. You've no money worth speaking of. Little chaps trust your honesty. They know you could have exploited your title and war record to collect directorships. You could give a respectable front to questionable ventures, clean up on the noble-lordship circuit. The little chaps I'm talking about share my respect for small bank accounts— more than they look up to a new chief justice who can suddenly afford to pop over to Fort Lauderdale and pick up a million-dollar pleasure boat."

Bracken sat quiet as a cat with a mouse. Cleats and rigging screws rattled against steel masts. Dark hulls swung with wind and tide. Securing lines created in the vast emptiness ahead.

"Finance Minister took off suddenly for Switzerland yesterday," Chilly burst out. "Acting governor's pissed off to London, saying he sees no legal objections to the Windfalls *going independent!* This new general workers' union is going to demand freedom from British oppression! My office is a confessional for folk who don't like such goings-on." His voice trailed off and then regained its vigor as some new thought struck. "And when was it ever put to the vote that we'd stop all visits by NATO warships?"

"I hadn't heard that," said Bracken, genuinely shocked. "You mean they're closing down even that miserable little maintenance base?"

Chilly tapped the side of his nose. "That old petty officer at Dockyard, minding war-surplus stores, told me."

Bracken seized his opportunity. "Dockyard's crammed with stuff, kept in mint condition by a chiefy called 'Pony' Moore."

"That's the chap!" said Chilly, and then rustled in his chair with embarrassment. "Belay that last pipe. Forget it. Shouldn't mention names. No names, no pack drill!"

Bracken saw him slipping from his grasp again. He said hastily, "The American tax men who came to see you? When was this?"

"Today."

"How'd they get here, if the airport's operating limited services?"

There was a short silence. Then Chilly said slowly, "I don't even know if they're really who they claim, come to think of it. The American consul's on leave. I just took them at their word."

"I'll have them checked out," Bracken said grimly. "If Gabbiya's making his final move, he knows exactly how to stir up the federal tax authorities. He certainly arranged that leak to the *Post*." He paused. "You served, didn't you, sir?"

The sudden change of direction took Chilly by surprise. "You know I did! A humble jolly jack-tar. First World War. I was just fourteen. Why?"

"Gives you seniority," said Bracken. "You'd be authorized to sign a letter of marque."

Chilly made a whoofing sound, like an old dog that doesn't want to be disturbed.

Bracken circled him again. "The weaponry at Dockyard's in tip-top shape. Some of us got a good look-see, last Trafalgar Day."

"Hah!" snorted the club commodore. "Hasn't been a

proper Trafalgar celebration since they abolished the post of Senior Naval Officer, West Indies."

"Old 'Pony' keeps the flag flying."

Chilly snorted again, and began to throw caution aside. "Their Lordships of Admiralty must've forgotten the old bugger. They used to tell a story about Chiefy Moore. Some nonsense about being court-martialed by the Home Fleet for poking a Shetland pony on the moors. His defense was, he thought it was a woman rating in a duffel coat. The court decided he'd had carnal knowledge, but with a *female* pony. 'Nothing queer about our Pony!' was the slogan went around Scapa Flow. That's how he got his name. Not," he added hurriedly, "that I believe a word—!"

Bracken smiled in the darkness. In such obscure ways, in Chilly's younger days, important island issues had been settled—by artful anecdotes, not in parliament, but on drowsy evenings in the club.

The shrill note of a bosun's whistle floated across the harbor where *Qurqūr* lay at anchor. "Wonder who they're piping aboard?" muttered the commodore. "Wonder who the Great Protector's fancy frigate is buying tonight for the frigging Republic of frigging Sahara, hey?"

"They've even got torpedoes at Dockyard," said Bracken. "And mines."

"Wouldn't mind putting a tin fish up bloody Gabbie's arse myself," grunted Chilly. "*What* did you say about letters of marque?"

Bracken let out a small sigh of relief. "The Queen's representative is off the islands," he said quickly. "There's nobody else around. After all, you *are* commodore of the *royal* yacht club."

"Hah!" said the commodore. "Hah, hah!" His joints creaked as he climbed to his feet. "You got wheels, me boy?"

Bracken's heart sank. He knew what was coming. There was no dodging it. "Actually, well, no, sir. I took a taxi here. Thought I'd be hoisting a few and they've already taken me off the road once this year for being—ah, inebriated while in control of a moped."

"Never understood why they say *in* control when they mean drunk and *out* of it," said the commodore. "You'd better hop onto the back of mine."

Bracken clenched his jaw at the prospect of clinging to the Ancient Mariner on a scooter.

Chilly added, with a fresh note in his voice, "I knew something was up when that daughter of yours started keeping company with some shady characters back of town."

Bracken pretended innocence. *"Shady?"*

"They're not shady in *my* book," Chilly amended hastily. "Chaps like Oyez Lem, the town crier, Seraphim and Gideon, the gardeners at Rose Hall, couple of marine constables . . . All, you might say, clients of mine at the bank and in the courts."

"Courts!" Bracken slapped his thigh as they emerged from the club into the moped parking lot. "That settles it! You're a Justice of the Peace! Marvelous! A bloody magistrate! *Perfect.* You will issue me a letter of marque, Chilly? You must."

"To fly that magnificent flying machine?" Chilly saw Bracken stiffen as if shot. "Come on, young 'un, there's nothing much I don't get to hear about. Except," he added sadly, "how Gabbie's robbing me of my

227

bank."

Bracken waited for the old man to get astride the moped. "My flying machine will carry a torpedo, mines and rockets. And Alison's *shady* company consists of ground crew, armorers . . . Dammit, *rebels* if you like. They're been ready to get me airborne a long time, Chilly, just as soon as they get word that what we fear is happening is happening. You must join us!"

"Hop aboard," said Chilly. "You talk too much." He kick-started the moped. Then he throttled back and lifted his crash helmet out of the wicker basket hanging from the handlebars. "Here." He handed the helmet to Bracken. "You can't take risks at your time of life, me boy."

CHAPTER 13

Alison putt-putted through the back of town to Rum Runners' Reef and slid her moped in among the customers' bikes. In the private bar she found two black Marine Police constables and four other sturdy islanders duly assembled. "Back-of-town" was avoided by tourists, who thought it must be the haunt of the drugged and the damned. But, as Sir Everard Chillingham well knew, it was only the gathering place for those who could not pay tourist prices or live on the expense-account economy of the offshore companies.

"A pint of bitter," she said in response to the invitation from Constable Mello. "Anything new?"

"Yus'm," said Mello. Half the Mellos in the Windfalls were black; the rest were white except Constable Mello, who was an even-handed coffee color. "Dem two johnnies, da revenuers, flew here in E. P. Geld's jet."

Alison gulped down her pint and ordered another. "Christ!" she said. "This is thirsty work."

Mello shifted uneasily. He disapproved of blasphemy.

"Sorry." Alison consulted a list. "My old man says we're to go sometime tomorrow night."

"Lord John says that?" asked a tiny black man, as tall as he was wide.

"He does." Alison glanced around. She trusted every man there save Oyez Lem — not that his spirit wasn't willing. His flesh was weak. "Listen here, Oyez," she said. "You won't carry cannabis?"

"No, mum."

She looked hard into the bloodshot eyes. "No marijuana? No ganja? No dope?" She didn't want him later to plead that she had failed to mention the specific drug he *did* carry. "Coke? Snow? Crack?"

"He be cleaned," interrupted Mello. "We be putting him through da wringer."

"The wringer." The word startled a memory in Alison's mind. TAX HAVENS GO THROUGH WRINGER. "That's another reason for action," she said, and told them about the Washington *Post* report.

"What's stopping us?" asked the other constable.

"Democratic procedures," said Alison. "We must have a majority of the voters behind us."

"Like a referendum?" suggested Mello. "Done secretly?"

"I suppose if it's secret it's not democratic," Alison mused. "It's more like a partisan uprising against enemy occupation. You've all got enough contacts to make sure we get popular support. The facts are plain. Zia Gabbiya's puppets have cleared the decks. They've got the chief magistrate, the police chief, the acting governor, off the islands or on their way. They've closed down our links with the outside world without any of it seeming suspicious. Tourist agencies have simply been warned hotels are being struck soon. The agencies are rerouting their customers. That always causes a loss of confidence abroad. Gabbiya's front companies can yank their deposits out of the bank at the push of a button. Then the two pillars of our economy crumble. We'll be broke. We'll wake up to find we're in hock to Gabbiya. Our real boss."

"But for why?" asked Constable Mello.

"Not sure. That's the other thing I want you to do, all of you. Keep your eyes and ears open." Alison's eye fell upon Seraphim and Gideon, gardeners in the tradition of their Portuguese forefathers, who had settled here after their ships were seized by Windfall privateers. "You especially. Find out what else is happening at Rose Hall since you reported to my father."

She looked at her list again. "We need extra derrick equipment."

"Doan' worry 'bout dat," said Mello. "We got block 'n' tackle, hawsers and grapnels enough to seize dat ship oursel's."

"The barge?"

"Ready at de police wharf. Sam Oysterman's in charge of loadin'."

Alison caught Oyez's eye. "You want to keep your town crier job?" she said.

"Aye, I do that." Oyez squinted up with a toothless grin. Tourists knew him as the relic of a bygone era

231

when honeymooners took night rides in his horse-drawn buggy. The Windfalls Tourist Board failed to mention in its literature that Oyez tended to get stoned and sometimes fell off his perch. Alison was constantly arguing for leniency in court, and Oyez owed her a fortune in legal fees. But he was built like a cannonball and Alison knew she would need him perhaps more than all the others. The only hold she had over him, short of letting him go to prison, was that as chairman of Nelson Harbour's Welcome Committee, she had gotten him the town crier job. He had the most power-ful lungs in the islands. The world at large also saw Oyez in ceremonial robes, bawling glad tidings. The world at large kept its distance, because Oyez made a considerable racket, so it did not see Oyez held upright by the mayor when blotto.

"Who'll watch Oyez?" Alison finally asked, still un-sure of Oyez could keep a solemn promise more than twelve hours.

Nobody looked keen.

"I'll arrest um," said Constable Mello.

"Oi!" protested Oyez. For once, he could look a policeman in the eye and sincerely declare, "I ain't dun nuffink."

"Pick him up for loitering," said Alison.

Oyez grabbed his battered top hat. He was still in his tourist coachman's rig of tails and striped trousers. His feet were bare. Oyez's honeymooners were not concerned with viewing his feet.

Mello stopped him at the door. "I won't be chargin'

you. I just be takin' you into custody for safekeeping."

"You be de boss." Oyez relaxed. Once, he had reached the peak of his fame as central figure in a travel poster seen from Paris to Hong Kong. When offshore companies became the larger source of revenue, though, his commercial value diminished. To get rid of Zia Gabbiya, symbol of Oyez's decline, he would do anything—even fly as ballast in Lord John's torpedo bomber.

That was a possibility never far from Alison's mind. Though not with Lord John as pilot.

CHAPTER 14

E. P. Geld always left on the same day of his annual visit to the Windfalls. He had never spent a night at Rose Hall since Amanda tore his heart in two.

This time he had no choice. Zia Gabbiya had created a situation from which E.P. saw no escape.

Amanda was his daughter, born out of wedlock, entitled to twist his guts and pour upon his head hot coals of shame. He had first brought her to the islands to keep the child from the mother's crazed clutches. The mother had killed herself. Then E.P. discovered what the mother had already known: Amanda was not normal.

She became his secret cross. E.P. had never admitted feeling guilt about anything in his entire life, but in some attic of his mind had accumulated great quantities of guilt inherited from forefathers or deposited by original sins of his own. The more E.P. rejected natural impulses toward human feeling, the more Amanda weighed upon his unacknowledged conscience. He had continued to postpone her transfer back to mainland America, reasoning at first that he could provide her with the best attention in seclusion. She needed more than doctors: she needed whatever money could buy to develop her incredible talent for music. She had her own staff, her own quarters, her own music room. As the years sped by, it became more and more easy for E.P. to convince himself that this was best for the girl. But he also went to extraordinary lengths to keep her existence hidden from those same glossy high-society magazines in which he was featured as the great-man-about-town, the most eligible bachelor. He had a horror of being laughed at. And somewhere in that attic, this shameful concern for his image was added to the mountain of guilt.

Let this cat out of the bag, risk Amanda making fool of him, and E.P. would have nothing to prop up his self-regard except his billions.

Now, in the night, he was drawn to the place where Amanda was confined for her own safety. He knew, as if an alarm had gone off, when it was low tide and he could wade across to the tiny island which was Amanda's tortured world. He was afraid to use the cable car and draw the attention of his own security guards.

The world's most eligible bachelor paused on the sandy isthmus. *Vanity Fair* had once called him that. Most eligible? After four wives? Amanda was the demon that drove him out of all those marriages: she was the demon that forced him to escape any woman the moment his physical needs were done. Once, long ago, he had in a terribly drunken moment considered putting her down. He had thought in terms of destroying a pet dog. It had been the briefest of moments, after hours of drunken self-pity. Kill his own daughter! The consequences of such a thought, however fleeting, were too dreadful to risk again. Nightmares had followed. He could only break the sequence by working days and nights on end without sleep. There had been the inevitable nervous breakdown. Even then, he would not consult a therapist. He supposed there were tycoons—stupid word, but the columnists used it all the time—who confided to their psychiatrists. But not E.P. He couldn't afford it. Not even without this shameful secret.

He heard the notes from one of the grand pianos. It was in tune. He'd have wrung the neck of the bonded piano tuner who was flown here monthly under discreet guard if it hadn't been. Everything had to be right for Amanda. This blob of land at the end of the isthmus was an extraterrestrial principality. There, she met only with love and kindness. If E.P. had thought about these things, he might have wondered if it was the love and kindness he had missed in his own life, or if it was the substitute that only money can buy. Just as he failed to recognize Casey's contempt, so he was unable to distinguish between true affection and the sycophancy through which he moved.

He tried to blot out the music. Debussy. Played by an idiot savant. Well, the quacks insisted Amanda was that. He put his hands over his ears. The gesture reflected his confusion. Once a year, he came to the islands; everyone assumed, to meet tax requirements. He had come to believe it himself. Every year, he rushed away before nightfall, afraid of the siren call.

He removed his hands and resumed his cautious journey. Whatever Amanda played, it was with style. It was not mechanical, or in any way symptomatic of an imperfect brain. Somewhere someone someday would unlock the door. Gabbiya's mysterious expert, perhaps. Everything Amanda played was automatically taped and sent to New York. In the privacy of a Manhattan penthouse known to very few, he would listen and convince himself over and over that here was pure genius.

He stopped again. The tapes! There was one person who knew about the tapes: Mellanie Blake. And it was only today he'd discovered her intimate relationship with Zia Gabbiya. Did that explain Gabbiya's boast of controlling an expert who had the answer to Amanda's problem? Zia's original approach in the case of Amanda had come via typically tortuous channels: through Alpha Chemicals in this instance, a multinational in which Zia's Matasuchi Metals and E.P.'s Royal Tin Corp. were partners. Zia's original feelers had been subtle: just the hint of secret access to a specialist; just a brief intimation that he knew about E.P.'s illegitimate daughter: and all couched in such obtuse language that middlemen would never understand this was not an exchange of notes on some industrial process. Zia's early probes grew, until now he talked confidently of the Soviet expert able to suggest a course of chemotherapy and psychotherapy to solve Amanda's problems. Only Lani had been in that particular penthouse. It contained thousands of Amanda's tapes. She could help herself to a few samples, enough to give the expert something to work on!

Even the richest men of commerce are capable of naive self-deceit in matters so simple that you would expect them to tread cautiously. E.P., though surrounded by financial genius and administrative brilliance, had already presided over an empire while it was being sapped by Gabbiya's better-paid agents. You would expect him to be full of suspicion, and doubly on his guard, because it was Gabbiya again who flashed his conjuror's hands and juggled his conjuror's hat. Instead, having now reasoned that Zia must have gotten hold of Amanda's music tapes through Lani, E.P. nursed a small fire of joy in his heart. Of course! The tapes were brilliant. That explained why Zia had been so confident about his expert's ability to cure Amanda!

Nanny Locke hid her astonishment when he appeared at one of the plate-glass windows of the gazebo. This was Amanda's house, anchored to a vast mechanical turntable so that the girl at the piano might either catch what sunlight there was or enjoy the glow of the sea at night.

She was lost in her music. She had been dressed as if for a formal dinner. Her clothes were not changed just twice a day, but several times, that she might be ever fresh, ever ready to be rushed into prominence if E.P.'s hoped-for miracle should ever occur. She was in her early twenties. Her face was the untroubled face of a child.

E.P. motioned Nanny Locke to remain where she stood, although in truth Nanny Locke would have had difficulty lifting one foot after another, so shocked she was by this unprecedented break in routine. Nanny Locke was not afraid of E.P.: she had been the sweet young governess from England who taught E.P. his ABC's. She was the only retainer, domestic or corporate, who had survived so long the storms, the whims, the sudden power trips. And so, rooted to the spot, she waited.

The house had eight walls of plate glass. There were window aquariums and splashy paintings of the world beneath the sea. The spire roof was like the top of an ornamental birdcage. And here, thought E.P., is my pretty polly. A sleeping beauty. With Zia's promise of a Prince Charming to wake her from this hideous somnambulism.

He slipped out of his loafers and trod softly across the grasslike carpeting. He stood behind her for a long time, admiring the shoulder-length hair of golden chestnut. The hair was beautifully groomed, like everything, like the face and figure, like the music and the place; all so perfect and different, so clearly out of this time and space, as if created for another level of existence.

He put up his hands to touch her shoulder, and stopped. From behind, she was the image of her mother. If she turned, he would be looking into the eyes of the young woman he had murdered by his actions.

Amanda stopped playing, so abruptly that it seemed an exquisite crystal globe had exploded into a thousand fragments. She twisted around and E.P. found himself looking into the clear windows of an empty house.

Then she screamed. There was no expression in her face. She opened her mouth and this awful cry escaped.

E.P. shrank back. He would have liked to take her in his arms and speak to her. The habits of a lifetime prevented him. He would have liked to tell her that he had not done this terrible thing to her, but Nanny Locke had uprooted herself at last and was tugging him away.

After a time, the girl stopped screaming. Soon the clear notes floated once more upon the night air.

"Nobody's fault," E.P. murmured, stumbling away from the gazebo, brushing past the guard dogs, letting himself out through the gate in the high steel fence. Nobody's fault.

But what if there was a tenant inside that strangely beautiful house that seemed so empty? Listening to the magic sound rising like a summer breeze off the water, he *knew* someone was there! Then, he must search, must be the butler to Zia Gabbiya's ambitions. If he didn't, then it *would* be someone's fault—his own.

Nanny Locke saw with her hands folded in her lap. The storm had passed. She pressed her lips together. In her private opinion, if anyone were to ask, and so far nobody ever had asked, Master Geld was as much out of touch with reality as his daughter. How she did wish the wretched child would stop plonking away at that doleful church music. Nanny Locke had, she didn't mind admitting it, a tin ear. But oh! how she missed a bit of noise and a good laugh and a bit of knees-up like they did it in the music halls back home.

Schroeder said into his walkie-talkie, "He's on his way back to the main house now."

"I'll be waiting," said Zia Gabbiya from the *Quarqũr*.

CHAPTER 15

Casey had played backgammon until his patience ran out, and with it his tolerance for remaining in Gabbiya's presence. There was still no reply from Vietnam by the time Lani uncoiled herself and expressed a desire for bed. Zia Gabbiya gave Casey an amused look, and offered him a cabin for the night. Casey gladly accepted. It turned out to be a paneled room, to which clung a woman's fragrance. The bunk might have been one of those Tokyo chicken-coop capsules you rent in the new assembly-line hotels, like a plastic coffin with headphones to deliver the word of the Lord and spigots to offer beverages of your choice. Something suspiciously like a deflated rubber doll hung in one of the adjacent closets. Beyond a steel door, he found the toilet bowl, a small wash basin, and a medicine cabinet. In the cabinet was a small curved knife. The blade was sheathed in wood bound in very fine silver wire. A jade ring was set in the handle. Casey had seen such knives in Vietnam. Girls carried them, curled inside their fists, just the ring showing, the blade sharp enough to de-sex a male attacker.

He was groggy from lack of sleep. He had no scruples about taking Gabbiya's hospitality. He saw no other way of learning what Big Vien wanted from him. He seemed to have just drifted off when someone gently shook him.

243

He was naked, lying with his head to the porthole through which filtered the barest hint of early dawn. He rolled over and saw Lani. He grabbed the sheets and sat up. "Excuse me," he said, and at once felt foolish.

"I was told to bring you this." She held out a sheet of paper.

The message was from Vietnam. It repeated the list of missing Americans and concluded: "Coincidence is the simultaneous concurrence of causally unconnected events." That was the answer to Casey's transmitted phrase: "What a coincidence." It was the confirmation he needed. He was indeed dealing again with Big Vien. Only Vien could have responded with Schopenhauer's line, for nobody else knew it had been the core of that nightlong debate inside the Zoo.

"You're satisfied it's genuine?" asked Lani. She leaned over the bunk's guardrail.

"I have to believe so," said Casey. He was struck by the thought, though, that Big Vien could just as easily be tapping out his telexes from another part of this very vessel.

"You *must* believe it!" She thrust an eraser-tipped pencil at him impatiently, almost angrily, then gave a slight toss of her head, as if to indicate the cabin door. From there, an observer might have gotten the impression she was vamping Casey. She wore a loose robe. It fell open as one of her hands moved over his body. He stared at her, baffled. She snatched back the message and turned it over, blocking it from the view of anyone near the door. Lightly penciled on the back were the words: SMITTY HARRIS/RUB OUT.

She flashed a smile. Her head bent over him, and the silky black hair cascaded over his chest. There was a staginess about all this that warned him. She was acting for the benefit of hidden microphones, or concealed cameras, or both. She swept the sheets from his lower torso and moved her head there, and at the same time she thrust pencil and paper at him. Hurriedly he rubbed out the dangerous words. Smitty Harris hammered in his head. That was the sole reality. Otherwise, he could have just as well been still asleep and dreaming.

She stood back. "There's more when you want it, Casey," she said in a penetrating, stagy voice. Then she left.

He rolled over. If Zia had told Lani to seduce him, it must have been to make a compromising record on videotape. Yet Lani had frustrated any hidden camera. So there had to be some other explanation. Where did Smitty Harris come in? The Irish Girl could know nothing about the prisoner's tap code. Unless—But the idea was absurd. It was impossible that Tony Rutgers' father, old Rotgut, could have told Lani . . .

The code had to be memorized. It had been invented for American fighting men who might be captured and isolated. It could be tapped out on jail plumbing, against walls, on cell bars. It was based on a 5 × 5 matrix containing letters of the alphabet. In the Zoo, practitioners of the code could communicate almost as if conversing. Pilots were good at it because they were accustomed to the clickety-click shorthand used during operational flights when radio silence was desirable. Each man could exchange signals with other squadron aircraft by flicking the microphone button on his throttle. In the brief time Casey had spent with Rotgut, they had talked about the code, and how it would maintain the moral fiber of prisoners who might be still in Vietnam. Rotgut had spoken of the U.S. Government's fear that the Communists would try to sell any surviving prisoners. Casey had said all Forget-Me-Nots were utterly opposed to making deals.

Now, staring at the closed porthole in his cabin, Casey thought that you didn't fight for your country and its ideas unless you were damned if you'd surrender that American dream. You didn't endure so much to become a commodity, to be sold by a regime dedicated to that dream's destruction.

He thought about Tony Rutgers. Thirty when shot down. If he was still alive, he'd be entitled to early retirement. A pensioner! The thought was staggering. If Tony was alive, as Big Vien's message claimed, he would never have collaborated. Casey knew the way the system worked. If a prisoner refused, he eventually became a nonperson. Casey had been released only because word had been smuggled to Washington that he *was* alive.

No man who lasted that long, who had not surfaced as a brainwashed propagandist, could possibly want his freedom purchased. He might welcome, however, some sleight of hand. Suppose Rotgut's son and all those other missing pilots could be exchanged for myself and IN-SPAD? Casey maneuvered his way out of the bunk while he thought about this. I've had a good long spell of freedom myself. What have I done with it? Had a few laughs, played my small part in my country's democratic processes, founded a business . . . C'mon, who're you kidding? Never once have you forgotten what you left behind in Vietnam!

He ached to lock horns with Big Vien again. If Vien really thought he was some big CIA spy, he could spin out the game forever. It wouldn't be hard to invent convincing crap about INSPAD's deep-tow vehicles and detection gear, and lure the bastard into wasting huge resources on fool's gold. First, he'd have to get his own men out. After that, hell, he might even learn if Vietnam was the tail wagging the Sahara dog.

He looked at the telex again. If he held it to the light, the imprint of the penciled words was still dangerously decipherable. He tore the paper into small pieces, then realized he could not throw it out the porthole. The porthole was sealed. As, no doubt, the door was locked. On the outside. He thought of flushing it down the toilet, but who knew the limits of Gobbiya's cunning? He probably had a trap in the plumbing below. Finally Casey bent over the wash basin and put a match to the bits of paper.

As he washed down the charred remains, a steward burst into the cabin. The intruder was squat, but his arrogance inflamed Casey. *"Who the hell do you think you are?"* Casey hurtled across the cabin. "You *knock!* Then you *wait!*" He jabbed a finger in the man's chest to emphasize each word. When the steward still tried to bob around him, eyes searching, Casey shoved him with the flat of his other hand, step by step, out through the opened door. "Get your goddam butt out of here!"

"Sir, *je regrette* . . . A matter of urgency . . . The fire alarm . . ." The steward fell back into the corridor. Something in his manner put Casey in mind of a strutting Napoleon: "the Corsican upstart." The Corsican, if such he was, had slammed shut the door. So much for fear of fire. Fire alarm? Of course! The moment Casey had burned the telex, the Corsican had rushed in. Casey began a search. Smoke detectors? Here, here, and here! And in the head! What about concealed cameras? Bugs?

247

Savagely he ripped out the linen from the bunk, turned the thin mattress, tapped wooden panels, poked behind lights. He found nothing more, but when he had finished, he had exhausted his anger and frustration.

A gong sounded. First call to breakfast.

Before he left, he remembered something and returned to the washroom. He took the curious ring-knife from its hiding place. It had been overlooked in a cabin clearly under surveillance. Was it another odd circumstance built into the situation by Gabbiya? Another of his conjuring tricks?

If Zia Gabbiya smelled trouble, he concealed it. He sat at a breakfast table set on the half deck above the pool. The early sun struck across the flat harbor waters and added gaiety to striped awnings.

"Help yourself." Gabbiya indicated chafing dishes spread across white linen. "American fare? Or English style? On such a day, I recommend Jamaican salt fish and ackee. Ackee is over there. Looks like scrambled eggs. Never eat ackee unripe, Commander. It may poison you!"

Casey rose to the challenge, annoyed with himself for doing so. To refuse the codfish and ackee would be like surrendering a piece on the chessboard. Gabbiya was playing the role of the Arab host who, when you admire something, says, "Take it!" He was dressed this time in a Nehru costume: collarless rough-weave white jacket and pantaloons, sandals. He had kicked off one sandal and hooked the bared foot over the other thigh. His curling black hair glistened from his hairstylist's attentions. Drops of water lingered on the tight red rose in his buttonhole. He peered into Casey's plate. "You choose wisely. I myself prefer ackee when in the West Indies. The most dangerous way to cook and eat ackee, of course, is the most exciting. As in all matters. What I do is pluck the ackee from the tree—" He paused and gazed anxiously at Casey. "This doesn't bore you, my dear chap? No? Good. Pluck it when it is bright red and lethal. I roast each section slowly. As the edges grow golden brown, tiny drops of oil come to the surface. It is the oil, Commander Casey, you must watch for. Then, while the edges of the fruit bronze, I sprinkle a measure of salt." Gabbiya kissed his fingers. "Mmmmm! The taste is like a celestial chestnut. Sometimes I think codfish and ackee is better than sex. Do *you* think good food, in the end, is the more satisfying?"

The question caught Casey in the middle of treacherous thoughts about cooking his host. *A target of opportunity.* That was what you looked for sometimes on a flying mission. Just ranging out over enemy territory, lazily watching for targets of opportunity. Zia Gabbiya would fry most marvelously.

"Do you, Commander Casey?"

"Hug?"

"Prefer the culinary to the bedroom arts?"

"My cooking's confined to some experience in boiling rice," said Casey.

Gabbiya's smile vanished. The reference to Vietnam was too crude for this early-morning exercise in conjuring rabbits from silk hats. These were finger exercises. Sawing the lady in half would come later. The smile returned. "But I must not divert you. First, enjoy. The coffee is the best. Also Jamaican. From Blue Mountain. I had it flown here specially."

The coffee *was* good. So was the salted codfish, magically intermingled with the ackee. Casey reminded himself that Zia Gabbiyas as a dead martyr might be a greater threat than the Protector alive. He felt a jab near his groin. It came from the ring-knife in his pocket, and it sharply reminded him that he was getting a little cuckoo. First the wild notion of exchanging himself for prisoners. Now this urge personally to get rid of Gabbiya.

The large meal and the humidity were bringing out patches of perspiration on his host's clothing. Twice, a waiter had to wipe Gabbiya's face with a towel. Casey watched in fascination: as in Vietnam, inhabitants of a hot climate seemed more vulnerable to the discomfort of great heat than Casey, raised in Illinois, where half the year was spent in arctic blasts. Casey felt cool as a cucumber, and it gave him an edge.

When the last plate had been removed, the last cup of coffee poured, Gabbiya asked, "You have read Vietnam's response?"

"Of course."

"No 'of course' about it." Gabbiya became less jovial. "I don't know everything that goes on. May I have it back?"

Jolted, Casey made a show of turning out his pockets. "I must have thrown it out."

"Surely a strange thing to do? With all that information?"

"It's not information I'm likely to forget."

"I suppose not." Gabbiya's tone suggested this was a circumstance he was not likely to forget either. He made a dismissive gesture, but his eyes remained cold. "You're curious about my ship, yes? No, don't deny it. You're a

250

naval man. It's normal. Come."

If this was Gabbiya's way of getting down to business, Casey had no objection. He was too grateful for the escape from the telex impasse.

"Let us start—how is your term? Aloft?" Gabbiya was already shinning up the companionway. The boyish burst of energy, the swift change of mood, were beguiling.

"You have heard of the great Arab pilot Ahmad ibn Madjid?" he asked, pausing just inside the deckhouse. "He was the best of our navy experts in the fifteenth century. I trace my bloodlines to him. Arab fleets controlled the seas then."

"Sailed up the Bosporus," recalled Casey. "Laid siege to the heart of the Byzantine Empire. Piloted even the great Vasco da Gama across the Indian Ocean, because Ahmad's brass quandrants were superior to European astrolabes."

"Good! Excellent!" Gabbiya clapped his hands delightedly and wheeled around. "See? A memory of my ancestor!"

The great Ahmad stood in marble behind the steersman's position at the wheel, a burnoosed figure in odd contrast to the electronic displays. Casey could not help being impressed by the combination of grace and savagery in the full-size statue. It was clever of Gabbiya to identify himself with Araby's mightiest navigator and warrior-seaman. His claim had become part of the fundamentalist Islamic legends sweeping the Moslem world. Zia, said the faithful, spanned the centuries. And the wheelhouse, thought Casey, perfectly bridged the gap in time. Wedged just above the marble navigator's line of sight were digital displays for the loran (long-range navigation system) and the ultra-new GPS (Global Positioning System). The GPS was a child of U.S. Polaris submarine navigators. With it, a ship groping for a fairway buoy in an alien harbor in fog would know where she was to within fifteen meters. Gabbiya caught Casey's interest in it, and described its capabilities with easy familiarity while Casey burned inside, wondering how the King of Terror had obtained it. The GPS had been exclusive to the U.S. Defense Department's Integrated Operational Nuclear Detection System (IONDS). What treacherous merchant had sold its secrets?

"Money buys anything," said Gabbiya, reading Casey's mind. "You don't look for ideologists to do your spying these days." His gesturing hand took in equipment better suited for the control center of a fighting ship than the bridge of a luxury yacht. "Here I marry Arab seamanship with the most modern technology. It is why I named her *Quarqūr*, after the most ancient of Arab designs, the carrack. It means a simple seagoing vessel."

The *Qurqūr* was anything but simple. Casey chased after Zia, whose enthusiasm accelerated as they climbed and slid down ladders, strode from one deck's end to another. Crewmen jumped aside, saluting. The sense of discipline, the quiet hum of generators, the soft murmur of orders passed over an interference-free loudspeaker system all reminded Casey of a well-run navy ship.

"The old Arab carrack had a bulging round hull and square sails," said Gabbiya, giving no sign of flagging. "I am a student of marine history and I can tell you the carrack lasted through many centuries because nobody made a better design. It was generally two-masted with beams protruding either side. From it evolved four-masters: spritsail, bowsprit, mainmast and foremast. Then they added another mast, the *bonaventura*. Did you know a famous Canadian aircraft carrier was named after it?"

Casey affected ignorance.

"I myself believe Arab ships sailed *these very waters*. Gabbiya came to a stop outside Casey's cabin. "One day I shall find their wrecks. Did you know we first built the *sambook* centuries ago, and it still sails the seas? It is fast and can face any wind." He struck Casey's arm. "You will help me find one here, perhaps?" The eyes he fixed on Casey seemed to fill with admiration. "It will appeal to your sense of adventure, your curiosity about inner space." He pushed open the cabin door and made Casey go in first. "Inner space is where we shall discover the riches of human history, and our greatest mineral riches, too. Not in outer space that costs more than humanity can afford . . ."

He really believes this, thought Casey. It's as if he's heard Bingo and myself saying the very same things.

". . . like this ship. She may look expensive to you, Commander. She has a dive pool most oil companies would envy, through which my men go down two hundred feet with ease. And my divers are *the very best*. Nobody pays more highly than I do. Yet with all this, and though you may think *Qurqūr* a very expensive toy, she costs a fraction of a single rocket needed to put a shuttle into space. And with her I can explore underwater with a freedom comparable to your shuttles! Why, even Lani—equivalent to one of your astronauts—her training cost virtually *nothing*. Nothing! Yet she's the best of my diving elite."

Casey wondered why they had not visited the moon

pool and its diving facilities. Gabbiya cut into his thoughts. "You like her, then?"

"Outstanding as a frigate when her hull was first laid."

Gabbiya fell back into a chair and released a great bellow of laughter. "The hull was laid—? No, no, no!" He thumped his chest. "The girl! Lani! The Irish Girl it is that—how do you say in America? That is laid!" He gasped for breath. "You will be the death of me, Casey. May I call you Casey? You do not listen. I was speaking of Mellanie Blake."

"Sorry, Colonel Gabbiya, I—"

"Zia. Please. I like my friends to call me Zia . . . You like her, then?"

"I don't really know Miss Blake."

"Casey, you know why I like you so much? You are brave, intelligent, experienced . . . and so old-fashioned. All I ask is, Do you like her?"

It was the third time of asking. Casey said cautiously, "Well, yes, of course; she's a nice girl."

"Then, you must have her."

"Oh, now, please." Casey decided to treat it as a joke. "Any lively young person would find me a very dull dog." He hoisted himself onto his bunk.

"Nonsense. You would lay her very well." Gabbiya stretched his legs and grinned like a schoolboy. He threw back his head and shouted through the open door, "Get me the Corsican! And bring coffee."

The Corsican . . . Once more, Casey had the odd sense of following someone's script. He had thought the man acted and sounded like a Corsican. Had he somehow heard him called by that name?

Gabbiya banged his heel on the deck. "You know where this one was laid? This hull?"

"Quebec. French Canada."

"You did your homework. Another reason I could come to like you as a brother. Yes, laid in Quebec. Like Lani's mother."

Casey swallowed his distaste. "If she's Irish from Quebec, she must be what the French call *formidable*."

A steward interrupted with a tray. As he withdrew, Gabbiya reached out a foot and kicked shut the door. "Okay, Casey, now let's talk. INSPAD. You could have full use of this vessel for your research. I would not interfere." He leaned forward and revolved a tiny cup under a copper spout. "Turkish coffee for this time of day. Forget my pretty speeches about Jamaican." He glanced up with a sly grin. "I learned from the British to roll out those extravagant tributes to other people's food. In my heart and in my stomach, I'm an Arab. By the way," he added casually, "if you are thinking of killing me, please don't. The ring-knife in your pocket. I feel safer if I see it here on the chart table. By the way, too: I found this table in Alexandria. It was made for a Portuguese navigator, in 1492 by your calendar."

Casey surrendered the knife, impressed in spite of himself. He felt like a small boy chosen to play patsy to the Christmas magician. He said nothing.

As if the knife had never existed, Gabbiya said, "You would remain president of INSPAD and you would be free to pursue your ideas. I would provide all the money you could possibly need."

Casey sipped his coffee, thick and sweet like treacle, and thought sadly that the things you desperately wanted never came in acceptable packages. Unlimited funds!

"I know how miserly your federal agencies can be,"

255

said Gabbiya.

"There's no government money in INSPAD."

"Naturally you have to say that. Why did Professor Rutgers put twenty thousand dollars into your Forget-Me-Not-Fund? For CIA research!"

Casey put down his cup to hide more surprise. He would concede nothing. "Why are you so interested?"

"Come, you're no fool. In matters of sex, yes, perhaps. But not in this affair. You've seen my ship. Once, it was the hunter-killer of submarines. Now it is at the leading edge of support systems *for* submarines."

"INSPAD is designed for very deep waters. Deeper than any submarine can go."

"Not the submarines we have in mind."

Casey noted the switch to "we." He said, "I can't give up INSPAD's work to hostile designers," while he prepared hurriedly to drop hints about nonexistent INSPAD projects. He must not let Gabbiya suspect for one moment that INSPAD had advanced little beyond his dreams in the Zoo.

"You would have access to principals," said Zia Gabbiya. "A journey to Vietnam might be very worthwhile from your point of view."

"And doubtless a visit to the Paracels?" In his mind's eye, Casey could see the islands, due east of Da Nang and some 400 kilometers southeast of China's Hainan. The pancake-shaped islands melted into a portrait of Big Vien's flat, round face.

"China claims them." Gabbiya paused. "China thinks possession is nine tenths the law. The Chinese know the Paracels to be valuable real estate."

"Is *that* what's at stake?" Casey slid off the bunk.

"Vietnam wants independence in oil. China wants to

prevent that."

"Where do you come in?"

"I thought I made that clear. Surely you should be asking me about prices, Casey? The money I offer is far beyond anything you could hope to get elsewhere. And I'll throw in your American prisoners, your MIAs, for nothing."

"I don't bend to blackmail, Zia."

"Your comrades will be released according to how much progress is made in our negotiations," Gabbiya continued as if there had been no interruption. "A simple signal to the effect that we have started to talk will result in the release of Anthony Rutgers. He could be home in Maryland with his family by the end of the week."

"That won't work with me."

"On receipt of a further signal, reporting things go well, they will release 'Bash' McCoy."

Casey had a sudden image of Bill McCoy, known as Coy and then as Bash for Bashful. His old Naval Academy classmate had been flying as his wingman the night Combat Information vectored them onto bandits heading from Haiphong. Bash had been catapulted first into a China Sea night of pitch black. A night cat shot, with jets at full blast, often meant a blackout for the pilot plastered against his seat by the force of acceleration from zero to 200 knots. Casey, waiting his turn, saw Bash's lights vanish. Loss of power? It was the ever-present nightmare. No matter how smoothly the cat slung you into the air, there was nothing to be done if you were flying on momentum alone. Bash could have been out there in the void, waiting for the explosion. None came. Casey requested immediate launch. He shot down the track, heard the thump of the catapult's bridle as he broke free. He was swallowed almost at once by fog. He kept climbing on instruments, calling "Bash" on the radio at regular intervals. They used nicknames instead of call signs to baffle the enemy. Finally he had heard, "Keep goin', Cat's Eyes!" So Bash was airborne. His generator, it turned out, fell off line when he took the shot. It was an eerie night: long streaks of horizontal lightning illuminated the bellies of storms sweeping down from China. The bandits, if there ever had been any, were nowhere to be found. Casey turned back, low on fuel. "You're the only man aloft," came the soft voice of his controller. "Launching tanker now, in case you miss the wires and bolt." A bolter would have meant Casey going around again, on emptying tanks. But what he had worried about was Bash. Where had he vanished?

Now the Great Protector was telling him Bash was alive. It was possible. It could be.

Zia, ignoring Casey's silence, continued: "If I report our negotiations approach a favorable conclusion, Baa-Baa Black Sheep will go free."

Casey concentrated on lifting the refilled cup to his lips without a tremor. Zia had slipped up. Lambe had been nicknamed Baa-Baa. Someone else, not a member of the Group, had added that nursery-rhyme reference. No pilot ever spoke of Baa-Baa Black Sheep . . .

"It would pay you," said Gabbiya, "to keep negotiations going. Even if you finally decide not to trade, you'll have engineered the release of seven men."

Casey refused to ask who the seventh man might be.

"This is not only in your own best interests," said Gabbiya. "It is in those of your country, too. You're not a politician. You're not out to make a splash. You're an honest patriot, Casey. It is another reason I like you so very much."

"Don't count on it," said Casey. His stomach had started to heave.

"But if you were not a patriot, you would have drawn that knife on me! You did not, because there are bigger things at stake. A clever test, was it not?"

"I'm in no moood to haggle."

Zia Gabbiya saw the nausea in Casey's face: nausea, contempt, superiority. The Protector rose and jerked open the door. "Stay here, Casey, and do some more thinking about all this."

Outside loomed the Corsican.

"Don't forget," said Casey, "E. P. Geld knows I'm here."

Geld? Achch!" Gabbiya hawked and spat.

The Corsican inserted himself between the two men. He carried a heavy Colt .45, an automatic for which Casey had little respect. It had proved unwieldy and inaccurate when he'd tried to escape capture in Vietnam. At these close quarters, however, it had a certain authority.

"Geld is one of your American cockroaches," said Gabbiya. "I do this to him if he steps out of line." He ground his heel into the deck, and left Casey wishing he had used the knife after all, while the Corsican grinned down at him.

CHAPTER 16

Alison had no court work that morning. She had spent much of the night mobilizing islanders. Sergeant Winston banged into her office for his elevenses. While she poured him a mug of tea, it struck her that she'd neither seen nor heard from Casey. She was annoyed by Winston's uncharacteristic loquacity:

"You're dead right, Miss Bracken, about ordinary people being secretive. It's in the blood. Even with Gabbiya, they've hardly said out loud what they think till now. They've been so long in the habit of discretion. The Windfall tradition! Overseas companies only come here on our guarantee of confidentiality . . ."

Alison was feeling panic at the recollection of her last words with Casey about the *panji* spike and the danger to his life. Winston's words brought her back to the islanders' awakening alarm. "We could revert to being an island only grows bananas," said Winston. "Plenty other islands prospered on the banana trade. Until nobody needed bananas. We'd rather be less dependent. My youngest brother was one of the best fishermen 'round here. Now he works in the Royal Palm Hotel's kitchens preparing fish frozen in New York and *flown* here! Where the fish practically jump into your boat!

You know the Royal Palm's owned by one of E. P. Geld's subsidiaries, and all profits go out of here, but people didn't wake up to this till now. You take my big sister, used to be a higgler, did her trading in the market. Now she works in the head office of this Texas multinational. A billion dollars flow into the Windfalls office a month. But them clams can flow out again just as quick. My sister *is* the head office. She tears the instructions off one telex machine and she retransmits on another without making any change except the address: Windfalls Corporate Headquarters. We may feel very grand with all these big corporations quartered here, but what good does it do us?"

"Pays your sister's salary," said Alison.

"She'd sooner sell cabbages. Except, who grows cabbages any more? They're all working for absentee landlords who pay them well enough to buy canned vegetables from overseas." His voice sharpened. "People are ready to rebel, Miss Bracken. They don't like outsiders like Professor Rutgers laughing about our toytown parades."

"Huh?" Alison looked up from a filing cabinet. She had been trying to end Winston's musings. "Rotgut—?"

"Was overheard by the barman at the Black Lion. Talking to another white man. Rutgers wasn't running us down, just poking fun at our royal Disneyland. What the prof didn't understand was that these are Windfall traditions, not just imperial splendor. The barman got mad. Said not a family here, black or white, didn't make sacrifices to develop and keep them traditions."

Alison woke up. Winston's unusual verbosity hid some purpose. "What are you trying to say?"

"If our people kept quiet till now, it's because they're not used to termites. They say, you don't notice termites until they eat out the inside of your house. We've been lucky. A robber broke into the house before we had to wait for the roof to fall in. Gabbiya was in too big a hurry, though he thinks he's been taking things nice and slow. Now we know he's out to rob us, people are saying we'd better remember the old law."

"What old law?"

"The old law giving us the right to protect our property. The law that says we can kill a robber if he's on our premises."

"Go on."

Winston put down his mug. "Your dad's health is bad. But he's the only hope we've got. Isn't he?"

"Except Casey." Alison cautiously voiced what had been in her mind.

"Are you *sure* about Casey?"

"He's had an outstanding record as a naval officer. Although as a jet fighter pilot, maybe he's spoiled by all those gadgets. The Stringbag looks primitive but you really have to fly her every inch of the way."

"Begging your pardon, that's not what I mean. This — ah, *honkie*, the white foreigner in the Black Lion. The name and address he gave on his tourist entry card don't exist. His passport and physical description fit a man on London's list of foreign agents. The same man talked about Casey with the professor. They were in the Black Lion together: Professor Rutgers and the other man." Winston repeated his assertion, unsure if Alison had understood its significance. He added: "The professor praised Casey's work in undersea research."

"That doesn't make sense. INSPAD — Inner Space

263

Development — is more dreams than reality. And a professional intelligence officer wouldn't stand in a bar talking—" Alison waved her hands in wonderment. "Not unless he *wanted* to be overheard," she added with sudden insight.

Winston rubbed his chin. He suspected why Alison had not been paying attention. "Are you in love with Casey, Miss Bracken?"

Alison flushed. Such a question, from anyone else, even from her father, would invite a tart answer. But Winston was in a position of special privilege. "In love with Casey?" she whispered, as if testing each word before admitting it to full consciousness. "Yes. Yes, I suppose I am."

A look of agony settled over Winston's honest face. "Then, you'd better find out what he's doing on Gabbiya's yacht."

Alison rose, and the color drained from her face. She trusted Winston implicitly. She had never known him, in any legal proceedings, to get his facts wrong. "Why didn't you tell me in the first place?"

The answer was in the sergeant's eyes: embarrassment, doubt, lack of any hard evidence, the possibility Alison knew that Casey was on *Qurqūr* and didn't want it generally advertised. What altered everything, though, was this revival of a theory that Casey was involved in intelligence work.

"I can't prove he's there," said Winston. "But Mary and Josh, over at Backgammon, haven't seen him."

"That proves nothing! Those two layabouts are hardly ever in the house." Alison opened a closet where her wig and gown hung from a peg, and removed her crash helmet. "I'm going over to speak to them now.

264

You coming?"

"Best not," said Winston. "I've got to find some excuse for getting on board Gabbiya's floating brothel."

"Phones be outa order, missie," said Josh the handyman when she burst into Backgammon. "That why you be findin' difficulty speakin' with us'n."

Mary chased him out of the kitchen. "Dat man!" she said. "Doan't have no come-from 'n' doan't have no go-to."

Alison had no wish to alarm either of them. Josh still lingered within earshot. She smiled. "Mary, you seen Mr. Casey lately?"

"No, mum. Nor sin yesdee . . . But doan't fret, missie. Dat woman cum early this mawnin collectin his'n clouts."

"A woman collected his clothes? What woman?"

"All bosom-shapes and thighses, da minx," said Mary with dark satisfaction. "Bold's brass in da scooter boat. Dem ladies! Dey's tease iggeren fellas like Josh here with their frills 'n' trills. Be better dey doan't wear nuffin. Den de mens knows where dey stand."

"What's she look like?" Alison demanded before Mary could get onto her hobbyhorse.

"I jes' dun tell'd you, missie. She's what dey call d' Irish Girl."

Josh edged back into the kitchen, reasserting himself. "Dey left dis on da beach." He held out a clip of 9-mm cartridges. "I didn't say nuffin because d' ole lady here, she doan't like guns."

"Where on the beach?" Alison stuck the clip in her pocket while Josh led them to the sea wall. He was

265

showing off a bit now. "Dey couldn' bin fishin', for twas wrong tide, wrong currents. See, dey run da boat up da sand."

The tide had receded as much as it ever does where Atlantic meets Caribbean. The marks of a boat, run ashore, still remained.

"Maybe dey wasn' fishin' for fish," said Mary. "But dat hussie sure fishes for de men. Orleddy she got da boat full."

"Full of men?" asked Alison.

"Well. One. Seemed like dere's anudder back of im."

"You'd better show me what this girl took away," said Alison, growing impatient with the pair of them.

Ten minutes later, Mary had to admit none of Casey's clothes seemed to be missing.

Alison faced them, hands on hips. "Now, then. What *really* happened?"

"Mis' Casey, he never seemed to mind if we cum in or not," Mary began hesitantly. "Specially after da poor dog was killed." She and Josh had been working overtime at the Ocean Beach Club the previous night. They had risen late and when they reached Backgammon, surprised Mellanie Blake in the garden. "She give us some work to do. Burn some rubbish dere, in back."

"What rubbish?"

"Dunno, not rightly. De man give us some papers."

Alison took a deep breath. This was like pulling teeth. "What man?"

Slowly, the full story came out. Lani had been with a "furriner" of such menacing size that Mary and Josh were intimidated. Lani had said she was fetching a change of clothes for Casey, went into the house, then returned with papers for Mary and Josh to burn as rubbish.

"Den de man goes down to da boat. D'Irish Girl, she goes back into the house." Mary imitated the girl's hip-rolling walk.

"What did she go back for?" asked Alison, trying to keep Mary's mind on more important matters than Lani's brazen sexuality.

"Doan't rightly know, mum."

Alison swallowed her exasperation. She went to where the remains of a bonfire smoldered. She sifted the ashes. She pocketed some charred bits of paper. The few decipherable words chilled her blood, though they made little sense. She tried the telephones again. They were dead. She warned Mary and Josh to make sure nobody else came into the house until the police arrived. Her cold fury finally impressed them.

Winston met her at Pretty Penny. They sat with her father on a veranda concealed from the lane and from the sea.

"Casey's definitely with Zia Gabbiya," the sergeant said when she finished. "Your story makes it seem he didn't go willingly."

"Then, bring him back," urged Bracken, peering up from the pad on which he'd been writing.

"Suppose he really is an American agent," said Alison.

"Tosh! Piffle! He's got too much sense!" Bracken consulted his pad, ticked off an item, and turned to Winston. "You promise the police barge for tonight?"

"No question."

"I'll need some of your special constables."

Winston took the list and scanned it. "No problem." The specials were civilian volunteers who put on police uniforms in an emergency. The last emergency had come in 1942. A mailman, clearing a remote postal box, discovered letters addressed to Germany. Crewmen had slipped ashore from a U-boat at night, the skipper correctly gambling on Windfall sleepiness and sportsmanship. The letters were duly forwarded through neutral Lisbon, but the islands stayed on twenty-four-hour alert just for the look of things. "Tonight's the night, then?" asked Winston after a pause.

"If you can get Casey off the *Qurqŭr*," said Alison.

Both men understood the implications. Her father started to say that he was perfectly able— Then he stopped. He wanted no argument about his ability to fly, with or without Casey.

Sergeant Winston coughed. "We don't want to be guilty of conspiracy," he said.

The word hung between them.

"Was Ralph Wigram a traitor for confiding state secrets to Churchill when he was in opposition?" asked Lord Bracken.

Alison laughed. "Wigram was an anguished English patriot—"

"Who helped Churchill conspire to stop the government submitting to Hitler," completed Winston. Alison's laughter broke the tension, but the sergeant still looked grave. "We used to go through channels to inform London of a situation that threatened us, even if the laws weren't yet broken. Those channels are clocked now."

"You don't need to break the law to get Casey," said Alison. "Just say the inquest on Professor Rutgers re-

268

quires Casey's presence as a witness. Yes, I know there's been no inquest called. But it'll give you the excuse to go on board."

"I hate to lie," said the sergeant.

"Then, say the investigation's reopened because of this." Alison drew forth the charred papers rescued from the Backgammon bonfire. "Can you trust the police labs to make an analysis?"

"With the police commissioner away, there isn't a soul in the department I would not trust," Winston said proudly. "But why — ?"

"Some words will show up under the scan. Some I've made out already." Alison carefully cupped the brittle paper. "Words like *deep-tow, seamount, mapping procedures, transponders* — and Professor Rutgers' name repeated over and over."

Edgar P. Geld slept through half that day after spending his first night in the Windfalls since he had built the Rose Hall gazebo-house and conservatory for Amanda. He had passed a portion of the early morning fretting over cable interruptions, aware that his companies and those of Gabbiya were the only ones able to communicate overseas. Finally he had faced the truth: no people in New York, or farther overseas, needed E.P. to tell them what to do. He was not missed. So he gave orders to the local staff that he was not to be disturbed.

He awoke to find disenchantment still weighed upon him. Nobody had ever yet initiated an action that might conceivably disturb him, waking or sleeping. Nobody needed him. Nobody would talk honestly with him. The most humble cog in his multinational machineries contributed more than he did.

He lay in the huge bed and watched the midafternoon sun spill across the high ceiling. He had broken his own taboo about staying here overnight, and now he felt unable to leave. He was deprived of the props that sustained the image of himself as the indispensable tycoon. No bustling secretaries. No faces around a boardroom table to give him importance. No crowded agenda, chauffeured limousines, hasty peregrinations from building to building or city to city. No personal jet, humble customs men standing aside, his own henchmen marching lockstep beside him across the awe-stricken tarmac.

He was just little Edgar, naughtily naked in bed because he'd forgotten to put on his 'jammies.

I must talk to someone about Amanda, he told himself. But who? Great wealth bears a penalty. Prominence spells publicity. And being the scion of America's best-known dynasty means that everything you say can be sold on Grub Street. The most faithful family retainer will spill out memoirs for a suitable sum.

Except Nanny.

Nanny came out of a different age, another tradition. Nobody would ever buy Nanny Locke. She knew Amanda's story; knew E.P. had loved the child from the moment she was born. Nanny knew that when it was clear a medical problem existed, E.P. had worked through intermediaries to scour the world for a solution. Then Zia Gabbiya's commercial empire became entangled with his own. Zia had crept into every nook and cranny of the E.P. empire, but that didn't bother E.P. half as much as the thought that Zia really did know someone who could help Amanda and that Zia might withhold the information if E.P. put a step wrong.

Before Zia, he had vented his rage and frustration on Amanda's mother, employing lawyers to keep the woman out of her daughter's life, producing fake records showing the mother had been treated for venereal diseases, threatening to make public the mother's guilt for the child's tragic flaw. Nanny had known all this, and quietly approved, for hadn't she herself raised little Edgar in defiance of E.P.'s feckless mother?

He got up, dressed, and moved down to the great hall. An unnatural silence prevailed. He had broken precedent. His overnight presence had unnerved the servants.

"Sir." Fat Herman Schroeder approached in a sidling motion that was half swagger, half sycophancy. For a man so large, he had an astounding ability to tie himself into a knot. "Colonel Gabbiya's helicopter is waiting."

"Waiting?"

Schroeder shrank. "It came two hours ago. With a message. From the Colonel. Himself." Schroeder, who had bullied and blustered and never before in his life called anyone sir, swallowed. "Sir? The Colonel expects you."

E.P.'s mouth became a firm line. Any thought of again consulting Gabbiya vanished. The Great Protector could wait. For Nanny.

"Sir?" Schroeder's concern pursued E. P. Geld through the vast vestibule. At the arched exit, E.P. turned. "Has that Arab's pilot been fed?"

"Well, no! I—we—were waiting for you. I—we—

thought it best to confine him to his machine."

"Take him to the servants' quarters and let him forage," said E.P. "I'm going out."

Nanny Locke's Scottish forebears had left her the gift of the second sight. She was expecting her Edgar. Yesterday, he might have been Mr. Geld, but not after last night. She knew he'd been wrestling with his conscience.

"Where is she? asked E.P.

"In the conservatory, where else?" Nanny Locke gazed up at him with firm blue eyes like marble chips.

The circular conservatory, designed to blend with the gazebo, followed the sun like a flower. Amanda sat inside, the most delicate of blooms, enclosed by tinted glass walls, banks of electronic sound systems and color-coded digital records. She had selected something E.P. did not recognize. She was staring out to sea, lost in the music. He came up quietly behind her to read the record notes: *A Mirror of Whitening Light,* by Peter Maxwell Davies, 1977.

He moved nervously to a chair. Amanda turned, acknowledging his presence with an abstract smile. She showed no recollection of her previous shocked reaction.

The sounds of the sea were in the music. A flourish of woodwinds ended the first movement. The calmness of the deep was intoned by a bassoon in a high, sustained C. A warning breeze rippled the waves with stringed glissandos. Whitecaps, small but quick, were evoked by sudden dance rhythms. Then came an ominous moan of wind in which the full orchestra joined.

E.P. was shaken by the growing force of the composition. A solo horn emerged from the echoes and floated high on plainsong: *Veni Sancte Spiritus*. It rose like the Old Man of Hoy, that bleak rock standing sentinel over Scapa Flow, for centuries the haven of the British Home Fleet. The composer had been inspired by Hoy and those cold northern waters. E.P. read this in the record notes, and felt himself sucked into a trough between rising waves as the music paused. The orchestra swelled, and he was borne up to the crest of a giant wave. There he fought for breath in a growing tumble of waters. He seemed to be drowning in a tumult of conflicting currents, of discordance and strife. Life, he thought with unexpected insight, is like this for Amanda. She is oversensitized. Her mind's too perceptive, too quick, to deal with the slow routine, the dissonance of ordinary existence. That's why she has to be held secure against the world's buffeting. That's why she takes refuge in music.

With this renewed sense of having divined something about Amanda justifying her exile, E.P. was briefly at peace. It took a moment to relate his new state of mind with the music: the underlying plainsong had come to the foreground as if sweeping him into the shallows of a receding sea. Death was in the deep silence that followed.

Amanda sat motionless, facing the sea, her face untroubled. He rose, made as if to touch her, then shrank back and tiptoed away.

"How did Amanda come by that disc?" he asked Nanny Locke.

"She hasn't stopped listening to it since it arrived." Still in a confusion of emotions, E.P. at first missed the implication. In his head, the crashing chords of the second movement had started up again. He tried to escape by pushing along the garden path to Nanny Locke's cottage. Incongruously, closed-circuit television cameras permitted Nanny to watch over her ward.

"Turn down the sound," E.P. implored the woman, and collapsed into an old rocking chair. "And would you make me some tea? The way you always liked it. Take your tea with me, Nanny, as in the old days."

Nanny Locke would have preferred a stiff drink at that moment. This was little Edgar peering at her from behind the skirts of Mrs. Geld, Sr. He sat dumb while she boiled a kettle of water. She fussed with the tin of Scottish shortbread she had always kept handy, even in the days of his infancy. She tested the teapot with her elbow and almost dropped E.P.'s cup when he said suddenly, "Why'd you suppose I've never before stayed here more than a day?"

"Business?" she ventured.

He stared up at her. "Come on, Nanny. You don't have to repeat the official line with me. You don't really believe that, do you?"

Nanny Locke sat down heavily. *Crikey!*

"Tell me what you honestly think," she heard E.P. say. She screwed up her eyes and examined the backs of her arthritic hands. Life in this climate was a trial, truth to tell. Back in England, her pension would go a long way. She hadn't much to lose.

"That child's the cause, Master Edgar," she said. "She's like the hunch on a hunchback to you. If other hunchbacks had your money, they'd do what you do, and abandon the hunch on an island far away."

"But, Nanny—"

274

"You do what you can, Master Edgar, by your lights. If any hunchback could take good care of his hunch, he'd put it somewhere safe and nourish and polish it." Nanny Locke's voice trailed away.

"That's a bad analogy," said E.P. "Amanda's not a lump—"

"No, the poor wee soul!" Nanny said with sudden animation. "And there's the truth of it. You can't bear to give her your time, because she's too much like you. That's why you stay away." There, she'd said it.

E.P. stirred his tea. His stomach felt hollow. "Like me? In what possible way is Amanda like me?"

"She's cut off from human contact by a curtain she cannot move. Just as you are."

He laughed uncomfortably. "What a strange fancy, Nanny! A curtain?"

"For Amanda, it's a curtain of iron, bless her heart. Someone else will have to help her pull it aside. But your curtain, you made yourself."

"What with?" E.P. frowned, uncertain if he wanted to hear more, but unable now to stop the conversation.

"Fear," said Nanny Locke. "Some of it you made with fear."

E.P. turned red.

"Greed," said Nanny Locke.

E.P. began to fidget.

"Self-indulgence." She was warming to her task now. "Suspicion. Arrogance. Master Edgar, I warned you against these sins when you were little. Your parents spoiled you. Not with love, but with things rich people shower on their children because they can't give love. You asked, and I'm telling you. You became a self-centered brat."

E.P. put down his cup. Then, because he didn't want Nanny to suppose he was afraid of her opinions, he tried to pick up the teapot. His hand was shaking.

"Let me, sweetie pie," said Nanny Locke, unconsciously reverting to nursery endearments. She was in full control. E.P. watched her pur, and a lot of things came back to him.

"I don't suppose you remember when first I wet-nursed you," said Nanny. "Fed you at my own breast, because your mother was too vain to do it herself."

E.P. could not take his eyes off Nanny's fearsomely upholstered bust as she put her hands around her tea-cup and hunched forward. "You're like little Amanda in that way too. You never growed up. Both of you. She can't help it. Perhaps you can't help it either. But if her curtain is made of iron, yours is gold."

"*Gold?*"

"Yes, Master Edgar. You used to think that was your name, did you know? Edgar Gold. You've been sitting on top of it all these years, afraid you'd be cheated out of it. And now the biggest cheat in the world is taking it all away."

E.P. had no need to ask whom Nanny Locke was talking about.

"That man has been searching and searching," said Nanny Locke. "And now he's found it. The hole in your curtain."

"What makes you say that?"

"This '*Colonel*' Gabbiya is leading you a dance with his tales of a cure for Amanda. A cure? As likely a story as that military title he gives himself, along with all them medals! The Victoria Cross, indeed! My poor dear grandfather would have a fit. A *real* colonel, he

276

was, in a real Highland regiment. *And* he won a real Victoria Cross, which is only given for the highest acts of courage."

"Some specialists have said there *is* a cure, Nanny."

"Aye, and I've heard sometimes there's genius hidden there," she conceded, busying herself with the teapot again.

"When she plays—" E.P. faltered. "She plays beautifully?"

"Oh, yes. Very nice, it is, so I'm told."

E.P. stood up. "Nanny! What makes you say the colonel's leading me a dance?"

"I've seen the doctors come and go."

"What doctors?"

"Those you sent to give her the tests."

E.P. frowned. To provide Gabbiya's unidentified "expert" with medical data, he had authorized some tests. He tried to keep the alarm from his voice. "You never answered my question, Nanny. Where did Amanda get that disc she's been listening to?"

"It came from the so-called colonel."

"I told you never to give Amanda anything without checking first with me!"

"I thought you knew." For the first time, Nanny Locke lost her self-assurance. "The man who brought it went back to the helicopter. He left me the copy of a note he said went to you in the Great House." She began searching her pockets. "Here. You're sure you didn't see it, Master Edgar?"

He scanned the carbon copy of a typed memo to himself: *The first step to recovery! Zia.*

He shook his head. "No, I knew nothing about this." He stared at the old woman. Perhaps he had missed the original message. Certainly the helicopter pilot had not attempted to hide his presence; the man had waited two hours to take him to *Qurqūr*. Perhaps the explanation was perfectly simple. An hour ago, E.P. would have fired half a dozen hirelings for inefficiency. Now he was deeply stirred; first by the music, and then by Nanny Locke's hitherto forgotten wisdoms. "I can't thank you enough, Nanny," he said, and then mistook her expression of surprise. "How can I repay you?"

The old woman recovered quickly. "Go back in there and make that daughter of yours *feel* you love her, Master Edgar. You never did that before. Go on! Give her a kiss and a hug."

He caught the echo of the pretty young nanny who in the old days had urged him, "Now then, Master Edgar, finish up your porridge like a good boy." Faintly astonished at his own obedience, he returned to the conservatory. Could it be the music that so discombobulated him? Amanda was still listening. He stood behind her and slowly lifted his hands to her shoulders. She made no move this time. He leaned gently forward until the long chestnut hair was soft against his face. Again he heard the waves crashing upon that wild shore; again felt himself swept into calm waters.

An hour later, Edgar P. Geld was on his way to see Colonel Gabbiya.

CHAPTER 17

Casey found no way to break the porthole seal. He felt as if Big Vien the Thimble Man had reached out to the *Qurqūr* to booby-trap him again. Vien's other nickname had come naturally to navy prisoners in the Zoo. Thimbleriggers swindled sailors who swarmed ashore with pay to squander. The shell game was one of the Thimble Man's favorite traps. Under what shell or thimble hides the pea? In what Vietnamese cell lies the unknown prisoner?

Casey tried the cabin door again, knowing it would still be locked. He paced back to the head and compulsively washed his hands. In the Zoo, the toilet had been a hole in the ground. You drank only when water dripped from a standing pipe, which wasn't often. Even now, Casey sometimes had to reassure himself that water really did run from shining chromium taps. He checked the mirror over the basin. For years in prison, he hadn't seen his face at all. When Vien's men prepped him for release, he'd almost fainted at his own reflection.

Dum-diddley-dum-dum / dum-dum!

Casey jumped. Shave-and-a-haircut two-bits!

The signal in the Smitty Harris Tap Code meant a fellow prisoner had to communicate.

It was insane! Casey examined his face in the mirror. Clean-shaven. Well fed. No prison pallor.

He opened the doors under the wash basin. The clicks became more audible.

He retreated into the cabin, pushed home the inside bolts of the door already locked from the passageway outside. He returned to the head and crouched by the exposed pipes. The same signal, repeated over and over!

Dum-dum. He tapped the largest pipe with the end of a safety razor supplied by Gabbiya's stewards. "I'm ready."

Dum-dum-dum (C) dum-dum-dum / dum-dum-dum (N) dum-dum / dum-dum-dum-dum (I) dum-dum / dum (F) dum-dum-dum-dum-dum (E). *CNIFE!*

Casey broke into a sweat. The code was engraved on his mind. He could not possibly forget the language he'd used for a decade in prison. But—*CNIFE?*

But of course! The letter C also served as K to reduce the alphabet to the twenty-five letters containable in Smitty Harris' five-by-five grid.

He tapped out the hurried acknowledgement: Dum-dum. The next coded word came back. IN. Again he acknowledged. CLOSET. After his double click, the mysterious sender signed off.

CNIFE IN CLOSET.

He straightened up and looked inside the cabinet above the basin. Nothing. He recalled the curved Vietnamese ring-knife, and stifled disappointment. He knelt down and transmitted: IF U MEAN RING

CNIFE ITS CONFISCATED.

WHO?

ZIA.

There was a pause; the kind of pause that Zoo prisoners had called pregnant. Pregnant with danger. Pregnant with news one did not want to hear. Then came: SCRUDRIVER UND BASIN.

He groped under the basin and felt a slender blade. He maneuvered out, with a sense of overwhelming triumph, a multipurpose screwdriver. He hadn't felt so pleased with himself since his first small victory over Big Vien: the painful assembling of a partial list of the Zoo's prisoners, by way of the Smitty Harris code. It had taken twenty months to put that list together. He had no intention now of wasting even another twenty minutes.

GOT IT / WOT NOW? he tapped out.

WAIT

He waited with growing impatience. Finally he clicked: WHO R U ?

Back came an exasperated WAIT.

Casey put his head against the bulkhead. Two hours had passed since Zia Gabbiya had politely — well, more or less politely — imprisoned him. There'd be serious repercussions if it got out that an American had been held against his will be a leader who sought world respect. Or had the rules been changed? Did the world now only show respect to the cowards who kidnapped, cudgeled and killed Americans? Perhaps Gabbiya was right.

Shave-and-a-haircut two-bits! rapped his unknown signaler.

Hurriedly Casey responded: Dum-dum.

ZIA CUMS. DO NOT RPT NOT KEEP TOOL ON UR PERSON.

Casey thrust the screwdriver back under the basin before he acknowledged. Already someone was banging on the cabin door.

"You always lock yourself *in?*" demanded Zia Gabbiya when Casey opened the door. "That shows a lamentable lack of trust."

"I was caged from the outside," Casey replied calmly. "The trust broke down when your man turned the *outer* lock." His gaze slid past Zia to where the Corsican and another man blocked the passage.

"Read these." Gabbiya tossed a package onto Casey's bunk. "You're authorized by the government of Vietnam to see what went on behind the backs of the poor American fools who fought that war." This was a nastier Gabbiya, not at all the same man who had recounted Arab maritime history while he showed off his ship. Or was this new guise just another magician's trick?

Gabbiya signaled to the third man, and said to Casey: "You will submit to a body search? To restore my trust."

The Corsican moved into the doorway, gun cocked. There was nothing Casey could do. The Zoo had taught him never to pick fights with jailers. He concentrated his mind on the searcher, as he had learned to do before. He told himself: I'll call this bastard Bounty. He's in that class of predators said by Lord Bracken to be the lawful prey of bounty hunters.

Gabbiya's face was black with apparent rage when Bounty finished the body search and reported—nothing. Casey wondered if the Protector could have intercepted the warning from the tapper in the next cabin. "Lucky for you," said Gabbiya with deliberate offensiveness, "that we found nothing hidden up your rear."

Casey stood for a long time after they'd gone, breathing hard. He tried to imagine ramming a two-ton torpedo up the Great Protector's anatomy. A twenty-foot steel shaft with high explosive in its head would be the cleanest, swiftest answer to the question Casey hadn't answered: You will submit to a body search?

He turned to the package on his bunk. It contained photocopied transcripts and messages, most in translation: a record of meetings and exchanges over many years. Familiar names popped up. There was a former director general of French Intelligence, later hired as "adviser" to the Ho Chi Minh government in exchange for southern rubber concessions. There were President Nixon and Henry Kissinger, listed alongside alleged promises of American aid to the tune of billions. There were "cultural figures of influence" in the Marxist jargon: busybody Hollywood celebrities and other travelers, publicity-seeking churchmen, and "useful idiot" traders scouring Asia for any kind of business at any kind of cost. There were former members of the 1956 Indochina Truce Commission: Poles and Indians who had given cover for Communist preparations to drive south from the conceded northern territories around Hanoi. Some of the material in the packet had been clipped to government notepaper from Ho Chi Minh City, the former Saigon, and some bore the imprint of the state-run petroleum agency now housed in the former U.S. embassy where Gabbiya kept his own Paracels head office.

Casey read, standing by his bunk, turning the pages and piling them neatly under the porthole. Big Vien again! Presenting a little more of the big picture. The basic message, boiled down, had always been a simple offer of men's lives for money. Vien still wanted American veterans to believe their buddies could be reclaimed in exchange for billions in interest-free loans, the provision of port-and-highway construction equipment, the underwriting of a new Indochina infrastructure. The demands had been fed through a bewildering variety of channels and rose as Vietnam's economic problems worsened. Suddenly it became clear to Casey what Zia Gabbiya's role had become. The Great Protector's immense wealth and influence would be placed at the disposal of the Communist world's best-armed and most intensively trained guerrilla army *if*—

If what? What was Big Vien trying to tell him? Casey stared at the papers. There was a hidden purpose to this—what did Zia Gabbiya call it?—*disclosure.*

Casey braced himself against the bunk and tried to reason it out. Vietnam was broke, an economic basket case. Gabbiya's Republic of Sahara was richer than West Europe and Canada combined. Vietnam wanted that wealth. What Colonel Gabbiya wanted was Vietnam's experience in jungle warfare to train terrorists.

Yet Vietnam was eager to deal with America, as these papers made clear. So—this must be Big Vien's way of threatening America. Pay up, or Vietnam will further employ its only usable currency, the wealth of expertise distilled from a series of unconventional wars in nearly fifty years of unending conflict.

A currency of violence. To be placed totally at the

service of the King of Terror. A resumption of Vietnam's jungle fighting in the concrete jungles of America? Was that it? Then, why make the setting the Windfalls? Why choose a high-profile villain like Gabbiya?

Casey scooped up the lists of missing Americans. Some had apparently written appeals, to be conveyed through Vietnam's go-betweens.

Interesting that none of those appeals carried the prisoners' signatures!

"You haven't learned, Big Vien!" Casey muttered. The Zoo's boss still underestimated Americans. He'd misjudged them in their cages. He misjudged them now. Not a single American prisoner had actually put his signature to any document purporting to plead with Washington to buy his release!

Casey was gripped by a desperate thirst. He returned to cup his hands under the running tap, and then he heard the tapping again.

He dropped to his knees and gave the clickety-click response. PUT SCRUDRIVER THRU PANEL RITE OF PORTHOLE came the message. Z HITS SAK NOW. GET OUT.

Casey replied: WOT ABT U?

I OK, replied the mysterious tapper, and gave a decisive signoff.

Were they trying to goad him into doing something stupid? Then, if Gabbiya retaliated, it could be described as self-defense. Casey could be shot dead as an unauthorized intruder who threatened the ship's owner. But, thought Casey, I'm only useful to Gabbiya alive. The mysterious tapper—could he be Vietnamese? After all, the Zoo's guards had eventually figured out the tap code.

He thought about the Vietnamese ring-knife. He had been directed first to CNIFE. Now the tapper wanted him to leave the cabin — GET OUT—. Via the porthole? It might be a trap. It even *looked* like a trap.

CNIFE. A memory leaped to mind. Mellanie Blake on the breakwater, raising one hand to sweep back her hair, her hand tight shut, the gesture nervous. On one finger, Casey had glimpsed a jade ring. The ring-knife was designed to be clenched in a woman's fist, only the jade ring on one finger visible. And Lani had been walking away from Rotgut's dead body!

Pieces of the puzzle seemed to be falling into place. *Or was there more than one puzzle?* Casey ran his fingers lightly around the rim of the porthole. Trap or not, he could see no other way to get out with the urgency required by the tapper. He sensed the outline of a panel tailored into the woodwork. He drove the screwdriver under one side of the panel. Nothing happened. He tried another side. And then another. Finally the panel flipped open. At the bottom of the shallow recess was a slot. He probed the slot until he heard a soft click and felt a slight decompression as the seal broke. A thin draft of cold air struck his perspiring face when the brass-bound porthole flew open. The sky outside was dark with an approaching storm.

He put his head out. He should have guessed there would be some quick way to unseal the port. All marine regulations forbade seals on conduits and exits. The *Qurqūr*, putting into foreign berths to refuel, would be subject to inspection. Gabbiya would wish to avoid needless foul-ups with meddling bureaucrats.

The porthole was large enough to allow the passage

of a thin torso. Casey stripped down again and lathered himself with soap. He bundled his clothes into a pillow case strapped with his trouser belt. The cabin was just above sea level. One of several rope ladders dangling from davits was within easy reach. His body slippery with soap, he eased his way through the porthole, reaching for the ratline with one hand. He grasped with the other hand the deadlight suspended above the port for use in rough weather. For a moment he swung from his arms, and then he gained a foothold on the ratline. He retrieved his bundled clothing by pulling on one end of the trouser belt. He tied the clothes to the ladder. He closed the porthole. Deadbolts fell back into place. The port was immovable now from his side. He could not escape back.

The gentle roll of the ship caused the ladder to sway so that his body scraped against the hull. The hull sloped slightly outward, providing just enough friction for him to maneuver. The tapping had come, he was certain, from the adjoining cabin. He was suspended between it and his own. He stretched for the brass deadlight above the second cabin's porthole, and pulled himself into a position where he could see into the cabin. It was illuminated inside, the curtains partly drawn. Casey glimpsed two figures.

He was spreadeagled across the hull, two hands gripping the deadlight, toes curled around a wooden rung of the ladder, his white body standing out against the black hull. He was grateful for the premature twilight caused by the swelling rain clouds. Each time the ship rolled to one side, he had to hang onto the deadlight for dear life. When the ship rolled back, the rest of his body crashed against the hull, knocking the breath out of him. He could have let go, let the rope ladder swing down, and dropped into the water to swim away. But each movement of the ship gave him another tantalizing, fleeting picture of something strange taking place in the second cabin.

The figures were those of a woman and a man. The woman appeared to be scantily clad. The man was pushing her against a bulkhead. The man's head turned, and for a second Casey recognized Bounty's flat features. With the next roll of the ship, Casey swung into a position where he stared directly through the gap in the curtains at the struggling figures. As he swung away again, he was certain he'd seen Mellanie Blake.

The harbor swell must have been rising. Each roll of the *Qurqūr* seemed a little worse than the last. Casey's arms were being wrenched out of their joints. Yet what he was watching—figures in a flip-book—was Lani being assaulted by Bounty. Each time he was snatched from the porthole, the positions inside the cabin changed slightly. A strap on Lani's shift broke. Bounty fell back from her raking fingernails. Lani was on her knees. Bounty dropped. The flip-book pages turned.

Casey felt the ratline jerk violently beneath his feet. Cold metal gripped his bare ankles. He was yanked from his spiderlike position and the ship's hull scraped his chest raw. The force of whatever had taken charge threw him back. His body arced over and came to rest upside down. He twisted, feet seemingly lashed to the ratline above, and got a grip on the last few rungs, his face half submerged in seawater. He craned back and up, and saw his feet manacled to the ladder. He collapsed back again and his mouth and nose filled with seawater. The water thundered in his ears; salt stung his eyes; his sinuses exploded. He wriggled like a fish on a line, knotting muscles, fighting for breath, tensing his stomach for another convulsive effort to raise his head out of the sea.

The rope ladder inched up a little. The blood was pounding in his head but he was breathing air again. He reached for the ropes where they scraped his thighs. He tried to pull himself up. He saw the ladder become rigid, pulled taut by a line disappearing into the sea. Someone shouted, "Breathe deep, Casey! You're being keelhauled!"

His body was jerked tight against the metal plates of the hull. The journey began. It was a journey seamen had feared for generations. It meant being hauled under the ship, from one side to the other. Casey drew himself up into a ball and prayed that Gabbiya would have had the decency to get the ship's bottom scraped.

" 'Fraid I don't know much about aerial torpedoes," apologized Sir Everard Chillingham.

"Oh, c'mon, Chilly!" implored Lord Bracken. "Bloody torps haven't changed all that much since you sailed against the Kaiser."

"What's this, then?" demanded Chilly, bending spindly legs to peer at the scarlet head of a black torpedo sitting in its wooden cradle at Dockyard.

"Duplex Pistol," answered Bracken. "It makes the tin fish explode on contact; or if it runs too deep, explode as it passes under the target ship. It's magnetically activated."

"What about degaussing, then, eh?" Chilly straightened up with a wince of pain, and glanced at the wizened little man watching from a distance. "Don't tell me Gabbiya hasn't thought about *that*, Chief!"

Chief Petty Officer Pony Moore inclined his head. His manner was stiff with disapproval. "Not for me to say, sir."

"Relax, Chiefy," said Bracken. "Sir Everard is here as commodore of the Royal Windfalls Yacht Club, not as chairman of the bank."

"I also served as a boy seaman in the 1914 war," added Chilly. "Finished up a killick."

Pony Moore unbent a trifle. "Once a seaman first class, always a first-class seaman."

"Yes, well." Bracken's sweeping glance took in the cavernous interior of the huge warehouse. Once, it had been the hangar for giant flying boats of the old British Imperial Airways using the Windfalls as a refueling base. The Royal Navy had reactivated the entire complex for World War II. With the decay of empire and the shrinking of the Navy, Dockyard had receded by the 1970s into near oblivion. The Falklands War had briefly restored London's interest, evidenced by the presence of stores Chilly had been astounded to see: projectiles, sidearms and heavier weapons, rockets and ammunition packed in grease, all guarded by CPO Pony Moore, who looked as if he should have been retired long ago. "Can you roll this torpedo down to the barge, Chief? That's the nub of it."

"Reckon," said the chief, signifying assent.

"Weighs a ton or two, I bet," objected Chilly.

"Manual hoist," said the chief.

"Right, then." The commodore advanced upon the

small gray figure. "You're conscripted."

CPO Moore swiveled his head in Bracken's direction. Two thick black eyebrows shot up in interrogation. "Who says?"

"I says." Chilly squared his bony shoulders. "How long you been caretaking Dockyard, Chief?"

"Nigh on twelve years. Officially."

"Your last direct orders from Admiralty—?"

"Official? 'Bout '79."

"Swinging the lead ever since, eh?"

"Guarding stores!" cut in Bracken quickly, before Chilly got the chief's back up. "Jolly fine job he's done too!" He dared not explain to the commodore that the chief's unofficial role was to keep the base shipshape despite the political decision to shut it down. Chiefy Moore, in the Nelson tradition, had turned a blind eye while Bracken helped himself to tools and matériel for the Stringbag. "Chiefy's retired now," he added encouragingly.

"You got Windfalls status yet?" barked Chilly, taking the hint.

"No." A faint note of interest crept into the chief's voice, for he knew the locals were choosy about who "got status" to enjoy full citizenship rights.

"Fix things tonight and I'll see you get it before the year's out."

The chief ran a hand along the smooth back of the torpedo. "None's got status if Gabbiya seizes control."

Bracken again interrupted. "Stores in good order?"

"Aye. In every way ready for sea."

"And that's where she's going." Bracken patted the torpedo's explosive head. "To sea. To sink the enemy."

Pony Moore's face lit up. Then caution reasserted

itself. "Isn't there a simpler way?"

"None. Our target will have considered every possible form of attack, and prepared against it. Except"— Bracken patted the torpedo—"this. Besides which, what delivery systems do you have?"

"None," admitted Chief Moore. "Unless you've got a frogman who could use some limpet mines."

Bracken shook his head. "Anyone who approaches *Qurqūr* underwater will go the way of the Commander Crabbe."

They all understood the reference. Crabbe had volunteered to secretly examine the underside of a new Soviet warship when Nikita Khrushchev visited England. Crabbe's decapitated body was washed up later, mute testimony to the pitiless efficiency of Soviet frogman guards operating from the warship's hidden dive pool.

Pony Moore said, "We never avenged Commander Crabbe. I'm still waiting. Waiting to hear someone speak straight out about *the enemy.*" His wrinkled features became less dour. "I'm tired of weasel words and high falutin diplomatic talk, Lord John. We was a fighting navy once. Old Nelson had it right. 'A man cannot do wrong that lays his ship against the enemy.' Let's do things proper, sir. I bin a navy man forty years. I've seen too many bad situations because a key man said, 'I signed nothing, you can prove nothing.' What I say is 'Get it on paper, get it in writing, get it signed proper,' sir."

Bracken allowed himself a small ray of hope. His big concern had been the chief's respect for regulations. So long as Bracken seemed only involved in restoring an old warplane, the chief had pretended to see nothing.

Now Bracken's plans required the chief's active help. Pony Moore was coming around but still obviously saw Bracken as the cocky young midshipman he'd known long ago. He had served Bracken first as a rigger on a MAC ship, one of the merchant aircraft carriers converted hastily from small mercantile tubs to meet the U-boat challenge when Britain was suddenly left alone in Europe against Hitler, and within an ace of being starved into defeat. He had followed Bracken through all the theaters of war. What he remembered was that Snotty Bracken frequently got in trouble for acting without *written* orders. Written authorization, to Pony Moore, was the one constant in the flux of naval operations. You couldn't get caught out by sudden changes, by erratic superiors, by sea lawyers looking for a scapegoat and twisting your intentions, so long as "you got it in writing, signed proper."

Bracken took a parchment sheet from the envelope he carried. "Righto," he said. "Here's the authorization."

For a moment there was nothing to be heard but the rain drumming on the metal roof high above and the first windy sigh of the gathering storm. In the deepening gloom, Bracken unhooked a maintenance lamp hanging from the torpedo cradle and held it over the sheet.

". . . hereby authorise said vessel, to wit Stringbag (otherwise known as TSR Swordfish RN Registration L 9781) to sally forth as a properly legalised ship of war to take reprisal against hostile forces." Pony Moore slowly spelled out the words. "But it's not signed, Lord John!"

"That's going to be done right now. By Sir Everard."

"Is this the letter of marque?" Chilly cried out. He peered at the parchment in Pony's hand. "I say, it looks jolly impressive."

Bracken thought it wiser to keep to himself Alison's employment of a calligrapher in the law office to inscribe the document and decorate it with suitably impressive seals.

Pony Moore perched half-moon spectacles on his large, bent nose and gave the parchment a second examination. He was remembering that time young Snotty Bracken had signed himself out on a long-range mine-laying operation . . . "Is it legal," he asked, "having Sir Everard sign?"

"In time of emergency, yes!" cried Chilly in alarm. "When the monarch and the monarch's representative were absent, such a commission was in the gift of the colony's chairman of the legislative council, which preceded parliament. As the only member of parliament here present, and as former Speaker of the House . . ."

"Well, so long as it's all proper-like." The chief exchanged a swift and secret smile with Bracken. It said: The old duffer's probably making up the tarradiddle, but we have to have something on the books. "It'll be like old times, Lord John." The chief quoted the old naval air-arm motto: "Find, fix, and strike."

"Ha!" Chilly paused in the task of unscrewing the top from his oldfashioned fountain pen. "Finding Gabbiya may not be that easy. Before I left the club this afternoon, Harbour Radio's schedule of ship movements came in. The *Ultima Thule*'s due to leave tomorrow."

"That's not our problem," said Bracken

"But I think it is." Chilly stared at the sleek torpedo. "Harbour Radio says the name of the ship's commander will be a Colonel Zia Gabbiya."

The yacht club commodore looked like a naughty child who lets off a firecracker in church. Enjoying the stunned expression on Bracken's face, he dropped to his haunches and tested the resistance of the small propellers in the torpedo's tail. "You've only got one of these tin fish," he said. "Don't waste it on the wrong ship."

"What's your suggestion?" asked Bracken in a resigned tone.

"You'd better involve me in more than just signing a letter of marque."

"I knew it!"

"I'll find out more tonight," Chilly continued, unperturbed. "When do I report for duty?"

"Be at Wreck Cay by crack o' dawn," said Bracken. "I'll stick you on the Stringbag's bonnet as my mascot."

Sergeant Winston took the blue marine-police launch out to the *Qurqūr*, armed with a warrant he had himself signed. Flying cloud obscured the harbor headlands, and rain drew a pale mauve curtain across the fading horizon. Lights were coming on where houses stood above the harbor road, and more lights picked out the silhouette of Gabbiya's yacht. At the foot of the gangway, he flourished the warrant, supported by a second document signed by Sir Everard Chillingham in his capacity as a Justice of the Peace. Chilly had used the imposing "Sloped Secretary Hand" of his Elizabethan forebears whose diaries and navigation logs he had lapped up as a boy.

"It's in the matter of an inquest," the sergeant told the yacht's quartermaster. "We'll be requiring the evidence of one of your master's guests, a Mr. Casey."

CHAPTER 18

Casey was dragged down into the sea. He glimpsed a seaman swimming nearby. Then the water closed over him. The light deepened from bottle green to black. Against the pull of the rope ladder, he moved hand over hand until he made contact with the cold steel of the metal cuffs on his ankles. The barnacled ship's bottom gave way to unexpectedly smooth, curved metal. He was hauled, feet first, into the blinding conflagration of the *Qurqūr*'s diving well.

He came up out of the water, twisting on the ropes like a netted mackerel. The ducking had been too abrupt to be a real keel-haul. Even upside down and fighting for breath, he knew he was in the moon pool, amidships. Hands grabbed his shoulders and swung him over the lip of the frogmen's open-mouthed capsule. Figures in black neoprene diving suits set him on his feet and released the manacles. They were laughing, slapping him on the back, shouting words in another language that sounded congratulatory. Through eyes blurred by salt, he saw a foaming bottle of champagne waving in front of him. His first instinct had been to swing at the nearest man. But the nearest man began to take the shape of King Neptune, and suddenly Casey remembered the first time he had crossed the equator on a ship, and the ducking given every rookie.

"Well done, Casey!" Now it was Zia Gabbiya who loomed up in front of him. "You've seen my ship every which way, stem to stern." The Great Protector wore a skindiving suit of blue and orange with red accent stripes. He was laughing. Casey felt his legs turn to rubber. Only his silent rage held him erect. Gabbiya, he thought, you look like a goddam fashion model.

"You had me fooled, Zia!" Casey wiped his face, and found blood on his hands. "In my navy, when we keel-haul, we do a real job of it!" He managed a grin.

Zia shrugged. "Two thousand years ago, our sailors devised a more amusing punishment. Americans, I think, would screech like schoolgirls." He motioned to his men.

Casey braced himself, but the men only began cleaning his wounds. "They're nothing," he said with another show of bravado. "Scratches." He heard the purr of machinery as the plates at the bottom of the moon pool closed tight, and the slurp of water being sucked out. He remembered Rotgut's analysis of Gabbiya as an egomaniac with manic-depressive tendencies who used his own violent swings of mood to release an almost superhuman energy. Casey wasn't so sure. This latest projection of Gabbiya's personality was more like that of a master illusionist, enjoying the fact that his victim was helpless to retaliate.

"I congratulate you on keeping your head," said Gabbiya, and roared with laughter anew. "Figuratively, of course. You also had the presence of mind to keep your clothes." Casey felt what he recognized to be a childish pride that the bundled clothing had remained with him on the ropes. "I will have them dried for you," said Gabbiya, suddenly sober again. It crossed Casey's mind that his encounters with Zia always followed the pattern of the Zoo and Big Vien: geniality, a test of wills, violence, then smiles and sweet talk before the cycle restarted.

Gabbiya tossed him a bathrobe with a kind of locker-room bonhomie, then left. A member of the dive team said in English, "You were not shown the moon pool, m'sieu? Of its type, it is the best." He seemed to have been instructed to show Casey the facilities. Like the tour of the ship, this appeared a deliberate attempt to show Casey everything. If I were intent on sabotage, he thought, I couldn't ask for more information.

"We dive every day," the Frenchman told him. "The Colonel has the pick of North Sea divers. We are of mixed nationality and it pays to practice teamwork." An alarm shrilled. The Frenchman said, "An emergency exercise. We have one each morning and night. It is the turn of the red team." Six men scurried across the duckboards, casting off deck clothing. The moon pool began to flood. To Casey, the scene was one of confusion. Not all the men were within his view at the same time. One by one, suited up, they vanished into the pool. He noted where the water stabilized about three feet below the rim. Above the noise, he heard the Frenchman talking into a mobile phone. "M'sieu, the Colonel wishes me to bring you to him." Casey followed, and wondered why Gabbiya had gone to such lengths to demonstrate his undersea defenses. Was it a case, again, of directing attention away from the real threat?

Gabbiya met him in the stateroom astern. "It would seem your presence is required at an inquest."

Casey saw Sergeant Winston standing at a distance. The sergeant gave no indication of recognizing him.

"I've no idea why the police should think you are here, but—" Zia Gabbiya gestured in a pretense of helplessness.

"Dey say you be da first did see dat professor's body," said Winston.

The sudden relief from tension, the welcome sight of a friendly face, brought Casey to the edge of laughter. Winston's self-mocking patois was hard to swallow. Casey said carefully. "I found a body that I was told later might have been that of an American professor."

"Den, we be needin' you to testify at de inquest."

"I'm ready when you are," said Casey.

"Your clothes, sah?"

"Commander Casey will get his clothes back in a moment," cut in Gabbiya. "We were playing a little joke on him, Sergeant."

"It was no joke," said Casey. "I saw a young woman being attacked in her cabin, Sergeant. You may know her as . . . the Irish Girl."

Gabbiya said very quickly, "Now, that's carrying the joke too far. By the Irish Girl, if you mean Miss Blake, she's not even on board."

Sergeant Winston interrupted. "Dat's a serious allegation. A girl attacked?"

Casey made the mistake, he realized later, of describing then and there what he had seen. It gave Gabbiya time to think.

"I must insist on seeing dis girl," said Sergeant Winston when Casey finished.

"But I told you. Miss Blake went ashore." Zia Gabbiya spread his palms. "She was going to a place I believe is called Rose Hall?"

"Some way I can check dat, dis minute?"

"Why, yes, there is," the Protector said pleasantly. "You can ask the owner, a Mr. E. P. Geld. He used the same launch that took the girl ashore. He got on as she got off. He's here now."

Edgar P. Geld sat, contemplating with a pop-eyed stare the Cretan designs in the mosaic swimming pool on the open deck. He still heard the crashing notes of *A Mirror of Whitening Light*. He wanted to ask Zia Gabbiya by what right had he given Amanda the music disc. Nobody, ever, trespassed on E.P.'s privacy. But he was gagged by fear of offending the one man who claimed to know how Amanda's mind could be unlocked. He blinked back tears and told himself they were entirely chemical, caused by thimerosal in his contact-lens fluid. He had been obliged to send to the local chemist for some unknown brand, the result of his unexpected overnight stay.

He stiffened. A steward behind the wet bar, a sailor by the companionway, two ship's officers at the guardrails, had all suddenly adopted that look of well-bred anxiety common among butlers at the approach of their betters. Two more officers scuttled into view. Behind came the Great Protector.

E. P. Geld remained seated. He gave Gabbiya a curt nod and ignored Casey and the police sergeant.

"I have explained to these gentlemen how our mutual friend" — Gabbiya bestowed upon the glowering Geld a conspiratorial smile — "our *dear* Miss Blake, went ashore with the launch sent to pick you up."

Casey was watching E.P., whose codfish eyes betrayed disbelief. The guard came up again in a flash, but Casey had glimpsed the confusion of a man in crisis.

"That *is* what happened?" prompted Zia Gabbiya.

"Yes," said E. P. Geld

Casey was sure he lied. "The question comes up, Mr. Geld, because I *saw* Miss Blake under physical attack."

"A joke!" Zia waved an arm. "Casey's been the victim of several jokes. Nobody likes to be made to look a fool." He flickered his fingers at Sergeant Winston. "So really — you must go now."

"Dis udder t'ing of d' inquest," said Winston. "I need Mista Casey for dis."

Casey saw the flat features of Bounty appear at the companionway.

"I be proceedin' on h'information received dat d' American professor was killed divin' in da vicinity of dis vessel registered in da name of" — Winston groped for the word — "dis, um, um, um, gen'lman." He jerked his chin at Zia.

"You need not concern yourself in this matter further." Zia gestured. "I am cooperating with your commissioner. A security veto will avoid any diplomatic unpleasantness. My man will show you the gangway."

Bounty came up behind the sergeant. Casey said, "That's the man assaulted the Irish Girl, Sergeant!"

Winston did not bother to turn, although he seemed half the size of Bounty, who was huge and predatory. "Doan't yore man lay finger on me," Winston warned in a lazy drawl.

Bounty rested his large hands on the sergeant's shoulders. Winston reached up, took a firm grip, bent forward, and let out an explosive gasp. Casey, the only bystander who had anticipated something like this, got a blurred impression of the stylized movements which sent Bounty flying over Winston's back and out over the pool.

Everyone looked in horror at Zia Gabbiya as Bounty hit the water in a reverse belly-flop.

"Well done, Sergeant!" said Zia.

Winston appeared to be the only one there who was not surprised by Zia's genial reaction. "He doan't look like he can swim," he said. "Dat man of yore'n."

"Sad," murmured Zia, "but true!" He snapped his fingers for the deckhands to snare Bounty with a lifesaving net. Then he turned his full attention on Winston. "The Republic of Sahara could use you," he said. "From now on, you work for me."

"After d' inquest, if de terms be right."

"No! There can be no inquest. I respect you, Sergeant. I have seen your file. You have a wife and two children. Your sons' education will continue wherever you please. You work for me on terms you decide." Gabbiya signaled for the dripping Bounty to be removed. "For you"—his eyes snapped back to Winston and weighed how big the bribe should be for someone reported to be the soul of honor—"an immediate

303

two hundred thousand American dollars in a Swiss account for your personal expenses."

Winston frowned.

"There would be professional expenses on a weekly basis, of course." Zia Gabbiya watched the other man's face. "Plus living allowances."

Winston rubbed his chin.

"We need more Black Muslims like you."

"I'm not a Black Muslim."

"Religious instruction will be arranged. There will be, naturally, the home of your choice in Sahara, first-class travel for you and the family, a car and chauffeur for your wife."

Winston sighed.

"A title goes with the job. Special Plenipotentiary for Foreign and Security Liaison. It will give you diplomatic status, with many privileges . . ."

Casey could not bring himself to look at the sergeant.

"Your own superiors have betrayed you," said Gabbiya. "You owe them no loyalty. Today you work for three hundred dollars a month. For what? To serve a government that has sold you out."

"You makin' me think, man," said Winston.

"Look at Mr. Geld, here, Sergeant." The creases bracketing Zia's mouth had whitened and stood out like sword cuts in the dark complexion. "He is very, very rich. Would he sacrifice a single red cent for you? Of course not! So why should you live in penury while protecting him? Now, I . . . I have the power to send him away from here. If I say his *household* must leave these islands, he and his household will leave!"

304

Geld turned beet red. "Sergeant, I have a daughter here in need of special care. That's what . . . what the colonel means by *household*."

"Regard the symbol of American wealth and power!" jeered Zia. "His Momma and Poppa did all the hard work and he certainly won't die for what he's got. Does he *deserve* your concern?"

Winston appeared deep in thought.

"Let Suleiman, here, take you below. Yours is thirsty work. Refresh yourself. We have much more to talk about."

Winston allowed himself to be guided out of the group by a suddenly attentive, respectful seaman.

Something in the spectacle tripped a wire in E.P. "You needn't look so self-righteous!" he snarled at Casey. "What's *your* price?"

"American prisoners," said Casey.

Zia's lips moved silently as if coaching Casey.

"Men betrayed by others," said Casey. "So our own government disowns them and says they're dead."

"When the truth is, they're alive in Vietnam," Zia told E.P., sounding like a rug merchant about to close another sale.

"You take this man's word against that of our government?" demanded E.P. What Zia had contemptuously read as cowardice seemed after all to cover an awakening.

"Colonel Gabbiya," Casey responded carelessly, "is nothing. Just a middleman."

Zia would not be provoked this time. He flashed his white teeth and said, "I was to be Casey's target, Mr. Geld. All to please that government he pretends to despise. But my Vietnamese colleagues are clever.

They have known everything since Casey was approached by such a highly secret government agency that now your President has been forced to disband it under public pressure!" Zia was enjoying himself hugely. "The Vietnamese proposed I switch roles with Casey, and make Casey the target. He has no friends now. No Professor Rutgers of the Double-D-C's! Surprised, Casey? But you know nothing is secret in Washington. I have counselors who once were security chiefs to powerful nations. It is all in the spirit of free enterprise! Sell a secret here, get a good price for a comrade there. Profits justify anything. If former CIA directors can be paid by foreign governments, why should I not pick up, say, a former director general of intelligence for the French when they were in Vietnam?"

Casey's face was wooden. He'd seen Tony Rutgers' service records and the original name had been Huguenot French: De Ruetgers. Was that what Zia hoped he'd conclude? That Rotgut was a French agent?

Zia had turned on Geld again. "You're in business. Everything's for sale. The morality of the marketplace is set by the highest bidder. That is your American ethic today. As my Latin friends in South America say: America is a corpse on which the maggots feed. Casey and his friends wasted their lives defending a corpse. But still they believe in their system, and so even Casey will sell. And you, Mr. Geld? A mewling daughter, an idiot child. For that, you sell your soul."

A cry of pain escaped from E.P. He lunged at Zia. Behind him, the Corsican struck out. E.P. twisted as he staggered away, hissing at Casey: *"The Irish Girl . . . I never saw her!"* Then the Corsican got in a second blow, chopping at the juncture of E.P.'s neck and shoulder.

Casey watched, open-mouthed, as Zia's voice arrested the Corsican. More words, in deadly soft Arabic, sent the crewmen scurrying to bring up a lounger on which they laid E.P.'s now suddenly limp form. Casey was certain nobody else had heard E.P.'s last words. *Lani had not left the ship.*

"My guests," said Zia, *"never* get such treatment! I am dishonored."

Casey stifled an urge to ask if keel-hauling was a Sahara social phenomenon, a community nicety like the amputation of limbs from purse snatchers and errant wives, now performed in modern, petrodollar hospitals. E.P.'s disclosure had started a plan forming in Casey's head. Offending Zia was not part of it.

"My man went beyond orders," said Zia, seeing E.P. coming around. "What do you want done with him, Mr. Geld?"

E.P. had a pop-eyed stare. He motioned. "My contact lenses! I've lost one!" He tilted back his head, rolling his eyes. "The other's under the lid, I think."

Zia ordered the Corsican to kneel, and struck him across the back with his gold swagger stick. "I will have him crawl for the missing lens, yes?"

Zia, like Big Vien, was changing his mask to suit the changing occasion, thought Casey. It was time to join the game. "We've too much to lose by quarrels, Mr. Geld," he said. "You and I must find an honorable path between betraying America and expending useless energy."

E.P. dropped his head forward and regarded him with fish-eyed vagueness. The Corsican shuffled around in search of the missing lens.

Zia said, "There is no question of betrayal. Business propositions are on the table. Agree. Or lose a lot."

"I'm pretty resigned to agreement," said Casey.

"Think carefully," warned Zia.

"I have." Casey stretched his legs. "Ten years I've thought, sitting in jail because of Washington's mistakes."

"Treachery is what foot soldiers commit," Zia said encouragingly. "Treachery is never done by those in power, for they decide its definition."

Casey nodded. He was beginning to enjoy himself. In the Zoo, they'd called his kind of crap *bafflegab*. It kept the jailers hopping, in the courteous periods between torture sessions. "A foolish consistency," he said piously, "is the hobgoblin of small minds. A dogged persistence is self-defeating. It prevents our going after targets of opportunity."

"Targets—?" Zia clapped his hands. "My very theory! The best scientists never follow a dogged path. The best science is done by those who break away to pursue a target of opportunity, some unexpected alley of research that opens up when least expected."

"You are a scientist, I'm told," said Casey, glad to have nudged Zia's mercurial mind in another useful direction. "As distinguished in underwater exploration as your illustrious ancestor, Ahmad the great navigator."

Zia came up to the bait with the glitter and dash of a prize trout. "That is true."

"And your excellent sources have told you how IN-SPAD demonstrated the theory you mention."

Zia preened himself. "INSPAD's work is well known to us."

Casey had to think quickly. Someone had been feeding Zia's and Vietnam's spies a rich line. He must be careful not to invent a story Zia would regard as palpably untrue. He said, "Dolphin sonar produces an underwater substitute for all-round vision." He was staring into Zia's eyes. There was no flicker of denial. "The new arrays on deep-tow submersibles, working more than three miles down, were the result of a young oceanographer forgetting his lab work to chase after an idea." It was about as far as Casey dared to go. He shifted onto another tack; one that Big Vien had certainly never been able to resist. "The young scientist has a philosophical nature and rebels against authority. I fully approve—"

Now Zia could not contain himself. "Are you a Catholic, Casey?"

It was a question Big Vien had often used in the Zoo to trap the unwary. The Communists believed a Catholic's actions were influenced by authority. A Presbyterian, they said, acted according to conscience. Once they'd categorized a prisoner, they felt able to manipulate him.

Casey sidestepped. "I've always wished I understood Islamic beliefs better."

E. P. Geld had retrieved the lens under one eyelid and was bent forward in his chair, helping look for the other. He twisted his head and said unexpectedly, *"It's a question of raising your mind above base mercantile and utilitarian needs of commerce!"*

Casey's pulse quickened. This was help from an erudite quarter. He pretended bafflement. "Are those the words of the Prophet?"

E.P. straightened. "A different kind of prophet. Conan Doyle. He wanted to drill into Mother Earth's skin, *beneath the sea.*"

"How is this?" demanded Zia. "You speak about the creator of Sherlock Holmes!"

"Who was a scientist ahead of his time," improvised Casey. The trick was to keep needling Zia's curiosity without taking away the flattering implication that he was intellectually equipped to debate higher philosophies. It had worked with Big Vien.

"He saw Mother Earth as a living organism," put in E.P., who was drawing on stories Nanny Locke had introduced him to long ago in the nursery. "He thought Mother Earth needed to be reminded there were human beings living on her skin. His heroes drilled holes into that skin to catch her attention."

"Which led him to foreshadow drilling for oil under the sea," added Casey. "But of course you're familiar with his book, Zia. *When the World Screamed.* It suggested the greatest of human aspirations was 'to know what we are, why we are, where we are.' "

"*To know what we are!*" Zia's eyes glistened.

The Corsican, on hands and knees, gave a loud grunt of triumph and carefully picked up the missing contact lens. Zia murmured. "*To explore!* An honorable ambition. It is why I need INSPAD—"

E.P. examined the restored contact. Casey thought, E.P.'s not quite the vulgar tycoon of legend, after all!

Zia said, "We must have more philosophical discussions," and stood as a crew member approached Ca-

310

sey with his clothes freshly laundered.

"You want to explore an INSPAD agreement?" Casey took the clothes. "We can talk now—"

"Not so fast!" Zia smiled. "Both of you go, think some more, then return with more convincing arguments . . ."

Casey pretended annoyance, but he'd expected this. He'd observed the technique in the Zoo. The victim was ground down until ready to convert. Then he was told conversion meant nothing unless reached through self-study, not coercion.

"Your agreement comes too readily," Zia was saying. "You must persuade me you really mean it." He picked up his swagger stick with an air of polite withdrawal.

Casey smiled inwardly. He'd never met a zealot yet who didn't think decadent Americans could be broken this way. Zia was becoming as self-destructively arrogant as the rest. Surprisingly, it had been E. P. Geld, looking a perfect idiot as he revolved his head to restore the contact into position, who had helped Casey maneuver the Great Protector into this unbalanced position. When it came to manufacturing distraction, E.P. was no mean magician himself.

Back on the water, it was dark. E.P. had shrewdly requested a *Qurqūr* launch instead of the helicopter. Zia could hardly refuse after claiming E.P. had come out by boat.

"You heard what I said about never seeing Lani?" muttered E.P. as they boarded the launch.

"Yes."

311

"Did Zia hear too?"

"I'm sure he didn't." Casey moved along the rail until they were concealed by the cabin structure. "I'm going back to look for the girl. Could you reach my partner without using Windfalls' communications?"

"Give me his name and details."

Casey did so, and squeezed the other man's arm in gratitude. The throb of the diesel rose. The launch surged forward. Casey went over the side with the next roll of the launch, his movements lost in the glitter from the rising bow wave.

E.P. tightened his grip on the grab rail. Something profound had happened. He wasn't sure what it was. He hated Gabbiya. He loved his daughter. Somewhere between those extremes, he had learned this much: It must have been more than fear of losing his reputation that made him keep Amanda in the Windfalls. He began to allow himself a small indulgence of hope. Perhaps he really wasn't the rat he'd always denied he was.

CHAPTER 19

By nightfall, Lord John had seen the police barge loaded. The crew of volunteers rounded up by Alison sailed from Dockyard with a cargo of propulsion rockets, old navy flares, kerosene lanterns and fuel, and deadly devices dominated by the sleek black-and-red torpedo.

The barge was navigated by Alison. Constable Mello nursed the ancient diesel bolted to the stern. His partner, Sam Oysterman, balanced against a portable derrick to keep it from swinging against the commodore of the yacht club. Chilly Chillingham was quietly relishing the prospect, after so many years glued to his chairman's chair at the bank, of a Real Adventure. The butcher of Nelson's Harbour, Tiddley Ridley, crouched forward, looking for rocks. The barge drew less than three feet. Water lapped over the blunt bow and soaked Ridley's bared legs. Oyez Lem, advertised abroad as the honeymooner's coachman and town crier, was for once sober and squatted before the torpedo's scarlet fore section to prevent any sudden movement in the event of a grounding.

Chief Pony Moore hunched over the torpedo's tail fin and mourned the time when an operation like this would have mobilized the fleet. Even American and French revolutionaries merited a gunboat and a sloop here. Those had been the glory days, when Britain looked ahead to making the Windfalls the Gibraltar of the West. Now the man Chief Moore regarded as the greatest evil of all time could only be tackled by a girl and a few men chugging at three knots over water smooth as a millpond. It needed to be smooth. One sneeze would upset the whole kit and caboodle.

They had crossed Great Sound when Bracken said just loud enough to be heard: "Wreck Cay coming up. Gravediggers, stand by."

Two more men rose from the shadow of the wheelhouse: Deacon Thomas, from the Anglican cathedral at Nelson's Harbour, was of Welsh mining stock. Fellow gravedigger Jamaica Tipoo was descended from runaway slaves. Each carried a big shovel from the cathedral's cemetery, ready to do the night's donkey work.

"Reduce power!" Bracken ordered Constable Mello.

The barge wallowed in the slight swell. Alison let the current sweep them between the reef's outcrops, toward the old ropemaker's wharf. "Us that are Moon's men," quoted Chillingham, "our fortune doth ebb and flow."

The barge ground against the broken stone wall.

"Moon men?" John Bracken loosened up as Mello cut the engine and Deacon Thomas with Jamaica Tipoo slipped into the shallow water. "Shakespeare was writing of *thieves* . . ."

"I was thinking of moonrakers," said Chilly, raising his eyes at the gibbous moon. The remark, clear in the sudden quiet, drew chuckles. All knew the local

314

folklore. Moonrakers had been those islanders who smuggled liquor into America during prohibition. Surprised by the U.S. excise men while raking coastal shallows for submerged kegs of smuggled whiskey, they professed to be simpletons raking the calm waters to capture the moon reflected there.

The confident mood was shattered by the growl of a powerboat. Bracken saw the danger and ran to help the two men guiding the barge to windward of the wharf. With a muttered curse, he jumped into the water and called for Jamaica Tipoo to throw him a line.

A vessel showing no lights pounded through the sound. The men in the water worked feverishly to secure the barge. The intruder's wash came grumbling along the shore. The wash was long and heavy, lifting the barge so that it crashed against the stones. Bracken yelled out in pain. The barge receded, and Mello and Oysterman hauled him back aboard.

"Careless bastard!" Bracken sprawled by the wheelhouse, trying to stanch blood from his leg.

"Not *careless*, look you!" warned Deacon Thomas. "He's coming round again." Both men splashed out of the dangerous gap, back to where they had worked before, on barge lines fore and aft.

"If he keeps circling, he'll stop us unloading," shouted Bracken.

The barge rolled heavily as the powerboat's wash again lashed the shoreline.

"Can we stop him?" asked Chilly. "We don't have guns."

"Rockets!" said Chief Petty Officer Moore.

"I've a better idea." Alison winced, hearing the

barge plates grind against granite. "We want to keep things legal. Surely you haven't forgotten how Wreck Cay got its name?"

Casey stood once more on the the *Qurqūr*, this time not at the owner's invitation. The ship was fully illuminated. Zia Gabbiya was not a man to hide his light under a bushel.

Casey had shinned up a rope ladder after diving off the launch. How E. P. Geld would explain his disappearance was of no concern. What mattered was that the tycoon had finally remembered he was also an American.

Now to find Mellanie Blake. She was the key.

A bosun's whistle sounded. Casey hid between life rafts as feet padded along the deck. The stern was suddenly bathed in more light. Casey heard the whine of winches. A drum of cable facing him began to turn. He felt the crew's attention focus astern, and he took the opportunity to dodge down a companionway.

He blessed Zia for the earlier guided tour, and headed for the cabin where he had been held. The next cabin forward was where he had glimpsed Lani being assaulted by Bounty. The door was open. He slipped inside and moved to the porthole. Through the loosely drawn curtains, he saw one of the *Qurqūr*'s launches drawing away.

A body in the bunk stirred. If this was the Irish Girl, she could hardly be here against her will. Both door and porthole was open. Casey froze.

The body rolled over. A face glistened in the dim light.

"Lani?" whispered Casey."

"Ye gods!" Casey jumped. "Sergeant Winston?"

"In person." White teeth gleamed. "Sorry about all that 'ole black Joe' vernacular. Topside, it seemed the best way"—Winston's words slurred—"to get by the great Lord Protector. As one of da Lawd's black chillun." He tried to swing his legs over the side, groaned, and grabbed his head. "Mercy! I don't know what went into the beer they gave me. It sure wasn't hops."

"You didn't take on the new job?"

"I fancied myself as Special Pleni—Plenipotentiary-airy for Foreign Liaisons. But on mature reflection, I'd still rather be the detective sergeant who turns somer— Aaah!" Winston caught his breath. "Turns somersaults for Windfall tourists, and not for the Lord Almighty on the upper deck."

"Where's Lani? The Irish Girl?"

"Last I saw, she was hustled out of here, hands tied."

"She *was* here, then!"

"Tied to this bunk."

"They put you together?"

Winston cranked out a laugh. "That's funnier than you think." He tried to stand and failed.

"Get back in the bunk," Casey ordered.

Winston climbed back and collapsed. "Lani was bound and gagged when I was put here. She was . . . naked. I reckon Zia was testing. See if I was made of the right stuff." Winston sounded like a man having a tooth yanked out. "The right stuff being, like, I'd rape her."

* * *

Winston had not been surprised to find Lani in the cabin. He never had believed that she'd gone ashore.

As soon as he was alone with her, he went to work on the ropes. The gag had been easily removed. She hissed, "Come closer."

She was tied upright, and looked like a blackbird nailed to a barn door, legs spread wide. He thought she was going to tell him where there was some means of cutting her bonds. What she did tell him was "Rape me!"

He thought he'd misheard. He had been given beer and sandwiches in the galley, and the beer left him feeling unusually woozy. He put an ear to her mouth. She said, "Cover me. I've killed the audio bugs, but they can still *see* us."

He was totally adrift. Her eyes blazed at his stupidity. "Rutgers!" she hissed. "I worked with him!"

He turned instinctively to the door.

"They'll leave us alone." Lani indicated with her chin the upper corners of the cabin. "They'll watch."

That sent a cold chill through poor Winston. He was happily married. The thought of hidden videotape cameras recording even his mimicry had made him almost faint.

"Fondle me, for Christ's sake!" Lani sounded as if she was ready to scream, and Winston had hurriedly positioned himself so that the cameras could only see his back and motions. He felt light-headed.

"Zia likes a cheap thrill," whispered Lani. "Get excited. Get your damned clothes off!"

Winston had tried to focus his eyes. If he was aroused, he'd want to free the girl's hands, wouldn't he? He worked at the ropes with his teeth. His head

318

was spinning, but not with excitement.

"I can get out." Lani's words were a controlled scream of frustration. "Don't you see? Zia wants you to *fail!*" One of her freed hands began tugging at the zipper on his pants.

He felt her grope between his legs. The beer had dulled his senses. He resisted her movements and she said impatiently, "You *must* help! Zia's sending me to the *Ultima Thule*. To plant the Vietnam flag on a seamount. *That's* the whole objective. Hanoi's takeover . . ."

She was tearing at his trouser belt. His natural modesty, his fidelity to his wife, his fear of being set up, all conspired to drive him away from her. But if she was speaking the truth . . . ? He dropped his pants. He was limp as a rag. That was what Peeping Tom Zia wanted, wasn't it? The pleasure of seeing a black man incapable of rising to the occasion?

And all the time, Lani kept talking in a soft, controlled voice.

"Man!" Winston stared up into Casey's twitching face. "That was some ordeal!"

"Shocking! You'll look back someday and find it . . . ah, kind of funny, too."

"Not if I look back at tapes. And what if Zia tries blackmail?"

"I think Zia's gone."

"So that's why they took the girl. To the *Ultima Thule* with Zia!" Fresh hammers beat inside Winston's head. "I need to get out. A swim will clear my head."

"You'd sink like a stone. You were probably slipped

319

several mickey finns. Maybe with Spanish fly to make you horny. Zia would love that, the depressant working against the accelerator. If you leave now, you'll be asleep before you hit the water."

"What if I stay?"

"Keep off the grog!"

"Funneeee! How'd make mysel' useful?" Winston's tongue felt too big for his mouth again. He hardly cared if he sank into the sea or into oblivion.

Casey shook him. "Sleep things off. Then get out. I'll do what I can to help you, but if things get screwed up—you know the name Bingo Harriman?" He smiled at Winston's mumbled assent. Of course the detective-sergeant had made it his business to know. "Can you warn him? Without going through commerical cable or phones?"

Winston muttered "Harbour Radio" and then jerked himself up onto one elbow. "Mus' get Lor' John!" He grunted with pain. "Mus' act. But. Not. Against." His head fell back.

"Against what? urged Casey. He slapped the sergeant's cheeks.

"You'll findem. Lor' John's crew. Wreck Cay."

And that was all.

Casey swam easy, drifting with the current astern of the ship. Harbor lights shimmered. The pull of the tide was strong. A few figures were silhouetted at the *Qurqūr's* stern rail. A subtle alteration in their stance suggested he'd been right: the owner was no longer on board.

He was not sorry when darkness swallowed up the

320

ship. His eyes had been on black holes in the ship's hull marking where garbage came down the galley chutes. Rotten food discharged from ships in harbor drew sharks. Casey felt more comfortable if he could see nothing to remind him of the fact.

He was indistinguishable from flotsam, carried in a great arc which would bring him to the dinghy club, favored by those who enjoyed mucking about in boats. He selected one with a light Seagull motor and a jerrican of gas, and hauled himself over the gunwale. The flywheel spun at the first tug. He pulled up the light anchor astern, slipped the buoy line, and headed out again, expecting some irate owner to howl and dance a jig of outrage. He needn't have worried. The boat belonged to Oyez Lem, but taped under its thwarts were rubber condoms stuffed with marijuana.

How could Lani have "worked with Rutgers"? The whole episode with Sergeant Winston could be another con. If she knew about Lord Bracken's cockeyed Stringbag schemes, maybe she was misdirecting attention to the *Ultima Thule* for reasons best known to Zia Gabbiya. Yet, why *invent* that mysterious mention of a seamount and planting the Hanoi flag?

Casey crouched in the powered dinghy, debating with himself. The Irish Girl could be lying. She had used the Smitty Harris Tap Code, but she could have learned it from the Zoo's Communist masters as readily as from Rotgut. That scene when Bounty assaulted Lani now seemed like a rehearsal for what had happened to poor Winston. Its purpose might have been to distract Casey's attention, or mislead him. Lani must have been under Zia's control when she tapped out the instructions for Casey to escape from the cabin. Zia's men had been ready for the mock keelhauling, after all.

Casey's feet were cold in the water swilling around the bottom of the dinghy. He was running the Seagull at full bore, but you can only get so much out of a 2½-horsepower outboard. He knew the marker buoys and marine lights; and there was the hunchbacked moon, as well, by which to navigate to Wreck Cay. He had time to juggle the puzzle.

Torpedo the *Ultima Thule?* If Lani was still Zia's agent, then there had to be some reason for steering Lord John Bracken onto that target. An international incident? Casey's hand tightened on the throttle. In that case, Lord John should be aiming his torpedo at the *Qurqūr*.

But — Zia had gone to such great pains to show Casey over the *Qurqūr*. To misdirect any saboteurs Casey might have up his sleeve?

Was the Protector cooking up real mischief on the *Ultima Thule?* Or playing the tricks he found irresistible, creating illusions, crooking a finger here to draw the eye away from what was really happening over there?

Lani had passed on a lot of information in that deceptive encounter with Winston. It should be possible to check some of it out. Mostly it concerned the *Ultima Thule*.

What Casey remembered about *Ultima Thule* was Virgil's *Tibi serviat Ultima Thule:* the last extremity.

Lani said the research ship of that name had served in U.S. geophysical surveys of the 1970s. Well, that made sense. It was a period when the inner space of deep ocean was thought to conceal huge mineral wealth. Excitement had died down when the nuggets were found to be not so readily recoverable from the seafloor. The *Ultima Thule* had become a maid-of-all-work research vessel, transferred from Trident Marine, of Fort Lauderdale, Florida, to the Texas-based Multi-Search Group in 1981. She carried a USCG Certificate of Shipping, was classed +A1 (E) by the American Bureau of Shipping, and flew the U.S. flag. After that, her movements became more obscure. Several U.S. universities used her as a floating laboratory, at least according to records. Lani said the universities could not substantiate this. Latterly, a parent company was traced back to Falconseek (Windfalls), a subsidiary of Mercantile Enterprises of Liechtenstein, established originally by the old French Bank of Indochina.

The Irish Girl had displayed professional skill in encapsulating that information. Indeed, she had shown the skill of a Rotgut protégée. But Rotgut's department in Washington had been liquidated by presidential order.

Perhaps that order had been a blind. *Perhaps* the department was continuing its covert activities. Or . . . perhaps the remnants of the department were carrying on, without the knowledge or approval of the higher-ups. If there was some sort of CIA rogue elephant charging around, Zia Gabbiya would certainly seize the opportunity to feed it false targets and precipitate a major crisis.

In which case, Zia would use Lani.

Casey was back full circle. He seemed to spin inside

a tiny radius of speculation, like . . . like the spinning flywheel that was the Seagull's only visible moving part as it thrust the dinghy forward.

He was navigating now by the automatic flashing light on the southern tip of Wreck Cay. It stopped flashing. He throttled down, sensing danger. The ancients, he remembered, had equated *Ultima Thule* with ultimate darkness. Then the black night was swallowed up in an enormous orange blaze of light. All Casey could think about for a moment was his schoolboy Latin and the double meaning of Virgil's ultimate extremity: world's end.

CHAPTER 20

The moment the intruding powerboat struck the reefs, Alison dowsed the lantern. The waters split open to release a flood of light. She glimpsed figures flying end over end, and she plunged back into the sea from her perch on the rock with no more hesitation than she felt about luring the boat to disaster. The urgent work of unloading the barge had been delayed for Wreck Cay's traditional welcome to strangers. Now that same tradition demanded she try to rescue survivors. She swam to where debris still burned, and heard the boiling-kettle rattle of a small and finicky outboard.

Casey, in his Seagull-driven dinghy, reached her as the last flames died on the water. Together they fished for the wrecked boat's crew.

On the wharf, Bracken's men spared little time worrying about the sunken boat. It had been making yet another circuit of the cay, treacherously jeopardizing the precious cargo overcrowding the barge's open deck, when Alison had severed the cable to the southern navigation light and waved in its place the old navy lamp.

"The wreckers of the last century or two would have been proud of her," gasped old Chillingham. "We've burned our boats now!"

"Bridges," said Bracken, tightening the slings under the torpedo. "It's bridges you burn behind you."

"It's bloody boats tonight," gloated Chilly. He was enjoying this excursion into piracy all the more because Alison had shown him there was a legal precedent: the War of 1812, when an American warship was lured to catastrophe by false beacons. It established, at least to his Windfall mind, a right "to secure the islands in such manner against hostile forces." Chilly's one memory of high adventure had been also unhampered by legalities: the Battle of Jutland. He wasn't sure if the British or the German Navy had won that clash of titans, but he still felt the joy of being a boy on a burning deck. Now it was someone else's deck that burned.

Oyez Lem summarized the general indifference to the enemy's fate. "Dey try sink us, dey deserve to git sunk." His opinion was held to be fairly balanced, for hadn't his great-grandfather sold gunpowder to General Washington while helping capture American ships during the Revolution? Unfortunately, Constable Mello then dropped into the dinghy that Casey brought alongside the barge. Mello recognized it as Oyez Lem's boat, normally moored at the dinghy club, and automatically ran his hand under each thwart. "Aha! Ganja!" he withdrew one sausagelike object after another.

Oyez Lem let out a cry of anguish.

"Doan't push yer luck," Mello advised him. "Keep yer mouth shut and dese men will take da rap." He pointed at two bodies in the bottom of Oyez's requisitioned dinghy.

Alison's voice sounded unnaturally loud. She was perched beside Casey. "Actually," she said, "there's only one man. The other's the Irish Girl."

John Bracken's first outraged impression was that Casey had been part of the troublemaking launch crew. Casey had to interrupt the bellowing by yelling louder: "We've got the man who killed the governor!"

That stopped Bracken cold. Someone shone a light into the dinghy. Buddha, the Vietnamese, sat shivering, knees drawn up to chin. Lani stared back defiantly.

"I just escaped from the *Qurqŭr*," said Casey. "I stole this boat to get here. The explosion happened right in front of me. The first one I saw was Alison."

With Alison, he had finally discovered Lani and Buddha, balanced on a submerged canopy of coral far from shore. Both had been blown clear of the launch.

"What the devil were you doing?" Bracken asked Lani. He was nursing his leg and had propped himself up against the wheelhouse. "Who told your boss we'd be here?"

"*I* told Zia Gabbiya," Lani replied calmly.

The flat statement arrested Casey in the act of leaving the dinghy. Bracken searched through the tangle of his beard. "Does anyone have a flask?" asked Lani, looking into the men's cold faces. The moon flooded the scene in a pale glow under a clearing sky. Buddha still lay in the dinghy, bleeding from a wound in the head. Everyone had heard Casey call him the governor's killer, and none seemed in a hurry to help him. Bracken yanked out a flat hip flask. "Here, Miss

Blake. Navy rum."

She tilted back her head and her long black hair cascaded over her shoulders and shimmered wetly in the eerie light. "Thanks." She wiped her mouth with the back of her hand. "There was no other way I could get off the *Ultima Thule.* That's where Colonel Gabbiya is now. I told him you'd be here. It was my only hope of getting away with him." She pointed to Buddha.

"Hey, Casey!" Bracken called over to where Casey remained standing in the rocking dinghy, his hands braced on the edge of the wharf and just his face showing. "Was Gabbiya on the *Qurqūr* when you escaped?"

"No," Casey began. Then he stopped. Let Lani tell her story first; and he'd judge how it stacked up against what Sergeant Wilson had already given him. "Miss Blake, did you deliberately put everyone in danger here?"

"*You* put *me* at risk," retorted Lani. "Colonel Gabbiya's always known about Wreck Cay. This man with me—"

"Buddha?"

"If that's what you want to call him . . . He reported an airplane burned here. From his account, it seemed obvious Casey set fire to it. That forced Gabbiya to reconsider, and fouled me up totally." Her voice rose slightly. "Don't strike at the *Qurqūr!* It's a booby trap!" She bent down until her face was level with Bracken. "I'll explain. But not in front of people I don't know."

Bracken heaved a great sigh. "Over here's Sir Everard Chillingham. You *must* know him—"

Lani gestured at the other listening men. They caught the tone, if not the whispered words, and began

328

to resume their tasks.

"That's it, boys!" called out Bracken. "We have a schedule to keep."

"Now hear me out," pleaded Lani.

"Go ahead. You already know my daughter, and Mr. Casey."

Lani acknowledged them. Casey kept his eyes fastened on her face, the light from a lantern catching it at odd angles. He would have liked to believe her, but he had large reservations.

Her first words were lost in the rattle of chains as Chief Moore began the task of transferring the torpedo. "We were on the research ship," said Lani, "when Gabbiya radioed the *Qurqūr* to dispatch an ACT team here. That's like in Action-Covert Team, right? They're frogmen trained in sabotage. I said it would take too long for them to get their act together. He thought that funny. He knows the divers are prima donnas and would have gone on a toot the second he turned his back. So he put . . . Buddha, as you call him, in charge of a powerboat to bring me here for backup." She caught the skepticism in their silence, and added, "I'm *very* well trained in undersea demolition."

"It was your bloody great wash nearly did for us," growled Bracken.

"Not mine. The first time we came round the island, I tried to dive over the side. He—Buddha—caught me." She turned sideways to the dancing light, raised her hair from the side of her face and neck. For the first time, they saw what appeared to be bruises and oozing blood.

"My dear girl!" exclaimed Chilly. "Let me get the

329

first-aid kit."

"When does this ACT bunch get here?" demanded Bracken.

"Not before dawn," Lani promised. "The divers went ashore on the spree. Our patrols will be beating the bars for them now. When they do arrive, look out! They've got a new, waterproof blowpipe missile."

She stopped while Chilly began to swab an area of matted hair just above the jawline. Bracken, sitting with his back against the wheelhouse, shifted his good leg impatiently. "That's fine," Lani said quickly to Chillingham, and gently pushed him aside. "Lord Bracken! You must believe what I'm telling you. Not for my sake." She swayed as if she was about to faint. "For the sake of Admiral Dalrymple. *Downwind* Dalrymple!"

Bracken's head came up with a jerk. Alison suppressed a gasp of surprise. Dalrymple's name meant nothing to Casey and Sir Everard Chillingham; but both men heard the curious softening of Bracken's voice as he said, "What is it you want me to do, Miss Blake?"

"Sink the *Ultima Thule.*"

"I've no idea where to find her."

"I have."

"Pray tell," said Bracken, struggling to his feet.

Lani retreated astern of the wheelhouse. Perhaps it was only Casey who saw she thus placed herself within earshot of Buddha, lying neglected at the bottom of the dinghy. But Casey would have been first to admit he was seeing more than most in this situation. His mind crawled with suspicion. The Irish Girl was Zia's whore, and also a procuress: the procuress of legend.

330

"There is always a good deal of *charlatanism* in procuring intelligence," the Duke of Wellington was reputed to have once said. Was that Lani's role: to serve the charlatans, to procure, to get the best of all worlds for her personal advantage?

". . . with the task of exploring six hundred miles of a complex undersea drainage system," Lani was saying. "That's the plan filed with Windfalls shipping control. Nothing odd in that. The *Ultima Thule*'s role is scientific research. She will begin combing an amphitheater basin some twelve thousand feet down in about"—she leaned forward and took Bracken by the wrist in a gesture that seemed strangely intimate; she looked at the glowing dials of his wristwatch—"in about nine hours from now, starting at Black Rock."

"Black Rock!" Bracken made some hasty calculations. "That's at least two hours' flying time from here, in the Stringbag."

"*Combing an amphitheater?*" Sir Everard Chillingham's voice quavered. "Oh dear, I feel so dreadfully out of date. What does it *mean?*"

"Zia Gabbiya's partners will be towing an unnamed submersible," said Lani. "Mapping the sea bottom, as advertised. Not breaking any laws, even if it were broadcast across America that their worst enemy was exploring their submerged coastline. But the probe is not for Zia. It's for Hanoi—" Her last words ended in a muffled scream as the Vietnamese rose from the dinghy and hit her across the back of the legs so that she toppled sideways. Casey caught her, Alison sprang in Buddha's direction. Out of the darkness shot the cannonball shape of Oyez Lem, who slammed into the Vietnamese and bore him down toward the water.

Buddha's skull struck the Seagull's metal flywheel with a crack like a snapping branch, and his body began to slide over the dinghy's stern. Oyez Lem scrambled out of the bottom of the boat, shook his head once, and eased the rest of the Vietnamese into the sea. The body floated face down, and Oyez gave it a shove with an oar. "Dat's anudder," he said happily, "with no more go-to."

The only sounds now were the sharp clink of axes where the gravediggers cleared bush along the ropewalk. Constable Mello, who had returned moments earlier with Oyez to jury-rig a second derrick, ostentatiously turned his back and got on with improvising a gantline for raising one end of the torpedo. The task lasted long enough for Buddha's dead body to be caught in the tidal currents and swept swiftly away.

"Right, chaps!" said Lord John Bracken. "We've less time than I thought to arm and fuel the Stringbag."

But Casey had other ideas.

It seemed altogether too fortuitous, the way Buddha had given credibility to Lani's story by striking at her. Sure, the Vietnamese had paid for it with his life, but that was the luck of the game. The way Lani stumbled had not convinced Casey that the Irish Girl had been in any real danger; when he caught her, she was well balanced and was twisting her body as if to turn the fall into a dive from the wharfside. The interruption had enabled her to break off at a dramatic moment without really proving her case. She had also stampeded Bracken.

There was no way to halt the action. And maybe

this was what Lani, for Zia, wanted.

The torpedo came up the ropewalk into the light of kerosene flares, dipping and rising on the iron wheels of a navy dolly, hauled by men stripped to the waist in the night's oppressive heat.

Casey had never paid serious attention to aerial torpedoes. They were not a fighter pilot's chief concern. You might encounter them in a carrier's hangar, below decks. You learned their characteristics in order to understand the limitations they imposed upon any torpedo bombers you might have to escort to the target ships. But he had not confronted one, so to speak, outside its habitat. This one crept up the avenue of twisted trees and heavy-scented tropic flowers with a writhing motion imparted by the dolly's unsteady platform. The sleek cylinder was as wide as Oyez Lem, who had one arm thrown across the red fore section to keep it pointing in the direction of the Stringbag waiting to receive it at the top of the hill. The detonator at the center of the scarlet head was like an angry eye.

Casey shuddered at the idea of harnessing this unruly ton of iron and gunpowder to the smooth aerodyanamics of the warplanes he had flown. It must marry well with an old dowager like the Stringbag, though. Its slug-smooth shaft was the cleanest thing about the torpedo, rooted in a pouch made up of stubby fins and a cowling that enclosed the propellers.

"Looks positively phallic, doesn't it?" Alison said cheerfully. She had Lani in tow, and paused beside Casey. Her father came up behind. Without apparent effort, he took up the task of keeping the Irish Girl under courteous guard. Alison waited until they had passed up the track. "What do you think?" she asked Casey. "Are we going to ram that into the wrong target?" She lifted her chin at the torpedo.

"There must be some way to check Lani's story," said Casey.

"There is." Alison stood aside for Sam Oysterman, pushing a barrow loaded with fuel cans. "There's time for me to check our fiction library and the shipping records."

"Good!" Casey gave her a long look. "What was the magic name she used to impress your father?"

"Dalrymple. A fellow Stringbag pilot." She lowered her voice as Chief Petty Officer Moore plodded past with a jerrican in each hand. "For Lani to know his name means she might have a connection with British Naval Intelligence."

"Or she got it from Gabbiya's spies." Casey summarized what had happened on the *Qurqūr*. "I'm not sparing your blushes," he concluded. "The woman's foxy."

"I'm jealous. She seems to have tied you men in knots."

"Then, get hold of Sergeant Winston. He'll have found a way to leave the ship. Talk to E. P. Geld. But be quick."

There was a note of authority in his voice that was new to Alison. "I've got a whaler at the mooring," she said. "If I slip away now, I can be back in an hour or so. Wait till I'm gone to break the news to my father, though." She kissed him and vanished back down the ropewalk.

Casey resumed walking up the hill and came upon Bracken resting on a tree stump.

"Where's Lani?"

"Don't worry," said Bracken. "One of the constables has her in charge. Blast this leg!" He made an effort to stand and failed. "I'll be fine in a jiffy."

Two men trotted past with wooden crates on their shoulders.

"They're like wartime partisans," said Casey, wondering how to bring up Alison's departure.

Bracken agreed. "Partisans is right. Ordinary chaps who pull together when threatened."

Casey stared up the ropewalk where the torpedo plowed on, iron wheels screeching and throwing off sparks, the men grunting with exertion. All he could remember from weapons school was that modern torpedoes were the result of careful breeding through several generations and grew brainier and brainier. Darwin would have seen in the evolution of the torpedo a dark side to man's creative impulse.

"She packs enough powder to blow Gabbiya to kingdom come," said Bracken.

"She's not going to blow up anyone yet," replied Casey.

"Cold feet?"

"Just sensible caution. There's the smell of a trap in all this."

Bracken groaned. "The world's been terrorized for years by this fella. Nobody ever wants to take action. You retaliate against his latest terrorist operations, and he threatens to take the war into your streets. So you talk about a trap!"

"Cool down. I've met him. You haven't. Everything's too pat. It's like the *panji* booby trap, so much part of the landscape that you suspect nothing."

Bracken fell into a respectful silence while Casey spoke of what he'd learned from a decade in the Zoo; and of the feeling Casey had of being led by Big Vien through another maze filled with closely coordinated surprises. "From the moment of the governor's murder," he said, "it's as if Big Vien's pulling the strings. He's got Gabbiya dancing to Hanoi's tune, because it delights Gabbiya to test us and find us wanting. The Vietnamese kill the queen's representative here and London does nothing. Gabbiya blows up airline travelers all over Europe and nobody does more than *talk*. It's leading up to something big, and you could be baiting the trap."

Bracken stood up and tested his leg again. He stamped his foot to restore circulation. He sniffed the night air. Then he said, "It all depends on whether we believe Lani, the Irish Girl?"

"She's the only person in Gabbiya's gang we *know* is aware your Stringbag is operational. But all along I've had a sixth sense about Big Vien. Sorry to sound like the Gypsy fortune-teller!"

"Widely separated particles continue to affect each other." Bracken set off, still dragging one leg. "Synchronicity," he said. "Don't apologize for something the scientists are just starting to take seriously."

Casey saw his opportunity. "I sent Alison back to Nelson's Harbour—" he began.

"Yes," said Bracken. "*I* had a sixth sense about that."

Sergeant Winston heard the voices of men taking in the warps. Some subtle change in the ship's noises warned him *Qurqūr* was preparing to up anchor. Zia

336

Gabbiya's hospitality had left him with a raging headache. He had a dim recollection of hearing the order "Darken ship!" piped, and of someone closing the scuttles. Like most islanders, he had a good feel for ships. In addition, he had served in the U.S. invasion of Grenada, part of the token forces drawn from the region to avoid America laying itself open to charges of exercising imperialist strength unilaterally. He had been attached to a British naval observer whose presence was *not* cosmetic: an admiral with a black eyepatch named Dalrymple.

The deck seemed to shift under his feet as he dropped from the bunk. It was time he made himself useful before swimming for shore, as Casey had suggested. He slipped into the unlit passageway. There was an eerie absence of the customary sounds, of distant radios, of boots clanging on metal rungs, of crewmen gossiping. He made his way down narrow maintenance ladders toward the moon pool. He had been over the ship's plans with Dalrymple in Washington. Along with others from the old island colonies on the American eastern seaboard, Winston had missed the comforting attentions of Her Britannic Majesty's Government, HMG, Big Momma, though he doubted if the Windfalls could defend themselves any better than Grenada without total U.S. help. Big Momma had seemed to doze off again after the Falklands War. Still, he missed her, and he had valued the blossoming friendship with Big Momma's man in Washington.

He swung down to a catwalk brilliantly lit from below, and moved forward until he could see through a narrow grating into the cavernous hold where five men stood around the lip of the diving pool. Two more were slumped against the porcelain cowling, their dive gear neatly bundled on the deckboards.

Winston lowered himself onto the valance of recessed fire curtain. He saw another man strutting almost directly beneath him. He recognized the Corsican's bullying voice and swagger.

"Drunken white trash! Swallow these pills. They'll sober you up fast. Nobody said you could take shore leave to get *drunk*." The men wore a resentful air, but they did as the Corsican told them, and dipped into the large jar. Benzedrine? Winston wouldn't bet on their chances if they dived now on a combination of alcohol and pep pills.

"Lucky for you the Protector is not here." The Corsican's awkward use of the ship's working language made the words more ominous. Winston listened while another track of his mind played back data he had previously memorized. He had not only gone over the ship's plans with Downwind Dalrymple. He had been *under* the ship, with Professor Rutgers. Later, he'd covered up the manner of Rutgers' death.

Now he'd have to get out the way Rutgers had. He tore off his undershirt and shorts. A black skin traveled best in the dark places.

The *Qurqūr*'s air-tank compressors came to a sudden stop. Tanks clanged as divers hoisted them from the racks. One of the men moved unsteadily away and leaned over a steel drum to vomit. The drum was around the curve of the diving pool's lip, beyond the Corsican's sight.

There was an explosion of decompressing air, and

Winston almost lost his grip as he slipped down to the deck plates. Faces turned to where someone fought to secure a valve: the seal on an air tank had failed. The diversion allowed Winston to dodge between shadows until he came up behind the straggler, still retching. He threw an arm around the vomiting diver's chest, and clamped his other hand over the mouth. He found the pressure point below the man's right ear and thumbed it hard. The sodden diver was already limp, and slid to the deck without a sound. Winston unzipped the neoprene wetsuit and stripped it off, like a Chinese medicine man skinning a cobra.

The drum was almost full of fresh water made murky by the immersion of diving gear being washed free of salt. Winston lifted the inert diver until he hung over the drum. He took the diver's knife and slid the razor-sharp blade across the windpipe, then tipped him in fast. Blood gushed down among the waving rubber fins and masks, the body bubbling with it. Winston felt no compassion for the dead diver. He had liked Professor Rutgers in the short time he knew him.

Black-hooded, the collar of the wet suit turned up to conceal part of his face, Winston struggled into weight belts and harness at the rear of the assembled ACT team. "Late for class again, Dawson!" roared the Corsican. There were a few sniggers. The men knew they had overstepped the mark. They were anxious to please. "You get the privilege," said the Corsican, "of going first. And don't head back to port, Dawson. You've got a target this time: Wreck Cay."

Winston went over backward into the flooded moon pool, and struck deep. For all he knew, the Corsican might be playing games with him the way Gabbiya and these men had played games with Rutgers.

It had been apparent to Winston, when he inspected Rutgers' body, that the professor had been drowned long before the blow to the head. And the drowning was accomplished by a magnetic device in the hull of the *Qurqūr* developed from wartime anti-mine equipment. The modern system disoriented any unfriendly frogmen, sent his compass needles spinning, could even arrest metallic working parts of a saboteur's gear. ACT divers wore a small countermeasures pack to neutralize the powerful magnetic impulses. Winston did not know if such a pack was routinely stitched into ACT life vests. He had no intention of staying around to find out. Instead, he kept on going down, then struck along what he hoped was a horizontal path without consulting his underwater compass. He took no air from his regulator, but kept swimming until he felt safely clear. Then he rose cautiously toward the surface. He saw the pale shimmering light and finally sucked air from the tank. His lungs were so close to bursting, he almost bit through the mouthpiece.

He floated up the last few feet to fix his position. The range of the antidiver device must not be very great. His compass agreed with the shore lights he knew. He treaded water until he located the old wooden naval pinnace which the Corsican had said the ACT team would take to Wreck Cay. "Time your attack as late as possible," he'd ordered. "We don't want too big a gap between the attack and the arrival of the Americans. We'll want to blame the incident on the American invaders." So an American invasion was expected. Dalrymple had indicated as much. Perhaps that explained Professor Rutgers' odd behavior.

The sergeant finned gently past the pinnace. It had been bought from the local sea scouts by an American tourist agency. Winston knew now the agency had been purchased earlier by a front company of Gabbiya's. He wondered how many other small craft were secretly Gabbiya's.

He came up to Fisherman's Quay, calmly going over his priorities. The first thing must be to warn his friend in Washington. He had other friends in Harbour Radio, with their own lines to the U.S. and Caribbean coast guards. He didn't thing Gabbiya could have bought out Harbour Radio.

He dumped his gear at the bottom of the quay and mounted the stone steps. He poked his head above the level of the street. Windfallers were seldom out along the waterfront after nine in the evening. Only a traffic policeman in the birdcage stood fast, for the benefit of any stray tourists. No cruise ships were in.

Sure enough, there was Constable Cooper-Slipper under the light, studying the shining face of the parliamentary tower clock. Winston came over the quay's edge at the double.

The constable was known to his colleagues as "Bluebell." He was a large, jovial member of the black branch of the Cooper-Slipper clan. He would have swung his truncheon at the apparition hurtling across the cobbles at him if he hadn't heard it yell his nickname: "Bluebell! It's me! Sergeant Winston!"

Bluebell laid the truncheon back over his shoulder, and an enormous smile spread over his round features. It wasn't often a constable got a chance like this. Not with Sergeant Winston. Running through a public place, improperly dressed!

"Indecent exposure," said Bluebell, thumbing open his notebook. "I'll book you on that charge, for starters."

But he very quickly changed his mind.

CHAPTER 21

Lord John was easing the torpedo forward between the legs of the Stringbag when he caught sight of Tiddley Ridley, the butcher, sticking a wooden match into the tip of a cigar. Bracken snatched away the cigar. "I detest seeing a man spike a good Cuban," he grumbled and licked the tip of the cigar. "There." He held it aloft and gently squeezed it open. "Seduction, not rape."

"You're not planning to light that thing, I trust," said Chief Petty Officer Moore, seeing Bracken turn again into the cheeky young midshipman who had been cured of smoking a pipe in the open cockpit only when a glowing plug of tobacco flew out with incendiary results.

"Sorry, Chief." Bracken flourished the cigar. He had guided the torpedo the last few inches after the men maneuvered its dolly to where the nose rested just short of a propeller blade. In the red glow of flare-path lanterns, the missile looked huge, angry, and menacing.

"Come on, Casey." Bracken jabbed the cigar upward. "I'll show you how to shove it in." He climbed onto the crinkly surface of the lower starboard wing.

"Not with my cigar, you don't!" called out butcher Ridley.

And not, thought Casey, with me. He waited while Bracken reluctantly returned the cigar, and then followed up through the bracing wires and struts.

"There's the tit you press to drop the tin fish." Bracken shone his torch into the front cockpit. "Top of the throttle, there. With your left thumb. The moment you release, the Stringbag surges up. So remember to hold her down with your right hand on the stick."

"Not with *my* right hand," said Casey.

Bracken chose to misinterpret this. "You jet jockeys," he retorted, "are spoiled by all those fancy-trick rockets. The torpedo may look big and awkward, but it bloody works. Marvelous feeling as you go down on the target. You stand on the rudder bar and look over the top of the wings. That's how steep she dives. Your head's in the wind, you're going down vertically, then *whammo!* You pull out at fifty feet, and charge at sixty knots."

"Sixty?" Casey's bowels turned over. Six hundred would have seemed slow enough.

"You get a better target sighting. And the enemy gunners *always* miscalculate. They can't believe you're moving that slow, so they allow too much deviation. Anyway, even if you're coming head on, the tin fish is already running under its own power. It can cover six thousand feet in four minutes." Bracken could hardly contain his excitement. "The torpedo sight is foolproof. See those little electric light bulbs, like you find in an actress' dressing room?"

344

Casey was tempted to say he did not frequent actresses' dressing rooms. Instead, he followed the dancing torchlight. What looked like fishing rods stuck out on either side of the pilot's windscreen. Small light bulbs hang from them. "The distance between each bulb," said Bracken, "represents five knots of speed made by the target ship. So if you drop at three thousand feet from target, you figure the ship's speed from where she sits on the light bulbs. If she's making twenty knots, the tin fish will strike her twenty-four hundred feet from where you first took aim. You allow for that when you press the old tit."

Casey felt like an idle passerby who straggles into a store with no intention of buying and then lets a sales assistant expend time and energy displaying a complicated gadget. Yet he could not stop Bracken, because he was already seduced by that heady mixture of smells lingering in all such cockpits: the tang of high-octane, the rubbery odors, the sharpness of metal, the oiliness. Impossible, really, to disentangle the components. It was the French perfume of every pilot's downfall, the irresistible lure that led to trouble. He squinted sideways at Bracken, whose face, even in the pale glow, betrayed guile. The old bastard knew what he was doing!

He cast an eye over the assortment of controls, valves, cocks, handwheels. *Primitive,* thought Casey. Primitive as a *spike.* The Stringbag was an equivalent weapon to Vietminh booby traps. Recognition came as a shock. How many times had he argued that America was losing the war by depending on elephantine technology? How often had he wished to booby-trap Big Vien? Well, here was his chance.

"What are those handwheels?" he asked.

"To trim elevator and extend flaps."

"And that?" He pointed to what looked like a simple barometer set into a chunk of wood and suspended under the crash pad.

Bracken gave an embarrassed laugh and unhooked it. "That's my—ha!—my personal touch. It foretells the weather." He held it closer under the light. "Storms ahead. Still a good distance out to sea, though. You shouldn't have any trouble getting off—"

Casey took a deep breath. "I wish you'd stop talking, Lord Bracken, as if I'm flying this . . . this contraption."

"Sorry, slip of the tongue." Bracken seemed dampened by Casey's sudden formality. "You're probably right." He replaced the weather forecaster. "Why should you trust an old fool who tells the weather by shark oil?"

"Shark oil?"

"That's the liquid in the tube. Turns cloudy when the weather's changing. With practice, you can read it quite accurately. Oh, but I shouldn't say that, should I? I mean, *I* can predict the weather ahead."

Casey suffered a pang of guilt. He knew how he would feel if another pilot made fun of his own aircraft. Bracken's torch was shining across one wing. Casey, to placate him, said, "There's some loose metal there, on the nearside strut."

"No, no!" Bracken gave an indignant snort. "That's the airspeed indicator!" He focused more sharply on the strip of red metal. "It's on a spring. The airflow

346

presses back the thingummy and you read off the speed against the scale on the strut."

"Ah!" Casey turned back hastily to the cockpit's interior. Without thinking, he let one hand wander over a metal ring. It looked like the metal ring you pull to open a can of beer.

"That's the inertia starter clutch control," Bracken said in a voice that was decidedly stiffer. "For winding up the engine."

Casey was afraid to breathe. A false word or gesture might be taken for derision. He was in that situation in which you seem doomed to say or do the wrong thing. He had a sudden image of winding up the elastic in a model airplane, and he coughed to cover a threatening burst of laughter. He heard Bracken say, "A couple of matelots stand on the lower wing and crank it up with a starter handle."

Casey got a grip on himself. "You need a reliable engine," he said cautiously. "I mean, carrying all that armament."

"You creep in at half throttle to deliver a torpedo," said Bracken, warming up again. "You just keep the old motor ticking over. The tin fish has to enter the water properly. If it bellyflops or porpoises—no bang."

"How do you know it'll keep ticking over, though? I mean, you're flying straight and level, just off the water, right into the target's guns . . ."

"I run her up regularly."

"Doesn't the noise advertise what you're doing?"

"No. I do the engine tests when the speedboats have their Sunday races across the sound. Compared with those souped-up marine bombs, my little Peg's no noisier than a sewing machine."

"Little Peg?"

"Pegasus III radial. Made by Bristol engines. *Never* stop."

"They stopped *making them* centuries ago—" Casey clamped his mouth shut, afraid he'd again given offense, but Bracken rattled on.

"This Peggy was in the Stringbag when I crashed her. I was showing the young 'uns how to outmaneuver enemy fighters. Both Hun and Jap were all much faster, and with tons of firepower. Three times our speed at the very least, and all we had was that ridiculous First World War Lewis machine gun on top of the wings."

"And you *outmaneuvered* them?"

"If the pilot knows the drill, it's not hard. If the bandit dives on you, which is the favorite attack, you pull the Stringbag up onto her tail. The bandit whizzes past and *has* to loop to get into position again. You dive for the sea. The bandit's got you plastered on his ring sight and forgets his aerodynamics. Generally, he flicks into a spin and can't recover before hitting the sea, upside down . . ." Bracken balanced over the cockpit coaming, demonstrating with his hands. "I was playing the role of the attacker when it happened. The new boy in the other aircraft pulled a stunt. He was turning on a farthing and I was turning on sixpence. I tightened up to get inside him. I forgot the extra weight of the three bods in the back. All three went for burtons."

"Bought the farm?" Casey knew all the euphe-

348

misms for death in aerial warfare. "These kites were coffins. Why didn't you raise holy shit?"

Bracken laughed. "If Gabbiya lands us in war, will you waste time arguing with politicians about the weapons we've got? *Our* politicians had been snake-charmed by Hitler. When he started his war, we grabbed whatever was to hand . . . Broomsticks, Stringbag, Faith, Hope and Charity."

"Faith who?"

"Three lone Gloster biplanes called Faith, Hope and Charity. They held off the fascists over Malta." Bracken twisted around to stare into the black hole of the rear cockpit as if into an open grave. "I never remember the names of those blokes I killed. Always think of 'em as the three Gladiators."

Casey sensed he was being offered another hook. He had to bite, though. *"Gladiators?"*

"Those biplanes at Malta. Officially named Gladiators. But our chaps said they were a final act of Faith, our last Hope, and we'd scraped the barrel to get Charity." Bracken lowered himself a few inches. "Come on, time we got back to terra firma."

Casey followed. Seduction, not rape, eh?

Below him, Lord John dropped the last few feet to the ground. A mawkish performance? Perhaps. Dishonest? No. He had conjured up the spirits of his dead shipmates in a good cause, although he'd stretched things a bit. The navigator's name had been Kenilworth. Not even his worst enemies thought of him as Faith. The last Bracken saw of him, they'd hit the sea and Kenilworth flew out, arse over tit, because he'd forgotten to secure his jockstrap, the

349

safety wire that clipped between the legs. The other two had drowned in gasoline; it had filled the rear cockpit before they could be knocked out by the crash.

Bracken had killed a lot of good men in his time; some his own, some the enemy's. He'd sunk a lot of ships. If he'd ever stopped to brood about it, he'd have stopped helping win the war. And if a man gives up the cause, he told himself, from fear of disturbing his delicate bloody conscience, it'll be the nasty buggers who'll win this time.

He turned, and his leg buckled. Casey jumped down in time to steady him.

"It's my Stringbag leg!" Bracken groaned and lowered himself onto an emptied handcart. "You have to push one leg against the rudder all the time you're flying her. She doesn't have a trim control to correct propeller torque—" He clutched his chest.

"I say!" It was Sir Everard Chillingham. He whipped the brandy flask from Bracken's pocket and forced it on him. "You can't fly in that condition, leaky heart and all."

Bracken took a long pull, coughed, shook himself. "I've had these things before," he said.

"But not in the air," said Chilly.

"Nobody else can fly the Stringbag." Chiefy Moore reminded them.

"You do Mr. Casey an injustice." Bracken tugged a pamphlet from his pocket. "Between what I tell him and these pilot's handling notes, we'll manage it together."

Casey took the notes. "You're not dropping out,

are you?" The Stringbag leg had become unserviceable at a convenient time.

"Only one leg is U/S," Bracken said cheerfully.

"Yeah. But your ticker suddenly seems not to be ticking so well too."

"I've a pocket filled with dynamite pills to keep the heart valves popping." Bracken tilted his beard at Casey. "I *want* to fly, if it's the last thing I do. Alison's been scheming to have you pilot the ship. She's scared I'll have another heart attack, in the air. She loves you, Casey. She wouldn't ask you to sail with me unless she was absolutely certain it was in a good cause!"

Sail? Casey looked up again into the network of wires through the wings like a ship's shrouds. In the wavering light of flares, the Stringbag did look like a seagoing vessel. Those great wings were sails to catch the wind. That wood-and-canvas hull, the tall rudder, the running lines and stays, the cleats, tackles and spars . . . He'd heard the parts enumerated when Lord John led him to the pilot's cockpit, like a sailor climbing ladders to the wheelhouse. They were all nautical terms. Deck-handling grips. Lashing tackle. There was even a dinghy stowed like a ship's lifeboat.

He glanced down at the pilot's handling notes. Inside, was a picture of a Stringbag flying the white ensign from the small flagstaff abaft the midwing section. Even the Royal Navy portrayed her as a ship!

"I'll sail if Alison's research tells her I must," he said finally. "Meanwhile, I might as well read the handling notes." He began to walk away, then stopped and turned. "What the devil is that . . . that *pastry board?"*

"It's for plotting gunfire," Bracken said defensively. He waved the square wooden frame. "It's called a Bigsworth Board."

Casey drew closer as Chiefy Moore retrieved the board and began clipping a chart onto the frame.

"It's also for plotting a course," Bracken added hastily.

"Like . . . to Black Rock?" Casey stabbed at a telltale cross on the chart.

"That's where the *Ultima Thule*'s supposed to be, at dawn."

Casey carefully set the Stringbag notes onto the handcart. "Before we sail in this thing," he said, "I'll want to see evidence, hard and irrefutable evidence, that the *Ultima Thule* isn't a decoy." He saw the look of dismay in Bracken's face. Casey remembered Faith, Hope and Charity, and stared up once more into the Stringbag's rigging. "Because," he added, "not even Big Vien ever invented a booby trap like this one. I sure as hell don't want to waste it."

Edgar P. Geld skimmed through the documents he kept in his bedroom safe. They recorded the history of his companies incorporated in the Windfalls. Now and then he scribbled down a name. His hand shook when he wrote.

The telephone rang. "Rose Hall," he said cautiously.

"Alison Bracken. Of John Bracken Partners."

"Thank God!" E.P. could not suppress the exclamation. He tried to steady himself. "Thank God the phones are working, I mean."

"Only domestic."

"I hoped—I've been trying to reach a Mr. Bingo Harriman. I seem totally cut off. I managed to get through from a call box after leaving the *Qurqūr*—" He realized he was babbling when the girl's voice cut in sharply.

"You left messages on our tape machines, at the office and at home. This *is* the Mr. Geld whose companies we represent?"

"Yes."

"Then, meet me at our offices. If it's as urgent as your messages say. Make it half an hour. Come through the back . . ."

Perhaps for the first time in his life since his nursery days with Nanny Locke, E.P. found himself submitting to female orders. He interrupted only once to implore Alison Bracken to wait for him if he should be late. "I have to pull together urgent information—"

"I'm working against deadlines too," snapped Alison. "Just be sure you get here by midnight."

E.P. replaced the phone. An hour. It seemed like a reprieve. But it also gave him too much time to think, to reconsider. If his suspicions were confirmed, he was finished. The Geld empire would collapse in scandal unless he acted to save himself. With cooperation from the local lawyers, papers could yet be doctored. It wouldn't take much to falsify what was, after all, already in the fiction library. He must distance himself from the subversive activities of those whose corporate bed he shared so unexpectedly. His original impulse, after the *Qurqŭr* launch had dropped him on a Nelson's Harbour quay, had been to dredge up all the documents and use them to denounce Zia Gabbiya.

Then he'd had second thoughts. Zia had treated him like dirt on board the ship; and returning in the launch, E.P. was braced against trouble if the crew discovered Casey missing. Instead, *nothing had happened.* The coxswain helped E.P. ashore, saluted, and away went the launch again. Of course the crew were a slack lot, secure in the knowledge of Zia Gabbiya's power. They might be simply careless of what passengers did. Worse, from their point of view, would be reporting to Zia that one had vanished.

E.P. had considered Zia's provocations, and even began to wonder if Casey had been part of Zia's scheme. Nevertheless, he attempted to make a payphone call from the waterfront to the Virginia numbers Casey had given him. He was not unhappy when an indifferent operator said, "We are taking no overseas calls." He had better luck phoning the estate for a chauffer.

Now Alison's call immobilized him again. He was nervous enough already at having to endure a second night in the Great House of Rose Hall.

In his original mood of active hatred for Zia, he had noted from Casey the cable address for Bingo Harriman. He had even tried to communicate through the estate telex machines, but they were also silent. Now he wondered if he should go down to the radio room. Or call the local Cable & Wireless office.

He stood at the windows and saw that the moon had dropped behind the tall casuarina pines, throwing long shadows across the dew-damp lawns.

The guard dogs barked, while his mind still danced from one extreme to another. Did he want to see the Bracken lawyers in order to sanitize the company archives? Or was it to demonstrate the extent of a conspiracy against America? If it were not for Amanda, he would do his patriotic duty. He had to believe that.

The barking dogs drew his attention to Amanda's quarters. He suffered a fresh attack of fear. It wasn't that he distrusted his staff. Amanda was safe behind the security fences, and guarded on three sides by the sea. There was something about Herman Schroeder's behavior that disturbed him, though. He never bothered to identify those individual employees who watched over the estate, but he thought the men tonight were unfamiliar and vaguely . . . dismissive? If Zia had infiltrated the E. P. Geld commercial empire, might he not infiltrate the Geld households? There was the damned Irish Girl, Lani, to prove Zia could penetrate all defenses . . .

Suddenly E.P. was in a state of extreme alarm. Amanda! Zia had put his filthy hands on everything else. Zia had called Amanda a bird in a gilded cage, and he wouldn't be above poking his fingers through the bars. But there was one thing neither Zia nor anyone else knew. E.P. was not easily made a prisoner in his own house. The radio room was in what had once been the mating chamber for slaves. It was reached by a spiral staircase. There, two keystones, intricately secured, finely balanced, guarded a tunnel. The tunnel had been built by the king-killers, never certain of their safety though smuggled to the Americas by Cromwell. It emerged among rocks standing sentry where the sands at low tide joined the estate to Amanda's place of exile.

Amanda had been playing, over and over, the record of *A Mirror of Whitening Light.* Nanny Locke sat waiting for the girl to declare her readiness for sleep, and occupied her usual position this late in the evening, facing the sea, the revolving mechanism of the gazebo switched off, and one of the glass walls retracted.

The music, by repetition, worked an enchantment. Nanny had noticed its effect on Amanda, and she had gently diverted the child from time to time. Always, though, the girl returned to it. Now the same hypnotic influence gripped the sturdy old woman, who stared out across the moonwashed waters. Immediately in front was the brief stretch of shoreline not embraced by the high security fence. Instead, the fence extended to a dab of rock, guarding against intruders from the sea.

The plainsong, the *Veni Sancte Spiritus,* rose out of the glissandos rippling like waves. Nanny Locke had read the notes sent with the record by Zia Gabbiya, and these had altered her first feelings for the music. The composer had been writing about a part of Scotland, the islands beyond Bloody Foreland and Cape Wrath, where Nanny Locke had grown up. She could imagine the Old Man of Hoy rising from the ocean and beckoning. He had always seemed to promise a tranquillity that all men seek, and some have found in the sea. She closed her eyes. The music washed away all care.

Amanda quite often sat motionless for hours listening to her records. She was capable of perfectly copying a composition by ear alone. Zia Gabbiya's gift, though she knew nothing of her benefactor, exercised a fascination unlike anything she had heard before. Her life had been spent responding to the rhythms of the sea. The only furniture that interested her consisted of the large window aquariums. She knew all the fish. If she was not playing or listening to music, she was looking into the aquariums or gazing at the pictures of undersea life.

She slowly turned her head and saw that the old woman was calmly sleeping. Then she did something she had never done before. She walked out of her gilded cage. She walked into the sea.

It was all over when E.P. got there.

Nanny Locke was shrieking for help. The dogs had started to bay long before. Beams of light played around the Great House at the top of the sloping lawns. Amanda's white dress floated in the water beyond Nanny Locke's reach. *A Mirror of Whitening Light* began to repeat itself again in the background.

E.P. waded in. He lifted his daughter up to meet the noncommittal gaze of a sky chalked white by the moon and smudged by stars. In death, Amanda's

357

face remained as calm as in life.

He carried her through the shallows, up the narrow stretch of beach, past Nanny holding her hands to her mouth, and placed Amanda on the hummocky grass without looking at her again. He was not going to fool himself with a display of lifesaving, a face-saving activity he knew would not be justified. Amanda was gone. The soul he had only once succeeded in touching, and that just hours ago, had fled.

He moved through the gazebo, through the conservatory, at an accelerating pace across the narrow isthmus and through the main gate. He shouldered aside two anonymous security men, thundered up the glistening lawns to the house, and raced back up to his own bedroom while servants stumbled and scrambled aside in sleepy bad humor which turned swiftly to fear when they recognized and were flummoxed by the reappearance of the master. He grabbed one of the manservants and had him stagger back down the stairways again with boxes of documents. He ran to where one of the estate BMWs stood idling. He yanked open the driver's door and his hands were like hooks as they took Herman Schroeder by the collar and wrenched him out of the car. He heard shouts, protests, and maybe warnings. He had only one thing in mind, and if every member of his staff had opened fire, that would not have stopped him. He saw the documents safely in the seat beside him, and it was only the speed of the car's acceleration that slammed shut the opposite door.

He need never have pleaded with Alison Bracken for more time. When they had spoken together on the telephone, he already had enough on paper to cook his own goose and that of Zia Gabbiya. He had delayed too long. He should have known there was a dark and sinister intent behind Zia's gift to Amanda. Those medical and psychological experts about which Zia had boasted were qualified not to cure but to kill her. This is what E.P. believed in these moments. He did not ask himself why Gabbiya would act so foolishly against his own interests. He just wanted to get Gabbiya. Like so many others.

The Windfalls are fortunate in having one of the best marine radio services anywhere along the American eastern seaboard. It comes under the Department of Marine and Ports and is situated at Fort St. George, overlooking the North and South channels, so that the conspicuous red-and-white flagpole and rotating radar scanners can be seen from almost any angle. Harbour Radio coordinates marine operations in and around the Windfalls, and it has telex communications with the U.S. and Caribbean coast guards (see Appendix B, Safety Equipment, of *The Yachtsman's Guide to the Windfall Islands*). The radio monitors and broadcasts twenty-four hours daily on two Call & Distress channels and on 500 KHz in Morse code. Anyone who tries to interfere with Harbour Radio automatically signals an alarm to the electronic world that is always listening, on hundreds of frequencies.

Nobody knew this better than Sergeant Winston. He dispatched the constable known as Bluebell on various errands. Then he made his way to Harbour Radio on a bicycle stolen from behind the nearest waterfront pub. You need a bicycle to get up the steep and winding dirt track that climbs to the station.

"Evening, Squire," he said to the elderly white man inside.

"Hullo, young Winston!" replied the other. "It's coming up to midnight and all's well—"

"Oh no it's not!" Winston stepped out of the dark doorway.

"Hell's bells!" The man addressed as Squire took a second look. "Did her husband catch you at it?"

Winston, naked under Bluebell's cape, glowered. "This isn't funny and I'm not here to play the fool." He told the radio operator as much as he thought he should know.

"Jesus." The operator thumbed through his log. "The only vessel to leave these waters was the *Ultima Thule*. She gave her skipper's name as Zia Gabbiya."

"Was he?"

"Here's the duty pilot's report . . . See, he took her out through the Narrows, then 'handed over command to Colonel Gabbiya.' "

"He couldn't be mistaken?"

"There isn't a cottage in the islands hasn't clipped out a photograph of Gabbiya from somewhere since the rumors began to fly."

Winston nodded. "Can you patch me through to this number in Virginia without attracting attention?"

The operator looked at the slip. "If I do it VHF to

shore, it can be overheard."

"Telex?"

"There's the reasonably secure Coast Guard line. You've got to be sure it's an emergency."

"It's an emergency," said Winston.

The operator looked him up and down. The sergeant looked dirty and oil-stained. The cape had been thrown aside, and Winston in sweaty nudity was not an imposing sight.

"Listen," Winston said threateningly, "when I'm done with this, I want some foul-weather gear and then I'm off. Meanwhile, just assume I'm in my sergeant's uniform."

"I really should have the okay from higher authority—"

"I *am* higher authority."

The operator rubbed his chin. "I could get fired."

"You bloody fool—Squire . . ." Winston choked back an urge to strangle the man. "We'll all be out of jobs, homes—we'll have lost these islands by tomorrow if you don't pull your finger out."

The operator nodded. He had heard the rumors, but he was the father of four children and he moonlighted during the day at a tourist bar. For the past week, he had excluded all the gossip from his conscious mind, being unwilling to face the implications. "What do you want me to send?" he asked.

The message addressed to Bingo Harriman of Spad Beer in Raleigh, Virginia, reached its destination a little late; and by then, copies had been distributed into nooks and crannies of Washington, D.C., where it caused considerable disturbance. At

Spad Beer the teletype spat out the words just as Sergeant Winston had written them with the thought in mind that Americans who read them might not immediately know who or what were Zia and the Windfalls: BINGO, he began chattily. PLEASE ONPASS ALL INTERESTED PARTIES. THE GREAT LORD PROTECTOR OF ISLAM COLONEL ZIA BEL-EL-BEY GABBIYA ALSO COMMONLY KNOWN AS GOLLIWOG GABBIYA ABOARD RESEARCH VESSEL ULTIMA THULE ENROUTE TO CLAIM SEAMOUNTS FOR REPUBLICS OF SAHARA OR VIETNAM OR BOTH WITHIN VICINITY BLACK ROCK 150 MILES EAST WINDFALLS (GROUP OF ISLANDS FORMING SELF-GOVERNING COLONY OF GREAT BRITAIN ROUGHLY 500 MILES EAST YOUR CAPE HATTERAS). INFORM ADMIRAL DALRYMPLE (AS IN QTE QTE QTE DOWNWIND UNQTE UNQTE UNQTE) COLONEL GABBIYA HAS RECEIVED WHAT APPEARS TO BE ADVANCE WARNING IMPENDING AMERICAN INVASION THESE ISLANDS WHICH HE WISHES ENCOURAGE SO AMERICANS LOOK IDIOTS BECAUSE HE WILL NOT RPT NOT BE HERE BUT NEAR BLACK ROCK CLAIMING INTERNATIONAL LAW COVERS HIS ENFORCEMENT NATIONAL SOVEREIGNTY OVER SEAMOUNTS. GABBIYA ASSIGNED FROGMEN DEMOLISH DALRYMPLES OLD SQUADRON MATE LORD JOHN BRACKEN WHO PREPARING AERIAL STRIKE ON ULTIMA THULE WITH ASSISTANCE YOUR REPEAT YOUR OLD SQUADRON MATE CAT'S EYES CASEY. CANNOT YET SAY HOW GABBIYA PLANS USING TERRORISTS AS AGENTS PROVACATEURS. SENDER IS REJOINING LORD BRACKEN AND CASEY. PLEASE DO NOT WALK INTO GABBIYA'S OR VIETNAM'S BOOBY TRAP. BEST REGARDS DETECTIVE-SERGEANT CHURCHILL SPENCER WINSTON OF ROYAL WINDFALLS CONSTABULARY.

"You're going back to Lord John?" asked the operator after he had sent the message. He was lost in wonder at the sergeant's heroism.

"You misspelled *provocateurs*" was all the sergeant said.

CHAPTER 22

Casey worried while he pretended to study the thin blue paperback *Royal Navy Pilot's Handling Notes: Fairey Swordfish Mark II*. He crouched under a wing, then found a perch on the aircraft's big Port Dunlop starboard mainwheel. The Swordfish — Bracken's Stringbag — must be launched within two hours to catch Zia Gabbiya at Black Rock. *If* Zia really was there. The danger was growing in Casey's mind that if it was a trap, and he were to be shot down, the raid would be represented as an American attack on Vietnamese interests, with fatal repercussions for his buddies in prison. Those prisoners were his *only* reason for being here, he reminded himself. His body, fished up from an abortive raid, could be used by Zia and Big Vien as proof of an illegal and hostile act.

Big Vien was in Ho Chi Minh City, though. Or was he? Casey had no way of telling. The cables on *Qurqūr* could just as well have been dispatched over no greater distance than stern to bridge. Given Zia's record as an illusionist, nothing was certain. Zia's ACT demolition team, according to Lani, was to start firing rockets at Wreck Cay by daybreak, ninety minutes away. But that, too, could be just another of Zia's deceptions.

Lani was helping Sam Oysterman. The constable had been instructed to watch her, and kept her busy repairing tears in the fuselage, using a sailmaker's needle and leather thumbstall. Casey had tried to coax more information from her, but the Irish Girl was on guard. She knew Casey had refused to fly until he was certain she told the truth. "Why waste my breath?" she said. "You won't believe me until Alison Bracken gets back. And if she doesn't get back, an ACT missile will confirm what I've already said. By which time, it will be too late."

Alison should have been back long ago. Once in a while, Casey had caught the sound of an outboard; but it was always some night fisherman trolling through the sound. Chief Pony Moore had reported an hour ago to Lord John that all weapons and stores were now hanging from, propping up or stuffing the inside of the Stringbag. The torpedo was locked snug under the biplane's belly. Oyez Lem and Constable Mello were tamping rocks under the wheels. Jamaica Tipoo and Dean Thomas had cleared several hundred feet of the ropewalk. Flares were laid down either side of the makeshift runway. Bracken had gotten Tiddley Ridley to help assemble the rocket-assisted-takeoff gear (RATOG). The butcher's sandwiches had been demolished and all the beer cans were empty. The last of the fuel had been laboriously siphoned into the tanks. Sir Everard Chillingham, the Ancient Mariner, darted back and forth like a dog with two tails. They're all waiting for me, thought Casey. And I'm not flying until Alison produces something to prove we can trust the Irish Girl.

He must have been nodding, because he failed to hear the putter of Alison's whaler. She appeared in the clearing, followed by a man.

"What's this?" Lord John burst out angrily. He motioned to Pony Moore.

"Mr. Geld," said Alison. She turned on Chief Moore. "You can put that down. He's joining us."

Chief Moore lowered an aircraft flare pistol. Instead, Jamaica Tipoo came up behind the newcomer, his gravedigger's shovel slung in readiness over his shoulder.

"I don't care if Geld's joining the boys' brigade or the heavenly host!" Bracken limped forward. "He's no business here."

"But he does." Alison beckoned. "He can confirm the Irish Girl's telling the truth."

Lani dropped her work near the tailplane, astonished by this version of the E.P. she thought she knew. His clothes were in disarray. She had never seen him less than sartorially perfect, except in bed. His hair flew wild, yet even in bed he'd always managed to preserve its pomaded, unruffled look. He had a fat portfolio under each arm, and she had never known him to carry anything bigger than an ashtray. Strangest of all, the weakness in his features was gone.

"I want Gabbiya dead," said E.P.

He caught sight of Lani. "You bitch." He shook with grief and rage. "You stole those recordings of my daughter's music. You gave them to Gabbiya." The portfolios fell, files spilled out over the ground, and he raised clenched fists to his head.

367

"I wanted to help," said Lani. "I really believe Zia has found experts—" She stopped, silenced by the way E.P.'s hands dropped and his body went slack.

Alison said quickly, "Tell them what *we* found, Mr. Geld."

E.P. nodded. He started. "After—" Then he shied away from Amanda, her exile, her death. He began again. "Gabbiya got into every fiber of my organizations. I started to discover this only because he wanted me to know. What he doesn't expect is that I no longer care about the consequences. He can't blackmail me." His eyes strayed over to Lani again. "That bitch threatened exposure. She brought me evidence of company operations unknown to me. Subsidiaries trading with Vietnam's Communist government. Links with arms dealers, and with drug smugglers. Gabbiya wants my cooperation. He's not as clever as he thinks." E.P. swayed and his face glistened in the pale light. He took a few paces to steady himself against one of the Stringbag's wings.

Alison said, "We found Gabbiya's own companies are in partnership with Vietnam."

E.P. made a gesture, as if relinquishing the story to her.

"Hanoi got hungry for INSPAD." Alison looked over at Casey. "Someone deliberately gave them the impression INSPAD—Inner Space Development—was a commercial cover to test very advanced deep-sea equipment in the field." She bent and retrieved a file. "This purports to be an INSPAD report: 'Mineral Deposits from Sea-Floor Hot Springs.' It says, only fifteen years ago scientists accepted the theory that

368

continents are continually in motion. Ocean basins open and close. In deep ocean, hot springs create rich mineral deposits: gold, tin, titanium, diamonds . . ."

E.P. suddenly revived. "One of my companies got into undersea exploration." He fingered his mustache in a faint echo of his old style. "It became a personal concern for me. Billions of dollars' worth of minerals were thought to be down there for the picking. In the form of nodules. We had twenty-three small research submarines in the North Sea alone in those days when hopes ran high. But the field became overcrowded, the pickings disappointing. Companies like mine went belly up. The scientists had to go back to the drawing board.

"Then the Russians tried a fresh approach. Word spread." E.P. turned to Alison, snapping his fingers. This was E. P. Geld in another guise. She handed him a folder. "Yes." He withdrew a sheet and held it under one of the working lights, reading aloud: "A variety of chemical and physical mechanisms precipitate the metals from solution along the upwelling zone within the crust and on the seafloor where the solutions discharge as metal-rich hot springs." He looked up. "The process is wherever the overlying seawater prevents boiling, which means at depths below six thousand feet."

He leafed through more papers, and Casey interrupted: "So your remarks to Zia about Conan Doyle and drilling under the sea didn't come out of the blue?"

E.P. shook his head. "The subject's a private passion. Any number of thinkers in other centuries saw the possibilities without knowing facts." He raised his eyes. "Of course *your* contribution to that encounter with Zia deepened the impression that you — IN-SPAD — knew very much more."

"But you said it was Hanoi wanted INSPAD," said Casey.

"Zia's greedy for control of everything that doesn't carry with it the burdens of an old-fashioned empire." This time it was Lani who spoke. "Hanoi's using his dreams to realize its own."

"Look here," interrupted E.P. "The Mid-Atlantic Ridge at the latitude of Miami is described as the region richest in strategic materials . . . nickel, copper, cobalt, molybdenum. And silver and gold. The site is known as the Trans-Atlantic Geotraverse (TAG) Hydrothermal Field." He held up a report. "There's no point going into technicalities . . . undersea volcanic chains, combinations of circumstance . . . The point is, these islands, here, could proclaim a two-hundred-mile 'exclusive economic zone' to cover such TAG seafloor deposits."

"The Windfalls?" asked Chillingham. As the islands' banker, his curiosity was reaching fever pitch. "What do our legal eagles say?"

Bracken gestured toward his daughter. She said, "The United Nations still has to work out aspects of a 1982 convention on traditional rights. They extend a maritime country to its coastal waters, usually twelve miles out. Meanwhile, all British territories have proclaimed two-hundred-mile zones. And possession is nine points of the law while the UN fuddles along."

"We'd better make *our* proclamation now!" exclaimed Chilly.

"Too late," said Lani. "The *Ultima Thule's* task is to put Sahara's flag on seamounts around Black Rock. Seabed rights will be claimed in a two-hundred-mile radius of each, *enclosing the Windfalls.*"

"Can Zia do that?" demanded Casey.

"The British got away with it on Rockall Bank," Alison said. "They hung the Union Jack on that bit of rock in the Atlantic and laid claim to the whole region's seabed."

"And that's what Zia will do tomorrow." Lani peered at Casey's wristwatch. *"Today,* I mean. It's gone midnight."

"What's his hurry?" asked Casey.

"It's Zia's booby trap."

Casey looked hard at the Irish Girl. "Why should we believe you?"

"I can't explain," she said desperately. "There's no time."

"There's all the time in the world." Casey kept his eyes on her face. "I'm not flying until I'm sure."

Alison saw how the other girl trembled, and interrupted with almost brutal force: "Lani, speak freely! Edgard Geld is here because his daughter just drowned."

There was an audible gasp from the onlookers. Their number had been growing as each task was finished. The Stringbag stood ready. The sky had darkened. A freshening wind sighed through the casuarinas.

"It's impossible," cried Lani. "Zia's chopper pilot saw her this afternoon."

"How do *you* know?" rapped Alison.

"I had him deliver a new record."

E.P. made a sound like an animal in pain. His hands fell loosely to his side. "That music drove her into the sea. You killed her, Lani!"

Lani opened her mouth, touched one hand to her lips, tossed back her hair. "Amanda!" The word seemed to stick in her throat.

"Steady on!" said Chilly

She leaned against his proffered arm. "You think I'm a whore," she said, turning to E.P. She straightened up. "Zia's whore. Everyone's whore. You must believe—" She had her voice back under control. "Never—I never for a moment thought Zia would hurt your daughter!" She looked around the circle of faces. She whispered, "I risk prosecution . . ." Her gaze settled on Casey.

"Prosecution?"

"The Espionage Act of 1916."

"Nineteen sixteen!" Casey stared back at her as if she had gone mad.

"The so-called 'spy' law?" asked Alison gently.

"Broadened to cover CIA agents," Lord Bracken added quickly. He nodded at some of the men, who quickly melted away, leaving him with his daughter, Casey, Chilly and E.P. "You'd better tell us the whole story," he said to Lani. "Right from the beginning."

"I'm a whore," she repeated. "I sold my services and got my kicks." Her voice was defiant. "I had a daughter of my own, you see. Once. In Vietnam."

* * *

She moved cautiously, testing each word of a tale she knew must pass muster, a story to catapult Casey into action. If she failed now, she truly had squandered herself, body and mind.

"I'm Irish from Quebec," she said. "I was at McGill University in Montreal when the Quebec separatists got a boost from France. I joined. It was a movement to brake away from Canada, strengthen the French connection. The French external security service, *Action*, the DGSE, recruited me, paying tuition, later bringing me to Paris. With my Canadian passport, I was particularly useful. Canadians can go anywhere, they're not a threat. And Canadians served on the Indochina Truce Commission, before America got into the Vietnam War.

"At the DGSE espionage school, I took top honors. I showed proper enthusiasm for the Gaullist concept of *tous azimuts*, all-round defense, which means equal hostility to the CIA as the KGB. The anti-American sentiment reached a peak when the Americans muscled into Vietnam and jeopardized new French commercial links with the Communists.

"I was sent to Hanoi, 'papered' as secretary to a permanent trade mission. I got access to Hanoi's Communist elite. They'd all been educated in Paris.

"My real job was to fuck what Party leaders I could," Lani continued savagely, lashing herself with vulgarities. "I fucked myself right into the confidence of North Vietnam's new director of terrorist training. He's a big man in Hanoi. He's their biggest earner of foreign currency. They kid themselves he's exporting Marxist revolution. What he really sells is the best training in the world for unconventional warfare. The Arabs and Africans respect Vietnam for defeating American technology with barefoot 'freedom fighters.' And men like Zia Gabbiya pay handsomely to learn how it's done.

"In Vietnam, they don't believe in birth control. They discourage using condoms by supplying those thick mainland-China contraceptives that feel like bicycle inner tubes. My friend the terrorism expert liked skin on skin. I had two abortions. The third time, he made me bear the child. A daughter. Then he assigned me to the jungle training school for Sahara."

"How did you square that with *Action?*" asked Casey.

"I got off the DGSE hook by simply deserting. Saharan gold looked a sounder proposition than devalued francs. My Vietnam lover knew this, but the Party was more important. The Party looked like benefiting when Zia Gabbiya took a fancy to me. It happened when Zia made one of his publicized trips to Moscow. The Soviets quarrel with Hanoi on many things, but *not* on Hanoi's reputation in guerrilla warfare. Zia flew to Hanoi on the regular military flight through Alma Ata. You know how those things are done. Big dignitary, busy schedule, lots of publicized meetings in Moscow. Then a couple of days obscured in the agenda while the famous man does his real business in secret. Zia was at the jungle school less than a day, but he zeroed in on me right away.

"You think the Communist bureaucracy is slow? But that's only when delay's a weapon. It's like greased lightning when someone like Zia needs to be pampered. I was on the plane back to Moscow with him that same night."

"You must have aroused suspicion, though," objected Casey. "Hanoi could easily check you out . . . Canadian passport, French trade assignment—"

"They *all* checked me out. Went back to my roots. Montreal's the most heavily infiltrated city in North America, and its security is an open book to any Communist agent. All of which helped me, because the information obtainable in Montreal was foolproof." Lani stopped dead.

"Nineteen sixteen?" Alison prodded.

Lani swallowed. "Yes, 1916. The Espionage Act of the United States. It's very hard to go against basic training."

"Let me guess," offered Casey. "*Basic* training was provided by the CIA? *They* first recruited you in Quebec, planted you in the separatist movement?"

"Because French separatism in Canada could spread to the traditionally French regions of the United States," said Lani. "Because separatism meant instability, and an unstable Canada was a threat." She spoke now as if the key had finally turned in a lock untested for many years; as if a door creaked open, and she was anxious now to walk through and get it over with. "My basic cover for the CIA was . . . anti-Americanism! Anti-Americanism was common to the French and to Hanoi's Communists, *and* to Moscow, *and* to those kids flooding into the terrorist training schools from the Mideast, Asia, Africa . . . yes, even from Europe. So long as my deepest cover remained intact, my real qualification was my reputation for hating America.

"When the political heat was on the CIA, my bosses shifted me to the Deep-Deep Cover department. Once inside Sahara, all two-way contacts were broken with the Double-D-C's. I was a sleeper in every sense. Zia invaded my senses and I had nothing for protection; no rubber goods, no CIA contacts. My lover in Hanoi was delighted to buy Zia's increased custom through me. And anyway, he'd got my daughter." She faltered. "He didn't know it would take more than my daughter to guarantee my loyalty to Hanoi. I'd already killed her in my mind."

She twisted her head to watch Sergeant Winston quietly joining her listeners. She had erased all sentiment from her voice. "I was abandoned to Zia for so long, I began to *think* like Zia. Then I came here. Professor Rutgers got into harness with me. He'd always known the risks I ran. He'd also seen how the efforts of agents like me get trashed, up on Capitol Hill. There was Zia, bullying and blackmailing America, getting away with endless *murders,* and America had an agent *sleeping* with Zia! And did nothing!"

Lani paused, seeing Casey stiff with suspicion. "There's so much to disentangle," she began again. "Rutgers alone could never fill in all the gaps. His concern became personal . . . his son! A navy pilot, like you, Casey. Told me that much, did Rutgers. Told me his boy was dead. My daughter . . . dead. And all the rest, Casey. All dead. I was smarter than the rest of you, Casey. I killed my little girl in my head. They couldn't blackmail me. They've jerked you around, Casey, because you wanted to believe your boys live: the Tex Graingers, the Bash McCoys, the Black Knights. But they're not alive. Except in your imagination. They live in the bits of paper Zia gives you. They're otherwise dead, Casey. Including the pilot Zia called Baa-Baa Black Sheep!"

Casey's head came up with a jerk.

"Rutgers tried to warn you. He knew your Forget-Me-Not Fund was being watched by Zia's men. Rutgers even put money into it, to sustain the illusion he was giving Zia. Rutgers played another haunted father, driven to recover his boy at any cost. He knew Leslie Lambe was known in the squadron as Baa-Baa. He planted the nickname as Baa-Baa *Black* Sheep, expecting Zia would add it to the list of those said to be alive, and that you, Casey, would spot the error."

"How the hell could Rotgut plant it?" asked Casey.

"Through a Frenchman. He contacted Rutgers here, told him his son was alive, showed him photographs he'd obtained in Hanoi. Rutgers knew damn well who the Frenchman was: *Action*. The DGSE often does its own way, ignoring French Government policy. This was a bit of free enterprise, to snare Rutgers. *Action* was after information on Hanoi's terrorist cells in Marseilles, and had to sell Hanoi a juicy tidbit in exchange —"

Alison said, "That explains the barman in the Black Lion," joining Lani in the effort to convince Casey. She drew the black sergeant into their circle. "Winston will confirm it."

Casey nodded the interruption aside. "Who planted the *panji* spike?" He fired the questions at Lani.

"What's *duck soup?* What was Rutgers trying to do with INSPAD?"

The girl hugged her shoulders. "Washington is applying the disclosure penalties *harshly*, Casey. You can get me hanged." She got no reaction. "You cold bastard," she said. "You got screwed by the Duck in the Zoo, and I got screwed by the Duck in Hanoi's Metropole Hotel. The Duck is Big Vien, and *the Duck is here!*"

They were all aware of the soft drone of an aircraft far above. It sounded like a long-range weather plane. Once in a while, the U.S. Air Force flew one over. John Bracken stared up, thinking it was the second high-flying aircraft he'd heard that night. "I'm getting jittery," he said. "The Duck and *panji* spikes seem academic right now."

"Not for me." Casey sounded angry.

"The Duck set the *panji* spike," said Lani. "He *meant* it to kill the dog. He meant *you* to be shafted by the old Hanoi fear quotient. It would put you into a 'reasonable' frame of mind for negotiations. Rutgers understood that. He told Bingo what he could, before returning here. Rutgers felt it was dangerous to make direct contact with you, Casey. He banked on you fitting the bits together. He figured you'd get some of it out of Lord Bracken."

Eyes turned to Bracken, who said, "Listen! Listen to the Doctor's Wind." The leafless branches of the tall casuarina pines leaned like soldiers. "It blows off the sea just before daybreak. Reaches its peak in about an hour. We'll need that high wind, to get off."

This time Casey raised no objecton. It was, thought

Alison, as if he'd quietly made up his mind to pilot the Stringbag and it wasn't any big deal. But it was a big deal for Alison. She was terrified to let her sick father take the controls, and she'd maneuvered to get Casey into the front cockpit—but that was before she fell in love with Casey. To defer a decision, she said to Lani, "What about INSPAD?"

Her father answered. "Dalrymple put it up to Rutgers . . . Matter of fact, it was when Lani spoke of 'Downwind' Dalrymple that I became pretty sure she'd be one of us. Admiral Dalrymple is Navy. Not just British Navy. Not just American Navy. *Navy!* We do things together that our governments don't always approve. In the end, Rutgers was doing something his department didn't approve. Our concern was something bigger than Zia, something that hid behind him. Bigger than Hanoi, but hiding behind Hanoi. Our public don't want to probe beyond the obvious, don't part the curtains around Hanoi, nor look beyond the neat Zia headlines. Behind all of that, though, is the Soviet Navy!"

Bracken let the words sink in. "There's a new generation of *very* deep-running Soviet submarines. All they need are servicing bases near the foot of seamounts, and they can remain indefinitely on station, *undetected.* They slip *under* existing defenses. If the West got on their track, by some miracle, the clues lead where—? Gabbiya? He's been getting away with murder for years. If we searched beyond Zia, we'd find Vietnam. Everything's sweetness and light now, because Vietnam wants our diplomatic recognition. So nobody's likely to bother risking more conflict there, right? If—

379

if—investigations went further, there stands INSPAD, run by Zia's petroleum corporation on Vietnam's behalf, quite legitimately." Lord Bracken limped over to the torpedo and glided his hand along it. "Here's the answer to all the trickery. It cuts through the bullshit. *But it must be done now.* Our enemies think they can't lose. They'll come out just as far ahead if Zia today triggers an American military response. They gamble that America will repeat what it's done all too often lately: start a surgical operation, then leave the patient neither dead nor alive. Experience *proves* this always strengthens the terrorists." He slammed his fist on the torpedo. "Let's best the bastards at their own game. *Boom!!!*"

"I wish you wouldn't do that," said Casey.

"It won't go off."

"It had better when the time comes."

"Ahhhh!" Bracken's beard waggled with glee. "So the time *is* coming!"

"If you'd just calm down a moment," cut in Alison.

"I *am* calm, dammit!"

"Then, listen, Father dear. If Lani Blake's suddenly such a credible witness, how come she was the last to see Rotgut alive and the first to be seen with his dead body?"

E.P., breaking a long silence, said, "And why's she done Zia's dirty work to this very day?"

"And what were you doing, burning papers at Backgammon?" Alison confronted the Irish Girl.

Lani shrugged. "My task was to maintain credibility with Zia. The department which assigned me that task is officially abolished. But Professor Rutgers gave me no reason to abandon it. I'm in the classic situation of an agent who returns to find his controllers gone, leaving the agent to explain away what seems treasonous conduct."

Sergeant Winston spoke up for the first time. "I know Miss Blake speaks the truth. I've already reported to Mr. Casey what transpired at Harbour Radio. There is, from a police angle, one outstanding problem. Miss Bracken raised it. Rutgers' death. You see, the professor *drowned*. The autopsy showed his head was bashed in later."

"I know," said Lani. "I bashed it in. But he was long dead by then."

This blunt statement was received in a conspiratorial silence. Everyone wanted to believe Lani now. She was part of the group, a feeling intensified by the fact that when anything untoward happens on a small island, everyone closes ranks. There is a sense of siege. Wreck Cay was a fortress in which, imperceptibly, those present had started to feel close bonds. They might still want further explanations from Lani, but the idea of her bashing in the head of a dead man was not one they were prepared to brood upon right now. There was widespread relief when Chillingham, secure in his seniority, spoke with the authority of a banker opening the doors for business. "It must be the hour to get airborne, gentlemen."

It was as if the bashing of Professor Rutgers' head had never been mentioned.

Lord Bracken ruffled his hair and said, "I'll need a good ten minutes to get off the deck. *If* I'm the pilot."

"I'll need fifteen," interrupted Casey. "The extra five

are for the cockpit check. I'll fly her, so long as you let *me* decide — in the air — if we're on a joyride or a mission." He caught Lani by the arm. "We'll sort out the rest of Rutgers later."

Bracken grumbled, "How the hell can you decide aloft?"

"You've got radio."

"Sort of."

Casey groaned. "Can you get Harbour Radio?"

"By unwinding the aerial and working the Morse key, yes."

"You should be in a straitjacket."

"What's Harbour Radio able to tell us that we don't know already?"

"Answers to more vital questions than how Rotgut got clobbered."

"Answers from duck-assed pen pushers, lumpish as our London humpty-dumpties." Bracken worked up a small rage. *"Blast* your *answers!"* He was stopped by Lani tugging his sleeve. "What is it?"

"Nobody's going anywhere if you argue any longer! Those ACT missilemen aren't amateurs. They're due here any minute."

They were all suddenly aware of that spiritual stillness preceding the dawn. The Doctor's Wind rose. There was the distant sound of a powerful vessel drumming out of Nelson's Harbour. The moon had dropped beneath the horizon. Clouds were gathering, the way they do over the Windfalls. The sky can be crystal blue one moment, and crowded with scudding cloud the next. Storms threaten, then dissolve. The weather is entirely unpredictable. But the sun and the

382

stars remain fixed in their purpose. The sun must soon appear, as the almanacs decree.

"You want answers," said Lani. "I'll give you answers. Up there in the back cockpit. I'll joyride, until you see why you've *got* to strike!"

It was her last, desperate attempt to convince Casey.

In the end, Lani's fate was settled by the rush of events. The final flight preparations required Bracken's full attention.

"You mean, I've got to *sit* on the stern?" asked old Chillingham.

"On the tailplane," said Bracken. "But not *sit*. Lie. As if you're out on the trapeze, sailing." He showed Chilly how to flatten himself over the port elevator, fingers hooked between the hinges. "Deacon Thomas will take the other side."

"You must think me a useless old fart," said Chilly. "Good only for ballast."

"*Ballast?* Christ!" Bracken's eyes popped. "You bloody well let go, soon's she starts to roll." Perspiration broke out on his face at the thought of an octagenarian glued to this Stringbag.

Oyez Lem took up position by the deck-handling grip of the lower port wing, and glowered at Constable Mello, forty-six feet away at the opposite wingtip. Their job was to run forward with the machine, steadying it before takeoff. Oyez cherished a vision of stubborn, duty-bound Mello hanging on like grim death as the plane soared. Mello *never* knew when to let go. Oyez still fumed at having his dinghy impounded, the marijuana confiscated.

E. P. Geld stood to one side of a main wheel, ready to tug the rope on an improvised chock. Beside him, Tiddley Ridley said, "I had you figured as a right old shit."

"I still am," E.P. warned the butcher.

Jamaica Tipoo stood by the other chock. Lani, still unsure what Bracken's decision would be about letting her fly, hovered nearby to lend a hand.

"You wan' I do you a mischief?" whispered Jamaica, waggling his rear.

"You better hang on grass," replied Lani. " 'Cos I goin' move *soooo* much!"

Jamaica moved suddenly away. She thought her prompt response to Windfalls sex-tease had frightened him. Then she heard, "I hears you, Lord John!" He returned to bestow upon her a lascivious smile. "He wants you up dere, honey."

Alison held tight to Casey. "You'll turn back if it smells wrong?"

He stood with one foot on the catapult spool, ready to scramble up the wing. "Yes, if by some incredible luck we get into the air. What's this?"

"A letter of marque. So if Gabbiya does get what he deserves, the world will only ever know you're a commissioned privateer. *If* the world learns anything . . ."

"You mean if we come down in the sea."

"Yes, you'll be a legal ship o'war."

"Small consolation."

"Oh, these things float for days," Alison said with forced cheerfulness. "So Daddy says. It's only him that

384

hits the water vertically."

"Who authorized this?" Casey waved the scroll.

"Chilly."

"Good grief, is he an admiral?"

"No, but he *was* a leading-seaman telegraphist. Their Lordships of Admiralty won't quibble. Better this than have Moscow raise a hullaballoo all through the Midwest and Asia about imperialist pirates . . ."

Lord John Bracken hauled himself up to the rear cockpit, fighting off dizziness. Sergeant Winston stood ready to strap him in. He tucked two of butcher Ridley's cigars into Bracken's shirt pocket and asked, "Have you enough of those dynamite pills?"

"Enough to stay conscious and steer Casey. It won't be easy. These navy jet pilots can drop onto a dancing deck at high speed, *and* stop inside the space of a living room. But it takes a good stick-and-throttle man to handle a Stringbag. We'll manage."

"Wish I could help," said Winston.

"You will. At Harbour Radio."

Casey swung his way through the rigging and glimpsed the Irish Girl matching his progress on the other side. So Lani was coming! What an irony! Alison would be left to face the ACT team. He found Bracken leaning over the gun mounting between cockpits, ready to hand him an old flying helmet with earmuffs and dangling rubber tubes. "I forgot to brief you on these," said Bracken. "They're speaking tubes. They connect three helmets."

Voice pipes! Casey thought: *What ho, the Jolly Roger. All ashore what's going ashore!* He pulled the helmet down over his head and heard Bracken's voice, all beef and

Yorkshire pudding, boom into his earmuffs. "There's a pack of solid-fuel rockets either side the fuselage to assist the takeoff."

"*Rockets!*" Casey blew down the voice pipe. "I refuse to get airborne riding a wicker wastebasket, on rockets."

"They're slanted so the thrust goes through the center of gravity."

"Through the goddam hull, you mean. No rockets!"

"You'll be off the ground in less than three hundred feet."

"In a ball of fire."

"C'monnnn . . . You just raise the tail, press the button, bring the tail down again, and — WHAMMO!"

"Whammo to you, too. The ropewalk's long enough for my kind of takeoff."

Silence.

Casey said, "What the hell's this, dangling from the joystick?" He'd been settling himself down in the seat, where what felt like angular cushions took the place of a parachute.

"Smoked glass. You look into the sun through it, if you think bandits are up-sun to jump you."

"Shan't need that, either."

"Yes you will!" Bracken was distinctly testy now. "See the hole in front of you, in the dashboard, directly behind the engine? You look through that hole to see the fuel gauge. It's a stick floating in the main tank. When the cylinders get red hot, the smoked glass helps shield the eyes."

"Jumping Jerusalem!" Casey was not much given to

vivid expletives, and suffered for his deficiency now. He felt a buckle sticking into his rear. Instead of a parachute, he was sitting on old-fashioned cork life jackets. "You'd better just take me through the cockpit check and forget the rest." He tried to wrench the oval chunk of smoked glass from its long string.

"Don't!" shouted Bracken. "You need that to see missiles, too."

"Who said anything about missiles?"

"Our Target Intelligence. She's standing right behind you."

Casey squirmed around. Lani had squeezed alongside Bracken in the rear cockpit. There was space to stack half-a-dozen Lanis, if they all stood. She blew through her own voice pipe and said, in what seemed a caressing whisper, "I'm giving Lord Bracken the statistics on the *Ultima Thule*."

"We've got 'em," mumbled Casey, distracted by the incredible cockpit.

"*Not* on the ship-to-air missiles," hissed Lani, at the very moment a brilliant scarlet glow expanded behind the forest. What had sounded like the soughing of the wind through the casuarinas became metallic and ugly. A projectile whistled overhead. There was an explosion, far enough away for Bracken to yell, "Elevation too high." He sounded like a gunnery officer spotting on Whale Island. "The second will fall short."

"Let's not wait for a third," urged Casey.

"I haven't taken you through the drill yet," objected Bracken, and Lani whispered, "It's only the ACT team. They're out of practice."

Casey shut his ears to them both and leaned over

the side. "Hey! Chief!"

Pony Moore's face showed white below.

"Wind her up!" cried Casey.

CHAPTER 23

Bingo Harriman was waiting for them. The odd little guy with the black eyepatch and the English accent had arrived earlier to warn him.

They wore no uniforms.

"You don't have a boardroom?" asked one of the generals.

"We don't even have a board," said Bingo. "There's just Casey and me."

"We need *somewhere* for this conference," said an American admiral.

"There's space in the bottling plant," Bingo suggested. "Back where we load the crates."

So they all trooped over to Spad's bottling plant.

Other cars kept rolling up. It seemed sort of funny to Bingo. Everyone was emphasizing secrecy; yet by now the citizens of Raleigh, Virginia, must surely have been rousted from their beds by all the activity.

They crowded into the loading bay and leaned or perched on wooden boxes. Bingo felt he owed them some kind of hospitality and told them to help themselves to beer. Nobody did.

"Gentlemen," said the American admiral, "I'm commander of Task Force Sledgehammer. Make your questions short. We need a decision by dawn or we're sunk." The admiral introduced himself as Davy Jones, which in the circumstances struck Bingo as an unfortunate name.

"What did you know about Operation Fly-Swat?" demanded a lean young fellow in T shirt and jeans. Bingo, vaguely recognizing him as a presidential adviser, replied: "Nothing. What is it?"

"An entirely unofficial mission," cut in the little man with the eyepatch. "I'm Dalrymple, by the way," he told the general assembly. "The chap mentioned in that message from Windfalls." He coughed. "My Prime Minister does not believe in the use of force. However, British naval tradition in the Windfalls region is older than the Prime Minister." He coughed again, and looked carefully around him. "I speak as among friends, I trust?"

There was a general murmur of assent, but only because everyone wanted Downwind Dalrymple to get on with it. The question of whether the friendship had been strained too far would be settled later. He put a large briefcase on the desk where Bingo's bookkeeper usually kept tally of outgoing crates. A screen popped up from the case, and on it appeared a smudgy picture of what looked like a spider.

"That," said Downwind, "is Operation Fly-Swat."

They all craned to see the Stringbag.

"I'm sorry about the photograph," said Downwind. "I had so little notice of this conference, I tore it from an old war manual." He was still surprised at the way Bingo Harriman had tracked him through the embassy. "This aircraft, Admiral" — he turned and smiled

390

at Davy Jones—"is capable of solving all our problems in one go."

Jones saw expressions of disbelief and outrage. "Can I cut in?" he asked. "Gentlemen, you should know Vice-Admiral Dalrymple flew machines like this, so he's familiar with their capabilities. I should add, he was nicknamed Downwind because he saved an aircraft carrier." Jones paused, weighing urgency against the need for a balanced judgment before daylight. "Returning to the carrier, he spotted a German U-boat's periscope, waiting for the ship to turn out of convoy to land him on. His fuel tanks were reading empty. His radio gear was shot away. He had to warn the carrier. So . . . he didn't wait for her to get into wind, but dived straight onto the deck downwind."

The atmosphere warmed up slightly. Dalrymple turned pink. He said, "John Bracken's better off. He's got a crack American pilot at the controls, if I'm not mistaken."

Bingo saw that at least one man was unimpressed. He was the only man wearing a shirt and tie. Bingo guessed he was from the State Department. The man said, "This gets worse and worse. You plan to get Gabbiya onto a third territory, not his and not ours. Then you leak the plan. And then you mount an invasion—" He was accusing Admiral Jones.

The task-force commander held up a hand. "There is *no* invasion as of this moment. Sledgehammer may yet be remembered only as a large-scale exercise."

"I trust so," said the man wearing a tie. "There was the devil to pay after Grenada. The Queen was furious because we didn't tell her."

"Security's bad enough without trumpeting these things to foreign monarchs," someone called from the back.

"There you are, you see," said the State Department representative. "You fellows don't even check these things out thoroughly. The Queen is not a *foreign monarch* in Grenada or the Windfalls. She is . . . the Queen. We only got away with Grenada because it was all over before the old girl found out."

"Which is why Bracken and meself cooked up Fly-Swat," Downwind offered in conciliation.

"Your people," said the man from State, sounding as if Downwind's people were a troublesome tribe, "have been planning this a long time. Not only did you not inform us, you also now place an American at the head of the operation." His eyes slid over to Bingo. "A foreign power, operating secretly on American soil, mobilizing American resources secretly, using its agents here to launch a lawless act of . . . of piracy . . . *Heads will roll, sir!*"

Into Bingo's head flashed the word "Falklands!" That war had been executed with dispatch, in greatest secrecy. He remembered now! There'd been a Vice-Admiral Desmond Dalrymple named as NA2SL, naval assistant to Britain's Second Sea Lord. Bingo did not much like the implied threat from the State Department, and now he noticed figures skulking around the plant. Everyone except Dalrymple had come to Spad Beer as if it were headquarters for a foreign military mission. The soldiers and the sailors and the presidential advisers were all looking at Bingo, and so he positioned himself in front of the screen and said, "I don't like any suggestion Spad employees have been acting as foreign agents. Casey, my partner, believed we were doing something for buddies left behind in Vietnam. Maybe if you guys had done something sooner about prisoners, we wouldn't face a crisis today with Gabbiya. Hanoi's used the possibility of prisoners to try and squeeze America. That's terrorism. It fits well with the terrorism of the Great Protector." Bingo took a deep breath. He waited for protests. How often, inside the Zoo, had he longed for this chance to tell the policy-makers how far off base they'd been? But nobody in his audience stirred. He thought to himself: Well, they're Americans, like me, and maybe our strength is that we *don't* agree, and that we rush off in all directions until a clear and visible enemy comes along. But what he said was: "What is it you want?"

"Can you contact Casey?" demanded someone who looked to Bingo like news photographs of the director of central intelligence.

"It's been impossible to reach him for some time."

"The islands are cut off," said Jones.

"Then we can't stop Fly-Swat?" someone else asked.

"Gabbiya's ACT team might," said Downwind. "You've all seen copies by now of the famous Sergeant Winston telex. But if you want my best guess, I think they'll have a hard time stopping this." He tapped a pencil against the Stringbag's silhouette on the screen. "This," he said, "took on the German battle cruisers *Scharnhorst* and *Gneisenau, and* the heavy cruiser *Prinz Eugen.*"

Admiral Jones stared at his feet, not wishing to

recall that every single Stringbag in that operation had been shot down.

"What about the Sergeant Winston reference to a booby trap?" inquired the national security adviser.

"That's just it!" said Downwind. "You go ahead with Sledgehammer, you play straight into Gabbiya's hands. First, he won't be there! Second, he's organized the financial structure in such a fashion that an American invasion would result in the flight of capital on a massive scale, enough to shake all our economies. Third, you haven't consulted London, and *this time* there will be the most awful row! Gabbiya will have driven a wedge between America and her allies; every one of your neighbors in the Caribbean and South America will be shrieking once again about Yankee imperialism—"

"And if you do go ahead with Fly-Swat?" the task-force commander asked gently. "Won't the end be the same—propaganda for our enemies? Gabbiya baited this trap with American prisoners." He glanced apologetically at Bingo. "I'm afraid one former prisoner, Commander Casey, could well become a prisoner again, for public exhibition, proof of Anglo-American perfidy."

Bingo shook his head. "You don't spend ten years in the Zoo," he said, "without learning how to get out of traps."

Admiral Jones sighed. "Gentlemen, we don't have alternatives. As of now, Task Force Sledgehammer will be ordered to stand down." He stood in front of Downwind's pop-up screen and studied the Stringbag. "I don't suppose an antique like this would have radio?"

"Wireless," said Downwind. "You know," he added, seeing their looks of pained horror. "Morse key and trailing aerial."

"Does anyone actually *use* Morse these days?" asked the State Department man.

"The Soviets." The CIA chief mumbled the words. "All Communist intelligence agencies operate on it."

"Then, they'll monitor our exchange and say it proves the American connection." There was a note of smugness in the State Department voice.

"Not at all," volunteered Bingo. "Not if it's in the Smitty Harris Tap Code."

"What, for God's sake, is that?" exploded one of the generals.

So Bingo told him.

And unseen by anyone else, Downwind and the CIA chief exchanged swift smiles of complicity.

CHAPTER 24

Daylight filtered through the trees on Wreck Cay as Chief Pony Moore scrambled over the slippery skin of the Stringbag's lower starboard wing and yelled for Alison above the *whooooshhh* of a second ACT rocket missile. Only he and Alison, among the work parties, knew how to wind up the Stringbag. She climbed on top of the dew-damp wheel to face Moore, who leaned on the engine starter handle. Their figures were illuminated in the glow of an explosion, showing Casey, in the front cockpit, that he should launch the starting procedures. Before the light died, he saw them cranking, and his hands moved swiftly around the controls . . . oil cooler bypass to IN, fuel cock to MAIN ONLY, throttle advanced half an inch.

Sweat pouring into her eyes, Alison waved frantically at Casey to engage the clutch: *"Contaaccctt!"* He switched on the ignition and hand starter magneto. The big, three-bladed prop began to flail.

Lord John Bracken cocked his head, trying to measure the roar of the Pegasus from his position in the rear cockpit. "Never mind power checks!" he called into the voice pipe. "She sounds good."

397

Casey switched off the starter magneto. He would not be rushed. He opened up slowly to 1,000 rpm. He trimmed the elevator three degrees nose up. There was no rudder trim, and he shoved his left leg forward so that he would be ready for the prop torque. He put the mixture to RICH, glanced at the few instruments, and leaned over the side to seek back down the length of the hull. Good! Two figures were sprawled across the tailplane, holding it down, shimmering in the slipstream. Another flash of light! This time the missile exploded dead ahead and lit up the sky. He pushed the engine to +2 boost and 2,200 rpm. The racket was awful, even when heard through the earmuffs. The ship shook from stem to stern. He pulled the goggles down over his eyes and gave the signal for chocks away to Pony Moore, who repeated it and slid over the trailing edge of the lower wing.

Casey was sure the next projectile would come dancing across his nose. He felt the Stringbag shudder as it ran forward like an old goat with pepper up its tail. Mello and Oyez Lem were running with her, steadying the wings. He brought the tail up, and the two men dropped away.

He was not going to get off before the end of the ropewalk!

"*Rockets!*" bellowed Bracken through the voice pipe.

Casey reacted automatically, and pressed the RA-TOG firing button with a split-second sense of defeat. He had been so sure he could coax her off by skillful handling! She weighed a deadweight ton. Nothing was happening. No great uplift. No rocket power. The end of Wreck Cay came upon him.

The surge hit as the Stringbag appeared to stagger over the edge. Suddenly she was riding on two pillars of fire. They were airborne!

"Good show!" Bracken's voice in the Gosport tubes sounded thin and distant. "Have to report . . . stowaway aboard!"

Lani! Casey's mouth formed a grim, thin line. No clear-cut decision had been made about taking her on this . . . joyride? Well, joyride it still would be, unless she convinced him absolutely that the *Ultima Thule* was the right target. He tested the control stick under his hands. It seemed sluggish, and the aircraft seemed unwilling to respond. Control stick . . . joystick . . . no joyride for any of us, Lani dear. Something's wrong with the elevators and we're nosing down into the sea.

Sir Everard Chillingham closed his eyes against the slipstream and hung on like grim death while his ancient bones rattled. He had been told to stay flat on the tailplane while the pilot ran up the engine. The run-up seemed to last a long time, and he curled his fingers inside the elevator hinges while around him the air banged and sizzled. His eyelids lit up red, warm air struck his cheeks. He opened his eyes and through the gap left by the elevator, he saw fire!

The blaze from the rocket-assisted takeoff packs died, and Chilly knew he was in trouble. His first instinct was to hook on more tightly. A good skipper always felt the presence of an extra body on a racing yacht: doubtless this skipper would turn smartly around and deposit the surplus bod back ashore. Chilly's second thought was that chances for landing this ship were slim, with someone out there firing missiles at the airstrip. So, rejoicing that the Great Adventure should end in just the heroic self-sacrifice he'd always regarded as essential to true drama, the commodore of the yacht club and chairman of the Bank of Windfalls, in his eighty-sixth year, let go.

The Stringbag sprang aloft as if relieved of a burden, the nose no longer pointing into the dark well of the sea. Casey used the control column back tenderly, felt the elevators respond, saw the red mercury in the small, thermometer-like tube on the dashboard start to bounce alarmingly. He was now dangerously nose up. He corrected and the Stringbag pitched and yawed. He had no idea of his speed: the red *thingumee* on a wing strut was bending back on its spring, but he could not decipher the figures on the scale in the uncertain light. He closed his ears to the shouts coming from the rear cockpit. He'd master this she-devil his own way.

He steadied the climb and reduced boost to + ½ lb. He was turning cautiously to port. Air slapped his left cheek, warning him that he was sideslipping. His vision was blurred despite the goggles, which seemed to spring leaks. He had gashed his hands against bits of metal. This was more exciting than elementary training in a prim little prop-driven monoplane. It was like nothing he'd done before. It was not powered flight as he knew it. Nor was it hang gliding. He was acutely conscious of all the bits hanging from wings and hull. And now they'd gotten Lani Blake aboard as well.

A beam of light struck out from the rear cockpit and lit up the airspeed *thingumee*. Wiping away tears, Casey squinted without his goggles and read 70 miles an hour. He leveled off. Something flashed under the wing. He was still in the turn. He really heard Bracken this time: "Tighter! Tighter!" He put the Stringbag almost on one wingtip, turning around a dark spot in the water. Another flash! He was aware of someone hanging halfway out behind him.

"Toggles . . ." Bracken was shouting. ". . . work the outboard shackles." Casey remembered something about anti-shipping flares in the pilot's manual, and Pony Moore saying there were two left. He groped for the toggles and pulled.

The underside of the Stringbag bathed in a fountain of light. Casey twisted in his seat and saw Lani standing in the cockpit behind him, flourishing a wide-barreled signal-cartridge pistol. For one neurotic second, he thought she was aiming at him. She was shouting down to Bracken, who called through the Gosports, "It's them all right. Scare the shit out of the bastards, Casey!"

The flares illuminated a long wooden boat with figures on the foredeck whose stance was only too familiar. Casey unconsciously braced for the next flash from the blowpipe on the lead figure's shoulder. The Strinbag twisted down as if she had instincts of her own. Casey flattened out as Lani fired the pistol.

An incandescent ball curved out. Casey saw the figures scatter. Then he was passing the boat and had to pull up over Wreck Cay. He flew low over the trees and peered into the ropewalk. Nobody was there to be seen, but from the center of the makeshift airstrip rose a thin column of smoke. He was back over the sea again in seconds, with the cay between the Stringbag and the ACT unit.

He started to turn.

"Don't waste time," said Bracken.

Lani's voice came over the Gosport tubes. "Gabbiya's men won't hang around," she said. "Their job ended when you got airborne."

Casey resumed the climb, but he hated the irony. He was stuck with a dubious female. And down there, Alison was going to have to take her chances. The strip was burning, even if the ACT unit had sheered off.

"Course to steer," said John Bracken, "is 320 degrees."

Casey's hands scrambled around the cockpit in a fresh fit of controlled panic. No gyrocompass. No blind-flying panel. No artificial horizon. No radio beacons or autopilot. No flight aids except a bubble in a tube, and a label: Reid and Sigrist Turn-and-Bank Indicator. And . . . yes, there under the gunsight was what looked like a ship's compass.

He twiddled the compass outer ring and perspiration broke out. "What's the magnetic variation here?"

"Fifteen degrees west."

Casey had to think hard. He did not feel like advertising his forgetfulness. But it was fatally easy to apply the correction the wrong way.

Lani's voice came down the tube: "Variation west / Compass reads best."

"Right!" said Casey, remembering the rest of the old mnemonic: "Variation east / Compass reads least." In an area of west variation, the compass was always the larger figure when converting. He had to quell a flash of annoyance at Lani's omniscience. Who'd trained her so well? The KGB, CIA or the Irish Republican Army?

"I learned that in convent school," Lani said meekly.

Casey was saved from disconnecting the voice pipes by Bracken's warning growl: "No backseat driving, *please!*"

But there was a good deal from the backseat that Casey would require later. Lani must know he would only complete the mission if the rest of her story measured up. First, he'd better haul this lumbering omnibus to a safe altitude. He could imagine Bingo wetting himself with laughter and asking, "Where's Cat's Eyes Casey, the hotshot flyboy, now?" The flyboy had misread the compass and put blue on red. The flyboy had very nearly flopped into the sea on takeoff. The flyboy had been so sure of getting airborne as smooth as shit off a shovel, he'd almost rejected those lifesaving rockets. Once, it now seemed a long time ago, this flyboy, in company with other solitary men, each alone in his jet-driven capsule, would have been scrambling for fuel-efficient cruising levels at around 33,000 feet. Now, thought Casey, I'll be lucky to reach a thousand feet in five minutes, I've no idea where we're going to land, and there's a good chance that if we have to fight head winds, we can't make it to Black Rock and back.

"Wizard takeoff." Bracken's cheery voice broke into these gloomy reflections. "Jolly good show all round."

Wizard show . . . Casey couldn't help swelling with pride. He felt like a rookie pilot hearing his instructor's first words of praise.

"Are you telling me, in the whole of the American armed forces, we don't have a man who can work a Morse key?" asked the national security adviser. His name was Joe Malloy. That much Bingo Harriman had managed to fit together while the scene in Spad Beer's bottling plant grew beyond comprehension. More vehicles had arrived. There were chauffeured limousines and sleek communications vans with satellite dishes that periscoped up and opened like umbrellas. He could hear the whomping beat of a chopper circling each time he went out to the loading ramp to help some newcomer join the group. He felt he was entertaining the White House and the Pentagon without having issued the invitations. And this continual harping about Morse communication was getting on his nerves! He protested yet again that Casey could read Smitty Harris taps as fast, almost, as the spoken word.

"That's beside the point," snapped Joe Malloy. "Somebody has to learn the damned system to transmit."

"I can," said Bingo.

"And if Casey is *not* the pilot, or isn't even on board?"

Bingo nodded heavily. He was torn between wanting to be useful, and suspecting that any message this bunch sent to the Stringbag would be to abort the mission. Perhaps it was best to let them mill around. Admiral Jones had taken over the bookkeeper's tally desk and turned it into a small intelligence center, with a portable scrambler phone and clipboards and charts. His own staff had fallen into protective positions around him. Jones began to look like a real seagoing admiral on the bridge, what with the wind blowing rain through the open side of the building. Someone was speaking urgently to him, and Bingo overheard, "Joe, we've been flying reconnaissance over the Windfalls all night—"

"Krrreeessst! Malloy gritted his teeth. "Didn't we agree to freeze *everything!*

"High-fliers," said Admiral Jones. "Anyone'd take 'em for commercial jets." The task-force commander snapped his mouth shut in sudden impatience and thrust a sheet at Malloy.

"Casey's airborne? Blast!" The security adviser rubbed his face.

"The *Stringbag* is airborne," corrected Admiral Jones.

An attractive, tweedy woman—Bingo had her figured as CIA—said briskly, "There's a reunion of Old Crows and Ravens at the Quality Inn."

The task-force commander frowned.

"Americans are Crows. Brits, Ravens. They were telegraphist / airgunners."

"Call them!"

"They're an older generation, Admiral. They might take unkindly to being called by a woman in the wee hours—"

"I'll deal with it," said her boss, suddenly galvanized.

The Association of Old Crows and Ravens is a unique body. Its members are drawn from World War II airmen on both sides of the Atlantic who were known as Tail-End Joes. Pilots were kings back then. Few suspected that men who wore the half-wing emblems of telegraphist / air gunners would someday become the wizards of electronic aerial warfare. Those who survived the least glamorized and most dangerous of aircrew duties drifted into peacetime work in the field which expanded so spectacularly out of "Sparks," the general name for wireless operators sparking their Morse keys. They were pioneers of *elint,* eloctronic intelligence.

The only Quality Inn anyone from the Pentagon ever means is in fact called the Pentagon Quality Inn and stands on the other side of the Potomac from the White House. The reunion there of wartime buddies had been a smash, with a banquet as its climax. Some members who were now presidents of their own *elint*-oriented companies later wandered up to the suite of their president, Niels Johannsen, who had been a Raven with the RAF after behind-the-lines work in his native Norway. They'd talked about new developments: a new ring laser that uses spinning mirrors and a laser to do the job of the old cockpit gyroscope and to provide navigation data quick as light; and about the new electronic shields that would be needed for a new generation of ultra-high-speed aircraft. Then they'd finally retired, tired and happy. Niels Johannsen was just nodding off to sleep when his phone rang.

"It's awfully late," said the caller.

Johannsen misunderstood, and apologized. "The boys haven't been on the tiles for years. I'm sorry if we disturbed you."

"No," said the caller. "You didn't hear all I said. I said this is a crisis. It's frightfully late."

Johannsen had lived a key part of his life on fragmented conversations like this. Now he recognized the voice, too, for he did a lot of business with the agency. So he grunted an acknowledgment and waited.

"You got anyone there who could work a Morse key, and *isn't rusty?*"

"Me," said Johannsen.

"It could be dangerous."

"No need to bother the others," said Johannsen. "I'll take it."

At Spad Beer the news was received with varying degrees of enthusiasm. Most of those present had been preparing for a different kind of action, where you dive into a bottomless mattress of political committees and bureaus, armed with explanations and charts: where you scale the enemy's ramparts made up of eleven separate defense agencies, nine joint commands, scores of subordinate bureaucracies and a tangle of thirty-two monitoring committees on Capitol Hill. Task Force Sledgehammer had developed its own impetus in strictest secrecy. Like the Grenada combined-services operation, it gambled on the fact that nothing succeeds like success. After Grenada, nobody had been ready to risk public disapproval by asking awkward questions about executive decisions taken without consultation. Now Sledgehammer was stalled: its paratroopers suspended with nowhere to go, its SEALS loitering aimlessly, its ships and aircraft held on leashes. Such delay made leaks inevitable, and already Admiral Jones was ready with a statement about extensive exercises . . . *But.* Much the best thing would be to let the CIA deal with this and take the rap, if any.

There was some surprise, therefore, when Joe Malloy responded the way he did to someone's warning that there was still the danger of Russian eavesdroppers recovering the Morse. "I'm taking a P-3 antisubmarine patrol out of Cape Hatteras," he said. "I'm taking Mr. Bingo Harriman and I'm taking this Old Crow. And I'm taking you," said the national security adviser to the CIA man. "I gather" — he glanced at the little British admiral — "that the Stringbag's, ah, wireless has very limited range. If we can, ah, raise the aircraft from close range, Mr. Harriman should be able to learn from his partner, Mr. Casey, *just what the hell is going on.*" He looked slightly flushed after letting his emotions break through in those last few words, and he added in a milder tone. "We'll base our final decision on what we find."

A growing sense of relief became evident to Bingo, who supposed that this secret gathering in Spad's bottling plant meant nothing need be on the record.

Those in high places need not fear a public outcry. There would be no embarrassing questions about the congregation of Combat Talon choppers from Fort Worth, the first-stage alert of Task 160 air strike unit, the disposition of Delta Force commandos and a grab bag of special forces. He had been listening to a general from the Joint Special Operations Command at Fort Bragg, North Carolina, so he had a rough picture of who was involved. It seemed fair enough that if anyone had to carry the can, it should be the poor sap at the pointed end whose final words, even in the dots and dashes of Morse masked by the taps of the Smitty Harris code, would be chronicled by a tiny few whose integrity was to be trusted. He thought the national security adviser was a rare bird in these days of political cowardice. He hoped the adviser wouldn't meet his Waterloo to the sound of an exploding biplane and a wooden Morse key singing *clickety-click-you're-out!*

"Shouldn't we let out the aerial?" came through the biplane's voice pipes.

That was Lani again. Casey sighed. He heard Bracken's voice: "Clever girl! You made your own cockpit check."

"I saw Morse key. You're in luck, Casey. It wasn't only navigation I learned at convent school. We had this marvelous nun, said you never could tell when these things might come in useful. Like how to sew, and cook, and send signals."

Casey sighed, lifted his goggles, and wiped his eyes

again. The physical labor of flying the Stringbag was making him sweat. He had an uneasy feeling things were going to become more difficult. He peered over the cockpit's side at the whitecaps below. A heavy swell was running. A new wind must have sprung up. Not the Doctor's Wind, but something faintly ominous, pushing him sideways. He looked up into the sky flecked with mares' tales of cirrus, very high, and sinister even though they looked pretty enough.

He sighed again. He picked up the mouthpiece of the voice pipe, harrumphed into it, and said, "Okay, Lani, let's decide if this is a joyride or not. Why did you burn papers at Backgammon? And why were you with Rotgut in his last moments?"

Her story of Rotgut's last days emerged through the rubber tubes. Her words resounded in his ears while the wind whistled around his head. Her voice remained steady. She delivered each sentence with a punch, as if she had joined him in the front cockpit and knew she had to fight for his attention against the demands of the rudder under his feet and the stick between his hands responding to the primitive forces hammering outside.

Lani had been shocked when Professor Rutgers came openly to see Zia Gabbiya on board the *Qurqūr*. She learned later that he was pretending to respond to Hanoi's same blackmail against the American Government and the relatives of possible prisoners. The professor was after the bait put out by Big Vien: the promise that Tony Rutgers, his son, would be released. Rotgut's real purpose was to seek out Big

Vien if possible, and to give the impression that deep-deep-cover operations really had been suspended.

"You mean they hadn't?" shouted Casey above the wailing wind.

"Only so far as officialdom was concerned," Lani called back. "Rotgut and a couple of others were strictly volunteers. They took over the wreckage before it sank. They ran it like a wartime operation, with an amateur or two manning the pumps."

The unpremeditated effect of publicly scrapping the Double-D-C's was to encourage the regular services and the Pentagon's war-horses to think big. They strengthened the Sledgehammer plan for seizing the Windfalls military.

Zia had responded to Rotgut as he did to Casey. There had been polite talk, exchanges of information, and then opportunities created for Rotgut to talk with Lani. She had no doubt anything that passed between them was monitored. She had to maintain Zia's impression that she was devoted to Saharan interests. Rotgut, of course, understood; and Zia's secret cameras and microphones only recorded Lani trying to worm things out of Rotgut in her own inimitable fashion. She had also learned, without being observed, that Rotgut's safe house was . . . Backgammon.

"Backgammon!" Casey's hands jerked on the control column. "So the South African millionaire, my absentee landlord—"

"Was one of ours. Rotgut couldn't risk telling you. His emergency priority was to learn Zia's reasons for

411

chasing Vietnamese dreams under the seas around here . . ."

Lani met Rotgut on Backgammon's beach for the first exchange of information. "I'd been on my own so long," she told Casey. "It's a bad policy, leaving a sleeper untouched, out of contact. We go rotten, you know."

Obviously, Rotgut had been assessing the Irish Girl's reliability after such neglect. Then, satisfied, he gave her material concerning underwater exploration financed by Zia's web of corporations. "It fit precisely with E. P. Geld's findings," said Lani. "Of course Rotgut didn't know that at the time. He was digesting facts and then using his scholastic skills to make a hypothesis. I locked the material in the library safe at Backgammon. We were the only people able to get into it. Rotgut intended to show you the papers if it became safe to meet with you. My job was to scour the *Qurqūr* for clues: *why* Zia was doing all this deep-sea stuff."

Piecing the fragments of Lani's final accounting together, Casey knew this had to be true. Little had changed since the mismatch between what fighting men observed in Vietnam and what Washington's intelligence establishment *wished* to see. Rotgut was a rebel against conformity because he had a son in the field. After the deep-deep-cover operations were publicly liquidated, in consequence of newspaper leaks, Rotgut seized his chance to keep the Double-D-C division going in his own, eccentric fashion. He had been appalled to discover Lani had operated for so long without direction.

"He made one dive under the *Qurqūr* himself," said Lani. "He needed to know the ship's capabilities, because he had a hunch Zia might transfer activities to the *Ultima Thule,* which is fully equipped, with unmánned submersibles and towing cables and laboratories. Then he took the biggest risk of all, and came aboard the yacht secretly. He wanted to give me a complete update. He was sure Zia's agents were on to him. He wouldn't chance a second meeting on Backgammon beach. He followed a good tradecraft rule: when you sense hostile surveillance, best shelter right under the enemy's nose. He was in my cabin when alarms went off. Zia's men suspected there'd been an intrusion under the hull, and the dive teams were ordered to make a search. I've told you, those divers form an elite. I could dive whenever I wanted. I'm as good as any man. Probably better. I kitted Rotgut out with my own gear. The others assumed he was me. Ship's officers have no authority down in the moon-pool area . . ."

Casey strained to hear her, with the wind blasting around the cockpit and the Stringbag bucking wildly. He was balancing on treacherous elements, the way Lani had balanced; little wonder that her manner was easily mistaken for steely arrogance; she had to protect herself against surprise. She was an intimate part of Zia's life, and desperately trying to remember she belonged in the other camp. The contradictions and gaps in her earlier statements had been inevitable. She said, "I was terrified. I had seen what Zia did to traitors. I went up on deck to get control of myself, knowing it would all be worth the risk if

Rutgers would finally get some action. I'd done filthy things in the name of patriotism, things that went against my upbringing, and the only justification had always been that I was doing them to destroy a filthier evil. I felt dirty. The dirt would be washed away if he succeeded in stopping Zia."

"Couldn't you have killed Zia?" Casey asked, thinking of the ring knife.

"I had the means," said Lani. "But you have to understand the discipline I'd been under. Receiving no instructions for all that time, I had to believe some plan was in hand. If I murdered Zia, it might be precisely what Washington did *not* want. I believed in *the wisdom of the higher levels . . .*" Casey could have sworn she laughed, but perhaps it was just the slipstream mocked them. "Once Rotgut entered the scene *here*, I saw assassination as the last resort. Ever since Hanoi, I'd reserved that ring knife for Pham Quac Vien . . ."

Big Vien! The man from the Zoo. Was it his laugh Casey heard, and not the mocking slipstream? Casey no longer doubted what he must do. The joyride had ended. He blew sharply into the Gosports, and shouted for Bracken. "Are we on course?"

"I've taken bearings on Drake's Point and the old cathedral spire," responded Bracken. "The crosswinds keep shifting. I'll give you a new course to steer in a jiff."

"How long to Black Rock?"

"At this rate, two hours."

Casey's heart sank. He turned back to Rotgut.

Lani said: "I was still on deck, half expecting Zia's

414

goons to jump me, when I saw something floating on the surface. It swept astern, fast. I had this conviction it was old Rotgut. I panicked all over again. If it *was* the prof, in *my* dive gear, I'd have awkward questions to answer. The Sea Eagle I use to go ashore was where it usually is, tied to the ladder aft. The guards were out, but they never challenge me. I'm Zia's woman. Or was. I caught up with Rotgut. It was him all right. He was dead."

Casey shouted, "It was morning when Alison and I saw you leave that boat with Rotgut in it."

"The previous night, I dragged the body behind the Sea Eagle, and dumped it in a tourist boat at the end of that causeway. I ripped my gear off Rotgut and returned to the *Qurqūr* to work things out. I figured Rotgut drowned when the alarms activated the antisabotage systems. I took an old wet suit from my dive locker, one that wouldn't be identifiable, and returned to the causeway. I wanted a public inquiry. For that, murder would be the guarantee. So I bashed in his head with a claw hammer, then dropped the hammer into the water."

"Why a public inquiry?"

"A murder would be hard to hush up. The news would reach Washington. Anyone who came to make inquiries, I could trust. Anyone who stayed in Washington, I would assume was part of the cover-up."

"Didn't you have confidence in anybody?"

"After what Rotgut told me? American prisoners were 'administratively buried' because nobody at the top wanted the embarrassment of admitting prisoners were alive. Careers had been staked upon statements they were dead. Besides . . . every administration's scared, politically, of another hostage crisis like Teheran. MIAs would be seen as hostages, and no American president or political party wanted to appear, like Carter, powerless . . ."

"So Big Vien thinks American cravenness will get him what he wants?"

"Same as Zia. They say America talks big and carries a small stick."

"Not a safe assumption."

They've allowed for the other option too. Zia and Big Vien knew about the scheme to lure Gabbiya onto a third territory, neither Saharan nor American, then hit him. So Zia advertised his presence here."

Casey fell silent. There was no need to spell things out. If an American military action was now launched against the Windfalls, Zia had cleverly arranged to be absent.

Nobody spoke. Lani had gone through a kind confession and felt shriven. She had grown so close to Zia, it had been difficult to hang on to her perspectives. Now the spell had been broken. A controlled rage gradually welled up from deep inside. She had been tricked. Tricked in a bumbling sort of way by her own people; and also tricked in the calculating way of a master magician by Zia. She let the fury burn. It kept pace with Casey's own surging anger. Casey's object of anger, though, was Big Vien. The battle between them had raged through half of Casey's life if you included the years since his release from the Zoo when Big Vien must have been quietly scrutinizing him—figuring, no doubt, Casey would

416

keep tabs on him in the same way. People like Big Vien and Zia didn't seem to understand Americans, and for that reason their behavior forced Americans to consider ways and means that went against their own beliefs and traditions. Political assassination wasn't what America was about. Casey's hands tightened on the control column, and he prayed that Zia and Big Vien would give him just one motive for torpedoing the *Ultima Thule.* For he was sure Big Vien was there. There at Black Rock, waiting for the stupid Americans.

"How's our fuel?" Casey turned his full attention back to flying the Stringbag. He still couldn't figure out the floating dipstick.

"There should be 150 gallons in the upper mainplane," Bracken guessed. From long-forgotten habit, the gesture automatic, he took out a cigar. He had positioned himself behind Casey, standing on his seat and peering into the front cockpit like a tourist admiring the view from a balcony. "Seventy gallons we'll need to reach Black Rock, but with these winds . . ."

"Is Black Rock big enough to land on if we have to?"

Bracken brayed with laughter. "If you can dance on the head of a pin, yes. Otherwise, no sir! Not to worry, though. There's an extra seventy gallons stashed between us."

Casey smacked the harness release and stood, twisting to see Bracken fiddling with a cork and a piece of string at the top of a black metal tank.

"Is that cigar lit?" yelled Casey. The tank was a firebomb.

Bracken spat out the cigar and it whirled away. "Forgot to pull the cork out after takeoff!" He yanked the string. The cork went the way of the cigar. "Petrol slops out during the takeoff. It comes out this pipe here. The pipe's an air vent to let the fuel run into the main supply line. The cork stopped the high-octane raining down on our heads."

Casey swallowed, and faced forward again. He should press Bracken for an alternative place to land. All his thoughts had been on the delivery run to target. He didn't feel like pushing the question now, because he had a suspicion Bracken's answer would be that if winds caused further delays, they had the whole wide ocean for a landing strip. If Bracken didn't set fire to them first.

The horizon had started to blur. Sea mists could mean a drop in wind, or a sudden change in weather. One thing Casey had learned was that Windfalls weather was not to be predicted by normal methods. He peered inside the cockpit until he found the shark's-oil indicator: the liquid had turned an ominously opaque yellow. "Should we climb over this stuff ahead?" he asked Bracken. "Or does this thing show up on radar?"

"*Thing?*" It was hard to decide if Bracken's tone was mock indignation or if he was really hurt. "*She* is wood and fabric. She fools radar. Stay low. She'll merge with the sea clutter."

Casey decided the tone was genuinely frosty. "One more good mark for the Stringbag," he said. "Modern radar can see anything . . . modern."

Bracken thawed. "Take her down to sea level,

there's a good chap."

I'm back in His Grace's good graces, thought Casey. He let the Stringbag drop close to the water. She had yawed frenziedly when he stood up to reprimand Lord John. Now, strapped in his seat again, he felt a new mood slowly envelop the craft. Craft and crew were melding into a single unit. The ship fell into a comforting rhythm. Voices murmured through the voice pipes. Bracken asked if anyone would like some bread and cheese. Lani said no, but where were the washrooms. Bracken said there was a pee tube at the bottom of the cockpit, and Lani, after a pause, announced she lacked the necessary delivery system. It had all become very matey. Until the fog closed in.

CHAPTER 25

Alison had listened to the fading note of the Stringbag's engine while her companions on the Wreck Cay ropewalk waited, briefly blinded by the antishipping flares. When she was sure the aircraft would not return, she told Pony Moore to forget about the grass fires started by the ACT unit's missiles. "Get the work parties into the caves, Chiefy."

"That last rocket fell smack in the wake of your father's takeoff," said E. P. Geld.

"You mean Casey's takeoff. Father wouldn't drop off the end of the cliff like that." She was still recovering from the fright. "If the men who fired those rockets come ashore, I want them to think we're gone. There's a cleft in the rocks over there. Impossible to find, unless you know."

E.P. indicated the Chief. "And how would he know?"

Alison offered no reply. She saw no reason to tell the American tycoon more than was necessary.

The cleft in the black lava was the mouth to a rock chimney. Pony Moore said, "Brace your hands and knees against the walls, and go down slow. You'll feel a ledge at the bottom. Pull into the cave

421

behind. It's above the high-tide mark. You first, Mello." He chose the youngest constable as the man least likely to panic.

"And you?" E.P. asked Alison.

"I have to move the barge."

"Isn't that dangerous?"

"I'm the only one armed." She could hear the pulse of a receding marine engine. Zia's men had been concerned only with the Stringbag. She told herself this, but kept a firm grip on the crossbow.

"Bow versus blowpipe," said E.P. "Primitive warfare."

"There are laws against firearms."

"Except for Gabbiya."

"You should know!" snapped Alison. She was only waiting until all the men were down, but she was glad to rest for a moment among the rushlike stems of Spanish broom. Later, she would take the barge out to sea and give the impression Wreck Cay was abandoned. What happened to E.P. was of no consequence to her. They had achieved a sort of intimacy during their frenzied midnight search through company records. She had glimpsed a small boy cowering inside the adult who looked so sure of himself, but a small boy who would have to do his own growing up.

"I've never broken Windfall laws," protested E.P., having misread her remark. "I've never knowingly broken laws anywhere. Now I'm holding the bag for improprieties under federal investigation. If I could be sure of an honest inquiry, I could do my country some good still."

"Like —?"

Before E.P. could reply, someone thrust up through the dense yellow flowers bordering the cliff. Alison reached for the crossbow at her feet. "Don't!" warned the newcomer. It was Jeff Fetherstone. Behind him rose Herman Schroeder, stripped to his considerable waist, carrying stick grenades.

"Thanks for putting all the eggs in one basket," said Schroeder, glancing over at the caves. "I can scramble the lot with one throw."

"Not if you're as bad a marksman with a grenade as you were with the rockets," said E.P. He surprised Alison by his sudden self-possession.

Schroeder laughed. "It makes no difference to us if that flying jalopy gets hit here, or by the *Qurqūr.*"

Alison stiffened. The fools thought Stringbag was attacking the wrong target. Schroeder misinterpreted her startled expression. "Might look like a yacht to you, but there's enough firepower there to blast Nelson's Harbour apart."

"And is that the plan?" asked Alison.

"We'd sooner make your father the cause," said Jeff Fetherstone. He faced E. P. Geld. "You'll help it look authentic."

E.P. took two steps forward and was halted by the gun in Fetherstone's hand. "I'm not surprised," said E.P. He looked down at Alison. "Fetherstone's learned to cringe and whine to maintain his champagne style. He had the makings of a merchant banker. But you didn't want to take the normal route, did you, Fetherstone? You wanted power fast. Like this barrel of lard."

"Careful," warned Schroeder. "We want you alive. But not that much."

"You're finished, E.P.," said Fetherstone. "Two things will happen to your empire. Either exposed as cover for a terrorist underground, or as cover for a loused-up attempt by CIA hoodlums to destroy the Great Protector of Islam."

The three men were watching each other carefully. Alison nudged the loaded crossbow farther from sight behind an outcrop of rock. She had to keep Schroeder and Fetherstone talking. "How did you get here?" she asked.

"Stuff it, lady," said Schroeder.

"No, tell us," demanded E.P.

Fetherstone stared at his nominal boss, puzzled by this unexpected display of backbone. Then he shrugged. "The rocket team put us ashore. This operation comes under me. I'm in charge."

"You talk too much," interrupted Schroeder. But Geoffrey Fetherstone had just started to enjoy the novelty of browbeating the man to whom he had kowtowed so long. He was not going to lose his advantage because of a crooked union boss. E.P. goaded him with another question. "In charge of what?" The tone suggested Fetherstone couldn't take charge of a milkmaid.

Fetherstone turned his back on Schroeder and said, "The Geld operation, *Mister* Geld. If you want to save your skin, you'll say you felt it your patriotic duty to collaborate. *Washington* needed your resources."

"And when do I say that?"

"After it's all over. Congressional hearings will undoubtedly follow the attempt on Gabbiya's life, and the military invasion."

"Invasion?" Alison opened her eyes wide.

"Already the rumors have disturbed foreign investors. I know the business world as well as Mr. Geld. A full-scale American invasion will cause an economic collapse here. And I've cooked up evidence to blame the CIA for killing Gabbiya. Mr. Geld, here, will be an important witness. So will Schroeder."

Schroeder's tiny black eyes flashed inside the rolls of flesh. "Five years in jail, that's where you learn about expert witnesses. I was in for life," He said proudly. "Gabbiya's guys got me out. Couldn't be done without the special-witness program." He gave Fetherstone a savage look. "Ask him about American justice. You got the money, you get the justice. I've bought and sold some of the biggest unions in the United States." He licked his lips. The sun had started to flood the top of Wreck Cay. He studied Alison crouching near him. She recognized that appraising look, and quite deliberately she shifted position. She was half lying, her legs slightly bent, one hip raised in what was already a provocative way. Her work shirt was half open and she twisted around slightly so that her breasts were partly exposed. She said:

"You mean you're a union tycoon, Mr.

425

Schroeder?"

Schroeder had heard that tone before. His experience with women was limited to those aroused by proximity to raw power. His tongue ran around his upper lip again. "I could show you unions whose bosses operate companies, out of union funds, bigger than some of the Fortune 500, lady. I've run them guys. I can show you unions so big, they can bring America to a stop whenever they like."

"But how, Mr. Schroeder?" Alison sat open-mouthed.

"Shit!" said Schroeder. "I got one union, runs the security guards for all the nuclear plants in America. We put pension funds, emergency funds, contributions—you name it—into private companies *building* new plants. Ain't nobody, from the local district attorneys to the Department of Justice, can stop us. 'Cause we got the money for better lawyers. We got the muscle to shut up any whistle-blowers. And we got Zia Gabbiya ready to lend a little help any time we ask. He *owns* them security guards, lady."

"Gosh!" said Alison, wriggling her body. "You mean, all those nuclear installations are under Zia's—well, under *your* control?"

Schroeder nodded. He removed the pin from one of his grenades as if to illustrate who really had control.

"You won't *use* that, Mr. Schroeder?"

"I never leave evidence lying around," said Schroeder, savoring the awe in Alison's face. "You say this ain't America. It ain't a nuclear plant, nei-

426

ther. It's nothing, lady. *Nothing.* I do as I please in these islands—"

Fetherstone watched his companion. The casual arming of the grenade arrested any thought of shutting Schroeder up.

"These islands belong to Her Majesty the Queen," said Alison. "You wouldn't take on the British *monarchy?*" She sounded breathless with excitement.

Schroeder measured with his eye the distance to the cave mouth. He said, almost absentmindedly, "Queen? Big Momma, you folks call her, right? I want Big Momma to get real mad when she hears how *Americans* landed here and fell into real *deep* shit. Can't let your pals down there live to say otherwise, huh?"

He was tensed to lob the grenade when E. P. Geld launched himself. The assault was so out of character that it took Schroeder completely by surprise. The rage was superhuman. E.P. saw in the giant braggart the bully responsible for Amanda's death, suddenly sure it was Schroeder who had reported to Gabbiya, stolen Amanda's tapes and arranged delivery of the fatal disc.

Alison heard the *plop* of an igniting fuse as the force of the attack broke the handle from the stick grenade. She cried out in reflex, not from fear but because the last thing she wanted was Schroeder or Fetherstone dead. "Don't!" she shrieked. "Don't kill—"

E.P. seized the grenade as if grabbing the ball in a scrum. Schroeder was thrown off balance and fell

427

backward. Hugging the grenade, E.P. kept running. Alison lay face down, covering her head. The sky ripped apart. Both Schroeder and Fetherstone were flat on their stomachs. The explosion echoed and re-echoed, the blast smothered by E.P.'s falling body.

Out of a nearby clump of dogwood hurtled Sergeant Winston. He landed on top of Schroeder, knees into kidneys, edge of a stiffened hand striking the back of the fleshy neck. His other hand swept the second grenade out of Schroeder's loose grip and hurled it over the cliff. There was no explosion.

Alison came up at a run as Fetherstone rolled over. He still had the gun in his hand. She pulled up short, legs braced, her crossbow up. The sighting crosswires stood an inch above the well-bred nose. The arrow was ready to split the skull fore and aft.

"Big Momma's sure gonna be glad to get yore confessions," said Sergeant Winston. He retrieved Fetherstone's gun. Contempt for lesser breeds drove Fetherstone into defiance. " 'Big Momma,' " he said with a sneer, "won't ever hear the story. This beer barrel"—he jerked an elbow at Schroeder—"has sewn up the key men in these islands. Your queen won't hear a squeak."

Winston gave a piercing whistle. Pony Moore appeared among the rocks, followed by Constable Mello. "I dun heard all I need f'r evidence. *Gag them!*" In an aside to Alison, Sergeant Winston added, "A drug dart might be better," glancing at the steel arrow in her crossbow.

"Why waste good anesthetic?" she asked.

Winston sighed. "Okay, *gag.*" He pushed his face into Schroeder's. "We be dumb in dese islands, but we's got a voice right in to Big Momma. It be called Harbour Radio."

"Too late to stop the big bang over *Qurqŭr!*" Schroeder managed to gloat before Constable Mello stuffed a rag into his mouth.

"Dat's right!" Winston banged his forehead. "Ain't no way we can stop dat ole Stringbag makin' fools of us, hey?"

Alison drew him away. "Stop the slapstick!" She was laughing.

But the sergeant only raised his voice so the prisoners could overhear. "Reckon da best t'ing be, I rush 'em back to da yacht to be part of dat big bang." He turned back to Alison, dropping his voice. "The imminence of execution should concentrate their minds. We won't even have to pay Scotland Yard to do the interrogating."

Bingo Harriman, flying in a navy P-3, began to see Tony Rutgers' father, old Rotgut, in an entirely different light. He had heard Downwind Dalrymple say to Admiral Jones, "The beauty of it is, Gabbiya himself chose to make the *Ultima Thule* his own booby trap. He picked up each one of Rutgers' clues . . ." Then the two men drifted out of earshot.

Bingo had finally persuaded his unexpected guests to accept samples of Spad's fine beer made from the purest spring waters with a special barley base and the distinct rice tang. He had also made intelligent guesses from such fragments of conversation. As a result, he was able to sink into a state of useful meditation aboard the antisubmarine aircraft dubbed the Whispering Giant. Its turboprops made little sound. It was jammed with more electronics than a computer trade show. The plane had been diverted from its Cape Hatteras patrol to scoop up the chosen few from Andrews Air Force Base, to which helicopters had delivered them from Spad's brewery.

It was absurd. Incredible. Yet when Bingo retraced events, testing each new hypothesis like a high-wire artist checking the cable tension, the closer he seemed to get to daylight. Rotgut himself had spoken of the frequency in Washington leaks surpassing a dangerous level. Then came the leaked story that Gabbiya had gone too far, that the United States was determined to get him *through a third country*. After years of rhetoric, with Gabbiya winning every verbal battle, the challenge was too much for the Great Protector. His world reputation was more and more dependent on humbling America. He had announced his intention to go beyond Third World and "nonaligned nation" concepts. He wanted to divide the world between those who hated the West and "American imperialism." Colonel Gabbiya's Arab neighbors loved and loathed him. Algeria found him a pestilental parvenu. Tunisia hadn't forgotten his attempt to overthrow its government; nor Chad, which he'd also tried to occupy. Egypt's leaders had been the target of his assassins. He squabbled with

Syria over Lebanon, criticized Iran for the Gulf hostilities, infuriated the Shi'a Muslims, who were the dominant revolutionaries in Lebanon.

But. Zia Gabbiya voiced Arab obsessions: hatred of Israel, hostility to America for propping up Israel, and the vision of Islam leading the anti-American world. The more he boasted about "getting away" with terrorism, about training suicide squads to kill more Americans, about plans to wreck the government of the United States, the more he won dreamland sympathy along the vast Islamic crescent from North Africa to Java.

He had goaded Americans. "Honk If You Want Gabbiya Liquidated!" read car stickers. "Reward for Zia's Nose!" advertised a Texan who wanted Gabbiya's nose to spite his face. Out of the White House came a jumble of counterthreats and retreats. American armed forces were paralyzed by a powerful civilian concern for legalities. If the Secretary of State said an outlaw was outside the law and therefore fair game, civil libertarians shouted him down. And always, the leaks made sure that any military plan would be killed through the media.

Gabbiya had won victory after victory, not just in blood-splashed airport lounges, but in this war of words. He was clever enough not to propel himself into conventional war, for then the democracies would stop wringing their hands, and act together.

Now Bingo Harriman felt flushed with an excitement he hadn't felt since his graduation as a navy pilot. That leak about luring Gabbiya to a third territory *had* to have been deliberate. So, too, the leak about the CIA's deep-deep-cover operations, resulting in official disbandment. Task Force Sledgehammer? There wasn't any question, forces had been mobilized around the Windfalls. But was it really true that Sledgehammer had been mounted without consulting Britain?

The official line — that is, the official *leak* — seemed to be that the Brits had been toying with a small-scale intervention. They sheared away, though, from risking another, post-Falklands avalanche of criticism, and left a few Royal Navy rebels to improvise Operation Fly-Swat. The "leak" would occur if anyone later secured evidence of the Stringbag's mission.

Bingo had obtained from Downwind Dalrymple the details of the Stringbag's performance. The machine was a logical consequence of recent events. The British had been forced to close down their Windfalls naval base; they dared not land forces there, because half the world would scream blue murder; the Falklands War had cost them their national treasure for the next decade, but . . . it had made the Brits search hard, like terrorist and peasant revolutionaries, *for simpler weapons*. Like the Stringbag. That weapon, thought Bingo, answered Big Vien's *panji* spike. Some genius must have rooted out the facts of Gabbiya's collaboration with Vietnam. That genius had to be Rotgut. Prosopography was his specialty, studying inaccessible figures — out of reach in time or in geography and politics—and then figuring out what triggered them into what kinds of action. The old prof couldn't confide too much, because of the blasted ever-present danger of genuine leaks. So he'd turned the leakers into unwitting allies!

And he'd calculated how true patriots would react in certain circumstances. Bingo's blood ran cold. Casey's out there, struggling to find, fix and strike Gabbiya. Unless my arithmetic is off base, there's no way Casey can make a dry landing after squandering fuel in a torpedo attack.

He became conscious of Admiral Jones creaking into the seat beside him. Jones was an old navy pilot too. He leaned past Bingo to look outside. "Weather's getting worse. Soon be down to the deck," he said. "Funny thing, your buddy's out there flying a fifty-year-old crate to do what we should be able to do, with all our technology, as fast and simple as the headman's ax."

Bingo knew then his guesswork couldn't be far wrong. "Everything's politics these days," he hazarded. But the admiral's smile was neutral.

This angered Bingo. He thought of the risk Casey was running. He thought of the billions of dollars spent each year on weapons and gadgets like the stuff crammed into this Whispering Giant. He told the admiral what he thought, and for good measure he threw in his frustrations over the way Americans in Vietnam had been forgotten. He resurrected from memory some lines Kipling had written about the way soldiers—British "Tommies" in Kipling's verse—

433

were trashed in peacetime: "For it's Tommy this, an' Tommy that, and 'Chuck him out, the brute!' / But it's 'Savior of 'is country' when the guns begin to shoot." Bingo surprised himself by his own eloquence, but he was thinking of poor Casey in a couple of hours' time, floating in the middle of the ocean on a sinking biplane.

The admiral listened, his leathery face set. Then he laid a hand on Bingo's forearm. "The Navy looks after its own, son," he said.

I sure hope so, Bingo thought. But if all this has always been part of a big White House conspiracy, isn't it more convenient if Casey and the Stringbag simply sink without trace?

CHAPTER 26

Casey flew through thick fog. A pilot's senses become dangerously confusing in such conditions. If he divides his reactions between his instruments and his disturbed sense of balance, he may conclude he is flying upside down, or diving steeply, or executing a steep turn. *Trust your instruments* is difficult advice to follow unless you are highly disciplined. Casey was all of that, but he had no instruments to trust.

He had an altimeter, of course. Sluggishly, it indicated if he was going up or down. He had the ball-and-needle that in its own good time declared approximately if he was slipping or skidding. Turn-and-Bank showed if his nose was above or below the invisible horizon, and if he'd gotten a wing high or low. In the world of modern aviation, these relics hardly qualified as instruments. On the other hand, as Casey reminded himself over and over, they were not subject to the whims of electronic gremlins who had grown up in the high-tech world of avionics.

To remind him that gremlins were as old as the Stringbag, the *thingumee* on the wing strut fluttered down the scale. His speed was falling! He overcorrected and went into a shallow dive, although it felt like a sudden climb. He glimpsed the sea under his wheels. The controls felt sloppy. He shoved open the throttle too fast. The engine coughed. He said a prayer. The engine picked up. Without warning, they burst into brilliant sunshine.

Lord John Bracken said nothing during this kangaroo act.

Casey adjusted for economic cruise again. The top of the mist scudded under his wheels. His "Stringbag leg" felt as if he had been pressing grapes on one foot in an Italian wine tub crowded with Sumo wrestlers.

"Jolly good, old sport," said Bracken. "She's a forgiving little lady, isn't she? You couldn't stall any other kite in a sea mist at fifty feet and get away with it."

"*Stalled?* I stalled?"

"Wouldn't scarcely know it, old bean. I noticed only because I've done it so often m'self. All she does is sink a bit."

"Phew!"

There was some conversation between Bracken and Lani in the back. Casey tuned it out. He was back to about five hundred feet above the murk. That extended visibility. He couldn't see what was on the sea now, though, because of the intervening mist. If he sank into the white blanket below, he would never be able to judge if it continued right down to the sea's surface.

"I'll have to stooge around until I find a hole," he said.

"Give it time," advised Bracken. "These fogs dissolve and come up again in the early morning.

You're sailing a good course."

Casey relaxed. Things happened faster in a jet; here, he had to learn to gear down to the more leisurely life of a sailor. He'd wait another twenty minutes before making a square search: four miles to west, four miles north, then eight miles east and eight miles south, and so on in a widening square that might find him the hole he needed.

At the same time, he searched out his feelings about Gabbiya. Did he hesitate about killing Zia because sinking a merchant ship in cold blood went against the grain? It would help if the *Ultima Thule* opened fire. Or was he thinking of Alison? He wouldn't have much of a future with her if he got caught. Soviet propaganda *and* the Western media would make mincement of him. Was he worried about Spad? Spad wasn't just partnership with Bingo Harriman. Spad was a pact with the missing. Dead or alive, they would want him to press home the attack. That must be the answer to his doubts.

"Wakey, wakey!" shouted Bracken. "There's a doughnut at ten o'clock."

Casey squinted the few points to port. In the cottony topside appeared the possibility of an opening, more like the hole you'd assume to be there if you studied a fluffy doughnut. He banked sharply. If the *Ultima Thule* was on the lookout and armed, his best hope was to get back down to the deck, even if it meant groping inside a gossamer funnel. Of course it would resolve all lingering doubts if Gabbiya tossed a few missiles at him. He blew into the tubes: "Lani, what were you going to say about sea-to-air missiles—?"

"Penguins," she called back. "A version of the Norwegian Penguin type. They're in use with the American Navy LAMPS III program."

"Some research vessel, this *Ultima Thule!*"

"That's what makes it so artful. Gabbiya's got a lot of gadgets on board he can pass off as 'research' if awkward questions are asked."

"Such as?"

Lani began to reel off the brand names. She had not been wasting her time, lying alone in Gabbiya's bed, reading the pornographic literature of the arms trade.

Casey realized he would have to improvise some evasive tactics. As the hole materialized into a purple canyon, he dived toward it like a ratting terrier, and reached for the piece of smoked glass.

It was *damn* dark in the hole. Even the smoked glass did not prepare his eyes for the abrupt change. He had been loping over hummocks of white cloud whose brilliance he only fully appreciated now. Still, as Bracken had predicted, the smoked glass did help prepare his eyes. Casey was becoming addicted to simple Stringbag solutions. How many times had his past missions been scrubbed because a tiny component turned temperamental? The literature had imprinted itself upon his mind, along with some bitter reflections when "a qualified UHF filter/coupler with band-pass filters of maximum sensitivity, minimum insertion loss and interface compatibility for microprocessor controls" suddenly didn't filter. If you had trouble with the Stringbag filter, you rubbed it on your sleeve.

He hung the smoked glass by its string and concentrated on holding the Stringbag in a tight descending turn. Shreds of cloud trailed from his wingtips. Rain splodged across the windscreen. He had no way of telling how far down the hole would take him. The vapor walls looked insubstantial, but the sea at the bottom would be solid enough if he hit it. The hole resulted from convection. Somewhere between sea and cloud there should be a layer of visibility. But you never knew.

The Stringbag gave a sudden jolt as if someone hammered on a wing. A thin chalk line shot out from under his wheels. He leveled out. Silver spray spurted away to port. Flying fish! But for their appearance, he might have failed to see the water, flat as glass. He juggled fuel mixture and throttle, reducing speed and looking for the most economic consumption. The aircraft was sandwiched between that deadly gray sea and a gray overcast so muggy it dripped into the cockpit. Forward visibility was poor, yet he could almost smell the target. He began a preaction drill; not that of a Crusader barreling along with six-foot rockets under the wings and 20-mm guns slung around the waist. It was a drill just learned. But a drill is a drill. And snug under his belly was the kind of cargo that once sank Nazi battleships.

The sea brightened.

"Watch for rocks!" roared Bracken. It was bizarre to hear such a warning in an airplane. They were flying so low, the Stringbag seemed waterborne. A

439

line of rocks came rapidly angling in, looking like the saw-toothed spine of a prehistoric reptile.

Bracken, doing his sums on the Bigsworth Board, was reminded of the prehistoric flying reptile *pterosaur*. He sent up a brief prayer of thanks to the Smithsonian, fabricators of that beast. It was they who had helped him resurrect this dinosaur too. He blessed their model, flapping across the Rose Garden, at the very time, perhaps, when the U.S. President was consulting his security advisers about how to deal with Zia Gabbiya.

"I'm picking up some Morse," said Lani. "It blanks out and then comes in very strong."

"Black Rock dead ahead!" Bracken burst out before she had finished. "Good show, Casey!"

Casey saw nothing except the first hint of a dark band where the horizon should be. "How far?"

"Give it another ten minutes. I just spotted Needham's Point."

"Want to go over the dropping procedure once more?" asked Casey.

Bracken took him through it again while the sky grew light and Lani jotted down the odd letters she could snatch out of the ether. The letters were jumbled. She wasn't sure if they were always in Morse and she was close to deciding she had more important things to do when she realized she was listening to the Smitty Harris Tap Code.

CHAPTER 27

Colonel Zia Gabbiya preened before his Saharan TV cameras on the bridge of the *Ultima Thule*, playing the role of the ancestor, Ahmad ibn Madjid, who took the Byzantine empire by storm and dominated the trade routes in that time when Arab sailors ruled the waves. Later, with the videotapes, he would board one of his own Fox Trot Soviet-built submarines. By evening, a Cuban helicopter would convey him to Havana's military airport. There a Soviet Tupolev waited to speed him home. In the Saharan capital, the press releases would have been distributed the moment the Americans made their moves: "Unprovoked white imperialists invade tiny black colony . . . Colonel Gabbiya outwits American adventurists . . . Saharan flag flies from uninhabited seamounts claimed personally by the Great Protector of Islam . . . Wall Street lackeys in armed attempt to stop joint Saharan-Vietnam venture to develop new resources for Third World . . ."

Zia stood out on one wing of the bridge at the hushed request of a cameraman. The wind tore at the long white strip of cotton cloth bound around his head. His loose white shirt filled out like a sail. He felt . . . unconquerable! The phrases of the speech he would broadcast, live, to the world tomorrow night swirled and thundered in his ears. The American President had called him the Devil's Godfather, King of Terror, the flaky barbarian that American power would destroy. And I, Zia, say *my* suicide bombers will make of your American streets another holocaust!

In London, his friends were standing by to begin the political movement that would unseat a conservative government manifestly unable to stand up to American power. In Moscow, his allies would emerge as guardians of the Arab world; Russian ships in these international waters already held erect an all-round electronic warning system with the *Ultima Thule* at the center.

Three decks below, the Duck, Pham Quac Vien, stood in the research vessel's laboratory, situated as close as possible to the bottom of the hull, and resonant with the beeps and whistles of side-scan sonar, echo sounders and returns from acoustical transponders.

Zia's soaring spirits made it hard for the ship's captain, a Frenchman, to catch his attention. The Protector stared at the slip of paper. From one of the unseen escorts, it reported the possible presence of a small aircraft. Ultrasensitive sound detectors had picked it up . . . seemed to be wood-and-canvas . . . one fleeting glimpse . . . biplane.

Zia ducked back onto the navigation deck. He

thought it unlikely the Stringbag was in the vicinity. So many false clues had been dropped to lead the pilot to attack the *Qurqūr*, even supposing the machine ever escaped the ACT rocket barrage.

Suddenly he threw his head back and roared with laughter. He looked at the message again, rubbed his hands, gestured to the cameras. So what if Casey didn't fly into the flaming trap of the yacht? A lot of effort would have been wasted, of course: the detailed tour of the ship to direct Casey's attention away from the tight-packed hold of explosives that would set yacht and harbor ablaze; the staged meeting with E. P. Geld so Casey would draw wrong conclusions from an American tycoon's humiliation; the representation of Lani as the crew's regularly raped slave . . .

But what a splash he'd make on all the TV screens around the globe, himself personally shooting down the evil American aggressor. He began issuing orders to the Saharan cameramen. What a scene, when they captured Casey alive! He did not doubt Casey was flying. Only a fool and a coward would have refused to follow the false trail, and Casey was—for an American—smart, and not lacking in a certain kind of impetuous American bravado. Zia reread the cautious Russian warning, and hoped it would prove warranted. He must tell Pham Vien.

Big Vien heard Zia's news over the intercom. He showed no surprise. He had expected Casey to sense his presence. They were destined to clash once more! Call it the "E P R paradox," synchronicity, the inevitable influence two particles exercise upon each other once they have come into contact. You could call it the result of years of tracking Casey through Vietnam's friends in the United States. Or you could toss the joss sticks into the sand trays of the temple beside what used to be called Le Petit Lac and then consult the old blind bonze seated behind the giant smiling Buddha among his dog-eared astronomical charts.

Vien had changed little in appearance since the Zoo days. He wore the same kind of baggy blue collarless jacket, the black cotton trousers; even the sandals were still made from old car tires. He was tall, thin, ascetic-looking; not your typical Tonkinese. His thinking had changed, though. He saw now that the Great Han chauvinism of the Chinese had taken Vietnam too far from the correct path to communism. Chairman Mao had been very wrong to start the schism with Moscow. It had been a wonderful day when the Party in Hanoi no longer relied on China for arms and doctrine.

He glanced sideways at Orlowski, the Russian. That was where Vietnam's guns had to come from now.

Orlowski was supervising the towing of an unmanned submersible at the end of four miles of cable. Another Russian operated the servo control, "flying" the vehicle through valleys twelve to fourteen thousand feet down. The Russian name for the vehicle translated as Towfish, for Deep Tow Unmanned Submersible. Its dolphin-type sonar reported up through the armored coaxial cable to shipboard computers that wove the information into the data from magnetometers and vertical sounders, generating two-dimensional images of the seafloor. They were mapping part of a trench between the Windfalls and the fifteen-thousand-foot-deep Blake Plateau, off Florida, not far from the Bermuda Rise, and in among the foothills of seamount which on dry land would qualify as a considerable mountain.

"We must land the Towfish now!" said Orlowski. He felt against a bathymetric recorder as the ship heeled.

From the bridge came Gabbiya's peremptory "No time!"

Big Vien busied himself with the charts. He could not take sides in this argument. Gabbiya financed Vietnam's desperate search for oil; Russia supplied the Towfish, the first of its kind. If Gabbiya persisted in sudden turns, the Towfish might easily crash into any one of multitude of obstacles on the imperfectly explored seabed. In some turns, the cable looped and sank. There was a risk the Towfish would crash-dive into the bottom. To bring it up to a safer level, the ship should increase speed while the cable winch revved up. The Russians were only risking the submersible because Gabbiya had given them a rare opportunity to fill in the details of those seamounts already earmarked for deepwater bases. "Down there," Orlowski had told Big Vien in a rare moment of candor, "it is possible to build workshops, as in outer space. Down there, oxydization of metal slows to a stop. Everything is in cold storage."

Orlowski called the bridge: "Comrade! I am winching in the Towfish. Please hold a steady course."

The reply did not sound comradely at all. "There is no danger. I must be free to maneuver."

Orlowski concealed his fury. Someone inside the United States was risking his life to warn them, transmitting in squirts of Morse. A Soviet submarine had the only decelerator and decoding equipment around, to handle the signals. That sub, too, took a risk, lying on the surface to receive and relay information to the *Ultima Thule* over a transmitter of calculatedly short range.

The black sail of the submarine looked to Casey like Black Rock. The conning tower was the first thing he saw when he flew out of the fogbank. He made a tight turn back into the covering mist. "I saw a ship, beyond Black Rock!"

"That wasn't Black Rock," called Lani. "It looked like one of Gabbiya's submarines . . . Fox-Trot subs."

"Saharans drive Soviet subs?" Casey was incredulous.

"They don't," said Lani. "They're manned by Russians, except in port. *Very shy,* the Russians. They'll dive the second the sub senses us."

Spoken like an expert, thought Casey. Which, he reminded himself, is what Lani is. "*Can* they sense us?"

"They won't intercept *this* conversation. The Russians have all the latest tricks, from trawlers to subs, to pick up everything *except* words spoke down rubber tubes." Lani laughed at the thought of the vast Soviet networks for electronic eavesdropping, even on domestic phone calls. "Perhaps America should convert to Gosport speaking tubes," she said.

They were still flying in zero visibility. Bracken said, "Try sticking your nose out again. I think that ship you saw was the *Ultima Thule.*"

"Sure." Casey broke into the clear at three thousand feet, hugging the dark side of what was turning into a thundercloud.

"Approach with the sun behind you," recommended Bracken. "You'll have the sub in direct line with the *Ultima Thule*. If you miss the first, you'll hit the second."

It was the order to strike, yet the words were so casually spoken. Casey's stomach tightened. "You're sure of our position?"

"Geographic? Or political?"

"Both."

"We're definitely in international waters. We carry no identification—"

"Except your letter or marque."

"Which says we have the legal right to defend the Windfalls."

"If we collide with that Russian, it will be read as

447

an act of war."

"Then, I shall chew it, and swallow it," Bracken shouted down the tubes.

While they talked, each made preparation. Lani broke away from trying to jot down the radio signals to secure her harness. Bracken checked the ancient Lewis machine gun on its flexible mounting. Casey eased his thumb over the torpedo control button.

A red glow burst from the bow of the ship. The flame rose to meet them. Casey considered it. A long yellow tail. An adaptation from ship-to-ship missiles, and fired too early. They must be scared. Discombobulated by what was coming at them.

"Hold on to your hats!" he yelled, thrust open the throttle, and dived to meet the missile. The sea filled his vision by the time he pulled up the nose and reduced power. The Stringbag's prop windmilled. Everything seemed to hang on it. The missile drew level. Casey kicked hard right rudder. The Stringbag fell into another dive. With power off, the Pegasus exhausts were no longer piping hot for the missile sensors. To track the aircraft now, the missile would need to loop back on itself.

Casey's maneuver was perfectly executed, just the way Bracken had taught it to rookie pilots long ago. *There's a lesson!* thought Bracken. The weapons change. The tactics, never. The young 'uns, the dead 'uns, are with us here now, vindicated at last. This is how you turn the tables on a superior enemy . . . He watched the orange-yellow flame stuttering away for good.

Casey recovered from the stalled turn. "All okay, back there?"

"You've got her!" yelped Bracken.

"I've got her!" rejoined Casey. It was the formal relinquishing of command, a time-honored formula. Whatever happened now would be on Casey's head.

He put the propeller into fully coarse pitch and again cut back the throttle. He was correctly positioned on the *Ultima Thule*'s starboard bow, some six thousand feet away. The Russian was closer. The vessels were on a parallel course, pacing each other.

"Tallyho!" Casey cried for Bracken's benefit. He had the nose pointing straight at the sea. He was practically standing on the rudder bar, the wind tearing at his goggles. The scarlet *thingumee* was pushed clean off the scale. He was making maybe two hundred miles an hour in an unmarked torpedo bomber. In his sights were a Russian sub where it had no business to be, and the Devil's Godfather, who had fired first. Moscow wouldn't want an incident. Sahara would never know what happened. Nobody could blame America or the CIA. Nothing, officially, would have happened. The missile from Gabbiya had wiped away all Casey's scruples.

This was flying! Jets of air bombarded him. The sea came up again, gravely smiling. His body burst its boundaries of skin and bone, and became one with the wings and membranes of the aircraft. He felt the tips of his wings vibrate. A jet's computers would have told him it was too late already to pull out of this dive. Even if he got the nose up, momentum alone must send him crashing into the sea. But now he was a creature of flight entire. This time, he trusted his senses absolutely.

He flattened out, the sub and the ship dead ahead. He moved the prop pitch control to fine. He worked the speed back down to a sensible 130 on the wing-strut scale. The Russian's sail loomed up, fine on the port bow but altering course away. He made a violent turn to stay ahead, then settled into the steady approach for a drop. The sail was rapidly diminishing in size. For a dizzying moment, he thought he must be flying backward. Then he understood. The Russian had started its crash dive. Discretion's the better part of valor, thought Casey, and turned his full attention to the *Ultima Thule,* steaming across his track.

Big Vien watched Orlowski fling himself up the companionway in search of Zia Gabbiya. The Russian was in a fury. The Towfish still gibbered away from the deep, sending needles jerking across charts and wavy lines of green light flickering across cathode-ray tubes. The deck TV monitors showed the winch winding in cable. It was all too slow. If the unmanned submersible went to the bottom for good—? Even Big Vien quelled a shudder. He followed Orlowski. The steel decks under their feet shook with the increased revs of the two General

Motors diesels, each big enough to drive a Siberian express.

Out on the afterdeck, a second Penguin launcher jerked awkwardly in an attempt to follow the Stringbag's erratic movements. On the other side, farther forward, a masked and helmeted figure loaded a chaff decoy rocket into a Plessey Aerospace launcher. Chaff was still the decoy of choice for deceiving target-seeking missiles, and nobody was sure if the spiderlike machine wobbling toward them had air-to-ship missile capabilities. The technicians had cut their teeth on rockets. The simple aerial torpedo was beyond their ken. It was not even remembered as a myth.

Saharan seamen blocked the passage of Orlowski and Big Vien until Zia gave the order to let them by. He was in charge. His ancestry spanned ships of the desert and hawks of the air and vessels of the sea. Zia was more than a match for this flying tinderbox. "Don't worry!" he advised the newcomers to the bridge. "I know this fool."

And so do I, thought Big Vien. Only, he's no fool! Moodily, he watched the Great Protector strike another attitude out on the bridge deck, and then his gaze slid past the Bedouin and fixed upon the silhouette jumping across the waves toward them. It was difficult not to cheer the approaching aircraft. Zia would have to be put down, someday. His only strength was his money and his influence over the mad mullahs. His arsenal was a flashy potpourri purchased in the modern bazaars of death. Big Vien sighed for the old days of the *panji* spikes, of the Malayan Gates, the hidden bamboo shafts, the Mace made of mud, rock and nails. The booby traps of Vietnam had defeated the technocrats of megadose death.

Big Vien froze. Simple weapons, he used to lecture his prisoners in the Zoo, will always beat your blind technology. "The primitive power of the peasant" was a favorite theme during his encounters with Commander Pete Casey, USN. "I hear you" was all Casey would say. Perhaps Casey had heard too well.

Zia Gabbiya saw Vien's grim expression. Why were the Vietnamese always so dour? He waved cheerfully. "Not to worry." The ship's deck space was limited and her avowed purpose restricted Gabbiya's deployment of weapons to the Penguins and a SHIELD decoy system. He gave the order to release chaff, which, according to the advertisements, "seduces the seeker." He had so much relished the phrase that he memorized it like a passage from the Koran and could give chapter and verse from the published literature: paragraph 4, column 2, page 61 of *Naval Forces,* No. 11, Vol. VI/1985: "Seduce the seeker by the creation of credible, correctly positioned false targets of suitable intensity so that the attacker abandons the real target." *Chaff.* That was the old word for it. The very heart of deception, at which Gabbiya had excelled all his life.

Casey held the Stringbag steady so that the bow of the *Ultima Thule* seemed to balance above the fourth bulb on the starboard rod of light bulbs. He guessed the ship's speed at eighteen knots. It would cover twenty-three hundred feet while the torpedo traveled three thousand feet from the point of drop. He ignored the fire and smoke from the ship's stern. It was vital to hold a steady course, even if an entire fleet opened up with gunfire.

Now! He pressed the tit, and almost drove tit and throttle through the floor. The Stringbag surged upward. He forced her down again. Like golf, if you pulled back on the swing, you hooked the ball. "Steady the Buffs!" he heard from Bracken. Another missile rose on a column of fire. Any lack of steadiness in this vital second would still cause the torpedo to hit the water at a disastrously bad angle.

Silver blossomed in the air ahead.

"Pull away," Bracken said. "Now!"

Casey eased into a turn. The Stringbag failed to pick up speed. Yet he had the throttle wide open. One wing cut through the edge of the glittering tinsel cloud. He put the stick hard over. The biplane shuddered. For a moment she seemed to stop stock-still, until she was lifted sideways, her belly exposed to orange light and waves of heat. He fought her back under control and saw smoke erupt from the twin funnels of the *Ultima Thule,* as if she belched from a kick to the stomach. A direct hit!

The sound of the explosion followed, heard because the Stringbag's engine had fallen silent. The aircraft rattled as the concussion grabbed her by the wings. The Pegasus jumped back into life. Casey swallowed. Another second's delay and he would have had to ditch downwind. Now the Stringbag was flying herself at an old-maidish gait and they were already at two hundred feet and climbing gently.

"What happened?" Casey coughed politely.

"Zia decoyed himself." It was Lani who answered. "You nearly ran into the chaff he sent up. It's meant to trick missiles, not ancient torpedoes."

"There was a second launching—"

"A proper missile," said Lani. "In Zia's book of instructions, it was the right trick. It would have homed on us. But we're made of wood and canvas. We had a dying engine that isn't in the book. The missile homed on the chaff instead." She was laughing with relief. "The torpedo went through everything in its ignorant, archaic way."

The strength returned to Casey's hands. The Stringbag had been showing a mind of her own. He forced her into a turn to check the scene below.

"The ship's settling," reported Bracken.

"Crew's in the water, swimming clear," said Lani.

"They'll be okay. Rafts and dinghies galore."

"Will the Russian pick 'em up?"

"He's still submerged."

There was a touch of hysteria in their shouts. The missiles had been a declaration of war. They were privateers celebrating the victory.

Casey sobered up. "The Russkies *won't* retrieve them." He was suddenly very sure. The Russians had always faded into invisibility in Vietnam. Their supply ships, their submarines, their manpower, always evaporated at the first sign of trouble. The Russians were not officially there, just as they were officially absent now. "Did you say the"—he stumbled and winced over the word—"the *wireless* is working?"

"Yes," said Lani.

"Can we transmit?"

"I tried. Nobody's listening."

"It's a fixed channel," said Bracken. "I could change it if I had the crystals."

Crystals? Casey felt like suggesting they break out the semaphore flags. But now a new emergency intruded. Fuel! He bent forward to squint through the gap in the dashboard. The fuel dipstick had dropped almost from sight. "The main tank looks empty."

"Bloody hell!" Bracken was suddenly peering over the cockpit coaming. "The extra feeds into the main." He hammered on the extra tank between the two cockpits. "I think we're out!" He collapsed back into his seat. "I *did* figure consumption on my Ouija board. Hang on." He fished up the Bigsworth Board and hunted among the crayon marks, greedy for hope. "The attack cost us an hour's cruising, we took two hours out, lost maybe forty minutes buggering around in cloud—"

"I want to know what we do, not what we did!"

yelled Casey.

"What we do," crowed Lani suddenly, "is fly west for fifty miles and land on the *Coral Sea*." She savored their spellbound silence. "The *Coral Sea* is an American carrier—"

"Never mind the lecture."

"The message kept coming in, repeated over and over. Not in Morse! In numbers. The tap code. I finally woke up—" She passed a large piece of Perspex into the front cockpit. Casey read the red-crayoned words: UR FRENDS WAIT CORAL SEA DISTANCE FIFTY MILES DUE WEST BLACK ROCK.

There was a mystery here too profound for them. "I haven't time to figure this one," said Casey. There wasn't even time to think how they could keep from getting their feet wet. Bracken had become suddenly busy, snuffling like a truffle hound in the bottom of the rear cockpit, wriggling his long, spare body into the storage section of the fuselage, emerging triumphant with a jerrican. "I stowed some extra gallons. I've just dumped them in the extra tank. You've got another half hour."

Casey rubbed the moisture from his face. "Lani?"

"Yes."

"Keep sending, just in case." He waited for her acknowledgment. Then he asked, "John, how does a hundred miles an hour, maximum weak mixture at five thousand feet sound?"

It was the first time he had ever called Bracken by

his first name. The older pilot's response betrayed pleasure. "You might make it, boy." *Boy* was the Windfall Islands' fondest honorific.

Bracken dropped back into his seat and wiped his hands with a fuel rag. "Thanks, Lani," he said. "The old gel might yet take her last cut with dignity."

Taking the last cut. In the front cockpit, Casey shivered. That was the euphemism for sudden death among American Navy pilots. Before the present age of "meatball" landing aides, a landing-control officer brought in the pilot by signaling with yellow short-handled bats. The final signal was crossed bats to signify "Cut engine." But if the aircraft failed to hook a deck wire, if the crash barrier came up too late, if there was just a ball of flame, the pilot took his last cut.

Perhaps to keep his courage up, Casey said, "Don't scrap the old girl. Smuggle her into some museum." He knew he was whistling past the graveyard.

"Yes, but have you noticed the woodrot?" Bracken chuckled. "I didn't bother you with such details before. Termites in the wings. No museum would take her."

Casey hastily changed the subject. "Suppose *our* people rescue Gabbiya?"

"Make no public announcement!" said Bracken. "Silence. Very unnerving to your enemies, it is, when nothing's said."

"Ha! An impossible dream, in Washington." Casey ducked his head. "Can't see the dipstick at all now. We'll fly straight in, if I can stretch it."

The Stringbag kept purring along. She seemed to know the last flight must end with a touch of class.

Casey's mind went back to the subject of museums. "What about the Smithsonian? After all, they helped you restore the old girl."

"Somebody would put two and two together. You Yanks can't afford the publicity."

Casey thought some more. He remembered an instructive afternoon in London, south of the Thames, at the Imperial War Museum. "I've another idea—" he began, but then it was time to start praying.

The spectacle of a carrier turning into wind is misleading to a pilot new to landing on a moving deck. The ship appears at first to swing so slowly. The pilot wonders if anyone down there knows he's coming in.

Casey was a veteran of hundreds of such landings. He had never tried one like this. He was approaching the *Coral Sea* in a shallow descent, keeping to port of the ship's wash. The big Pegasus radial engine obscured the round-down aft on the carrier's flight deck. He dipped a wing until he could see, between the cylinders, men scooting across the heeling flight deck. Yellow bats flashed in a frantic wave-off.

"The engine's running on spit and they're telling

me to go around again!" he said to nobody in particular. He wondered where the bats came from . . . He was accustomed to the meatball on the port side, flashing green when he got too high, red if his approach was too low, and a new breed of landing-signal office, the LSO, telling him what was happening on the radio hookup.

So what was going on? The carrier's bows were almost imperceptibly turning. He looked for the violent surge of water aft. It would confirm the ship's stern was kicking the other way. She should have been well into the great swinging arc required to head up into wind, but he was closing on her too fast. The huge bulk of the carrier began to shift with a rush. He would be landing in the worst of situations; with a wind blowing athwart the deck, tempestuously unfriendly. He had no choice. He was draining what little fuel was left from the carburetor, sideslipping in, nose lower than desirable.

The yellow bats came up at an alarming rate. He kicked on rudder, straightened up, then pulled back on the stick until he was hanging on the prop. If it stopped now, they would drop into the broiling wash astern. The deck was angled into the turn and rose like a vast steel block flung at a fly. The yellow bats were violently crossed, to signal the cut. There was no need to pull the toggle to cut ignition. The engine had stopped, though the Stringbag still floated . . . and floated . . . Buoyant as a celluloid ball on a jet of warm air, it soared along the deck.

The tail hook struck first with a screech. He had time for some fancy waggling of wings so that both tires touched down together despite the heeling deck. Warm sea air breathed against his left cheek. He was not out of the woods yet. He applied coarse rudder to bring her parallel with the centerline, fore and aft along the flight deck. The hook caught an arrester wire. The sudden deceleration tripped the Stringbag. He thought he had bent a propeller blade and then felt the Stringbag surge up. The combination of wind and the ship's speed had started to kite her into the air again.

"Fold wings!" Suddenly Bracken was crawling all over him, was coming headfirst from the rear cockpit, was yanking at a wooden handle labeled WING LOCKS. "My fault!" shouted Bracken. "'M' own modification. Forgot to tell you." At that moment, the wings fell back under pressure from the wind. Casey watched, awestruck. The movement was majestic: like a giant Atlas moth folding its wings after the long glide through a tropical forest.

Nobody on deck spoke. Nobody gesticulated. The flight-deck crews in their varicolored skullcaps formed a protective circle. Firefighters in cumbrous white asbestos suits lumbered forward, anticipating a bonfire. Lani looked down into a web of wires and felt like a newly boated fish entangled in the nets. The wings lay back on either side the hull, from midships to rudder, no more buoyant or aerodynamic than a crude fish trap of bamboo poles and chicken wire.

Casey put one hand on either side of the cockpit and stood on his seat with his head out in the fresh sea wind. The transition from airborne to shipborne, the hot fumes in the cockpit, churned his stomach. He saw Bracken lean out over the deck twelve feet below. He heard the preliminary gurgle of a man trying to keep down his breakfast. The sound was not helpful.

On the bridge, the skipper of the USS *Coral Sea* measured with his eye the distance the Stringbag had run on the refitted deck. The biplane had traveled barely far enough to catch the first wire. To strike it down one of the forward elevators, a tractor would have to tow it the length of a football field. It had stopped in the space between two goalposts.

"Lordy me!" he said, reaching for binoculars. "I've flown with pilots who got airsick, and I've flown with pilots who got seasick, but I never saw two pilots at one and the same time being both."

His companion, commander of a Tomcat squadron, nodded dumbly. When he did speak, it was only to repeat. "And it even folded its wings!"

"I rigged the bats when they told us what to expect," said the landing-signal officer. He was cock-a-hoop and couldn't stop talking. "I'd just seen some Hollywood movie where they used clips from that wartime documentary on a carrier . . . *Fighting Lady*,

461

I think it was called. I remember the old batsman stuff, you know? Wave-off, more throttle, too low . . . ?"

Casey hadn't the heart to tell him that with empty tanks he had ignored the signals.

"That first wave-off," bubbled the LSO, "was to give the big VIP chopper a chance to get clear."

"Chopper?"

"Bringing in the White House eggheads."

Lord John Bracken had gone straight up to report to the bridge. There was a certain amount of organized confusion after he had pinpointed the location of survivors from a ship he was careful to say he thought might have hit a rock and sunk. After the rescue helicopters had been ranged, the skipper of the USS *Coral Sea* invited Bracken to his duty cabin. "Thought you might want a change of clothes," he said.

Bracken glanced down at his Wreck Cay hermit rags. He was still feeling a bit unsteady. He wished it was the old days when a chap could dodge down to the wardroom for a pink gin. "I'm quite comfortable," he said. He had heard that, in the privacy of their quarters, even American chaps, despite their "dry" navy, could sometimes summon up a bracer or two. "I'm tremendously thirsty," he added.

"We've the best coffee in the fleet," said the skipper.

There was no mention of the *Ultima Thule*, or Task Force Sledgehammer. The skipper spoke vaguely of a contingency plan. Planes and ships were all dispersed. The *Coral Sea* just happened to be steaming outside Cuban waters. He said, "I suppose, though, I'll have to record something in the logbook to explain that, ah, airplane's presence."

"Will this do?" Bracken tugged Sir Everard Chillingham's letter of marque from inside his tattered shirt.

The skipper studied it. To Bracken's delight, he said, "It was King James, wasn't it, in the 1600s, dished out knighthoods like candy bars. More than eight hundred in his first year! A whole bunch roved the Caribbean under 'commissions' from the Duke of Savoy." He rubbed his chin. "But if I put you down as a privateer, how do I explain you landing here?"

"Say I needed to refuel and thought you were one of ours," said Bracken, and keeled over.

CHAPTER 28

They put Lord Bracken in the sick bay under the name of Wally Raleigh. They diagnosed a serious heart problem. He knew that already. They decreed lots of rest. He was restless in captivity. They said it was nonsense to regard himself as a prisoner. But he was thinking of the *Ultima Thule* survivors when he said to Casey, "There's no better place than an aircraft carrier to hold men for questioning without lawyers or public fuss." Finally they agreed to fly Alison in from the Windfalls. It was the second day of the *Coral Seas*'s extended patrol, and the first clandestine shuttle between the carrier and the islands.

She burst out laughing when she saw her father's nom de guerre.

"It was the skipper's idea," said John Bracken. "He's a sentimental sort of fellow, a real old navy hand."

"Sir Walter Raleigh!" Alison hugged him. "That is really the most handsome compliment. He practically gave birth to America. He was the first great advocate of sea power—"

"I suspect it's Raleigh-the-pirate that the skipper had in mind."

They hustled Alison out of the sick bay, explaining he was in no condition to talk about serious things. They suggested Alison could do the talking for him. Mostly they wanted to know legally how to clear up the complexities of the E. P. Geld empire wherever it was allied with Gabbiya's offshore companies. Admiral Downwind Dalrymple was there for the British. Admiral Jones introduced some high-level visitors from the Justice Department. "The carrier's in quarantine," said Admiral Jones. "Until we can cool down our political hot potatoes, we'll stay out to sea."

One of those hot potatoes was Zia Gabbiya. He'd been selling dreams along with his scattered acts of violence. Within a very few days, questions about his whereabouts would have to be answered. The dreams would be shattered—unless . . .

"We can choose to simply announce you're dead," said Casey.

"On the other hand, I could be useful . . . *alive?*" Zia grinned. In his megalomania, he had decided to elevate Casey close to his own level. A worthy enemy.

"Yes, you could be useful, because Sahara obeys you," Casey said frankly. "You could be a force for good, if you'd listen to us."

"Never!" declared Gabbiya.

He remained obstinate, though he reacted well to the tour Casey gave him of the *Coral Sea*. They had to dress Gabbiya in an American officer's uniform. He turned necessity into a compliment. He quite enjoyed the figure he cut. They gave him another name, of course, and the areas he visited were cleared of all but essential personnel. He was impressed by the technology. He kept casting sly glances at Casey, as if to say: We know better now, don't we?

This was the trouble with Gabbiya. His love of fantasy made him dangerously unpredictable. They might have squeezed some sort of commitment out of him, in exchange for agreement on what story to make public. They could say Zia's genuine obsession with undersea exploration had been the inspiration of an experiment in U.S.-Sahara collaboration. The *Ultima Thule* (which was, after all, U.S.-registered and nominally owned) had met with an unfortunate accident. But they stuck on the fact that Gabbiya just flatly refused to publicly thank America for rescuing him.

The *Coral Sea* took excellent care of its guests. There were twenty officers and men from the *Ultima Thule;* and then there was Orlowski, who had to be confined to his cabin, since it was hard to explain away his dour expression and invincibly Russian accent.

Big Vien they left pretty much to Casey. The former Vietnamese political boss seemed unsurprised by the reversal of roles. He enjoyed being treated as an intellectual, just as he had in the Zoo days of his

467

ascendancy. He and Casey again discussed philosophical matters late at night. The theory of synchronicity still fascinated Big Vien. He pointed out that it could be applied to enemies as well as friends. He had actually been in Paris, visiting his old French *amis* from colonial days, when the experiment called the "E P R paradox" was performed. "Two particles continue to affect each other simultaneously, no matter how far apart, once they've been near each other," said Big Vien. "Human beings can be substituted for particles, even hostile ones, and there's no limit to the numbers . . . millions of Vietnamese and millions of Americans." At first Casey wasn't sure where this was leading. He even wondered if this sudden imprisonment—however polite and comfortable—had affected Big Vien's mind. That was usually the case when men of great power fell. Then he understood. Big Vien was saying Vietnam knew more about its former American enemies than it did about its so-called allies. A grudging respect had evolved. The two countries were intertwined.

Casey's big concern was to surprise information out of Big Vien about American prisoners. The Vietnamese Party ideologue continued to play games, though. Sometimes he indicated that some of them could still be alive, then he would drift into a long harangue about how America owed Vietnam billions in reparations.

Both Zia and Vien severely tested Casey's patience. He remembered that past villains could rely upon fashionable fainthearts to gabble away about this or that dictator being the inevitable manifestation of social disorder; and America only had to understand the underlying causes. He could imagine the chorus of protest that would go up if anyone made public the *Coral Sea*'s "illegal" confinement of the two tyrants.

The dilemma grew more acute. After three days, there were signs that politicians in London and Washington scented scandal. Those in power would naturally disown responsibility. Bingo Harriman was flown to the *Coral Sea* after the intervention of the national security adviser, Joe Malloy. When Bingo could get Casey alone, he tried to make clear the awesome nature of the discovery he thought he had made.

"Rotgut set the whole thing up," he finally managed to tell Casey. "He was *the* expert on predicting how people react. He saw how we'd go through the same old song-and-dance routine about hitting Gabbiya, and then not. He figured out a way to express the people's will without being hamstrung by the people's representatives. His deep-deep-cover department was under sentence of death anyway . . ."

It made sense. Rotgut had been quite willing to sacrifice his own life. He'd selected the key figures, and set them loose to bump into characters like Lord Bracken. "Democracies are never ruthless," agreed

469

Casey. "It's always some maverick who saves us from ourselves. Why don't tyrants ever kill one another?" Bingo's reply was, "That's a thought."

That evening, Bingo had a long talk with the three civilians who'd been ferried in. They were known as "funnies" among crew members because they looked like spooks or FBI agents. Later he said to Casey, "Gabbiya and Big Vien are getting together for a private dinner. Big Vien's been bitching, about 'solitary' and feeling like a prisoner in isolation."

Dinner was served in Zia's cabin. The two men were left to talk freely . . . in front of concealed cameras. Zia must have guessed he was going on record. His conversational style was to harangue Big Vien, who remained silent. On the *Qurqūr*, discussion had been confined to practical matters; the rest of the time, the Vietnamese had kept to himself. Now he was the sole target of rhetoric normally aimed at peasants. It was an insult to a French-educated Marxist who had spoken of Plato with Camus, who had been in the forefront of revolutionary conflict and all the major wars of the past forty-two years.

Zia made revolution sound like a cottage industry, and war a matter of paper tigers. Sahara's collaboration with Vietnam was never more clearly exposed as opportunistic, to spread Zia's word among the Moslems in Big Vien's neighborhood, through the great archipelago of Indonesia and the peninsula of Malaysia. Zia's plan for social justice was elementary: stamp out the white man. "I am training North

470

American Indians," he boasted. "I am pouring a fortune into stirring up the grievances of every racial minority in the West. The whites talk big about destroying me!" Zia tossed his curls and looked down his nose at Big Vien in that stiff-necked manner known to millions of TV-watchers. "But they cannot destroy me, or my movement. I have molded my people for generations to come. History will remember me as the hand of God, returned to save Islam. I am a divine wind. Americans cannot stop it, because they are hooked on the drugs of self-abuse and self-indulgence. Spending, spending, spending, they lay waste their powers."

He was rather proud of that last bit and his square face joggled under Big Vien's flat stare. He tilted back his chair. His hands hung loose. He twisted his head as if presenting his best profile to the cameras.

Casey had not been comfortable watching all this on one of the monitors. Now, though, he had a sudden sense of knowing exactly what was passing through Big Vien's mind. *Go on!* he thought. *Do it!* Big Vien is finally seeing the light. He's in the hands of a religious maniac and he must be thinking that Hanoi killed millions of Catholics—only to have fanatics of a fundamentalist faith spring out of the graves.

There was a steak knife thoughtfully placed at Big Vien's elbow. He picked it up. The Devil's Godfather was still talking, head thrown back, long neck exposed. Big Vien rose unhurriedly and with a gesture almost too graceful for the unseen watchers to comprehend, he sliced the knife across Zia's windpipe. Then he sat down again.

Nobody ever heard from Big Vien's own lips what made him do this. Zia had shown himself as a crude threat to Big Vien's political beliefs, whereas the West, in its democratic fashion, had always found a thousand arguments for inaction. Big Vien had simply come to a conclusion. Then he acted on it. Afterward, he sat awaiting his fate, wearing a gentle smile that suggested he was happy to have been spared endless debate about the rights and wrongs of getting Gabbiya.

That night, someone else died too. Lord John Bracken passed away quietly in his sleep. He knew from Alison that his beloved Windfalls were safe. He heard about Zia's bloody end. He closed his eyes and murmured to his daughter, "It wasn't coincidence." Those were his last words.

There was a swift burial at sea, very early next morning. Lord Bracken was committed to the deep, sewn up inside lead-weighted canvas in the fashion of his ancestors.

Zia's body was put on ice. Ironically, though Big Vien had carried out the execution, the same old Western indecision hovered over Zia's further disposal. "I know what Rotgut would have done," observed Casey to Bingo Harriman. "He'd have lamented the loss of Gabbiya in a marine accident, chucked the corpse overboard, then shown Big Vien the tapes and pictures of himself murdering Zia, before sending him back to Hanoi to work for us." This remark was made in rather a loud voice during a coffee break that morning. The skipper and Joe Malloy, the national security adviser, both overheard it. "The other great thing about aircraft carriers," Joe Malloy would be heard to argue later, before a congressional committee on procurements, "is, they don't leak."

The only person openly distressed by Zia's death was Mellanie Blake. But, as Alison found out, not for the reasons a cynic might suspect. "I could have killed Zia long back," Lani confided. "I could have saved all the subsequent turmoil."

"Not in cold blood you couldn't," said Alison. "And anyway, you knew assassination would never be Washington policy."

Privately, Alison wondered if Lani had fallen under the Protector's spell. Perhaps she was simply a professional who felt she'd botched things. Lani did say something more that was revealing: "I *enjoyed* breaking my own moral code. 'Duty' was a wonderful excuse to commit every sin forbidden by the convent." She shuddered. "Zia had some strange tastes. Don't you go feeling sorry for me. Even an abused donkey misses the whip."

She's what they call a burned-out case, thought Alison. She's lost her cover and can't go back to her

473

old trade. In this, though, Alison was wrong.

Three months later, the restored Stringbag was quietly inserted among exhibits at London's Imperial War Museum. There was no public ceremony. The museum had closed for the day when Churchill Spencer Winston drove to the adjoining street in Southwark. He was starting law school, fees underwritten by a small legacy from Bracken and an anonymous grant for services rendered. It had required the combined efforts of the U.S. Navy, the Smithsonian and a special fund to dress up the Stringbag as an artifact from World War II. The *Coral Sea*'s carpenters diagnosed woodworm in her timbers and injected the appropriate chemicals. The ship's workshops also put extra dents in the engine cowling, slapped on some authentic war paint and created a set of plausible identification marks.

Sergeant Winston's passengers were the president of Spad, Pete Casey, and the chairman of INSPAD, Bingo Harriman. Mrs. Casey was also present for a brief and impromptu viewing of the new exhibit. The bride's father was not; he was represented instead by a brass plaque stating: "Underwater research vehicle, Towfish, courtesy of the late Lord John Bracken." This took Alison by surprise. She had heard about the Soviet-built submersible, and how it had been cut adrift when the Russian submarine crash-dived and cut through the *Ultima Thule*'s towing cable. "But . . . here?" she asked Casey.

"All the experts have finished with it. They agreed to leave it here until the Soviets claim it. If they dare. The Forget-Me-Not Fund is paying the freight."

"That fund covers a multitude of sins," murmured Alison, hugging Casey. The fund's patrons now included two former presidents, three ex-prime ministers and several admirals, to lend it respectability. Its purposes had broadened too, from being narrowly focused on American victims of just one form of terrorism, although the prisoners in Vietnam remained a priority.

Explaining the museum, Winston said, "It used to be called Bedlam, the House of Madness and Folly." His face shone in the twilight. "The real name was Bethlem Royal Hospital. For lunatics. Someone was having a private joke when it was turned into a war museum."

An elderly guide took them through the First World War trenches, showed them a German Vengeance rocket from the Second, a Russian MiG from Korea, a bicycle bomb from Vietnam . . .

"Now this, here," said the guide, coming to a stop in front of the Stringbag, "is wot you might call going from the sublime to the ridiculous." Not knowing who his listeners were, he launched into the account of a flying dinosaur that faced extinction even before it saw battle.

"A ship," observed Casey, remembering his lessons

in Windfall talk, "with no come-from and no go-to."

The guide understood. "It done a fearsome lot of damage. Like you say, sir, the enemy never knew where it come from nor where it would go." He warmed to the theme long stirring under his peaked cap. He had never enjoyed a more attentive audience. "It were born in a time when weapons was built for specific targets. This old lady was a wicked one. She just waited for targets of opportunity. The perfect booby trap, you might say."

On the other side of the world, Mellanie Blake sat in what had been the U.S. embassy in Saigon, behind a door still bearing the Paracels Petroleum sign.

"You are either very brave or very foolish, Miss Blake," said Big Vien.

"My protector is dead," agreed Lani, "but Saharan corporations belong to the nation, not to one man. And I was Colonel Gabbiya's expert in these business matters."

Big Vien nodded. "What do you bring us?"

"Technical data." She had already placed the charts and bound reports upon his desk. The whole interview was a charade.

"You think your principals do a better job than the Russians?" He flipped through a report with the title *Paracels Undersea Oil.*

"That's our study in depth. Forgive the pun."

Big Vien showed his teeth. "In our waters? With,

ah, your submersibles?"

"Exactly. None of your great and good allies detected a perfectly routine U.S. geophysical study. It's in its *fifth* year!"

"The price?" Big Vien angled his head to see through the flyblown windows into the austere street.

"Our private corporations will exploit these resources under contract to your government."

"I see." Big Vien looked up at the ceiling fan. It had long stopped turning. "Would INSPAD be such a corporation?"

"They have a deep-tow vehicle suited to this area."

Big Vien sighed. "And how is Commander Casey?"

Lani weighed her words. She hated to rub it in. "When word leaked out about how he 'rescued you from the shipwreck,' he faked that illness to avoid the press. He wasn't really sick at all."

A silence fell between them. The sounds of a city in economic defeat drifted through the windowpanes still crisscrossed with paper against bomb blast. Big Vien would have liked to hear more: how, for instance, the Saharan crewmen were bought off; and how long it would be before unauthorized eyes saw the replay of Zia's murder. It was a bitter pill to swallow, this triumph for Casey.

Finally he said, "I suppose there is a special hook in all this *duck soup?*"

His eyes lifted to meet Lani's sharpened gaze. She said, "Poor Duck . . . We want the return of all prisoners, of whatever nationality." She saw the same certitudes in those eyes that she had seen in Zia's. Her white cotton blouse stuck against her back. She felt perspiration trickle along her spine. She widened her knees to let air circulate inside her blue denim skirt. "No more training of terrorists," she said. "No more hostages."

Big Vien spread his hands. "Hostages are the currency of the deprived. Without them I have no guarantees."

"You have me," said Lani.

THE FINEST IN FICTION
FROM ZEBRA BOOKS!

HEART OF THE COUNTRY   (2299, $4.50)
by Greg Matthews
Winner of the 26th annual WESTERN HERITAGE AWARD for
Outstanding Novel of 1986! Critically acclaimed from coast to
coast! A grand and glorious epic saga of the American West that
NEWSWEEK Magazine called, "a stunning mesmerizing perfor-
mance," by the bestselling author of THE FURTHER ADVEN-
TURES OF HUCKLEBERRY FINN!
    "A TRIUMPHANT AND CAPTIVATING NOVEL!"
      — KANSAS CITY STAR

CARIBBEE   (2400, $4.50)
by Thomas Hoover
From the author of THE MOGHUL! The flames of revolution
erupt in 17th Century Barbados. A magnificent epic novel of bold
adventure, political intrigue, and passionate romance, in the
blockbuster tradition of James Clavell!
    "ACTION-PACKED . . . A ROUSING READ"
      — PUBLISHERS WEEKLY

MACAU   (1940, $4.50)
by Daniel Carney
A breathtaking thriller of epic scope and power set against a background of Oriental squalor and splendor! A sweeping saga of passion, power, and betrayal in a dark and deadly Far Eastern
breeding ground of racketeers, pimps, thieves and murderers!
    "A RIP-ROARER"
    — LOS ANGELES TIMES

*Available wherever paperbacks are sold, or order direct from the
Publisher. Send cover price plus 50¢ per copy for mailing and handling to Zebra Books, Dept. 2571, 475 Park Avenue South, New
York, N.Y. 10016. Residents of New York, New Jersey and Pennsylvania must include sales tax. DO NOT SEND CASH.*

ACTION ADVENTURE

SILENT WARRIORS (1675, $3.95)
by Richard P. Henrick
The Red Star, Russia's newest, most technologically advanced submarine, outclasses anything in the U.S. fleet. But when the captain opens his sealed orders 24 hours early, he's staggered to read that he's to spearhead a massive nuclear first strike against the Americans!

THE PHOENIX ODYSSEY (1789, $3.95)
by Richard P. Henrick
All communications to the USS *Phoenix* suddenly and mysteriously vanish. Even the urgent message from the president cancelling the War Alert is not received. In six short hours the *Phoenix* will unleash its nuclear arsenal against the Russian mainland.

COUNTERFORCE (2013, $3.95)
Richard P. Henrick
In the silent deep, the chase is on to save a world from destruction. A single Russian Sub moves on a silent and sinister course for American shores. The men aboard the U.S.S. *Triton* must search for and destroy the Soviet killer Sub as an unsuspecting world races for the apocalypse.

EAGLE DOWN (1644, $3.75)
by William Mason
To western eyes, the Russian Bear appears to be in hibernation — but half a world away, a plot is unfolding that will unleash its awesome, deadly power. When the Russian Bear rises up, God help the Eagle.

DAGGER (1399, $3.50)
by William Mason
The President needs his help, but the CIA wants him dead. And for Dagger — war hero, survival expert, ladies man and mercenary extraordinaire — it will be a game played for keeps.